OUTLAW MOUNTAIN

J. A. JANCE

An Imprint of HarperCollinsPublishers

This is a work of fiction. Names, characters, places, and incidents are products of the author's imagination or are used fictitiously and are not to be construed as real. Any resemblance to actual events, locales, organizations, or persons, living or dead, is entirely coincidental.

HARPER

An Imprint of HarperCollins*Publishers*
10 East 53rd Street
New York, New York 10022-5299

Copyright © 1999 by J.A. Jance
Excerpt from *Betrayal of Trust* copyright © 2011 by J.A. Jance
ISBN 978-0-06-199897-3

First Harper premium printing: January 2011
First Avon Books paperback printing: May 2000
First Avon Books hardcover printing: July 1999

HarperCollins® and Harper® are registered trademarks of Harper-Collins Publishers.

Printed in the United States of America

Visit Harper paperbacks on the World Wide Web at
www.harpercollins.com

10 9 8 7 6 5 4

*To the Special Olympians
and to all the people
who make Special Olympics possible*

OUTLAW MOUNTAIN

🌵 PROLOGUE

"AL . . . ICE. Come . . . find . . . me."

The faint but drawn-out words, wafting on the chill November air, drifted in through the open window of Alice Rogers' aging Buick Skylark. Even though she didn't hear the taunting call or understand the words, the sound alone was loud enough to disturb her and rouse her from her Scotch-induced slumber. She woke up, shivered in the cold and blinked at the unremitting darkness that surrounded her. For a confusing, disorienting moment, Alice was afraid she had gone blind. She had no idea where she was or how she had come to be there. Fighting panic, her hands flailed out in search of clues. The first thing her trembling fingers encountered was the icy, smooth surface of the steering wheel. Next she ran her fingertips across the familiar worn plush of the Buick's upholstery.

Breathing a sigh of relief, Alice leaned back

against the headrest. She was in the front seat—the front passenger seat—of a car, her own car. She had fallen asleep there. Again. The best she could hope for was that maybe none of the neighbors had seen her. If they had, word was bound to get back to the kids. That was one thing Alice knew from bitter experience. Tombstone was full of gossips who were only too happy to carry tales.

Alice stayed where she was and rested for the better part of a minute, waiting for the momentary panic to subside, for the frantic beating of her heart to slow and steady. Hoping to get her bearings, she squinted through the darkness, trying to sort out some familiar landmark that would tell her where she was and how she had come to be there.

As dark as it is, she told herself, *it must be almost morning. Where the hell am I?*

Vaguely she remembered something about going to dinner at Susan's house, but now she had no recollection of having driven the twenty-some miles from Tombstone out to Sierra Vista. She didn't remember coming back, either. But a taste for Scotch was one of the few things Alice and her grown daughter shared in common. And knowing how dinners with her daughter and son-in-law often turned out, not remembering every blow-by-blow was probably for the best. Alice had never held her son-in-law in very high regard. In her opinion Ross Jenkins was nothing but an arrogant jerk. The problem with drinking Scotch in his presence was that the booze might have loosened Alice's tongue enough for her to come right out and tell him exactly what she thought of him.

Not good, Alice scolded herself. *Not good at all*. But then again, even if she had shot her mouth off, Alice realized it wouldn't be the first time she had infuriated her daughter and son-in-law. Most likely it wouldn't be the last, either. Beyond a certain point, that was all a mother could do for her children—hang around long enough to drive them crazy.

Alice found she was calmer now. She still didn't know where she was or how she had come to be there, but for some reason the possibility of having yanked. Ross Jenkins' chain made her feel somewhat better.

Outside the open window, the chilled Sonora Desert was deathly silent. Into that silence came a sound that resembled the rattle of castanets. Several seconds passed before Alice realized that the noise was coming from inside her own head, from her upper and lower dentures clacking rhythmically against each other. The brisk November nighttime air had reached deep into Alice's bones, leaving her whole body shivering and quaking.

Automatically, Alice reached for the button that operated the Buick's power windows, but when she pressed the switch, nothing happened. The window stayed wide open.

"The key, stupid," Alice muttered aloud. "You should know by now that the window won't work if the ignition key's turned off."

In the all-enveloping darkness, she reached

out again. This time she aimed her searching fingers toward the steering column, groping for the key. But where her fingers should have closed around her dangling key chain, there was nothing at all—nothing but air. The key was missing.

"Damn!" Alice exclaimed. "It must have fallen out. How am I going to find it in the dark?"

Holding the steering wheel for balance, Alice leaned down and ran her hands across the rubber-covered floorboard. She didn't find the keys. Instead, her hand shut around the neck of a bottle—an almost empty bottle, from the feel of it. In the dark Alice couldn't read the label, but she didn't have to. Long acquaintance made the round shape instantly recognizable. Dewar's, of course. The singular lack of booze in the nearly empty bottle went a long way toward explaining everything else.

Carefully, Alice checked the bottle lid to make sure it was screwed on securely. No sense in spilling whatever was left. Once the bottle was propped on the seat beside her, she bent down once more and resumed her search for the missing keys.

"Alice," someone called. "Wake up."

Wide awake now, she heard the voice distinctly. It seemed to be coming from right outside the car, from a distance of no more than a few feet.

Startled, Alice jerked upright and turned to look, but she saw no one. Still, the nearby presence of that unseen voice filled her with gratitude. That meant she wasn't alone out here in the desert after all. Someone else was here with her. Maybe whoever it was had taken the car keys.

"I am awake," Alice called back. "I just can't find the keys. If you could come help me find them . . ."

"I can't," the person called back. "You have to find me first. You're it."

Straining to listen, Alice wondered what was wrong with that voice. The odd falsetto defied identification. She couldn't tell if the singsong voice belonged to a man or woman; to a child or grown-up. Perhaps it was a child pretending to be a grown-up, or maybe the other way around. Whoever it was, the familiar words tugged Alice out of her failing body and back to the world of her childhood. "Come and find me," the words beckoned to her from across the years. "You're it."

A spark of memory flared briefly in Alice's heart. Was it possible that the person calling to her from the darkness just outside the Buick was someone from that far-off time in her life when she was just a child? Through the haze of booze she realized that whoever it was had to be someone who had known Alice Monroe Rogers back then, when she was a little girl. Maybe it was one of Alice's three sisters summoning her once again to an old-fashioned game of tag. Maybe it was time to resume a game of hide-and-seek that had gone unfinished for over seventy years.

As the youngest of Mary and Alfred Monroe's seven children, being "it" had been little Alice's lot in life. Being "it" had been her fate—her curse for having been born the youngest, for being the baby. As such, she had borne the brunt of countless jokes and pranks. No doubt, she decided, this was more of the same.

The insistent voice called to her once again through a fog of memory. "Alice. Are you coming or not? What are you, a fraidycat?"

A wave of goose flesh swept over Alice's body. The temperature in the car hovered in the upper thirties, but the sudden chill she felt had nothing to do with outside temperatures. Fraidycat! Like being perpetually "it," that well-worn phrase came directly from her childhood, too. That was one of the terms her three older sisters had hurled in Alice's direction to devil her. And it wasn't just her sisters, either. Alice's brothers had called her that as well. "Fraidycat! Fraidycat. Fraidycat."

Which of those voices was calling to her now? Alice wondered. Was it Jean, or Jessie, or Rosemary? Or could it be Thomas, William, or Jack? No, that wasn't possible. Rosemary was dead. Had been for years. So were William and Thomas. They had gone away to World War II and never returned. William had died at Guadalcanal and Thomas in a POW camp in Germany. Jack lived in an Alzheimer's group home up in Cottonwood. According to Alice's sister-in-law, Jack no longer remembered his own name, let alone those of his four sisters. Jean also lived in a nursing home, one over in Safford, near where her son and daughter-in-law had settled. She wasn't in much better shape than Jack was. Jessie, the old maid of the family, was eleven years older than Alice. At eighty-seven she still lived in Douglas in a roach-infested assisted-care facility only a few blocks from the rambling brick house on G Avenue where the seven Monroe kids had grown to adult-hood.

"Al . . . ice. Come . . . find . . . me."

That's who it has to be, Alice decided at once. *Jessie.* Jessie Monroe had always been a great one for practical jokes.

Reaching for the handle, Alice wrenched open the door. She almost spilled out onto the ground as the heavy door swung open, pulling her with it.

"Jessie," Alice called back, once she righted herself. "Is that you? Are you out here? Where are you?"

Assuming that she and her invisible playmate were all alone in the vast desert, Alice blinked in astonishment when she lurched to her feet and found a great mass of people looming along the road on the far side of the broad, bull-dozed drainage ditch that lined the black-topped ribbon of pavement. The ghostly crowd of onlookers stood tall, eerie, and silent, watching her expectantly—watching and listening.

"Who are you?" Alice demanded of the crowd, but no one responded. No one moved. No one spoke. It was as though they had all been rooted to the ground and struck dumb at the same time.

"What's the matter? Cat got your tongue?" Alice asked. Still there was no response. "Suit yourselves, then," she told them.

Reaching back inside the Buick, she dragged out the old, fraying sweater she kept there in case of emergencies. She put it on. Then, pretending the still silent crowd wasn't there, Alice cupped her hands around her mouth. "Ready or not," she called to Jessie. "Here I come."

Gamely, Alice Monroe Rogers set off across the desert, closing her mind to the cold, disregarding the darkness, and ignoring the loose pieces of rock and gravel that threatened to turn beneath her feet. It wasn't until she crossed the ditch that she discovered the ghostly shapes weren't people after all. What she had taken for a crowd of silent men and women was actually a thick stand of cholla. The tall, spine-covered cactus branches reached out in all directions, grabbing at Alice's clothing as she staggered past, snagging her skirt and tugging at the thread in her too-skimpy cotton sweater.

As she dodged between cacti, Alice came to a sudden puzzling realization. *Jessie's on a walker. What in God's name is she doing out here in the middle of the desert? Susan and I must not be the only ones who are dipping into the Dewar's.*

Panting with effort, Alice stopped and took stock. "Jessie, come on out," she called. "I give up. You win. It's too cold to play anymore, too cold and too dark. Come help me find the car keys so we can go home."

She stood still and listened. There was no answer, but there was something—a rustling of some kind that came from almost directly behind her. Alice was just starting to turn around to check on the noise when whatever it was crashed into her from behind. Because of her half-turn, the full body blow that should have sent her face-first into the nearest cactus hit her from the side instead. She reeled under the jarring impact and then went tottering sideways. She screamed as needle sharp spines plunged deep into her paper thin flesh, then she fell.

The cactus was far taller than Alice, but it was also far more delicate. The brittle, spine-covered branches dropped some of their needles and then broke off as she plowed into them. Under her weight, one shallowly rooted trunk broke off at ground level and collapsed. That first towering plant keeled over, and an accompanying domino effect brought down several of its near neighbors. When the cacti came to rest, so did Alice. She found herself lying face-up, her body impaled on a thousand razor-sharp, three inch-long needles, each of which burned into her body with the appalling intensity of an individual bee sting.

For a moment she lay there in agony, so stunned by shock that she didn't dare move or breathe or even open her eyes. Locked in a pain-filled daze, she failed to notice the muffled sound of nearby footsteps. When they finally penetrated her consciousness, Alice realized someone was standing over her. That's when she opened her eyes.

The awful pain remained but the terrible all-consuming darkness—a darkness that had verged on blindness itself—was gone. Overhead, beyond the shadow of whoever was standing above her, the sky blazed with the light of a thousand pinprick stars. It was still night, but the glowing starlight made it seem almost as bright as day.

My glasses, Alice realized at once. She had been

wearing her glasses, the heavy-duty wraparound sunglasses Dr. Toon had given her after her cataract surgery. The act of falling had knocked the glasses away and turned the solid darkness to silvery light.

If the cholla hadn't hurt so damned much, Alice might have laughed aloud, but this was no time for joking around.

"Jessie," Alice managed. "I'm hurt. I've fallen in the cactus. You've got to help me up, but be careful the cholla doesn't get you, too."

That's when she noticed that the person towering over her wasn't on a walker. He or she was far too tall and too broad to be Alice's sister Jessie. Not only that, the face was all wrong too. The features were distorted—mashed together in a strange, monstrous way. Through the haze of pain Alice realized that the person leaning over her was wearing a stocking over his face.

When she spoke again, whatever booze might have once been in her system seemed long gone. "Please help me," she begged. "If you'll just take my hand . . ."

At once a gloved hand reached out and took Alice's, but instead of making an effort to lift the woman to her feet, the fingers clamped shut around her wrist, imprisoning it in a bruising, viselike grip. Roughly the gloved fingers peeled back the cuff of Alice's worn sweater, exposing the bare skin of her forearm. Alice yelped in pain as the yarn in the sweater moved across the cactus barbs impaled in the other side of her arm, driving them farther into her flesh.

"Stop," she commanded. "Please don't try to move the sweater. It hurts too much. Just help me—"

That was when she saw the syringe for the first time. Somehow it materialized from nowhere, appearing in her captor's other hand. His rubber-gloved fingers held it upright, ready to plunge it into the naked flesh of Alice's captive wrist.

Alice's son, Clete, was a diabetic and had been for years. As a consequence, Alice was no stranger to syringes and needles. She knew them as distributors of the life-sustaining insulin that had kept her son alive, and as devices that had delivered the pain-killing drugs that had helped ease her husband through his final illness. At first she thought the person standing over her was trying to help her, that the needle held some kind of painkiller that would somehow counteract the poison pumping into her body from the cholla needles. Maybe he was giving her something that would combat the mind-numbing pain.

The metal part of the needle flashed briefly in the starlight and then she felt the sharp jab in her wrist. "Thank you," she murmured. "I'm sure that will help. Now, if you'll just help me up."

Instead, the man produced another needle and shoved that one into her arm as well.

What if this isn't a painkiller at all? Alice wondered. *What if it's something else, like poison, maybe? What if he's trying to kill me?*

"What are you doing?" she asked. Her tongue seemed to grow thick in her mouth. She had a hard time forming the words, but by then he had pulled yet a third syringe out of his pocket. She struggled and tried to yank her arm free, but even the smallest movement ground hundreds of cholla spines deeper into her back, legs, and arms. Once again the needle of a loaded syringe plunged into her arm.

"Stop!" Alice commanded, but this time the word came out as little more than an unrecognizable gurgle. She moaned in agony.

"Be still, Alice!" he growled. The falsetto was gone now. It was definitely a man's voice, but whose? It sounded familiar, but Alice's pain-fogged brain couldn't make the connection.

"Who are you?" she tried to say. "What do you want?" But the words were so slurred that they sounded like gibberish, even to her.

In reply, the man dropped her wrist. Alice lay still and watched him through a confusing, misty haze as he pocketed the third syringe and gathered up the other two from where they had fallen to the ground beside her. He stuffed them into his coat pocket as well. As he turned to walk away, Alice felt a small object land on her abdomen and then roll off onto the ground.

At that moment, what was happening seemed to be of little concern to her. The body lying on the cold, hard ground might have been someone else's rather than her own. There was no getting away. Alice had no strength or breath left to scream or cry out for help. There was nothing to do but submit and hope that eventually the pain would stop.

Her tormentor walked away, and after that,

time seemed to dissolve as well. The world spun out of control. Despite the cold, sweat popped out all over Alice's body. The sudden unaccountable dampness of her skin made her feel that much colder. Even so, she somehow remembered that something had fallen on her—something small and hard that had rolled off her body and onto the ground.

Unable to turn her head without driving the cholla needles deeper into her flesh, she patted the earth next to her until her groping fingers closed around something small and smooth. It was a bottle, a tiny glass bottle.

She knew what the tiny vial was without even looking—knew what it must have contained and what the inevitable result would be. The cholla needles were nothing compared to the hurt and betrayal that flooded through her in that awful moment of realization. Grasping the bottle in her fist, she closed her eyes and let the tears come. Hours later, when Alice Rogers finally stopped breathing, the little glass vial was still clutched tightly in her dying fist.

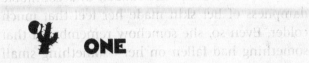

ONE

EASING THE porch swing back and forth, thirty-
year-old Sheriff Joanna Brady closed her green
eyes and let the warmth of an early-November
Sunday afternoon caress her body. Nearby, on the
top step, sat Joanna's best friend and pastor, the
Reverend Marianne Maculyea of Canyon United
Methodist Church. Without speaking for minutes
at a time, the two women watched their respective children—Joanna's eleven-year-old Jennifer
and Marianne's three-year-old Ruth—at play.

Both sets of mothers and daughters were studies in contrast. Joanna's red hair was cut short in
what Helen Barco at Helene's Salon of Hair and
Beauty called a figure-skater cut. On this Sunday
afternoon, Marianne's long dark hair was pulled
back in a serviceable ponytail. Jenny's fair, blue-
eyed face was surrounded by a halo of tow-headed
white hair while Ruth's shiny black pageboy
gleamed in the warm autumn sun.

The last week in October, a surprisingly fierce cold snap had visited southeastern Arizona, bringing with it a frigid rain that had threatened to drown out most of Bisbee's Halloween trick-or-treating. Two days later, when bright sunlight re-emerged, the cottonwood, apple, and peach trees on High Lonesome Ranch seemed to have changed colors overnight. In the sunny days and crisp nights since, dying leaves had drifted from their branches and had fallen to earth, carpeting the yard in a thick mantle of gold, red, rust, and brown.

For little Ruth, recently rescued from life in a desolate Chinese orphanage, the crackly, multi-colored leaves were a source of incredible wonder and delight. Together the two girls raked great mounds of leaves into piles, then dived into them with a chorus of shrieks alternating with giggles.

For a while both of Jenny's dogs—Sadie, a blue-tick hound, and Tigger, a comical-looking half pit bull/half golden retriever—had joined in. When Sadie tired of the game, she retreated to the relative quiet of the porch along with Joanna and Marianne. With a sigh, the dog lay down on the top step and placed her smooth, floppy-eared head in Marianne's lap. Tigger, however, continued to throw himself into the festivities with all the antic energy of a born clown.

On Jenny's command to "stay," the dog, quivering with eager anticipation, would lie perfectly still and allow himself to be covered with a mound of leaves. When Jenny shouted "okay," the dog would erupt from the leaves, tuck his tail between his legs, and then race around the yard as though pursued by a pack of ravenous coyotes.

Each time the game was repeated, Ruth clapped her hands in childish delight. "Again, Jenny," she crowed. "Do again!"

Watching the simple game and enjoying the gales of gleeful laughter, Joanna Brady found herself nodding and smiling. She was about to comment on the beautiful afternoon and on the two girls' unrestrained joy. When she looked in Marianne's direction, however, she saw a single tear snake its way down her friend's solemn face. Seeing that tear, Joanna opted for silence. For the space of another minute or so, neither woman said a word while Marianne's hand absently stroked Sadie's soft, velvety muzzle.

"What is it, Mari?" Joanna asked finally. The question wasn't really necessary because Joanna knew exactly what the problem was. In August, Marianne's other newly adopted daughter—Esther, Ruth's twin sister—had died of complications following heart-transplant surgery. It seemed certain to Joanna that watching two little girls at play on this warm, jewel-clear afternoon had reopened Marianne's aching wound.

Joanna Brady herself was no stranger to the grieving process. The death of her husband, Andy, had thrown her own life into a personal hell of pain and loss. She understood how a perfect moment in a gemlike day could darken and then be dashed to pieces by the sudden realization that someone else was missing from the picture, that a certain loved one wasn't present to share that special moment. At times like these, the perfection of the present would fade to a muddy gray, shrouded behind an impenetrable fog of hurt. Watching one daughter at play, Marianne had no doubt been stricken by a terrible longing for the other child, one who wasn't there and never would be again.

Convinced that she knew exactly what was going on with Marianne, Joanna was confused when, after another minute or so, she heard her friend's clipped response. "I'm going to quit," Marianne said.

At first Joanna didn't make the connection. "Quit what?" she asked.

"The ministry," Marianne replied. "I'm going to resign effective immediately."

Somehow Joanna managed to stifle her gasp of dismay. "Surely you don't mean that!" she said at last.

"I do," Marianne said determinedly. "I've never meant anything more in my life. My letter of resignation is all written. It's sitting in the computer waiting to be printed. There's a church council meeting on Wednesday evening. I'll probably turn it in then."

Stunned, Joanna fell silent. Through the turmoil following Andy's death, Marianne Maculyea and her husband, Jeff Daniels, had been never-failing sources of comfort and support. With their help and encouragement, Joanna had slowly battled her way back to emotional stability. They had walked her through months of painful grieving—through the inevitable stages of denial and anger—until she had at last achieved a measure of acceptance.

That summer, when tragedy had visited her friends in the form of Esther's death, Joanna had done her best to return the favor. She had strived to provide the same kind of understanding and strength for them that they had given her. Now, Joanna realized that her efforts had fallen short. She must not have done enough. Why else would Marianne be sitting on the front porch, basking in the warm afternoon sunlight, and drowning in despair?

"What's going on?" Joanna asked softly. "It's not like you to just give up."

Marianne's gray eyes darkened with a film of tears. "It's the Thanksgiving sermon," she answered. "Because of bulletin deadlines, I'm always working two weeks ahead. I've been trying for days to think of something meaningful to say, but I can't do it. I'm not the least bit thankful right now, Joanna. I'm outraged. If Marliss Shackleford tells me one more time how lucky we are to still have Ruth, I'm liable to punch the woman's lights out."

Marliss was a busybody columnist for the local paper and one of Marianne's parishioners besides. She wasn't one of Joanna's favorite people, either. In fact, when it came to Marliss, Joanna had long since given up turning the other cheek. "It might do the woman a world of good," she said.

Marianne favored Joanna with a wan smile and then looked off in the other direction, all the while continuing to stroke Sadie's unmoving head. In times of crisis Joanna herself had drawn comfort from the dog's uncomplaining, stolid presence, but she wondered if, given the present circumstances, merely petting a dog offered enough solace.

Marianne's continuing crisis of faith was something the two friends had discussed often in the months since Esther's death. Joanna had assumed that over time things would get better for Marianne, just as they had for her. But clearly the situation for Marianne wasn't improving. Rather than pulling out of her morass, Marianne seemed to be sinking deeper and deeper.

Struggling to find something useful to say, Joanna rose from the porch swing and raked a few more leaves into the small bonfire where a collection of foil-wrapped potatoes was roasting. Raking leaves and baking potatoes in an autumn bonfire was something Andrew Roy Brady had done first with his father, Jim Bob, and later with his daughter, Jenny. With Andy gone, this was one of the small family traditions Joanna had been determined to carry on. She had worried that reviving that old custom might bring up too many memories for both mother and daughter. Instead, Jenny had thrown herself wholeheartedly into playing with Ruth and Tigger, while Joanna was too caught up in Marianne's heartache to remember her own.

What can I say that won't make things worse? Joanna wondered, as she leaned the rake against the fence and returned to her spot on the porch swing. *Or would I be better off just keeping quiet?*

But keeping quiet wasn't part of Joanna Brady's

genetic makeup. She was far too much her own mother's daughter. "Have you talked to Jeff about this?" Joanna asked as she resumed her place.

Marianne's eyes flashed with sudden anger. Her reply was sharp, aggrieved. "Of course I have," she snapped. "He thinks I should have my head examined."

Any other time, such a comment might have been nothing more than a light-hearted quip. Here it was no laughing matter. "What do *you* think?" Joanna asked.

"I already told you what I think," Marianne replied. "If I don't have anything of value to contribute, I should quit. I can type. I can probably get a regular job. Somebody around here must need a secretary or receptionist."

Joanna closed her eyes. In her mind's eye she visualized the Marianne of old standing behind the pulpit preaching. Before Esther's death, and comfortable in her faith, Marianne's face used to glow with certitude as she delivered her sermons. There had been an inner joy about her that had backlit everything she said. For months now, though, that glow had been absent. Joanna doubted she was the only one who realized that her friend was simply going through the motions, but even Joanna had never considered the possibility that Marianne's inner glow might have dimmed for good.

"Have you thought about seeing a doctor?" Joanna asked.

"A doctor?" Marianne sneered impatiently. "See

there? You've jumped to the same conclusion Jeff has. You think I should see a shrink."

"I didn't *say* shrink," Joanna corrected. "And I didn't *mean* shrink, either. I saw what happened today at lunch. You hardly ate anything at all. You pushed the food around on your plate until enough time had passed for the meal to be over. The only food that actually left your plate was what you gave Ruth. You're not eating properly, and you look like you're melting away to nothing. You've got deep, dark circles under your eyes."

"I wasn't hungry," Marianne cut in. "Food makes me sick these days. I can barely stand to look at it, much less swallow it."

"And I'll bet you're not sleeping properly, either," Joanna continued doggedly. "You know yourself that eating and sleeping disturbances are standard symptoms of grief—grief and depression both. You're depressed, Mari. You need help. Go see a doctor."

"And what good will that do?" Marianne demanded. "All he'll do is plug me full of antidepressants—dose me with some kind of chemical joy juice. Take two of these and then wait for a sermon to pop up on the computer screen?"

"Not necessarily," Joanna replied. "But seriously, Mari, maybe there's something else wrong—something physical—that's causing all this."

"Come on, Joanna. Give me a break. Don't you see? It's not physical at all. I'm not a hypocrite. I've spent my whole life first believing and then preaching that life is eternal. Now that Esther's gone, I don't feel that anymore. I feel empty. There's nothing left of that hope but a huge black hole and everything—my whole life—is collapsing into it. I don't know what to do about it. If I'm not capable of living my beliefs in my own life, what business do I have passing them along to anyone else?"

"Maybe that's what the sermon should be about," Joanna suggested.

"About what?"

"About being thankful for the black hole," Joanna said. "The people down front—the ones sitting out there in the pews—probably think they're the only ones who've ever felt that way. A sermon like that coming from you would show them they're not alone."

Before Marianne had a chance to reply, a telephone rang inside the house. Joanna hurried to answer it. "Hello."

"Sheriff Brady?" an unfamiliar male voice asked.

With only a few seconds of emotional buffer between her private life and her public one, Joanna switched gears. "This is Sheriff Brady," she replied. "Who's this, and what can I do for you?"

"What's the deal with this Frank Montoya guy?" her gruff caller continued. "Is he some kind of a dim bulb, or what?"

Chief Deputy for Administration Frank Montoya, along with Chief Deputy for Operations, Richard Voland, were Joanna's primary aides-de-camp in running the Cochise County Sheriff's

Department. Both men had initially opposed Joanna's candidacy for the office of sheriff, but once the election was over, both had assumed important roles in her administration.

Listening intently, Joanna couldn't quite place the voice, although she was sure she had heard it before. "Chief Deputy Montoya is anything but a dim bulb," she replied. "He's a dedicated and talented police officer. Who's asking?"

"Mayor Rogers," the man replied. "Mayor Cletus Rogers of Tombstone."

Joanna sighed, took a seat, and prepared herself for the worst. In the aftermath of a bitterly divisive city recall effort, Clete Rogers had been the successful write-in candidate for mayor during a special election the previous July. A restaurateur with all the diplomacy of a mountain goat, Clete Rogers had assumed mayoral duties in the Town Too Tough to Die. Once sworn into office, he had immediately set about consolidating his power base by firing anyone who disagreed with him. One of the first victims of his displeasure had been Dennis Granger, formerly the town's chief marshal.

Rogers had planned to fire Granger and replace him with a crony—somebody who would be more to his liking. Granger, however, refused to go quietly. After turning in his badge and city-owned weapons, he had filed a million-dollar wrongful-dismissal lawsuit. With litigation still pending, both sides were forbidden from discussing the matter in public. In the meantime, the

Tombstone city attorney had advised Mayor Rogers that he had best not fill the marshal's vacancy since, legally, the vacancy did not yet exist. Which was how Sheriff Joanna Brady and her department had been drawn into the fray.

Mayor Rogers had asked the county supervisors to allow the sheriff's department to assume control of the town's four remaining marshals. The job was more supervisory than anything else—a matter of assigning and coordinating the officers left to do the actual work.

In the Cochise County Sheriff's Department, Chief Deputy for Administration Frank Montoya was Joanna's right-hand man, but before signing on with the county, he had served as marshal for the city of Willcox. Montoya's background and experience made him the logical choice to take on the Tombstone assignment. He had been there—working out of city hall, staying in a motel, and with the city of Tombstone paying his salary—for the better part of two months. But as litigation threatened to drag on and on, both Frank and Joanna were beginning to wonder if he'd ever return to his office at the Cochise County Justice Complex outside Bisbee. Not only that, from what Joanna had heard, Mayor Rogers didn't seem to appreciate Frank's performance as marshal any more than he had Dennis Granger's.

"What's the problem now?" Joanna asked.

"I'll tell you what the problem is," Rogers returned. "My sister Susan is the problem. She came into my place of business just before noon and started a disturbance. Frank Montoya was sitting right there eating his lunch when it happened. He didn't raise a finger."

"What kind of disturbance?" Joanna asked.

"Do you remember the Smothers Brothers?" Rogers asked.

"The Smothers Brothers?" Joanna asked dubiously. "Who are they?"

"That's right," Rogers snorted. "You're probably too young. Years ago, in the sixties, they were a comedy team. Used to have a great show called 'The Smothers' Brothers Comedy Hour.' I loved it. Some of their best routines were all about how their mother liked the other one best. Believe me, when it comes to that, Susan could have given those guys lessons."

"You're saying the argument was about your mother, then?" Joanna asked.

"That's how it started, and things went downhill from there. It ended up with Susan grabbing a tablecloth and pulling a whole table's worth of glasses, dishes, and silverware onto the floor. Broke two plates, one mug, three water glasses, and four wineglasses. That's more breakage than we usually have in a month. Make that a year. Those wineglasses especially are damned expensive. And what did your pal Montoya do about it? I'll tell you what he did—nothing! Not a damned thing!"

"Is your sister still there?"

"No. Montoya did do that much, I guess," Rogers admitted grudgingly. "He talked her into going outside, but he should have arrested her, by God! For disturbing the peace, if nothing else, for trespassing, or even for assault. With all that glass flying around, it's a wonder somebody didn't get hurt, If not one of my customers, then one of my workers. It was right in the middle of the Sunday after church rush, too. The place was packed."

"And this incident was all about your mother?" Joanna asked.

"About her boyfriend, really. Farley Adams. I'm sure Mother's mentioned him to Susan the same as she has to me, but now that it looks like things might turn serious, Susan's all pissed off that I haven't done something to stop it."

"I take it your sister disapproves of the boyfriend?" Joanna observed.

"Our mother is something of a free spirit," Rogers said. "But my sister is an uptight middle-class prude with delusions of grandeur. She can't stand the idea that our mother still has some feminine juices flowing. I'm sure she'd like to think of Mother as a shriveled old prune. The fact that the old girl's still capable of sowing wild oats drives Susan wild."

"So what exactly caused the fuss?" Joanna asked.

"I suggested Susan mind her own business. I also hinted that maybe she should try reading *Lady Chatterley's Lover*. That's when she went ballistic on me and started breaking up my restaurant."

Joanna felt as though important parts of the story were missing. "Why did that upset your sister so?"

"Have *you* read *Lady Chatterley's Lover?*" Rogers asked pointedly. "The randy caretaker and all that?"

"You're saying the boyfriend, this Mr. Adams, started out as your mother's employee then, as a gardener or something?"

"Right, as her handyman, but he's graduated to something else, evidently. According to Susan, the two of them drove up to Laughlin, Nevada, a couple of weeks ago and stayed for three whole days. I doubt they had separate rooms. And I doubt they spent the whole time playing slot machines or blackjack, either."

"All right," Joanna said. "So your sister disapproved of your mother's choice of friends, but how did that cause trouble between the two of you?"

"Susan evidently found out about the Laughlin trip just last night. Mother went out to Sierra Vista to have dinner with Susan and her husband and told them all about it. Rubbed their noses in it, was the way Susan put it. She asked me if I had known our mother was drifting in that direction, and why hadn't I done something to stop it. I told her it was none of my business, any more than it was hers."

"Where's your sister now?"

"Not in jail, where she should be. Montoya told her to go home and cool off."

"And your mother?"

"At home, as far as I know. I haven't talked to her today so far, but she usually comes by for dinner later on in the afternoon. That's one of the disadvantages of being in the restaurant business. Some of your relatives give up cooking completely. As far as Mother is concerned, though, it's the least I can do."

In the course of the conversation, Clete Rogers sounded as though he had cooled off some. He had needed to vent.

"So things are pretty well under control at the moment, is that correct?" Joanna asked.

"Well, yes. I suppose so."

"Are you interested in filing any charges?"

"Oh, all right. Probably not. If Mother found out, it would only upset her, wouldn't it?"

"Most likely."

"I'll just let it go, then. But you tell Montoya to give Susan the word. Have him tell her that she's not to come around here again. That from now on the Grubsteak is totally off limits."

"It might be best if you told her yourself instead of dragging Deputy Montoya into it," Joanna inserted smoothly. "Better yet, you might consider having your attorney go to court and obtain a restraining order. That way, if Susan comes anywhere near your home or your place of business, either one, then there'll be grounds for officers to arrest her. That will go for your town marshals and for my deputies, both. It'll give everyone a legal basis for removing her."

"Okay," Clete Rogers said, sounding mollified. "I'll think about it. Sounds like good advice, but right now, I've got to go. My cashier is waving that she needs something. I'll let you know about the restraining order later on."

When he put down the receiver, Joanna sat for some time listening to the dial tone. Nobody had told her how much the job of sheriff had to do with public relations. After half a minute or so, she punched the speed-dial code for the department. When Lisa Howard, the weekend desk clerk answered, Joanna asked to be put through to Dispatch. Tica Romero took the call.

"Afternoon, Sheriff Brady. What can I do for you?"

"What do you hear from Deputy Montoya?"

"Not much. Things must be pretty quiet over in Tombstone this weekend."

"Not totally quiet," Joanna countered. "Try to raise Frank on the radio and ask him to give me a call at home. Tell him I've had a call from Hizzoner Mayor Rogers."

"Will do," Tica said.

"Is there anything else going on?" Joanna asked.

"Nothing out of the ordinary," Tica told her.

"Good," Joanna said. "Let's hope it stays that way."

When Tica dropped off, Joanna returned the phone to its cradle. Then, thinking better of it, she picked up the receiver, stuffed it into the pocket of her jeans, and took it with her when she returned to the porch.

"Who was it?" Marianne asked. "Butch and Jeff?"

Butch was Butch Dixon. Over Joanna Brady's initial objections, he had meandered into her life and, invited or not, assumed the role of "boyfriend." While attending police academy courses in the Phoenix area, Joanna had happened into Butch's Roundhouse Bar and Grill up in Peoria. The two of them had hit it off. Joanna had enjoyed Butch's company when he was around, but she hadn't exactly encouraged the relationship.

Concerned about public reaction as well as Jenny's feelings and her own, Joanna had thought it far too soon after Andy's death for her to become involved with anyone. Had it been left up to her, she would have relegated Butch to a back burner and let him stay there. He, however, had taken matters into his own hands. When the opportunity presented itself, he had sold out his business holdings in Peoria and moved to Bisbee. Once settled into his new digs in Bisbee's Saginaw neighborhood, he had gone to work on his life-long ambition of writing a novel. He had also set himself the task of being useful to Joanna, and to her friends as well.

A bad case of writer's block and a mutual interest in old cars had drawn him into an easy friendship with Jeff Daniels and his business, Auto Rehab. The two men had joined forces to recondition a '56 Chevrolet Bel Air. Working together, they had bought the car for a song and then refurbished it on speculation. The previous afternoon the two men had gone off to Scottsdale together, towing their pride and joy behind Jeff's International and hoping to unload the Bel Air for a modest profit at one of Scottsdale's collector car auctions.

The fact that Jeff and Butch were both out of town was one of the reasons Joanna had invited Marianne and Ruth out to High Lonesome Ranch that Sunday after church. She had thought waiting for the menfolk together would be more fun than waiting separately.

"It was work," Joanna said, in answer to Marianne's query.

"Is something wrong?" Marianne asked. "Are you going to have to go in to the department?"

"I doubt it. It sounds as though everything is under control, although Frank Montoya will probably be giving me a call in a little while."

By then Ruth had tired of the leaf game and clambered up onto the porch, displacing Sadie's long-eared head from Marianne's lap. The child lay there, struggling to keep her eyes open while a worn-out and panting Tigger flopped down in the grass nearby. Jenny, both elbows planted on the ground, lay beside him. She looked up at her mother.

"I hope he doesn't call," Jenny said with a pout. "You never used to have to work on Sundays. Now you almost always do."

"We've been over this before many times, Jenny," Joanna said. "The kind of job I have now doesn't come with set nine-to-five hours."

Unconvinced, Jenny tossed her blond hair. Still pouting, the child turned to Marianne. "What about you?" she asked.

"What about me?" Marianne returned.

"Don't you hate it that you have to work on Sundays?"

For the first time all day a seemingly genuine smile spread across Marianne Maculyea's haggard face. "I never have minded," she said, "but I must confess, I never thought about it quite that way."

TWO

AS THE sun sank behind the Mule Mountains, a sudden chill settled over the porch. Raking the steaming, foil-wrapped potatoes out of the remaining embers, Joanna announced it was time to move the party inside. One by one, the fully cooked spuds were divested of blackened foil and scooped onto dinner plates where they were smothered with butter, sour cream, and chopped green onions and joined by thick slices of freshly baked meatloaf. After hours of play, the two girls were famished. Joanna, too, was surprisingly hungry. Once again, however, Marianne Maculyea pushed food around on her plate and made only the slightest pretense of eating it.

Dinner was over, the table cleared, and dishes mostly in the dishwasher before the telephone rang again. Joanna had left the cordless phone sitting by her place at the dining room table. Jenny raced to answer it before her mother could dry her hands.

33

"It's for you," Jenny announced, carrying the handset into the kitchen. "It's Butch. I already told him we're saving him a potato and some meat-loaf."

"Does that mean Jeff and I are invited out to the ranch when we get home?" Butch Dixon asked when Joanna came on the line.

"Sure," Joanna said.

"Anything besides potatoes and meatloaf on the menu?" Butch asked.

Knowing his slyly stated question had nothing at all to do with food, Joanna ducked her face away from Marianne and Jenny in order to conceal the crimson blush that swept up her neck and face. Her best line of defense was to ignore his remark altogether.

"Where are you?" she asked.

"Tucson," he said. "We're making a pit stop, getting gas, and grabbing some coffee."

"When do you expect to be home?"

"Not much later than an hour and a half."

"Where are they?" Marianne asked from across the room.

Joanna held the phone away from her mouth. "In Tucson," she answered. "Getting gas."

Marianne nodded. "Have Butch tell Jeff that Ruth and I will meet him at home. If we don't go home until after he gets here, it'll be too late for Ruth to have a bath before bedtime. Tell him we'll bring his dinner home and he can eat it there."

"Did you hear that?" Joanna asked Butch.

"Got it," he said. "I'll have Jeff drop me off at

my place so I can pick up my car. I'll be out at the ranch as soon as I can. See you then."

"Be careful," Joanna said. The warning was out of her mouth before she could stop it. No matter how hard she tried, Joanna could never quite forget that she had failed to say those cautioning words to Andy as he left home on the morning he died—the morning he went off to work never to return. With Butch those once unspoken words were never far from her lips or her heart.

"Don't worry about Jeff and me," Butch replied. "Neither of us is big on taking chances."

By the time Joanna put down the phone, Marianne was already gathering her stack of traveling-mother equipment—a diaper bag, an old briefcase packed with toys and books, as well as a purse. She loaded the collection into the backseat of her venerable VW bug. When it came time to strap Ruth into her car seat, the weary child turned suddenly cranky. She fought the seat belt and was screaming at the top of her lungs as they headed down the road for the seven-mile trip back uptown to the Canyon United Methodist parsonage in Old Bisbee. As Ruth's earsplitting wail receded into the distance, Joanna felt a sudden wave of gratitude that Jenny had grown far beyond the unreasoning tantrums of toddlerhood.

"Come on, Jenny," Joanna said. "Fun's over. Time to do the chores."

Six days a week Clayton Rhodes, Joanna's octogenarian neighbor, took care of the animal husbandry duties on High Lonesome Ranch. Sunday was Clayton's one day off.

For the next half hour Jenny and Joanna worked together, feeding and watering the High Lonesome's menagerie of animals. There was Kiddo—Jenny's quarter horse gelding; four head of cattle; two dogs; and half a dozen noisy, squawking chickens. The flock of birds had started out as cute and cuddly, living decorations for in-town children's Easter baskets, but once the chicks sprouted feathers and stopped being cute, they had all been discarded. The animal control officer who had convinced Joanna to take the first one knew when he had found a soft touch. He soon brought her several more, and she took those as well.

Joanna Brady found something life-affirming and grounding in watching animals munch their oats and hay. On Sundays when she had time to do her own chores, she found that performing those menial tasks gave her respite from the day-to-day pressures of running her department. Not only that, sharing those mundane duties with Jenny made Joanna feel that she was keeping faith with Andy—that she was continuing to raise their daughter in the way they had both intended.

"Is Marianne all right?" Jenny asked once the feeding frenzy was over. Mother and daughter were standing outside Kiddo's stall, and Jenny was reaching through the wooden slats to scratch the big sorrel's smoothly muscled shoulder.

"Why do you ask that?" Joanna returned.

"No fair," Jenny pointed out. "Remember, you're not supposed to answer a question with a question. If I can't, you can't."

Joanna laughed. "That's fair enough, I guess. And no, Marianne's not all right."

"What's wrong with her? Is she still sad about Esther?"

Joanna nodded. "I think that's it," she said.

Jenny considered that answer for some time before she spoke again. "When somebody dies, it takes a long time to get better, doesn't it?"

Joanna reached over and ran her fingers through Jenny's tangle of blond hair. "Yes, it does," she agreed. "But then, you and I both know something about that, don't we?"

Jenny nodded. "I guess we do," she said.

Back in the house and putting things to rights, Joanna was dimly annoyed by the fact that so much time had passed without Frank Montoya's returning her call. In fact, it wasn't until well after dark and after Jenny had scooted off to the bathroom for her evening bath when the telephone finally rang.

"What took you so long?" Joanna asked when she heard her chief deputy's voice on the line.

"It's hunting season, so naturally we've got spooked deer everywhere," Frank replied. "Right after you called, a big buck put himself through the windshield of a motor home just outside the Tombstone city limits. The Department of Public Safety officer who responded to the incident needed some help, and I happened to be handy. Sorry about that."

"What about the accident?" Joanna asked. "Not a fatality, I hope."

"It was fatal for the deer," Montoya answered. "The people in the motor home both got hit by flying glass. The seat belt did a pretty good job of bruising the woman's collarbone, but other than that, I think she and her husband will both be fine. What was it you wanted?"

"To know what's going on with Clete Rogers."

Frank sighed. "That's another whole can of worms. I'm just now getting ready to file the missing person's report."

"What missing person's report?" Joanna demanded.

"On Clete's mother—Alice Rogers."

"She's missing?"

"Evidently. According to the family, she drove to Sierra Vista yesterday afternoon to have dinner with her daughter and son-in-law, Susan and Ross Jenkins. Ross owns Fort Apache Motors, the Chrysler dealership on Fry Boulevard. According to the daughter, Alice left their place around eight-thirty, but she never made it home. At least, that's the way it looks so far. And if that wasn't bad enough, there was also a problem earlier at noontime between Susan Jenkins and her brother."

Joanna cut in. "I know about that. Mayor Rogers himself called to give me a full report."

Frank Montoya groaned. "Which was probably none too complimentary regarding yours truly."

"Right. Clete couldn't understand why you didn't arrest her. I've been wondering about that myself. If the woman was doing property damage, why didn't you?"

"Because they were *both* out of line," Frank Montoya replied. "I don't suppose Clete mentioned that."

"No."

"No surprises there," Montoya continued, "I've worked with the man long enough to know that when it comes to points of view, he has only one—his. I can also tell you that Clete Rogers doesn't exactly exude sweetness and light. By the time brother and sister finished bitching one another out in the middle of the restaurant, I had two choices. I could either arrest them both or let them off the hook. It was a judgment call, Joanna. Considering the current political climate, I chose the latter. I sent Susan Jenkins on her way. Told her to go home and cool off. She didn't, however. Instead, she went over to her mother's house looking for her. My guess is she planned to raise a little more hell, except her mother wasn't home. The Sunday paper was still on the porch.

"Afraid her mother might be sick or something, Susan let herself inside. She had a key. Once there, she found the place looked like it had been ransacked. Instead of calling us, she climbed right back into her car and drove out to Gleeson and proceeded to raise more hell, this time with Farley Adams."

"Her mother's boyfriend," Joanna supplied.

"Right," Frank responded, "although that's not what Susan Jenkins called him. Scumbag, for one. Gold digger, for another, along with a few other choice expressions that shouldn't be repeated in mixed company. I tell you, that woman's a piece of work!"

"You were there?"

"For part of it. He told her to leave—he lives in a mobile home parked at Alice Rogers' mining claim on Outlaw Mountain. When Susan refused to leave, he called for reinforcements. After what happened at the restaurant earlier, I didn't waste any time getting there. She was still raising holy hell with the man when I drove up. That's when she told me her mother was missing. I asked Susan if she suspected foul play, and the woman fell all apart on me. She went to pieces—hyperventilating and the whole nine yards. I ended up having to call her husband to come drive her home. The thing that really corks me is that Clete Rogers is probably right on this one—I should have arrested her to begin with."

"Where is she now?"

"Back home in Sierra Vista. Once I unloaded her, I went back to Tombstone and checked out the mother's house myself. And she's right. It looks as though the mother has disappeared, all right. At least she didn't come home overnight. Her car's gone. Somebody has ripped through the old woman's house and torn it to pieces, although there's no way to tell what, if anything, is missing."

"Did you have a chance to talk to the boyfriend?" Joanna asked.

"A little. Not that much because, like I said, I

had my hands full with this Jenkins woman. Then, after that, I was helping with the car wreck."

"What did Farley Adams have to say?" Joanna asked.

"He claims the last time he saw Alice was when she came out to his place yesterday morning. According to him, she planned on leaving home early in the afternoon because she had some errands to run in Sierra Vista before she was due at the Jenkins' place for dinner. Adams claims he hasn't seen or heard from her since. He says that he wasn't particularly concerned about that—about not seeing her earlier this morning—because he expected to see her later. They were supposed to have dinner together tonight."

"What time did you say Alice left her daughter's house last night?"

"About eight-thirty. Susan says she usually takes the Charleston Road back and forth to Tombstone."

Charleston Road, named after a long-gone mining town near the San Pedro River, was a short cut from Sierra Vista to Tombstone. It was a ribbon of cracked, curvy, up-and-down pavement. Because it crossed the San Pedro River, Charleston Road had its own share of meandering animals that sometimes came to grief with speeding vehicles.

"Had Alice Rogers been drinking?" Joanna asked.

"Some. According to the daughter, they had drinks before dinner and wine with the meal."

"There's not much nighttime traffic on Charleston Road," Joanna said. "Is it possible she hit a cow or a deer? Maybe she ran off the road somewhere between Sierra Vista and Tombstone. Her car may be out of sight in a ditch or a wash. Maybe that's why no one has spotted her."

"I already thought of that," Frank said. "I contacted Patrol and told them to have a deputy take a run out that way to see if he can find her. Just to be on the safe side, I also plan on filing a missing persons report. I don't want to give His Honor the Mayor anything else to complain about."

"Good thinking, Frank," Joanna said. "And good job, too, although I'm not sure it's going to help much. Clete Rogers is the kind of man who would complain if he was hanged with a new rope."

"Thanks, Chief. Always glad to be of service."

She put down the phone just as a pajama-clad Jenny emerged from the bathroom. "Was that Butch?" she asked.

"No. It was Frank Montoya calling about work. Did you want it to be Butch?"

For months now, Joanna Brady had watched from the sidelines, observing her daughter's reaction to Butch Dixon's increasing presence in their lives. It was a concern for Joanna, one she approached with more than a little misapprehension. She was glad Jenny seemed to like the man, but she was worried that if Butch walked away from a long-term relationship with Joanna, Jenny would end up suffering yet another devastating loss.

So far, though, things seemed to be all right.

Butch Dixon was the kind of man who had been born to be a father. Since he had no children of his own, he had thrown himself into an affectionate, easy kind of relationship with Jenny. Seemingly effortlessly, he had assumed the role of a beloved uncle.

And why shouldn't Jenny adore him? Joanna wondered. Butch was fun. He took every opportunity to spoil the child. Still, Joanna niggled away at the idea that under the placid surface of their friendship, something else was at work. Jenny's adoration went only so far. Much as she seemed to like the man, she maintained a certain distance as well. Maybe Jenny, like her mother, couldn't bear the risk of having her heart broken once again.

Jenny shrugged and studied her toes. "I guess I wanted it to be him," she admitted.

"Well, Butch is on his way, but he probably won't be here until after you go to bed."

"Oh," Jenny said.

Joanna waited to see if Jenny would say anything more. When she didn't, Joanna chose the easy way out. If Jenny wasn't ready to talk about Butch Dixon, neither was Joanna.

"Your homework's all done?" The motherly question was a cowardly attempt at sidestepping the issue.

Jenny sighed, flopped down on the couch beside Joanna, and snuggled in under her arm. "Of course," she said. "You know I always do my weekend homework on Friday afternoon right after school."

Joanna knew something was going on, even

though she couldn't quite put her finger on it. "Why are you worried about whether or not that was Butch?" she asked.

Jenny shrugged and said nothing.

"Come on," Joanna urged. "Give."

"I just need to talk to him, that's all."

"What about?"

"I can't tell you," Jenny replied. "It's a secret. Girl Scout's honor."

The lack of an answer bothered Joanna, but she tried to let it go. "All right, then," she said. "If it's Scout's honor, I won't try to pry it out of you. But it's getting late. You'd best scoot off to bed."

Jenny stood up. "Okay," she said. "But when Butch gets here, have him come talk to me."

"Only if you're still awake," Joanna said. "If you're already asleep, it'll have to wait until morning."

"Sadie, Tigger, come on," Jenny ordered. "Let's go to bed."

Obediently, both dogs got up and padded after Jenny into her bedroom. Long after the bedroom door had closed, Joanna sat there thinking about what had been said.

What kind of secret? she wondered. Everybody seemed to have secrets these days. The topper still had to be her mother, Eleanor Lathrop, hauling off and marrying Dr. George Winfield, Cochise County's new medical examiner, without saying a word to her daughter in advance of the nuptials. Even though Joanna had come to see that Eleanor and George were blissfully happy, she still wasn't over that initial sense of betrayal. Now she couldn't help wondering what kind of conspiracy Jenny was cooking up with Butch Dixon and what emotional traps would be laid for Joanna in the process.

She had gone just that far in her thinking when Butch's new Subaru Outback drove into the yard. Rather than risk having the dogs start barking in Jenny's room, Joanna opened the bedroom door to let Tigger and Sadie out. A quick check of Jenny proved she was already sound asleep.

Pulling on her jacket against the November chill, Joanna hurried outside. With the dogs on her heels, she met Butch at the gate. Using one hand to fend off an ecstatic greeting from the two pooches, he drew Joanna into a quick embrace and gave her a glancing kiss on the cheek.

"Nothing like a couple of dogs and a good woman to make a guy feel at home."

"Be quiet and come inside," she said. "It's too cold to stand around out here making jokes."

Butch followed Joanna into the kitchen. With his shaved head and stocky build, Butch looked far older than his chronological age of thirty-six. "Where's Jenny?" he asked.

"Asleep."

That announcement caused Butch to gather Joanna in his arms once more for a far more serious kiss. By mutual agreement, when Jenny was around, both Butch and Joanna consciously limited displays of affection. And since that one weekend in August when Jenny had been off in Oklahoma with her grandparents, Butch had never again stayed overnight in Joanna's house.

Dodging out of Butch's arms, Joanna took left-over baked potato and meatloaf from the fridge and popped them into the microwave. Then she brought out the butter, sour cream, and chopped onions.

"Jenny wanted to talk to you," Joanna said, as she stood watching the readout on the microwave count off the passing seconds. "I told her if you got here too late to see her tonight that the conversation would have to wait until morning."

"Any idea what's on her mind?" Butch asked.

Joanna shook her head. "I asked her, but she wouldn't tell me. Said it's a secret. Do you know what it is?"

Butch shrugged. "You've got me," he said.

Joanna set a place for Butch in the breakfast nook. When she put the plate of steaming food in front of him, she slipped onto the bench beside him.

"How was it?" she asked.

"The auction?"

Joanna nodded.

"Okay. We made some money on the deal. Of course, if we'd had to pay wages for all the work we did, we wouldn't have made a dime. The good thing is that several of the collector types got a chance to see the kind of work Jeff does. I think they were impressed. My guess is he'll get some more business out of it. Advertising. The main thing we did, though, going and coming, was talk. Jeff's really worried about Marianne."

"That she's going to quit the ministry?"

Butch turned to study Joanna. "She told you then?"

"This afternoon. She says her letter of resignation is written and ready to hand in at the next board meeting."

"That's what Jeff's worried about. In their family, Marianne has always been the major breadwinner. Jeff has the garage, and he does excellent work, but Auto Rehab, Inc., is a long way from making a profit or from being able to support a family of three. Jeff doesn't know what they're going to do. Did you say anything to Marianne, try to talk her out of it?"

"I tried to talk her into seeing a doctor," Joanna said. "She's depressed, and understandably so. I told her she needs to give herself a chance to feel better before she does anything rash."

"Is she going to?" Butch asked. "See a doctor, I mean?"

"I don't think so. I've known Marianne Maculyea since we were both in junior high. She's always had a mind of her own."

Just then, the phone rang. Joanna hurried across the room to answer it.

"Sheriff Brady?"

Joanna recognized the desk sergeant's voice as soon as Lisa Howard spoke. "Yes, Lisa. It's me. What's happening?"

"You remember that missing person's case Chief Deputy Montoya filed earlier this evening?"

"On Alice Rogers?"

"Yes," Lisa answered.

"What about it? Have they found her?"

"They haven't found her yet, but they did locate her car."

"Where?"

"At the border crossing in Nogales. Four young Hispanic juveniles tried to drive it across the line. When Border Patrol ordered the vehicle to stop, they all bailed out and made a run for it. Three of them were picked up by Federales. They're in jail in Nogales, Sonora. The fourth one wasn't armed but he looked like he was. He was shot in the leg when officers opened fire. According to the Santa Cruz County dispatcher, he's being airlifted to Tucson. University Medical Center or T.M.C., I'm not sure which. We're hoping that he'll be able to tell us where they left Alice Rogers."

"How bad is the kid hurt?" Joanna asked.

"No way to tell at this point. I talked to one of the EMTs who treated him at the scene. His best guess is that once they get him to Tucson he'll go straight into surgery."

Unaware that she had been holding her breath, Joanna let it out. The word "juvenile" could cover a lot of ground—from relatively harmless joyriders to cold-blooded gang-based killers. Depending on which variety Alice Rogers had encountered, she was either more or less likely to have been left alive. Unfortunately, the clock was ticking. With each passing hour the odds of her continued survival were vastly reduced.

"Has anyone let Frank Montoya know what's going on?"

"I called Chief Deputy Montoya first thing,"

Lisa Howard said. "Just before I called you. He said to tell you that he's heading down to Nogales to see what detectives on the case have to say. After that, he'll go to Tucson. He wants to be available when the suspect comes out of surgery and can speak with investigators."

"Thanks for keeping me posted, Lisa," Joanna said. "Tell Frank to let me know what develops."

"Regardless of how late it is?"

"Regardless."

Joanna hung up the phone and put it back down on the counter. Butch Dixon was studying her from across the room. "Bad news?" he asked.

She nodded. "A missing person," she told him. Briefly Joanna filled Butch in on what had happened.

"Are you going to have to go in?" he asked.

"I don't know yet, and I won't for a while."

Butch stood up and began to clear his place. "This wasn't exactly how I hoped the evening would end," he said quietly. "With Jenny already in bed and asleep, I had something more romantic in mind rather than a dinner followed by a missing person's investigation."

Joanna gave him a weak smile. "So did I," she said quietly.

She watched him carry his plate to the sink. He rinsed it, then loaded the plate and his silverware into the dishwasher. She liked his purposeful, economical movements. Liked the way he made himself a contributing part of the household rather than a guest. He seemed to be quietly weaving his way into the fabric of her life, but without making unreasonable demands. Joanna found Butch easy to be with, even though he knew they would most likely spend whatever was left of the evening waiting for the telephone to ring.

"I don't deserve you," she said quietly.

He grinned. "Yes, you do."

He came across the kitchen then and gathered her into a tight embrace. He held her for a long time, and she made no attempt to pull away. Finally, he was the one who broke it off.

"Come on," he said. "Bring the phone and let's go sit on the couch where it's comfortable. And that's where I'll spend the night—on the couch. That way, if you do have to go in, someone will be here to look after Jenny when she wakes up."

THREE

WHEN JOANNA awakened the next morning, that's exactly where she found Butch—sound asleep on her living room couch. They had waited up for some time, expecting a phone call. When none came, they had finally ventured into the bedroom. Sometime after Joanna fell asleep, Butch must have crept out of bed. Joanna was grateful for his discretion when, moments after she reached the kitchen to make coffee, Jenny appeared at her side.

"What's Butch doing on the couch?" she asked.

"Sleeping," Joanna said.

"I know that. But why?"

"Because if I had been called into the office during the night, somebody would have been here to look after you."

Pouring herself a bowl of cereal, Jenny scowled. "To baby-sit, you mean. I'm not a baby."

"No, you're not. But eleven is still too young to be left here alone at night."

By the time Joanna finished showering and dressing and returned to the kitchen, Butch was seated in the breakfast nook drinking coffee and chatting amiably with Jenny, who was munching her way through a peanut-butter-slathered English muffin.

As soon as Joanna entered the kitchen, the conversation ground to a sudden, awkward halt. By the time she had poured her own cup of coffee, Jenny had taken her dishes to the counter and was busily stowing them in the dishwasher. Joanna took Jenny's place in the breakfast nook. "I hope I'm not interrupting something," she said.

"Oh, no," Butch replied with a conspiratorial grin. "We're all done, aren't we, Jenny?"

From the kitchen doorway, Jenny looked back and nodded. "And you won't tell? Promise?"

"Cross my heart."

Satisfied by his words of reassurance, Jenny disappeared into the living room. Joanna turned an appraising eye on Butch. "Does that mean you really won't tell me?" she asked.

"Yup," he said. "That's what it means."

Joanna shook her head. She was grateful that Jenny and Butch clearly liked one another, but it bothered Joanna to discover their sharing secrets that didn't include her. It felt as though they were ganging up on her, double-teaming. It made her feel out of the loop and more than slightly resentful. If there was something important going on in her daughter's life—some important issue that required an adult consultation—Joanna felt she was the one Jenny should have turned to for guidance.

"You're awfully quiet," Butch said a minute or so later. "You're not upset about this, are you?"

"Upset?" Joanna repeated. "Of course I'm not upset. Don't be ridiculous."

Her misgivings to the contrary, Joanna agreed to let Butch drive Jenny to school. Meanwhile, Joanna continued to mull over the secrecy issue as she drove herself from High Lonesome Ranch to the Cochise County Justice Complex three miles away. Those private concerns left her the moment she stepped inside her office. Within minutes she was pulled into an escalating whirl of activity that allowed little time for introspection.

Monday morning roll call was the one time a week when as many of her far-flung deputies as possible assembled in the conference room. That gathering was one Joanna tried to attend on a regular basis. It was a way of staying in touch with officers in the field. Once roll call was over, Joanna retreated to the privacy of her own office for the daily briefing with her two chief deputies.

As usual, Chief Deputy for Operations Richard Voland was on hand and on time. He brought with him the routine sheaf of incident reports that had come in county-wide over the weekend. Tossing the papers onto Joanna's desk, Voland eased his bulky frame into one of the captain's chairs in front of Joanna's desk.

"I don't know where the hell Frank Montoya is," he grumbled. "I was told he's up in Tucson chasing after the kid who stole Mayor Rogers' mother's car. Isn't it about time he got his butt back here to Bisbee and started tending to business? I'm sick and tired of having to cover for him—of having to do my work and his, too."

Relations between Joanna's two chief deputies had never been cordial. Frank Montoya's temporary posting to Tombstone had made things worse. Not only that, Frank's continuing absence meant that Joanna and Dick Voland were thrown together alone for much of the time.

In public, Dick carried on with total professionalism. Alone in Joanna's office, however, the man's continuing infatuation with her was growing more and more apparent. He often came to the morning briefing with two cups of coffee in hand. When he gave Joanna hers, fingers brushing in the process, his face would flush—whether with embarrassment or pleasure, Joanna couldn't tell. She did know that a call to her from Butch Dixon while Dick Voland was in her office would be enough to send her Chief Deputy for Operations into a day-long funk.

It bothered Joanna that, once the briefings were over, Voland would often find one excuse after another not to leave her office. He would linger in the doorway, making small talk about anything and everything. Sometimes those doorway discussions were official in nature, but more often they revolved around personal issues—around Voland's bitter divorce and his difficulties as a part-time father. Joanna knew the man was searching for sympathy, and not undeservedly so. But she worried that any personal comments or kind gestures on her part might be misinterpreted.

Before her election to the office of sheriff, Joanna's experience with law enforcement had been entirely secondhand, as the daughter of one lawman and, later, as the wife and widow of another. Because she had come to the office as a novice police officer, she remained largely dependent on the professionals who worked for her to give her much-needed advice and direction. Richard Voland was an eighteen-year Cochise County Sheriff's Department veteran. As such, she needed his counsel and help, but his increasingly personal attachment to her forced Joanna to walk a fine line between not alienating the man and not leading him on, either.

On this particular morning, she welcomed Dick Voland's ill-tempered griping about Frank Montoya. Focus on work usually helped keep personal issues at bay. Without replying, Joanna buzzed her secretary, Kristin Marsten, whose desk was just outside the door.

"Did Chief Deputy Montoya call in to say he'd be late?"

"Actually," Kristin returned, "he's on the line right now. I was about to buzz you when you beat me to it. Do you want me to take a message or should I put him through?"

"Let me talk to him," Joanna replied.

When her line buzzed seconds later, she punched the speakerphone. "What's up, Frank? Where are you?"

"Still in Tucson," Montoya answered. "Sorry to miss the briefing, but I wanted to stay with this thing. I was afraid if I didn't stick around and keep prodding, Pima County would drop the ball."

"What's going on?" Joanna asked.

"Everyone has this one filed as juvenile joyriding, which makes it a pretty low priority. When the kid came out of surgery, they didn't even have any Santa Cruz County detectives here to talk to him. I was it. His mother was there and so was a hotshot attorney who happens to be the kid's uncle.

"All I wanted to know was where they picked up the car so we'd have some idea of where to go looking for Alice. The kid's name is Joaquin Morales. His attorney wouldn't let him talk to me without having some kind of deal in place first. I tried to tell him that if there was a chance Alice was still alive, we needed to find her as soon as possible. The uncle didn't buy it. He insisted that I call in someone from Pima County. Since the missing person is from Cochise and the shoot-out happened in Santa Cruz, the guys from Pima County weren't exactly chomping at the bit to come out.

"Finally—reluctantly—Pima County sent out a pair of detectives. According to them, they've talked to the kid. He told them he and his buddies found the car out on Houghton Road. If his doctor will release him and if the county attorney will agree to drop all charges, he's willing to show us where the car was."

"Wait a minute," Joanna objected. "That doesn't

make sense. How can anybody put together a deal when they still haven't found Alice Rogers and when they have no idea whether she's dead or alive?"

"Good question," Frank said. "I'm a little curious about that myself. Morales' attorney made a big squawk about how this is Joaquin's first offense. I don't think so. This is just the first one he's ever gotten caught on, but no one's particularly interested in my opinion. Besides, all I'm trying to do right now is find Alice while there's still a remote chance that she's among the living."

"I'd say there's not much of a chance right now," Joanna murmured.

"You're right," Frank agreed. "She disappeared on Saturday night, and now it's Monday morning. That means she's been missing at least thirty-six hours. An older woman like that, if she's been out in the weather all that time, she's probably succumbed by now—hypothermia if nothing else."

"So what's the plan?" Joanna asked.

"I'm going to hang around here. If Pima County cuts a deal and they take Joaquin out to look for the crime scene, I intend to ride along."

"Good," Joanna said. "Keep me posted."

Switching off the speakerphone, Joanna turned back to Dick Voland and business as usual. Ten minutes later, the phone rang again. "The Pima County attorney gave Morales his sweetheart deal. If Joaquin leads us to the crime scene, all charges are dropped. That's where I'm going now—someplace out on Houghton Road. Morales and the Pima County cops are going in one vehicle and I'm going in mine. Once we get out in that general direction, we're supposed to rendezvous with a Search and Rescue team."

"Has Clete Rogers been informed about any of these latest developments?" Joanna asked.

"No," Frank said. "I haven't called him. Up to now, I didn't think I had enough information to clue him in. Once we locate where the kids picked up the car, we'll have a probable place to start looking for his mother. Now is most likely a good time to bring him up to speed. Clete Rogers may be a complete jerk. Even so, he deserves some advance warning about what's going on. And, taking all the political implications into consideration, Joanna, you're the one who should tell him," Frank added.

Not so very long ago, Joanna Brady herself had been on the receiving end of a next-of-kin notification. She knew how much that kind of news hurt—knew that it tore people apart from the inside out. Not only that, her own wounds were still fresh enough that there was no way for her to distance herself from other people's hurt. Those were her private concerns, but she was careful not to make them part of her voiced objection.

Across the polished surface of Joanna's desk, Dick Voland shook his head. "Don't look at me," he said. "I've got too much work to do."

"Look, Sheriff," Frank Montoya said in a placating tone that was calculated to win her over, "I know how this guy operates. Clete Rogers is an arrogant jerk, but he's also a master manipulator. You'll be doing yourself and your whole department a big favor if you handle this in person. Clete will be a lot less likely to get his nose out of joint and make trouble if news of his mother comes to him sheriff-to-mayor rather than deputy-to-mayor. Most people don't give a rat's ass about who gives them the bad news, but Clete Rogers isn't most people. He's a guy who walks around with a huge chip on his shoulder just waiting for somebody to cross him or slight him in any way. That's why I ended up in Tombstone in the first place. Rogers somehow got the idea that the previous marshal wasn't *respectful* enough toward him, regardless of whether or not he deserved anybody's respect."

"In other words," Joanna said, "if I don't do this, Mayor Rogers is going to make your life miserable for as long as you're stuck in Tombstone."

"My life and yours, too," Montoya told her. "He'll pull out all the stops."

Sighing, Joanna glanced at her watch. "What about the board of supervisors meeting this morning?" she asked. "If I can't go and you're not going, who will handle that?"

"Let me guess," Voland grumbled from the far side of Joanna's desk. "I suppose that's going to wind up in my lap. I'll take care of it. I'd much rather do that than have to deal with Clete Rogers."

"Okay, then Frank," Joanna said. "Since Dick has agreed to handle the board meeting, I'll be responsible for notifying Rogers. But what about his sister? Who's going to notify Susan Jenkins? If Clete merits the benefit of the full deluxe treatment, including a personal visit from the sheriff, shouldn't his sister deserve similar consideration? What if *she* feels slighted?"

"Let me point out that Susan Jenkins isn't an elected official with a sizable voting constituency," Frank said. "I'm sure someone should go talk to the woman in person, but that someone doesn't have to be you."

"Good," Joanna breathed. "Maybe Dick has some stray deputy or other he can spare long enough to send out to Sierra Vista."

The Chief Deputy for Operations was already examining his duty roster. "There's Deputy Gregovich," Voland said. "He and Spike are heading that direction first thing this morning. They're due at the Oak Vista construction site outside Sierra Vista. If he stops by to see Susan Jenkins, it won't be that far out of his way."

Oak Vista Estates was a new mammoth-sized housing development being built at the southern end of the Huachuca Mountains. The previous Friday afternoon, sign-carrying protesters—people who preferred grassy, oak-dotted foothills to freshly bulldozed urban blight—had held hands across the development's construction entrance in an unsuccessful effort to block the arrival of flatbed trucks delivering bulldozers, backhoes, and front-end loaders to the site. In the end Mark Childers, the developer, had carried the day by simply waiting out the protesters. He had delivered his equipment after the tree-huggers had all gone home for the night.

Now, in a new week and with work on the

project underway in earnest, no one knew quite what to expect. Which was why Voland had dispatched Deputy Gregovich and Spike to the scene in hopes of preventing trouble before it could start.

Terry Gregovich was a Bisbee native and a former marine who had been riffed out of the service after two tours of duty. Back home in Cochise County, Gregovich had done such outstanding work with the Search and Rescue team that Joanna had brought him on board, hoping to turn him into a detective. That plan had been shot down by budget considerations, but when Frank Montoya had located grant money to establish a K-9 unit, Terry's previous K-9 experience working airport security with the military as well as time spent as an MP had put him on a fast track. He and Spike, an eighty-five-pound German shepherd, were the Cochise County Sheriff's Department's newest rookies. They generally worked nighttime shifts, but Voland had posted them to days to help handle the Oak Vista protesters.

"Terry's pretty new on the job," Joanna observed. "Do you think he can handle talking to bereaved relatives on his own?"

"No doubt about it," Voland said. "Terry may be new to our department, but it's not like he's never been a cop before. He'll be fine."

"And what about Spike?" Joanna asked.

"What about him?"

"Here's Clete Rogers getting a personal visit from the sheriff herself while his sister ends up with a rookie officer and a slobbery German shepherd besides. It sounds a little inequitable to me."

Dick Voland didn't seem to appreciate the joke, but Frank Montoya laughed aloud. "No doubt Hizzoner will approve. I'm not so sure about Susan Jenkins."

"It's Gregovich or nothing," Dick Voland growled. "He's the only deputy I can spare this morning."

"All right," Joanna said. "That settles it then. I'll head for Tombstone as soon as I can. Talk to you later, Frank." With that she once again switched off the speaker and focused her attention on Voland. "Anything urgent before I hit the road?"

"Nothing that won't keep," he said. With that Dick Voland stood up and lumbered toward the outer office. This time he marched straight into the reception area. Breathing a sigh of relief, Joanna followed him. At a desk just outside Joanna's office, Kristin Marsten was busily sorting through a stack of mail.

"I'm on my way to Tombstone to talk to Clete Rogers," Joanna told Kristin. "Just put the mail on my desk. It'll have to wait until I get back."

Letting herself out of her private entrance and into the parking lot behind the building, Joanna was faced with a decision. As sheriff, she had two vehicles at her disposal—a battle-scarred Chevy Blazer and a shiny and relatively new Crown Victoria. Because she wanted to make an impression on Clete Rogers and because she wasn't anticipating driving through any four-wheel-type terrain, she opted for the Crown Victoria. Other jurisdictions sometimes referred to Crown Victoria cruisers as "Vics." Joanna and Frank Montoya preferred to call them Civvies.

The twenty-five-mile drive from Bisbee to Tombstone gave Joanna plenty of time to contemplate how Cletus Rogers would react to the news that his mother's car had been stolen and that, although she was still officially missing, it was becoming more and more likely that she was dead. Like Frank Montoya, Joanna feared the mayor of Tombstone would come unglued and overreact. *What if he decides to go traipsing up to Tucson himself?* Joanna wondered. *Having him show up at a crime scene will drive the Pima County guys crazy.*

Thirty minutes later and still dreading the task ahead, Sheriff Joanna Brady pulled into the parking lot of Clete Rogers' Grubsteak Restaurant and Saloon on Allen Street. The clapboard-covered building, complete with phony white shutters, looked more like a refugee from a film set than a genuine product of the Old West. As Joanna stepped up on the sidewalk, she noticed, on closer examination, that the exterior paint was chipped and peeling. And when she pushed open the front door, she noted that the carpeting in the front entryway had been tacked down with a few strategically placed strips of duct tape.

Stationed in front of an old-fashioned cash register stood a well-endowed peroxide blonde holding a stack of menus. "Smoking or nonsmoking?" she asked.

Joanna hauled out her badge and flashed it. "I'm looking for Mr. Rogers."

The hostess stuck a pair of red-framed reading glasses on her nose long enough to examine the ID. "Mr. Rogers is busy," she said in a brusque manner designed to forestall any further discussion. "He's upstairs in his office and on the phone long distance. Monday's order day around here. He's not to be interrupted."

"I'm sure he'll want to speak to me," Joanna said. "It's about his mother."

The hostess sniffed disdainfully. "Well," she said. "It's about time someone started looking into that. We've had that useless deputy hanging around here for weeks on end, but as soon as there's a real problem, he up and disappears."

"Frank Montoya didn't disappear," Joanna corrected, coming to her chief deputy's defense. "He spent the whole night working on this situation, first down in Nogales and now up in Tucson."

"Oh," said the hostess, sounding somewhat mollified. "If you'll just take a seat, I'll try to catch Mr. Rogers' eye the next time he's between calls. Care for a cup of coffee while you wait?"

Joanna was finishing her second cup of coffee when Clete Rogers finally appeared. He was a large, rawboned man somewhere in his mid-to-late fifties. His eyes had the look of someone dealing with life on too little sleep. As soon as he had settled into the booth across the table from Joanna, the hostess hurried up behind him and set a large tumbler of orange juice on the table in front of him.

"Are you all right?" she asked solicitously. Her double chins waggled when she spoke. So did the ample cleavage that showed over the top of her peasant-style blouse.

"Goddamn it, Nancy!" Clete Rogers grumbled at her. "I know if I'm fine or not! Leave me the hell alone. Don't hover, and get back to work!"

Behind red-framed glasses, Nancy's enormous blue eyes filmed with tears. Her lower lip trembled right along with her chins, but after a moment she seemed to pull herself together. "Well, excuuuse me!" she snapped back at him, and flounced off.

Clete Rogers looked after her. "Sometimes it's hard to tell who's the owner around here and who's the employee."

Even though Frank Montoya had warned Joanna about Clete Rogers' arrogance and ill temper, she was nonetheless surprised by his shabby treatment of someone who was, as far as Joanna could see, a fiercely loyal employee.

Finished with what appeared to be an unwarranted attack on Nancy, Clete turned his attention back to Joanna. "So what's the deal here, Sheriff Brady? Have you found my mother or not?"

"We've located her car," Joanna said carefully.

"Where?"

"A group of juveniles were stopped while attempting to take it across the border into Mexico."

"What about Mother?" Rogers asked. "Where's she?"

"We don't know," Joanna said. "Not for sure. We haven't found her yet."

Clete Rogers took a swig of his juice. "What exactly does that mean?"

"Just what I said. It means we're looking for her. So are authorities from Pima and Santa Cruz counties. According to Frank Montoya, they've just received what they regard as an informed tip up in Tucson. There's a Search and Rescue group heading out there now. They'll be concentrating their efforts along Houghton Road between I-10 and Old Spanish Trail."

Clete Rogers raised his hand. Despite having been ordered not to hover, Nancy appeared from nowhere as if she'd been hanging fire to see what, if anything, her lord and master might require.

"I'm leaving," he announced. "Have Ken put together a care package for me. The usual. I'm driving up to Tucson. I don't want to be stuck out in the middle of nowhere with nothing to eat."

"Excuse me, Mayor Rogers," Joanna said. "As I said, there is a search, all right. But it's being conducted by members of the Pima County Sheriff's Department. Since it sounds as though that's where your mother's car was stolen, officers from Pima County are the ones in charge at this point. I doubt very much that they'll want any unauthorized onlookers clambering around under hand and foot and possibly disturbing crime scene evidence."

"And let me remind you, Sheriff Brady, that the person those people are searching for is *my* mother," Rogers put in. "Like it or not, I'm involved, and I'm going to stay that way."

Inside her purse, Joanna's pager buzzed, sending out a warning that sounded for all the world like a rattlesnake. She reached inside and stifled the thing before Clete Rogers seemed to notice what was going on.

"Really, Mr. Rogers," she said. "I don't think your showing up there is wise. As I said before, the more people milling around a crime scene, the greater the chance that important information will be overlooked or destroyed. I believe we'd be better off if—"

"I didn't hear anyone asking for your advice or your permission, Sheriff Brady. Are you coming with me or not?"

It took all of two seconds for Joanna to make up her mind. No way did she want to be trapped into three hours' worth of car travel with this overbearing jerk, but she also wanted to be on hand to defend her department and her people in case Rogers launched into an all-out attack over how his mother's case was being handled.

"Not," she replied. "I'll head on up to Tucson as well, but I'll drive my own vehicle. In fact, I think I'll leave right now. How much for the coffee?"

What Joanna had left unsaid was that while Rogers waited for his "care package," she would go on ahead and help run interference for whoever was in charge. Hopefully, she'd have enough of a head start to beat him to the crime scene.

"Never mind about the coffee," Clete Rogers said. "It's on the house."

Reaching into her purse, Joanna pulled out two ones and slapped them down on the table beside her empty cup. She wasn't going to be beholden to Clete Rogers for anything at all, including two cups of unbelievably bad drip coffee.

"I'll see you there."

Out in the car, Joanna checked the pager. Not surprisingly, the number listed was Dick Voland's direct line at the department. She called him on her cell phone. "It's Joanna, Dick," she said when he answered. "What's up?"

"Frank Montoya just called in. They've found Alice Rogers."

"Alive or dead?" Joanna asked.

"Dead, unfortunately. The kid—Morales—showed them where he and his friends found the car. Search and Rescue turned a dog loose, and he went right out and found the body. It's six miles east of I-10 on Houghton in a big stand of cholla on the south side of the road."

"They're sure it's Alice Rogers?"

"Pretty sure, pending an official identification from a relative. The clothes the dead woman is wearing match the ones Susan Jenkins told Frank her mother was wearing when she came to dinner Saturday night."

"What did she die of?"

"No way to tell. Not so far. According to Frank, they found her in the middle of a grove of cholla. He says she's full of spines. She must have fallen down in the stuff. Not a nice way to go. Frank was hoping to give you a heads-up while you were still in Tombstone so you could let Clete Rogers know."

Glancing in the rearview mirror to check for traffic, Joanna eased her Crown Victoria onto the street. At that point it would have been no trouble at all to return to the restaurant and give

Clete Rogers the news. The bottom line was, Joanna didn't feel like it. The mayor had been quite specific in saying he wanted no part of her advice. No, let him find out for himself.

"Negative on that," she told Dick Voland. "You're too late. I'm already on my way to Tucson. So's Clete Rogers. If you want to give anyone a heads-up, Frank's the one who's going to need it. Let him know Rogers is coming so he can pass the information along to whoever's in charge for Pima County."

"Clete's going to the crime scene?" Dick Voland asked. "The boys from Pima County aren't going to like that at all."

"No kidding!" Joanna told him. "In terms of interagency cooperation, his showing up will probably put us back ten years. They'll be ecstatic when a whole crowd shows up. Which reminds me, you'd better send Detective Carpenter along as well. If Pima County has homicide detectives on the scene, so should we."

FOUR

Two miles east of I-10 on Houghton Road, Joanna could already see the flashing lights several miles farther east that indicated the presence of several emergency vehicles parked on either side of the road. She stopped directly behind a van from the Pima County Medical Examiner's office. As Joanna stepped out of the Crown Victoria, the familiar figure of Dr. Fran Daly emerged from the back of the van.

"Well, if it isn't Sheriff Brady," Fran Daly drawled, dropping a man-sized equipment case onto the ground between them. "Long time no see," she added, wiping her hands on the worn leg of her jeans before proffering one of them in greeting. "We've got to stop meeting like this."

Fran was a tough-talking chain-smoker who had, during the previous summer, worked on a series of homicides with Joanna's department. When George Winfield, the Cochise County medical examiner, had taken off for Alaska on a honeymoon cruise, the board of supervisors had opted to contract with a neighboring county for whatever forensic services might be necessary in Winfield's absence. Fran Daly, the assistant medical examiner for Pima County, had been drafted into service. At the time the arrangement was made, no one could possibly have anticipated that during the two weeks Dr. Winfield was out of the county, Joanna's department would unmask Cochise County's first-ever serial killer, uncovering the remains of several brutally mutilated victims along the way.

Joanna's first encounter with the pinch-hitting Dr. Daly had been anything but cordial or smooth. The sheriff and the ME had first butted heads at a crime scene where a termite-infested floor had threatened to collapse beneath them at any time. Gradually, though, as one after another of the Cascabel Kid's tortured victims came to light, the two women had achieved an uncommon level of mutual respect. In the process Joanna had seen beyond Fran Daly's gruff and overbearing manner to the consummate professional underneath.

"How's it going, Fran?"

Dr. Daly grinned. Reaching into the pocket of her Western shirt, Fran pulled out a pack of cigarettes. She shook a Camel loose from the pack and then lit it by striking a match across the huge silver-and-turquoise buckle on her leather belt.

"Can't complain," she said, blowing a plume of smoke. "Of course, I'm overworked and underpaid, but then what else is new? By the way, what are you doing here? From what the dispatcher told me on the phone, I was under the impression that the victim was found well within Pima County boundaries. Or has Cochise County annexed this portion of Houghton Road and nobody's gotten around to telling me?"

"This is Pima County, all right," Joanna said with a short laugh. "But if the victim turns out to be who we think she is, she disappeared from her home in Tombstone sometime Saturday night. The Border Patrol down in Nogales stopped her vehicle when four juveniles tried to take it across the border Sunday evening. So, depending on where you say death occurred, this may turn out to be our case or yours. If it happens to come to us, I don't want to be last in line when it comes to information."

Fran Daly nodded. "Fair enough," she said. "Do you have detectives here then?"

"Not yet, but they will be. One of my homicide guys, Detective Carpenter, is on his way from Bisbee even as we speak. For the moment Frank Montoya, my chief deputy, and I are the only ones here. Unfortunately the victim's son, His Honor Mayor Clete Rogers of Tombstone, is also on his way."

"What for?"

Joanna shrugged. "Who knows? I told him he's got no business here, but the mayor isn't big on taking other people's advice. He's also an elected official who thinks his office gives him carte blanche to do any damned thing he wants."

"In other words," Fran said, "the man's an arrogant son of a bitch."

"You could say that." Joanna grinned in reply. "But please don't let on that I'm the one who told you so."

"Your secret's safe with me," Fran said.

Just then a uniformed Pima County deputy emerged from a thick stand of cholla, trotted across a shallow dip, and approached Fran Daly. "Howdy, Dr. Daly. Want me to give you a hand with that?" he asked, nodding toward the equipment case.

"No, thanks, Sergeant Mallory. I'm used to lugging this crap around. I can handle it by myself. Do you happen to know Joanna Brady here? She's the sheriff down in Cochise County."

Claude Mallory was tall, rangy, square-jawed, and thick-necked. He might have been good-looking had it not been for the fact that his eyes were set far too close together. He favored Joanna with an appraising glance that seemed to imply: *What the hell is she doing here?*

"We're not sure who gets this one," Fran Daly explained in answer to Mallory's unasked question. "It could be ours; it could be theirs. In any case, Sheriff Brady and her people will be on the scene, and they're to be allowed the same access as officers from Pima County."

Mallory nodded. "It's gonna be pretty crowded," he said.

Fran Daly shrugged. "The more the merrier," she said.

Mallory started away from them. "The body's over this way. If you'll both just follow me."

But Fran Daly was not yet done with her smoke. "How long before that detective of yours gets here, Sheriff Brady?" she asked.

"I sent for him as I was leaving Tombstone," Joanna returned. "If Detective Carpenter left the office right then, he can't be more than twenty minutes behind me."

Fran nodded. "All right. I'll go on up to the scene, get set up, and snap a few pictures. I won't do anything critical, though, until after Carpenter gets here—just as long as he's not too slow about it. By the time I finish taking photographs, he'll probably be here. In the meantime, Sergeant Mallory, are you the officer in charge?"

"At the moment. The two detectives are up with the body."

"According to Sheriff Brady, a man who's the son of our suspected victim is on his way here from Tombstone. What did you say his name is again, Sheriff Brady?"

"Rogers," Joanna replied. "Cletus Rogers."

"Right. Rogers. You got that, Sergeant Mallory? When Cletus Rogers shows up here, you're not to let him through. I don't want any civilians blundering through my crime scene. You let Mr. Rogers know that if he's planning on doing an identification of the body, he'll need to come to the morgue in Tucson after it's been transported."

"Gotcha, Doc," Mallory agreed. "I'll handle it."

"Good." With that, Fran Daly ground out her cigarette butt on the pavement. Then she picked it up and dropped it into a small rectangular box of the red-and-white Altoid variety. Only when the box was closed and shoved into her hip pocket did she once again heave her equipment case off the ground.

"Now then," she demanded of Sergeant Mallory. "Where is it we're going?"

"This way. It's not far, but the cactus grows so thick you can't see inside it."

As Claude Mallory and Fran Daly walked away, Joanna started to follow them. She went as far as the ditch and then stopped. Fran was dressed in proper crime scene attire—a long-sleeved shirt, jeans, and snakeskin cowboy boots. Joanna was in high heels, a silk blouse, and a cotton-knit blazer and skirt. One glance at the thick grove of spiny cactus convinced her that what she had worn into the office that morning—clothing that would have been entirely appropriate for an appearance at a board of supervisors meeting— wasn't going to cut it at a cholla-studded crime scene.

Remembering her mother's old adage about an ounce of prevention, Joanna retreated to the trunk of the Crown Victoria and dug into the small suitcase of "just-in-case" clothes she kept packed at all times.

She extracted jeans and a worn pair of tennis shoes as well as an ankle-length cotton duster straight out of a Clint Eastwood spaghetti western. After changing, she was just starting to cross the ditch when a battered Ford F-100 pickup pulled up beside her. It screeched to a halt with

Clete Rogers at the wheel. Parking half-on and half-off the road, he rammed the pickup into neutral and jumped out.

"All right, Sheriff Brady," he demanded. "Where is she? Over there? In that stand of cactus somewhere?"

Joanna had hoped Clete Rogers wouldn't arrive until after Sergeant Mallory had returned from leading Fran Daly to the crime scene. That way, someone from Pima County could have taken the flak for sending the mayor of Tombstone on his way. Unfortunately, Sergeant Mallory had dodged the bullet.

"You can't go there, Mayor Rogers," Joanna said, stepping into the path and barring his way. "As I told you earlier, crime scenes are off limits to civilians."

"You can't tell me what to do," Rogers objected. "This isn't Cochise County. You've got no authority here."

"Yes, I do," Joanna told him. "I've spoken to Dr. Fran Daly of the Pima County Medical Examiner's office about this. She made it clear she doesn't want you here. You're to go to the Pima County morgue in Tucson to make an official identification. If you'd like, you can go there and wait."

"How long will that be?"

"No telling."

"Is it hours, then? Days?" Clete Rogers demanded. "What are we talking about here?"

"As I said, there's no way to know."

Another car pulled up and stopped. This one was a cherry-red Chrysler Sebring convertible with an auburn-haired woman at the wheel. She, too, parked without first bothering to move her vehicle entirely out of the path of traffic. She jumped out of the car. Leaving her door ajar, she came striding up to where Joanna and Clete Rogers stood.

"What's going on here?" she asked.

Clete turned to Joanna. "If I'm not supposed to be here, why is she?" he demanded. "Who told her?"

An angry woman marched up until she stood within inches of Clete Rogers' face. Belligerently she stared up at him. "She's my mother, too," she stormed. "And it happened just the way I said it would. I tried to tell you the guy was bad news— that he was trouble. But you're always so much smarter than anyone else. You knew all about this long before I did, but you didn't bother to lift a finger. If you had told me what was really going on, I might have prevented this from happening, but oh no. Not you. And now Mother's dead because of you, because you're such a closed-mouthed son of a bitch. I hope you're happy."

"Wait just a damned minute here!" Clete railed back at his sister. "You're saying what happened is all *my* fault? No way!"

"You should have made her break up with him."

Clete hooted with laughter. "Sure," he said. "Me *make* her. When did anybody ever make Mother do anything she didn't want to do?"

Joanna remembered what Frank Montoya had said about the previous day's incident in the Grubsteak, about the two-sided fight between

Susan Jenkins and her brother, and the scuffle that had included a table's worth of flying crockery and glassware. Before they could start whaling on one another, Joanna attempted to soothe the raging waters.

"Excuse me," she began calmly, holding out her hand. "You must be Susan Jenkins. I'm the—"

"You stay out of this," Susan snarled back. "Who the hell do you think you are? If I want to tell my brother he's a jackass, it's nobody's business but ours. Now leave us alone."

"A jackass!" Clete choked. "Why, of all the—" He clenched one massive fist and drew back, as if preparing to deliver a brain-crushing blow.

Joanna's mind echoed with all the police academy cautions about the danger of stepping into the middle of a domestic dispute. She knew the statistics involved—the textbook recitations of cops killed and injured nationwide when summoned to intervene in family disturbances. Even so, as Clete Rogers wound up to deliver a haymaker to his sister's skull, Joanna had no choice but to act.

"All right, you two," she said, stepping into the fray and inserting her own body between the bristling pair, both of whom towered over her. "Knock it off!"

Surprisingly enough, Clete complied immediately. Susan Jenkins, however, held her ground. "I told you to leave us alone."

"And I said knock it off!" Joanna repeated.

"I don't know who the hell you think you are—"

"I'll tell you who I am," Joanna told her. "I'm Sheriff Joanna Brady, and I'm ordering you back to your vehicle. Now!"

"Why? If my brother's allowed to be here, I should be able to—"

"Return to your vehicle immediately, Mrs. Jenkins. Otherwise I'll be forced to place you under arrest."

"Under arrest!" Susan screeched. "Me? My mother's dead. My worthless brother turned a deaf ear and let her boyfriend kill her, and you're telling me I'm the one who's under arrest?"

But even as she objected, Susan Jenkins took a backward step. Joanna stepped after her, hoping to keep her moving in the right direction. "All the way to the car, Mrs. Jenkins," Joanna urged. "I want you to stand behind your vehicle. Spread your legs and place both hands on the trunk."

The big danger in domestic disputes is always the possibility that both combatants will stop fighting with one another and turn on the police officer. Concerned that Clete Rogers might come at her from behind, Joanna glanced over her shoulder. She was relieved to see that rather than joining in, he had moved away, backing up until he collided with the rear bumper of Fran Daly's van. It took mere seconds for Joanna to see that he posed no threat, but that momentary lapse of attention was enough for Susan Jenkins to launch a full-scale attack. By the time Joanna realized what was happening, the enraged woman was almost on top of her.

Dodging to one side, Joanna reached out, grabbed Susan by one arm and then tossed her over an outthrust hip. One moment Susan, bent on attack, was rumbling forward. The next she was sailing skyward and flipping end over end. She landed on her back with a thump that sent the air whooshing out of her lungs. For several long moments she didn't breathe. She simply lay there, staring bug-eyed into the sky.

With her own heart pounding, Joanna placed one foot on her opponent's shoulder. She was in the process of wrestling her Glock out from under the billowing duster when another car—a familiar white Econoline van—stopped beside her. Her burly, middle-aged homicide detective, Ernie Carpenter, vaulted from his vehicle and into the fray. "What the hell's going on?" he demanded.

"Cuff her, Ernie," Joanna ordered, moving away. "I don't think she's armed, but you'd better check."

By then, Susan was coughing and gasping for breath. Ernie reached down, hauled her to her feet, and then spun her around to secure her wrists behind her. Meanwhile, Joanna hurried to check on Clete Rogers, who was leaning against Fran Daly's van. His face had gone dangerously white.

"Are you all right?" Joanna asked.

He nodded. "I'll be okay," he said. "I've got some medication in my truck. Just help me back to it."

With him leaning against her for support, Joanna led him back to his pickup. "You're sure you'll be all right?" she asked. "I can call for an ambulance and have them take you to a hospital in Tucson."

He waved her away and then reached for a lunch-box-sized cool chest on the seat beside him. "No," he said, as he opened the lid. "Just let me be for a little. I'll be fine."

Sergeant Mallory appeared at that moment. "What's going on?" he demanded, looking from Joanna to a dust-covered but still belligerent Susan Jenkins.

"I want that woman arrested," Joanna said, pointing at Susan. "She's to be charged with assaulting a police officer."

"Who is she?" Mallory asked.

"Susan Jenkins, the dead woman's daughter."

Mallory looked puzzled. "I thought the son was the one who was on his way."

"They're both here," Joanna told him. "Clete Rogers is over there in his truck. Somebody had better check on him. He may need medical attention."

Mallory whistled. "Nice family."

"Isn't that the truth!"

While Mallory went to check on Clete Rogers, Ernie walked over to Joanna. His thick, bushy eyebrows were beetled into a frown. "Are you all right?" he asked.

"I'm fine."

"As I drove up, I saw what was happening," Ernie continued. "The woman was coming right at you, Joanna. She's so much bigger than you are, I thought for sure you were a goner. The next thing I knew, though, she was flying through the air like some kind of rag doll. Nice move. Who showed you that one?"

As relief flooded through Joanna's body, she remembered those countless summertime sessions out in the yard at High Lonesome Ranch where Andy had taught both his wife and daughter a collection of self-defense moves. He had taught them to use a thumbhold that could bring even the most burly opponent to his knees. Not only that, Andy had shown Joanna and Jenny how an attacker's own body weight could be used against him. Or her, as the case might be.

On wrestling mats Andy had borrowed from one of his old high school coaches at Bisbee High, they had practiced time and again until they had perfected their technique—until Joanna could throw Andy and until Jenny, in turn, could throw her mother. At the time it had seemed like little more than a game—something inexpensive that the financially strapped family could do together. Back then it had never occurred to Joanna that those very skills might one day mean the difference between life and death—between walking away from a fight as opposed to being carried away on a stretcher.

"It's a gift," Joanna told Ernie.

Ernie's frown deepened. "You mean it's something you were born knowing?"

Joanna shook her head. "No, I mean it's something Andy taught me before he died. A gift from him."

"Well," Ernie Carpenter said. "It's pretty damned impressive."

Frank Montoya came up behind them. In his early thirties, Frank was a tall man with a medium build. In hopes of disguising his receding hairline, he kept his hair barbered in a precision crew cut.

"Ernie!" Frank exclaimed. "You're already here. Good. Doc Daly sent me to find you. She's almost ready to start the proceedings, and she was hoping you'd arrived." Frank stopped and looked around at the collection of haphazardly parked cars. "What's going on?" he asked. "Was there a fender bender or something?"

Joanna chuckled nervously. "No. Chapter two in the Rogers family feud. I've asked Sergeant Mallory to place Susan under arrest. Other than that, everything's fine."

"You're sure?" Frank asked.

The very real concern fellow officers showed one another never failed to touch Joanna. "Really," she said, "I'm fine, Frank. Lead the way to the crime scene. Let's not keep Fran Daly waiting."

"If you expect me to arrest her," Mallory objected, "what about statements? I'm going to need to talk to both you and your detective here."

"We won't go back to Bisbee without talking to you, Sergeant Mallory," Joanna reassured him. "But right this minute, working with Dr. Daly takes precedence."

As Joanna followed Frank Montoya and Ernie Carpenter into the cholla grove, she slipped her cell phone out of her pocket and dialed Dick Voland's number. "I just had a little run-in with Clete Rogers' sister," she told him. "She seems to think her mother's boyfriend may have had something to do with all this. His name's Farley Adams or Adams Farley. I forget which. Anyway, if Detective Carbajal turns up there, you might have him take a run to the mining claim out on Outlaw Mountain. Regardless of what Susan Jenkins thinks about the guy, we owe him the common courtesy of letting him know what's happened to Alice. I don't think anyone else is going to do it. Besides, in the process, between Sunday and now, maybe he'll have remembered some little detail that might help us."

"Will do," Dick replied. "Besides, regardless of whether or not they're suspects, it never hurts to chat with survivors."

"Also, you may want to have one of the town marshals over in Tombstone slap some crime scene tape across the entrance to Alice Rogers' house until we have a chance to process it and make sure whatever happened didn't happen there."

"I'm one jump ahead of you there," Dick Voland told her. "By now, the crime scene tape should already be in place."

"Thanks, Dick," she said. "I knew I could count on you."

Talking as she walked, Joanna had been threading her way into the thick grove of ten-foot-high teddy-bear cholla. Not paying close enough attention, she came too close to one of the monster cacti. A gust of breeze caught the end of her duster and blew it against one of the buds of new growth at the end of a branch. Instantly, a spine-covered ball the size of a baseball came loose from the branch and attached itself to the duster. Before Joanna could disengage it, the next gust of wind whipped the duster, cactus and all, against her shin. Several of the needle-sharp barbed spines sliced through several layers of material and jabbed into her leg. Yipping in pain, Joanna reached for her leg, only to knock into another branch with her elbow.

Alerted by her yelp, Frank turned around just in time to see Joanna pull away from the second cactus with a second spine-covered ball sprouting from one elbow.

"I always thought they called cholla jumping cactus because the *cactus* jumped," he observed with a smile. "I see now the cactus stays put. It's really the *people* who jump."

"Don't be a smart-ass," she ordered curtly. "Come help me. This hurts like hell."

Without another word, Frank pulled his Leatherman multipurpose tool from the pouch on his belt. Flipping it open to the pliers configuration, he used that to remove the two offending cactus segments. Once the spines had been pulled free from her body, Joanna stood alternately massaging first her burning leg and then her arm. Even though the needles were gone, her flesh still hurt. It felt like the aftermath of a bee or wasp sting. Adding insult to injury, under her fingertips she felt a run tear through her brand-new pair of

No Nonsense panty hose. When it came to crime scene investigation, panty hose were the most common casualty.

"Thanks," she said gratefully as Frank restowed his Leatherman. "I couldn't believe how much those spines hurt."

Frank shook his head. "If you think this was bad," he warned, "just wait till you see what happened to Alice Rogers."

They both moved forward then. Deep in the grove of cacti they came to a small space where the cholla wasn't as thick. Several of them appeared to have been knocked down. In the middle of the fallen cacti and on top of one—impaled on the three-inch spines—lay a small female form that was covered with ants and surrounded by a cloud of buzzing flies. Hundreds of needles dug deep into the woman's back and sprouted from her legs and arms. The slightly bloated body was clad in a print dress and a light-weight sweater. There were torn nylons on her legs, but no shoes. Her vacant, empty eyes stared upward. One tightly clenched fist rested on her breast. The other lay outstretched on the rocky ground, as if searching for the pair of wraparound sunglasses that lay in the dirt just out of reach.

Fresh from her own excruciating encounter with the cacti, Joanna had difficulty looking at the cholla needles piercing Alice Rogers' insect-covered sunbaked flesh. She didn't want to think about how much the poor woman had suffered. It hurt Joanna to realize that she had died in such a horrific way—alone and in appalling pain.

A stiff breeze, blowing out of the west, swept across the scene and filled Joanna's nostrils and lungs with the awful stench of death. Once she would have turned and fled from that all-pervasive odor. Now she simply waited, hoping that eventually her gag reflexes would settle and that her nostrils would adjust.

Engrossed in what was going on around her, Joanna lost track of the fact that Frank was standing at her elbow. When he spoke, she started reflexively, almost as though she had been awakened from a sound sleep.

"Well," he said. "I've heard of people sleeping on a bed of nails, but this is ridiculous."

It was a nonsensical comment, and it certainly wasn't funny, but somehow it did the trick. The bile that had been rising dangerously high in Joanna's throat receded. What came out of her mouth was a chuckle—a hoot of utterly inappropriate, necessary, and life-affirming laughter.

"It's ridiculous, all right," she agreed when she finally sobered enough once again to be capable of speech. "Ridiculous but deadly."

FIVE

FRAN DALY proceeded through the examination process with Ernie Carpenter and the two Pima County detectives, Hank Lazier and Tom Hemming, observing her every move. With four people crowded around the body, there was no room for Joanna and Frank Montoya to move any closer. They remained on the edge of the clearing. They were close enough to hear most of the crisp comments Dr. Daly spoke to the detectives and into a small tape recorder but not close enough to see what was happening.

Losing interest, Joanna turned to Frank. "You were here when they found her?"

"Not right here," he said. "I was over by the cars. When the Search and Rescue guys found the body, Lazier and Hemming took off like a shot. I stayed put because I wanted a chance to talk to Joaquin Morales. I figured it was probably the only shot any of us would have at him without his attorney hanging on every word."

"What did you find out?"

"That his lawyer negotiated a real sweetheart deal."

"What do you mean?"

"All he had to do was lead us to Alice. Once he did that, he walks. Blanket immunity. No arrest, no charges, nothing. When his buddies come to trial, he doesn't even have to testify."

"Come on, Frank," Joanna objected. "That doesn't make sense."

"It makes sense to someone," Frank countered. "They claim it was a humanitarian gesture based on the fact that at the time there was a chance Alice Rogers was still alive, since finding her in a timely manner might have saved her life. The other considerations have to do with the fact that Joaquin Morales is only fourteen. He comes from one of Tucson's fine 'old Pueblo' families, and this is supposedly his first offense. His pals are older and, according to him, their hands are anything but clean. Once they're extradited, they'll be up on charges of grand-theft auto and murder."

"Not car-jacking?"

"That would make it a federal case. According to the detectives, the county attorney is looking forward to next year's election and won't let this one out of his personal jurisdiction."

"What exactly did Joaquin Morales tell you?"

"That there were several carloads of kids. They came out to the desert for a keg party on Saturday night. He says they were on their way back to town from the kegger when Morales and his buddies came across Alice's Buick. He claims it was just sitting abandoned by the roadside with the windows wide open and with a mostly empty bottle of Scotch sitting in the front seat. After the kids polished off the rest of the booze, they decided to take Alice's car out for some late-night drag racing. He claims he never even saw the old lady, but it could be he was too drunk to remember."

"He wasn't so drunk that he didn't remember where they found the car," Joanna pointed out.

Frank nodded. "That's true," he agreed. "So on Sunday, after the kids had sobered up, one of them came up with the bright idea of driving the car down to Nogales. He said he knew someone across the line who would pay good money for a car like that, no questions asked."

"Sounds perfectly plausible," Joanna said with a grimace. "And I'm sure Joaquin is pure as the driven snow. What do Lazier and Hemming think happened?"

"They think the old lady pulled over and stopped. With the booze in the car, there's probably a good chance she was drinking, too. Maybe she had pulled over and was passed out in her car. Maybe she had stopped to take a leak. Whatever, Lazier theorizes the kids found her, chased her into the cactus, and left her there. Since her death happened in the course of the commission of a felony, that makes it murder."

"But only for perpetrators who don't have connections or a sharp wheeler-dealer attorney," Joanna said.

"Right," Frank agreed. "Whoever said the world is fair?"

"Justice is supposed to be," Joanna countered.

She glanced around the area. "Any sign of footprints?" Even as she asked the question, she saw the futility of it. The terrain was far too dry, rough, and rocky to retain usable prints.

"None," Frank said.

As he spoke, a shadow fell across Frank's face. Joanna looked up. High above them a buzzard rode the updrafts, drifting in long, lazy circles, hoping for access to the feast. Seeing the carrion eater, Joanna realized that the agreement Joaquin's attorney had negotiated may not have saved Alice's life, but it had, at least, forwarded the investigation. Without the fourteen-year-old's help in locating the body, it might have been months or even years, before anyone located Alice Rogers' remains. And with the desert's numerous carrion eaters always on the lookout for their next meal, there might not have been much left for Fran Daly to examine.

Meanwhile, Frank Montoya moved on to a different topic. "I came up just as Ernie was putting the cuffs on Susan Jenkins," he said. "What happened?"

"Pretty much the same thing you had to deal with in the Grubsteak on Sunday. Susan showed up all pissed off that her brother hadn't done something about their mother's boyfriend. She's

of the opinion that Farley Adams is behind whatever happened to Alice Rogers."

"I doubt that," Frank said. "I met the man
Sunday afternoon. Talked to him in person. He
seemed genuinely mystified by Alice's disappearance. And in view of what we've found here, he
sure as hell didn't strike me as the kind of guy
who would be the mastermind behind a gang of
juvenile car thieves."

"You're probably right," Joanna told him. "But
with Clete Rogers second-guessing every move
we make, I don't want to leave any stone un-
turned. I've told Dick that we need to go over Alice's house from top to bottom. I want it treated
like a crime scene even if it isn't one. I've also
asked that Jaime Carbajal stop by Outlaw Mountain and talk to Farley again, now that we've
found the body."

Joanna paused and looked back toward where
Fran Daly was still working. "I'm not being of
much use here, so I could just as well go back to
the cars and talk to Sergeant Mallory about Susan Jenkins. He needs statements. I can give him
mine now, and he can take Ernie's later."

Leaving Frank in the clearing, Joanna headed
back to where the cars were parked. On the way,
her pager went off. Once again Dick Voland's
number appeared on the screen, followed this
time by the word "Urgent." Without waiting to
get back to her radio, Joanna used her cell phone
to return the call. "What's up, Dick?" she asked.

"After I talked to you last, I sent Detective Carbajal out to Outlaw Mountain just the way you

asked. He called in a couple of minutes ago. He said nobody's there. Farley Adams is gone."

"What do you mean, gone?"

"Jaime tried peeking in some of the windows. He says it looks like the place has been emptied out. The clothes closet was standing wide open and empty. The dresser drawers are empty, too. I'm sending Deputy Pakin uptown to get a search warrant. I'm betting Farley Adams is our killer."

That theory didn't square with Frank Montoya's ideas about Farley Adams. Nor did it work with the Pima County cops' hypothesis that Alice had died as a result of being hassled and/or frightened by a gang of juvenile-delinquent car thieves. In her time as sheriff, Joanna had come to realize that often unimportant leads—ones that don't seem to go anywhere—provide the critical details that point investigators in entirely different directions, leading them eventually to things that are important.

"A search warrant is probably a good idea," she told her chief deputy. "Anything else?"

"Nothing that I know of," Dick told her. "Later on, once Pakin gets the search warrant, I'll follow him on up to Tombstone. With you, Frank, and Ernie all tied up in Tucson someone should go oversee the situation in Tombstone."

"How was the board of supervisors meeting?" Joanna asked. "Did you go?"

"Oh, I went all right. I told you I would, so I did. The whole thing was nothing but a gigantic waste of time."

"No surprises there," Joanna said. "Those meetings usually are."

"You mean you don't like attending them, either?" Dick Voland sounded surprised.

"Fortunately for both of us, Dick, Frank Montoya actually gets a kick out of all that political wrangling."

"Is that so," Voland said wonderingly. "Maybe the guy has some redeeming qualities after all. Just don't tell him I said so."

Joanna laughed. "My lips are sealed. Now, how about putting me through to Kristin?" Seconds later, Joanna was speaking to her secretary. "Any messages?"

"Your mother, for one," Kristin said. "She's called three times so far. There was also a call from Father Thomas Mulligan. You know, the head of Holy Trinity, that Catholic monastery over in Saint David. He asked to speak to you directly. I told him you were working a case and asked him if it was an emergency. He said no, but that he did want to speak to you as soon as possible. Here's the number."

Pulling a notepad from her pocket, Joanna jotted down Father Thomas' name and number. "Anything else?"

"Nothing out of the ordinary."

"Good." Joanna glanced at her watch. The afternoon was speeding by at an alarming rate. It was already past time for school to be out. Jenny usually called the office in the afternoon, just to check in. "Jenny will probably call once she gets to Butch's house," Joanna said. "Tell her to try reaching me on the cell phone."

Walking as she talked, Joanna emerged from the cholla and was now within sight of the cars. She was shocked to see Susan Jenkins, freed from Ernie's handcuffs, standing beside her Chrysler and smoking a cigarette. An unconcerned Sergeant Mallory stood nearby, talking to another uniformed deputy.

"Wait a minute," Joanna said. "Why's she still here, and where are her cuffs? I asked you to place her under arrest, and I thought someone would have hauled her away by now."

Folding his arms across his broad chest, Sergeant Mallory sauntered over to Joanna. "Before we did, I talked to my lieutenant about it. He said no dice."

Joanna's temper rose. A sudden flush fired her cheeks. "What does that mean?" she demanded.

Mallory shrugged. "You know how it is," he said. "My supe wanted me to get those statements first. In other words, no paper, no jail."

Over by the Sebring, Susan Jenkins ground out her cigarette and came walking toward Joanna and Mallory. Preparing for the possibility of another attack, Joanna tensed, but as Susan came closer, it became apparent that the woman had been crying.

"I'm sorry, Sheriff Brady," Susan Jenkins apologized at once. "I don't know what got into me. I was so mad at Clete right then, I couldn't see straight. All the way here, I kept thinking that if only he had listened to me yesterday or if he had used his brain before that, maybe none of this would have happened. Maybe our mother would still be alive."

Much as it hurt her to do so, Joanna had to admit that right that minute there was nothing the least bit threatening about Susan Jenkins. With her faced blotched with tear-stained mascara, she looked just like any other bereaved relative—brokenhearted but not dangerous.

"You and your brother have both suffered a terrible loss," Joanna said. "And you both have my sympathy."

"It is her then?" Susan asked, nodding in the direction from which Joanna had come.

"Yes. Pending positive identification, of course. But yes, we're pretty sure."

Susan Jenkins' eyes filmed with fresh tears. She buried her face in her hands. "I kept hoping the cops would be wrong, that it would turn out to be someone else."

"What was your mother wearing when you saw her last?" Joanna asked.

"A dress," Susan said. "A pink dress."

"What about a sweater or coat?"

"Mother was very warm-blooded. She hardly ever wore a coat. She wasn't wearing a sweater when she left my house the other night, but she might have had one in her car."

Susan cast a wary look in the direction of the cholla. "Should I go over there and look—tell them whether or not it's really her?"

Joanna thought about how it would feel for a

daughter—any daughter—to see her mother lying on a deathbed of cactus and teeming with marauding insects. It had been hard enough for Joanna, a stranger, to see Alice Rogers that way. For a grieving daughter, the sight would be a nightmarish one that would haunt the rest of her life.

"No," Joanna said kindly. "It's probably better if you don't see your mother right now. As I told Clete earlier, that kind of ID is usually done after the body has been transported to the morgue. Speaking of your brother, is that where he went?"

Susan shook her head. "I don't know. He didn't say a word to me. He just drove off in his pickup truck."

Joanna turned to Sergeant Mallory. "Did Mr. Rogers tell you where he was going?" she asked.

"He said he wasn't feeling well and that he was going home."

"Typical," Susan said, with a trace of anger leaking back into her voice. "Clete always talks a good game, but when it's crunch time or when there's some kind of real crisis, looking for him to do anything useful is like leaning on a bent reed. I can understand his not having guts enough to do something about Mother and Farley Adams, but if Clete had bothered to mention the situation to me, I'll bet I could have."

Joanna was tempted to put a stop to that whole line of reasoning, to tell Susan Jenkins that there was nothing either she or her brother could have done to keep Alice Rogers from tangling with a gang of car thieves. That would have been the kind thing to do. But in the back of her mind, Joanna kept thinking about her phone call from Dick Voland—the one telling her that it looked as though Farley Adams had packed his gear and left Outlaw Mountain.

"Tell me what you know about your mother's boyfriend," Joanna said. "Had you ever met him?"

"Sure," Susan said. "He started out about a year ago doing yard work for her—trimming and pruning, mowing the lawn, raking, hauling out some of the old dead century plants. I didn't actually meet him until he was building the wall. Mother had always dreamed of having a wall around her place—one of those six-foot-high stucco affairs that looks like it came off a Spanish hacienda. She was thrilled when she finally found someone who could do the work for her. When the wall was finished, I expected Farley to move along. The next thing I knew, she had booted her previous renters out of the mobile home on Outlaw Mountain so Farley Adams could live there and work her claim. Even then, I didn't worry about it. I thought it was strictly a business arrangement.

"But Saturday night, she told me what was really going on—that the two of them were in love and getting married. Mother and I had a big fight about it. A huge fight. I told her she was crazy, that the man was just after her money. After all, Farley's at least twenty years younger—closer to my age than hers. What else could it be?"

What else indeed? Joanna thought. She couldn't help empathizing with Susan Jenkins in that moment. After all, Joanna Brady had felt exactly the same kind of shocked disbelief about her own mother and George Winfield when the medical examiner had finally worked up the courage to tell her that he and Eleanor Lathrop had eloped. Joanna had been so stunned at the time that she had almost driven off the road. And ever since, even though she liked George—even though she could see that the marriage between Eleanor Lathrop and George Winfield was clearly a love match—there was a small hard corner of Joanna's heart that couldn't quite forgive the love birds for their sneaky, underhanded maneuvering.

For a moment Joanna considered offering Susan Jenkins the benefit of some of her own hard-won experience. In her old life, that's precisely what she would have done. But now she was a cop—a detective—and it was her job and responsibility to ask questions. Counseling could wait.

"How much money's at stake?" she asked.

"Quite a bit," Susan returned. "It's not liquid. It's mostly in real estate. Daddy was always a great one for buying up property. There was a time in the early fifties when most of Tombstone was up for grabs. In those days, he and Mother worked like crazy to hang on to what they'd bought. Now, though, all the mortgages are mostly paid off and the rents keep going up. Consequently, Mother's been growing what should be a healthy little nest egg, from her rental income alone. There'd be more than that if she hadn't been such a soft touch where Clete was concerned."

"What do you mean?"

"Who do you think Clete's landlord is? And not just for his restaurant, either. He was supposedly paying Mother rent on the house he lives in, too, but he hasn't paid a dime. Mother should have evicted him years ago. That's one blessing anyway. At least I won't have to listen to that anymore—to Mother telling me how I have to make allowances for poor, sickly little Clete."

"So your mother had a fair amount of property in Tombstone," Joanna observed. "What about the mine at Outlaw Mountain—the claim Farley Adams was supposedly working. What kind of a mine is it?"

"Turquoise, mostly," Susan replied. "Dad picked it up years ago for back taxes. That was sometime in the forties, I think. For years he dinked around with it, working a vein of high-grade turquoise. He had some Indians he sold to—silversmiths up on the Navajo Reservation. I guess after Farley Adams went to work for her, Mother went back to selling to craftsmen on the various reservations. There never has been a whole lot of money in it, but I think Mother got a kick out of being a captain of industry."

"Let's go back to Saturday night," Joanna said. "You told me the two of you had a big fight about Farley Adams. Then what happened?"

"She left. She told me I should mind my own business and she left."

"What time was that?"

"I don't know. Eight or eight-thirty. Maybe later."

"Was she drunk when she left your house?" Joanna asked.

"Well, we'd all had a few drinks before dinner

and wine with, but she didn't seem drunk, not to me."

"How do you think she got here? Houghton Road is a long way from Tombstone."

Susan shook her head. "I don't know. It just doesn't make any sense."

"What did you do after she left?"

Suddenly Susan looked wary. "Why are you asking that? You don't think I had anything to do with what happened?"

"It's a routine question, Mrs. Jenkins. We'll be asking everyone."

"I went to bed."

"Alone?"

"Yes."

"Is there anyone who can verify that?"

"No. My husband had an appointment of some kind."

"An appointment Saturday night?"

"Yes."

"With whom?" Joanna asked.

"I'm not sure. He must have told me, but you'll have to ask him. Tyler, my stepson, never liked being around my mother much. He was out, too, with some of his friends."

"My detectives will need to verify where they were and who they were with."

"I'm sure that won't be a problem."

"What time did your husband come home?"

"I have no idea. As I told you, I went to sleep. But Sunday morning when I woke up, the more I thought about what was going on, the madder I got. That's when I went to see Clete. He's a pretty useless human being, and I don't like him much, but I didn't want to see either one of us cheated out of what our father and mother had built up. It just didn't make sense to hand something like that over to some gold-digging outsider."

"After you left your brother's restaurant, where did you go?"

"To my mother's first. When she wasn't there I went to Farley Adams' place on Outlaw Mountain."

"What happened?"

"I gave that worthless son of a bitch a piece of my mind. I told him I knew what he was up to and that I'd figure out some way so he wouldn't get a dime."

"And what did he say?"

"What do you think? He told me that he loved her, that he wasn't after her money. Do you know what he did then? Laughed in my face. Told me that Mother would never give him up. That was a lie, of course. He must have known then that she was already dead. He told me to leave, to get out. He treated me like I was some kind of interloper on my own mother's property. Acted like he already owned the place. I was dumbfounded! I guess things got a little bit out of hand about then. I do have a bit of a temper, you know," Susan added ruefully.

A bit of a temper, Joanna thought. She did indeed know. It was such a gross understatement that Joanna had to struggle to keep from laughing aloud.

"You attacked him?" she asked.

"Well, I would have, but he went inside and locked the door. Then he called nine-one-one. That's when the deputy showed up—the same one who was at Clete's restaurant earlier that day."

"Frank Montoya," Joanna supplied.

"Right. Well, he came out to Gleeson. It was while he was talking to me that I finally realized what had probably happened, that my mother was already dead. I was upset, I guess. Deputy Montoya called my husband to come drive me home."

Joanna thought about that. She was looking for motivation, and what Susan Jenkins was telling her didn't quite add up. "If, as you believe, Farley Adams killed your mother or had her killed in hopes of inheriting her estate, how would he do that?"

Susan looked puzzled. "What do you mean?"

"Do you think they were already married?"

"In secret, you mean?" Susan asked, incredulously. "Why, that's crazy! Who would do something like that?"

Joanna knew several people—herself and Andy included—who had done that very thing, but there was no sense in saying that to Susan Jenkins. "Supposing he and your mother were already married. If she died, as her surviving husband he could go against an earlier will and inherit at least the spouse's share of her estate. Or maybe she had already rewritten her will and put him in it. That way he could inherit regardless of whether or not they had gotten around to tying the knot. Without one of those two options, Farley Adams doesn't have an obvious motive."

"I remember Mother did go on a road trip a few weeks ago. She said she drove up to Laughlin, Nevada, for the weekend. Until Saturday, I was under the impression that she went by herself. It turns out I was wrong," Susan added bitterly.

Thinking about her mother and George Winfield, Joanna knew very well what else might have gone on in Laughlin, Nevada. "Those things do happen," she said. "But what about a will? Did your mother have an attorney?"

Susan nodded. "Her name is Dena Hogan. She's a friend of mine with an office out in Sierra Vista. A few years ago Mother went to one of those living-trust seminars and she got all riled up about the high cost of estate taxes. She asked me if I could recommend a good attorney, and Dena was the only one I knew. I gave Mother the phone number and Dena's the one she called."

"Did Ms. Hogan ever discuss the terms of your mother's will with you?"

Susan shook her head. "Absolutely not. I told you, Dena's an attorney, and a good one, too. I trust her completely. She never discussed my mother's business affairs with me, and I'm certain she didn't discuss mine with Mother, either."

Joanna nodded. Looking over her shoulder, she saw Frank Montoya coming out of the cacti and motioning toward Sergeant Mallory. That probably meant Fran Daly was ready to have someone come pick up the body and load it for transport.

"You'd probably better go on home now, Mrs. Jenkins."

"That's it? You mean I'm not under arrest after all?"

"No. I can see that earlier you weren't in full possession of your faculties. Considering what all's happened to you these past few days, that's not too surprising. Go on home. Try to get some rest. Over the next few days you'll probably have several detectives needing to talk to you, but they'll call and make appointments. In the meantime, don't attack any more police officers."

Susan grimaced and nodded ruefully. "What about identifying Mother's body?" she asked. "Should I drive on up to Tucson and do that today?"

"Why not talk it over with your brother first," Joanna advised. "Either he should do it, or you should. Or even, possibly, the two of you could do it together. After all, with your mother gone, isn't it about time the two of you buried the hatchet? Maybe that's something you could both do in her honor."

For a moment, Susan Jenkins' face almost dissolved in tears, but then she got a grip on herself. "You're right," she said with a sigh. "With Mother dead, it's about time Clete and I grew up."

"Try to keep a handle on your temper," Joanna advised. "You've been lucky so far, but one of these days, it's going to land you in jail."

"I'll do my best," Susan said.

She went back to the Sebring, climbed in, and started the engine. She was about to drive away when Joanna thought of another question.

"What about your brother?" Joanna asked. "How badly does he need money?"

"Clete always needs money," Susan replied. "There's never been a time in his life when he didn't. When we were kids, he used to come to me, begging to borrow some of my allowance. Now that he's been elected mayor, he can act like he's a big deal and throw his weight around all he wants, but he wouldn't be where he is today if Mother hadn't bailed him out of trouble time and time again."

Susan Jenkins paused and frowned. "Wait a minute, you're not suggesting Clete might be responsible for this, are you? Surely not. He's an A-number-one jerk at times, but he loved Mother to pieces. He'd never do anything to hurt her."

"I'm sure he wouldn't," Joanna agreed soothingly, but in the back of her mind she knew it was still far too soon to rule anyone out. The Pima County detectives might well be placing their bets on four young joyriding punks, but in the course of one afternoon, Joanna had found several other people, all of whom stood to benefit substantially from Alice Rogers' death. As far as Joanna was concerned, it was far too early in the investigation for her to rule anyone out.

If nothing else, Alice Rogers deserved that much consideration.

SIX

WHILE JOANNA waited for Alice Rogers' body to be hauled out from among the cacti, a maroon Chrysler Concorde with dealer plates pulled up beside her and stopped. When the driver rolled down the window, Joanna peered inside. The man behind the wheel was wearing a buckskin jacket complete with six-inch-long fringe. His hair fell in shoulder-length golden locks.

"I'm looking for my wife," he said, "Susan Jenkins. I heard there'd been some trouble out this way. I thought I'd better come check."

Now that he had identified himself, Joanna recognized him. His picture often showed up in local newspaper ads along with his signature "Li'l Doggie" bargain vehicle of the week. "You must be Ross Jenkins," Joanna said.

He clambered out of the car. He was a tall, broad-shouldered man, with a deep tan and movie-star-quality good looks. Peeling off his Stetson, he walked toward Joanna, holding one hand extended. "Yes, ma'am," he said. "That's correct. Ross Jenkins is the name. Who might you be?"

"I'm Sheriff Joanna Brady," she told him. "And your wife's already on her way back home. I'm surprised you didn't meet up with her along the way."

He shook his head and peered back up the road the way he had come. "That woman drives like a bat out of hell," he said. "She always has. The insurance premiums on that little red jitney of hers run me a fortune. So she's gone then?"

Joanna nodded.

"What about that?" Jenkins jerked his head in the direction of Fran Daly's van, the one bearing the logo of the Pima County Medical Examiner's office. "What's going on?"

"We're waiting for them to bring out the body," Joanna explained.

"It is Alice then?" he asked.

"We don't have a positive ID yet," Joanna told him, "but that's how it looks."

"In that case I'd best be heading on home," Jenkins said, turning back toward his car. "I don't want Susie Q. to have to deal with this all on her own."

After Ross Jenkins drove away, Joanna berated herself for not asking him at least one or two questions before he left. About that time, Fran Daly emerged from the cactus grove leading what looked like an impromptu funeral procession. Only when the body-laden stretcher was loaded into a van and hauled away and when the other vehicles had left the scene did Joanna settle into her Crown Victoria and switch on the ignition. Before putting the car in gear, she stopped long enough to consult her notes and find Father Thomas Mulligan's phone number. She hadn't yet punched it into the keypad when the cell phone chirped its distinctive ring, one that mimicked a crowing rooster.

"Hello."

"Joanna," Eleanor Lathrop Winfield announced brusquely. "Where in the world are you?"

Sighing, Joanna held the phone with one hand and eased the Civvy onto the roadway with the other. "Hello, Mother. I'm at a crime scene up near Tucson. Just leaving there, actually. I'm out on Houghton Road."

"Houghton. That's in Pima County, isn't it?"

"Yes."

"Well, that's a relief anyway," Eleanor said. "This should be one case George won't be called out on. We're having company for dinner. I don't want him coming home late."

Dr. George Winfield, Eleanor's new husband, was also Cochise County's recently appointed medical examiner. At first Joanna had been concerned that her position as sheriff would create impossible complications with a medical examiner who also happened to be her stepfather. So far those worries had proved unfounded. If anything, her working relationship with George Winfield had become better since the wedding. On the other hand, relations with her mother continued to be thorny.

"And that's what I'm calling about," Eleanor added accusingly. "Dinner. I've been trying to reach you all day long—since early this morning— but you've been out. In fact, I called your house right around eight. Butch Dixon answered."

Eleanor stopped cold. Joanna waited for her to continue, knowing the last sentence was more accusation than comment. "And . . . ?" she said finally.

"I said, he answered the phone!"

"Of course Butch answered the phone," Joanna replied. "I had to leave for work and, as usual, Jenny was running late. He offered to take her to school."

"I spoke to Jenny," Eleanor said stiffly. "She told me that Butch spent the night."

There it was, out in the open—the source of Eleanor Winfield's outrage. Butch Dixon had spent the night at Joanna's house without Eleanor's having approved the sleep-over in advance. The irony of the situation wasn't lost on Joanna. She still remembered her own dismay the first time she had dialed through to George Winfield's number and her mother—Eleanor Lathrop herself—had answered his phone bright and early in the morning. In that instance, it turned out that an unannounced but properly conducted wedding had already taken place.

At the time, however, Joanna had been bowled over by the thought of her mother fooling around. Living in sin, as it were. Since that stunning revelation, Joanna had been struggling to come to grips with the idea of her mother as a sexual being. Joanna had also been forced to accept the idea that Eleanor had a right to live her own life however she chose.

From Joanna's perspective, it seemed clear enough that those kinds of rights ought to be reciprocal. Sauce for the goose and sauce for the goose's daughter.

"Yes, Butch spent the night," Joanna said. "Things were happening at the office, and I was afraid I was going to be called out overnight. I couldn't have gone off and left Jenny there on the ranch all alone. Besides, on school nights it's too hard on her when I have to drag her out of bed and drop her off at Eva Lou and Jim Bob's place or at yours."

Eva Lou and Jim Bob Brady, Jenny's other grandparents, maintained an extra bedroom in their home that was reserved for Jenny's exclusive use. Usually, they were the emergency baby-sitters of choice. In a pinch, Jenny could have gone there. Joanna knew that, and so did Eleanor. Joanna also realized that out of deference to family harmony, she might have mentioned that Butch had spent the bulk of the night on the living room couch—that Jenny had found him there in the morning rather than in her mother's bed. If Joanna had disclosed that fact, it might have gone a long way toward soothing Eleanor's ruffled feathers.

Right that minute, however, Joanna Lathrop Brady was far more interested in establishing some privacy ground rules than she was in getting along. As a thirty-year-old widow—one local voters had chosen to elect to the office of sheriff—it seemed as though it was high time for Joanna to stand up to her own mother. Eleanor's response to Joanna's declaration of independence was utterly predictable.

"What in the world must Jenny think!" Eleanor exclaimed. "And what about everyone else? You're a public figure in this town, Joanna. An elected official. You can't have people going around talking about you this way."

"How are they going to find out about it, Mother?" Joanna asked. "I'm not going to tell them. Are you?"

"Certainly not!" Eleanor huffed. "I'd never mention such a thing, but Jenny might. After all, she told me, didn't she? Just like that. As though it's the most natural thing in the world."

"It is the most natural thing in the world," Joanna countered. "Birds do it. Bees do it. I suspect even you and George do it on occasion."

When it came to Butch Dixon, Joanna was tired of sneaking around. With everyone but Jeff and Marianne, Joanna and Butch had acted with such vigilance and discretion that most people in town probably thought of them as little more than nodding acquaintances. Suddenly Joanna found herself running out of patience with keeping up appearances. Butch deserved better, and so did she.

There, she thought. *Now it's finally out on the table. Let the chips fall where they may.*

Which they seemed to be doing. As Eleanor's ominous silence lengthened, Joanna knew she had crossed into some kind of emotional no-man's-land from which there would be no return.

"Mother," she said at last. "Are you still there?"

"I'm here," Eleanor said in a small voice. "I'm thinking about Jenny."

"What about her?"

"She's suffered so much already. How in good conscience can you put her through this kind of emotional wringer?"

"What do you mean?" Joanna asked.

Eleanor heaved a great sight. "Jenny's not ready for a new father, Joanna. It's way too soon."

Joanna's temper switched into high gear. "Who said anything about her having a new father?"

"But if you and Butch are . . . well . . . you know, then obviously you must be planning on getting married or something."

"We're not *planning* on anything," Joanna said. "We're enjoying ourselves. We're enjoying getting to know each other. It may lead to something more serious, and then again, it may not. In the meantime, Mother, it's our business and no one else's. Now, Kristin said you called three times. Is this why, to bawl me out about Butch, or was there some other reason?"

"I was going to invite you to dinner." Eleanor's arch, unbending tone wasn't likely to win friends, or daughters.

"Were," Joanna repeated. "Does that mean that now you're not?"

"No. Of course not. You're still invited—you and Jenny both."

Jenny and I, but not Butch. Definitely not Butch.

"I'm working a case, Mother," Joanna said. "I have no idea what time I'll finish up. I wouldn't want to keep you and your other guests waiting. I've got to go now. There's construction on the highway, and I need to concentrate on my driving."

Ending the call, she put the phone down and drove for several seething minutes before she picked it up again and scrolled through until she found Butch's number. He answered on the second ring. When he realized who was calling, the pleasure in his voice was unmistakable. "I was hoping you'd call long before this so I could take you to lunch."

"I missed lunch," she said, realizing it for the first time. "I've been out on a crime scene."

"Skipping meals isn't good for you," he observed.

"Neither is talking to my mother."

"Why? What happened?"

"Jenny told her that you spent the night. She's on the warpath about it."

"You settled her down, didn't you?" Butch asked. "You did let her know that I slept on the couch?"

"No," Joanna admitted. "I didn't. I let her draw her own conclusions."

There was silence on Butch's end of the call. "Why did you do that?" he asked finally.

"Because I'm sick and tired of her trying to run my life; of her telling me what to do. I want Eleanor Lathrop Winfield to mind her own damned business and leave me alone."

"Well," Butch observed thoughtfully. "Your mother didn't like me very much to begin with. I doubt this will improve the situation."

"So you think I did the wrong thing?" Joanna demanded. She was beginning to think so herself, but she didn't want Butch to share that opinion. And, if he did, she didn't want to hear it. That would only make it worse.

"No," he said with an easy laugh. "Not wrong. But you never choose the easy way out, do you, Joanna," he added. "That's one of the things I like about you—one of the things I love."

The word slipped out so smoothly, so naturally that for a second Joanna wasn't sure she had heard him correctly.

"Oops," he said. "That probably counts as pushing, and I promised you I wouldn't—push, that is. Especially not over the phone."

Joanna's initial reaction was to tell him to take it back, to unsay it. And yet, if she didn't want him to care about her and if she didn't already care about him, what the hell was the fight with her mother all about?

Joanna took a deep breath and decided to sidestep the issue. "Mother's position is that if we're sleeping together, we ought to be getting married or we should already *be* married. She also thinks, because of Jenny, that it's far too soon for us to even *think* about such a thing."

"In other words, we're damned if we do and damned if we don't," Butch said.

"Right."

"See?" he said. "Like mother, like daughter.

Eleanor Winfield isn't known for taking easy positions, either. Has either one of you thought about asking Jenny for her opinion?"

"Butch, she's only eleven. What does she know?"

"You might be surprised," he said. "Now if we're not having lunch, why are you calling?"

"Is Jenny there?"

Lowell, the school Jenny attended, was only three blocks from Butch's newly refurbished house in Bisbee's Saginaw neighborhood. On days when she didn't have after-school activities, she usually went to Butch's house to have a snack, do her homework, and hang out until Joanna got off work and could come pick her up.

"She's up the street riding her bike. Do you want me to go find her, or do you want to leave a message?"

"A message will be fine. Tell her I'm on my way to Tombstone to check on a crime scene investigation, and I'll probably have to stop off in Saint David on the way. It may be late before I get there to pick her up."

"Don't worry," Butch said. "She can stay as long as she likes. I'm making a pot of beef-and-cabbage soup. Soup and freshly baked bread are always a winning combination on a cold winter's evening. There'll be plenty for you, too, when you get here."

"Thanks, Butch," Joanna said. "By then I'm sure I'll be hungry. I have to hang up now. I need to make another call."

"Take care," Butch said.

"I will."

Joanna drove down I-10 all the while rehashing both conversations. Butch had slipped that four-letter word into the conversation so unobtrusively that she might well have missed it altogether. Still, he *had* said it—had admitted aloud that he loved her. Now the ball was in Joanna's court. Was she going to let their affair grow into something more? Did she love him back or not? And if so, how long before she'd be ready to admit it to herself, to say nothing of anyone else, including her own mother?

Turning off the freeway in Benson, Joanna belatedly realized that she still hadn't called Father Mulligan. She used the pause at one of Benson's two red lights to key his number into her phone. He must have been waiting beside the phone. Joanna's call was answered after only one ring.

"Father Thomas Mulligan here."

"It's Sheriff Brady," she told him. "I'm returning your call. What can I do for you?"

Joanna had met Father Mulligan when she had come to Saint David for a Drug Awareness Resistance Education meeting, along with her department's DARE officer, earlier in the fall. Joanna had been surprised to encounter the man at an evening PTA meeting in the local public elementary school, since he was prior of a Catholic monastery in a largely Mormon community. She had also been surprised to learn that the priest himself had been instrumental in raising money to fund that year's worth of DARE activities and prizes in the community.

"We've got a little problem here."

"What kind of problem?" Joanna asked.

"Well, we had our annual autumn arts and crafts fair here over the weekend."

"Yes, I know," Joanna said. "My department helped out with traffic control, remember?"

"That's right. Of course I remember. And there was absolutely no difficulty with that. Your officers were terrific."

"So what's the trouble then?"

"It's a lost-and-found problem."

Joanna knew that in the aftermath of local festivals, rodeos, and fairs, lost-and-found items could include everything from livestock to motor homes.

"What happened?" she asked. "Did somebody wander off and forget they left a Bounder parked in your RV-park?"

Father Mulligan didn't laugh. "Actually," he said seriously, "it's a bit worse than that. And since I know you personally, I thought you'd be the right person to call to discuss it."

"So what is it?" Joanna asked.

The priest took a deep breath. "Someone left their son here," he said. "His name is Junior. I found him in the church this morning before mass. He must have slept there overnight."

"You need to call CPS," Joanna said at once. "Child Protective Services has case workers who are trained to take charge of abandoned children.

They get them into foster care, locate their parents, that kind of thing. The sheriff's department just isn't equipped—"

"He's not a child," Father Mulligan interrupted. "I can't tell you exactly how old he is. He could be fifty or so, maybe even older. He told me his name—his first name—and that's about it. He couldn't give us his parents' names or the name of the town where he lives. I checked to see if he was carrying any kind of identification, but he wasn't. And then I thought maybe there'd be some identifying mark sewn into his clothing, maybe on the labels. But there aren't any labels on his clothing, Sheriff Brady. They've all been removed. I think someone cut them out on purpose, so we'd have no way of following a trail and finding out where they and he came from."

"What do you want me to do about it?" Joanna asked. "I can't very well put him in jail."

"You might have to," Father Mulligan said. "He was all right at breakfast this morning, probably because he was famished. But at lunchtime he was agitated. As near as we could tell, he wanted his mother. He wanted to know where she was and when she was coming for him. I had a meeting right after lunch. I left one of the sisters in charge of Junior. I thought he could sit quietly in the library and look at books. He got restless, though, and wanted to go outside. When Sister Ambrose told him he couldn't do that, he knocked her down and went outside anyway. I found him wading in the reflecting pond, chasing the fish. So you see, we can't keep him here. It's not that

we're uncharitable or unchristian, but some of
the brothers and sisters are quite elderly. They
can't be expected to handle someone like that—
someone that unpredictable."

"No," Joanna agreed, "I suppose not. I'm on my
way, Father Mulligan. I'll be there in a few minutes. I'm just now crossing the San Pedro River
on the far side of Saint David."

She ended the call and immediately radioed
into the department and spoke to Dispatch. "Do
we have any missing persons reports on a developmentally disabled male, named Junior, forty-
five to fifty-five years old, and last seen at the
Saint David Arts and Crafts Fair yesterday afternoon?"

"Nothing like that," Larry Kendrick, Cochise
County's lead dispatcher, told her. "Why?"

Joanna gave Larry a brief summary of everything Father Mulligan had told her. "What are
you going to do with him?" Larry asked when
Joanna finished.

"I don't know yet."

"It sounds like it could be iffy for you to handle
this alone. Do you want me to send out a deputy?"

"Who's available?" Joanna asked.

"Nobody right this minute," Larry replied.
"We've had a bit of a problem out at Sierra Vista.
Those environmental activists showed up on the
Oak Vista construction site right at quitting time.
They came armed with sledgehammers and spikes
and sugar to put in gas tanks. In other words,
they came prepared to make trouble and to do
as much damage to the contractor's equipment

as possible. It was quite a donnybrook. Terry Gregovich had to call for reinforcements. Dick Voland ordered every available deputy out there on the double."

"I'm the sheriff," Joanna said brusquely. "Why wasn't I notified?"

"I've been trying to page you ever since it happened, but your pager must be off line and your cell phone's been busy. I figured if you were in your car you would have heard the radio traffic and would have known something was up."

Guiltily, Joanna glared at her radio. She had turned down the volume while she was making her phone calls. And the pager, back in her purse, must have somehow turned itself off. "Sorry, Larry," she said. "I didn't mean to be incommunicado. Should I forget about Saint David and head out to Sierra Vista?"

"No. Chief Deputy Voland was on his way to Tombstone, but now he's going to Sierra Vista instead. He said if you called in, you'd better go check on the two teams working in Tombstone. Detective Carbajal is there, but other than that, the crime scene investigators are on their own."

Joanna shook her head. Even with almost two hundred people working for her, the Cochise County Sheriff's Department was chronically short-staffed. On those occasions when several major things happened at once, that chronic shortage instantly turned critical.

"All right," she said. "Radio Chief Deputy Voland and let him know I'll take care of Tombstone. And Saint David," she added under her breath.

After all, someone has to do it.

When Anglos first showed up in southern Arizona, the area along the San Pedro River, a few miles south of what is now Benson, was a mosquito-infested, swampy wasteland. Despite the hardships, a few hardy souls had settled there. When a severe earthquake rocked the Sonora Desert on May 3, 1887, no one in the Saint David area was injured, nor was there much structural damage, primarily due to the fact that so few people lived there. The non-killer quake left lasting evidence of its handiwork by instantly draining the swamp and forcing much of the San Pedro watershed underground. The former swamp turned into a fertile farmland oasis studded by ancient cottonwoods.

It was late afternoon when Joanna Brady slowed her Crown Victoria at the three wooden crosses that marked the entrance to Holy Trinity Monastery, a Benedictine retreat center beyond the eastern boundary of Saint David. The center had been there for as long as Joanna remembered. It was only as an adult that she had considered it odd for the Catholic Diocese in Tucson to have established a retreat center in the middle of Mormon farming country in southeastern Arizona.

Nestled under the San Pedro's towering cottonwoods, the monastery contained a small, jewel-like church—Our Lady of Guadalupe—a bird sanctuary, a pecan orchard, an RV park, and a library/museum, as well as a used-clothing thrift store. Living quarters for monks, sisters, and resident lay workers consisted of a collection of mobile homes clustered about the property in a haphazard manner. Throughout the year Holy Trinity held Christian Renewal retreats for various groups from the Catholic Church. Twice a year—spring and autumn—the monastery hosted a fund-raising arts festival and fair.

Shimmering golden leaves captured the setting sun and reflected off the surface of a shallow pond as Joanna parked in front of the church. As soon as she switched off the ignition, a tall, angular man in a long white robe and sandals came flapping out of the church to meet her.

"I'm so glad you came right away, Sheriff Brady," Father Thomas Mulligan said. "I've been quite concerned."

"The sister who was left with him wasn't hurt, was she?"

"No," Father Mulligan said. "She bruised her elbow when he knocked her down, but other than that she's fine."

"Where is he now?"

"In the church. There are lots of lighted candles in the sanctuary, and he seems to like them."

"Is it safe to leave him there alone?" Joanna asked.

"He isn't alone. Brother Joseph is with him. Back when Brother Joseph was a high school gym teacher, he taught judo. According to him, judo is like riding a bike. You never forget the moves."

Half-trotting to keep up with Father Mulligan's long-legged stride, Joanna followed the priest into the adobe-walled church. The setting sun, shining in through stained-glass windows, filled the small, carefully crafted sanctuary with a muted glow. Two men sat in the front pew. One was an elderly white-robed priest. The other was a wizened, hunched little man whose huge ears and doleful face reminded Joanna of an elf.

"Junior?" she said, holding out her hand.

Slowly he raised his eyes until he was staring up into her face. Politely, he held out his hand as well, but his grip barely clasped Joanna's.

"Hello," she said. "I'm Sheriff Brady."

Without a word, Junior scooted sideways in the pew until he was huddled next to Brother Joseph. Then, burying his head in the priest's robe, he began to moan. "Didn't do it. Didn't do it. Didn't do it."

"Didn't do what?" Joanna asked.

"Not bad," Junior wailed, pressing even closer to the priest, who by then had wrapped a protective arm around his shoulders. "Junior not bad. No jail, please. No jail. Don't hurt me. Don't hurt Junior."

Seeing that he was utterly terrified of her, Joanna stood for a moment trying to decide what to do. Then, from some far recess of memory, she recalled one sunny spring afternoon years earlier. She had been in her Brownie uniform, stationed in front of the post office in Warren, hawking Girl Scout cookies. A man had ridden up to her on a bike, a girl's bike. He had stopped and stood beside her, staring down into her wagonload of cookies.

He had stood there for a long time, and his silent staring presence had worried her. After all, he was wearing a badge and a holstered gun. Jo-

anna had been petrified that she was doing something wrong, that he was going to arrest her for it.

Then a gray-haired woman had emerged from
the beauty shop next door to the post office. The
man had smiled at the woman, called her Mama,
and pointed at the cookies, saying he wanted some.
That was when Joanna realized there was something wrong with him. That he was a grown-up
who was also somehow still a child. His mother
had bought a box of cookies—Thin Mints—and
she had explained that her son "wasn't quite right,"
that he liked to "pretend" to be a policeman. Both
the gun and the holster were toys. The sheriff's
badge was a prize from a box of Cracker Jacks.

From that long-ago memory came the seed of
inspiration.

"I'm not here to take you to jail," Joanna said.
"Did you ever want to play policeman?"

Junior quieted and peeked up at her from behind Brother Joseph's robe. "Play?" Junior asked.

"Yes," Joanna said. "Would you like to play
policeman?" Reaching into her pocket, Joanna
extracted her leather ID folder and handed it over
to him. Inside were both her identification and
her badge—the badge with the words "Serve and
Protect" engraved in square gold letters. Looking
at it, Junior's eyes bulged with excitement. He
fingered the metal.

"Would you like to put it on?" Joanna asked
kindly. "You could wear it while we go for a ride
in my car and look for your mother."

"Junior wear it?" he repeated wonderingly.
"Me wear it?"

"Yes," Joanna said. "But you'll have to come with me. Okay?"

Junior nodded his head emphatically, eagerly. "Me wear. Me wear. Put on. Put on now."

Carefully Joanna pinned the badge to the pocket of Junior's shirt. "All right now, can you raise your right hand?"

Both hands shot high in the air. "Do you swear to be a good deputy, Junior?" Joanna asked.

Junior's face split into a wide smile and he jumped to his feet. "Me good," he said. "Junior very good de-de-deputy." It took several times before he could finally make his lips form the unfamiliar word. "Go now," he added. "Go right now. Get in car."

"Right," Joanna said. "We'll go get in the car."

Junior raced down the aisle, with Joanna and Father Mulligan following behind. "That was very impressive," the priest said under his breath. "Whatever gave you that idea?"

"Desperation," she told him. "Desperation plain and simple."

♣ SEVEN

Between Saint David and Tombstone, Joanna said little and Junior said even less. He sat huddled in the far corner of the passenger seat with his arms clutching his chest. When Joanna asked him a direct question, he ducked his head and stared out the windshield without any acknowledgment that she had spoken to him.

What the hell have I let myself in for? Joanna asked herself. Obviously Junior didn't belong in jail, not even in protective custody—as if that would be protection enough from some of the casually abusive thugs populating the Cochise County jail. The county hospital down in Douglas contained a mental ward, but Joanna was sure Junior wouldn't qualify as a mental patient, either. He may not have been in possession of all his faculties, but he certainly wasn't crazy. He was lost. Abandoned. And, as Joanna could see, terribly, terribly sad.

So if jail and the hospital are both out of the question, what do I do with him? she asked herself. In the past she would have gone straight to Marianne Maculyea with that kind of thorny problem. Marianne had the unerring knack of knowing just where to turn for help in sticky situations, but at this point in Mari's life, she was at such a low ebb that she couldn't even help herself. How on earth, then, could she be expected to help someone else?

That was as far as Joanna had managed to noodle the problem by the time she reached Tombstone. Once there, she had to call in to Dispatch to get directions to Alice Rogers' home. It was on the far northern outskirts of town, past the dusty pioneer cemetery, and off on a dirt track called Scheiffelin Monument Road. At the far end of that road was a rocky cairn containing the worldly remains of Ed Scheiffelin. Scheiffelin was a hardy prospector whose silver strike had been the original foundation of Tombstone's fabulous if short-lived mineral wealth.

Joanna's father, D. H. Lathrop, had venerated the cussed independence of Ed Scheiffelin and others like him. With the Sonora Desert alive with marauding Apaches, Scheiffelin had left Tucson alone and on foot with little more than a mule, a chaw of tobacco, and a dream of achieving impossible wealth. And when that dream came true— when the silver claims other people had scoffed at came to fruition—Scheiffelin had gone on to wealth, fame, and high living without ever forgetting his humble roots. Years later, before he died in Oregon, he had asked to be returned to Arizona and buried near the site of that initial mining claim.

For D. H. Lathrop, people like Ed Scheiffelin epitomized the heroes of the Old West in a way the good guys and bad guys—the Earps and the Clantons—did not. Lathrop had filled his daughter's head with stories about Ed's greedy partners who had done their best to cheat him out of what was rightfully his. Her mother had disparaged everything about Tombstone—the clapboard buildings, the phony gunfights, and the tacky tourist souvenirs. For Eleanor Lathrop the place was little more than a vulgar tourist trap—something to be despised and certainly not patronized.

Joanna had grown up with her father's love of legends on the one hand and with her mother's unflinching disapproval on the other. Thinking about Alice Rogers, it made Joanna sad that as far as she knew Alice and her father had never met. She sensed that D. H. Lathrop would have had much in common with a woman whose whole life seemed to be tied in with Tombstone's fabled mineral wealth. In fact, Joanna wondered now: Did Alice's mining claim at Outlaw Mountain have anything to do with her death?

Joanna pulled up to the group of cars parked on both sides of the road. Alice's house was completely surrounded by the thick six-foot-tall adobe-and-stucco fence Susan Jenkins had told her about. Stopping for a moment outside the arched wrought-iron gate, Joanna considered the workmanship. Regardless of how much Farley Adams had been paid for building the fence, it was clear the construction project had been a labor of love. On either side of the gate and set at ten-foot intervals were beautifully wrought sconces made of turquoise-shaded stained glass and powered by carefully concealed wiring.

Having seen the fence, Joanna expected the house to be a luxurious hacienda-style affair. Instead, she found herself looking through the gateway toward a modest slump-block building that looked as though it had been thrown up on the cheap sometime in the fifties. With Junior tagging along, Joanna couldn't risk venturing inside for fear evidence might be disturbed or destroyed. Instead, she flagged down a deputy and sent her into the house to locate Detective Carbajal and send him back to the gate.

In the deepening twilight, Joanna noticed that lights showed at every window in Alice Rogers' house. An ordinary passer-by, seeing those lights and all the extra vehicles, might have assumed there was a party going on inside. *It's a party, all right*, Joanna thought grimly. *Your ordinary crime scene fiesta*.

A harried-looking Jaime Carbajal hustled down the walk. "Hello, Sheriff Brady," he said. "What's up?"

"I wanted to check on how things are going."

"Okay, I guess," he replied. "We're working the problem. Looks like a straight-out burglary—no TV, no radios, no jewelry. We're finding lots of prints, and we're collecting them all. Between this house and the other one, that's a lot of ground to cover. It's going to take time."

The detective paused and glanced questioningly toward Junior, who clutched his arms and gazed skyward, saying nothing. "Who's this?" Jaime asked.

"I've run into a little complication," Joanna explained quickly. "Junior here got separated from his family, and we're trying to help find them. Which means, by the way, that I'm not going to be able to go out to Gleeson to check on your other crew."

"That's no problem. They're about to close up for the night anyway. Besides, you're driving one of the Civvys today, aren't you?"

Joanna nodded. "Be advised," Jaime Carbajal said. "The road to Outlaw Mountain is a mess. Strictly four-wheel-drive. We're having to ferry the crime scene guys in and out in one of the Broncos."

"What all are you finding?" Joanna asked.

He nodded toward Alice Rogers' glowing house. "It's just like the daughter said. This place has been ransacked. No way to tell exactly how much is missing, since we don't have any idea what was in the house to begin with. We'll have to get relatives to help us with an inventory. The mobile home over in Gleeson looks like somebody did a fast job of packing rather than tearing the place apart. If you're asking for my best guess, I'd say whoever left there did so in one hell of a hurry."

"As in on the run?"

Carbajal nodded. "Maybe."

Joanna thought about that. Farley Adams taking off in a hurry didn't square with Pima County's kids-as-killers program, but it was something to check out. If Farley Adams had nothing to hide, why had he run away?

"Do we have any idea what kind of vehicle he'd be driving?" Joanna asked.

"We do have that. A vintage Jeep, a post–World War II Willys model. It belongs to Alice Rogers."

"Why is everybody so intent on stealing Alice Rogers' cars? And how did you find that out, Department of Transportation?"

"No," Jaime said. "I talked to Nadine Harvey, Farley Adams' neighbor. She runs that junkyard in Gleeson right at the turnoff to the mine. As near as I can tell, she spends most of her life standing out in her yard sweeping chinaberries out of the dirt and watching everything that goes on."

"Did she have any idea when Farley took off?"

"She knew exactly. Said it was yesterday afternoon. She claims Adams came hauling ass down the road about an hour or so after Frank Montoya left."

"Yesterday afternoon," Joanna mused. "That means he has a long head start on us, over twenty-four hours. Have you done anything about finding him?"

"Not yet. I've had my hands full, but I will. What do you think, an APB?" he added.

"No. I think that would be premature. Besides, a Jeep that old isn't going to be hard to find. He may have headed for the border, where he can still buy leaded gas. For now, let's post the Jeep as a stolen vehicle and wait for somebody to spot it for us. That way, by the time we locate Farley Adams, we may know more about what we're up against."

Next to Joanna, Junior stirred restlessly, shifting from one foot to the other, moaning softly. "Go," he whimpered, making his first sound in almost an hour. "Go. Go. Go."

Glad that he was speaking to her at last, Joanna did her best to reassure him. "It's all right, Junior," she crooned. "We'll be leaving soon. Just let me finish talking to Detective Carbajal." She turned back to Jaime. "Sorry I can't be more of a help right now," she told him. "As you can see, I—"

"You've got your hands full, Sheriff Brady," Jaime said. "Don't worry. You take care of him. I can handle this."

"But I'll want you at tomorrow morning's briefing," Joanna said. "With everything that's been happening today—here, in Tucson, and out at Sierra Vista—we're going to need to start the day with firsthand information on all fronts."

"Yes, ma'am," Jaime said. "I'll be there."

By now, Junior had edged away from Joanna and was skittering down the road. He had already passed the Crown Victoria by the time she was able to dash after him, catch him by the arm, and bring him back to the vehicle.

"Go," he said again, more urgently this time. "Junior go. Junior go now!"

"All right," Joanna agreed. "We're going. Come get in the car."

He tried to shake loose of her hand. Remembering what had happened to Sister Ambrose, Joanna held firm. After a momentary struggle, he quieted. For a matter of seconds Joanna wondered if she should lock him in the backseat rather than letting him ride up front with her, but by then he was no longer fighting. She helped him into the front passenger seat and buckled the seat belt across him. Then she hurried around the car and climbed in herself.

She had started the car, backed up, and completed a U-turn when the sharp and unmistakable odor of urine flooded her nostrils. Her heart sank with the sudden realization of what Junior had really meant when he said he wanted to go. She knew instantly that Junior's particular brand of "go" was going to play havoc with the Civvy's cloth-covered interior.

Embarrassed for Junior and angry with herself for not understanding his urgent plea, Joanna floorboarded the gas pedal. There was no point then in stopping the car and trying to hustle him into a rest room. The damage was already done.

What are the guys in Motor Pool going to think when I bring this one in? she wondered.

On the seat beside her, Junior buried his face in his hands and sobbed. "Sorry," he wailed over and over again. "Junior sorry."

"It's all right," Joanna said, swallowing her own anger in hopes of calming him. "You tried to tell me and I didn't understand. We'll be home soon, Junior. We'll take care of it."

He raised his head hopefully. "Home?" he said.

A feeling of total helplessness washed over Joanna. She had no idea where his home was or how to take him there. In his innocence he thought she did and trusted her to make good her promise. How could she do that? And how would she deliver on what she had told Father Mulligan, that she would take care of Holy Trinity's little lost lamb?

Where would she find something as simple as dry clothing for him to wear? There was nothing out at High Lonesome Ranch that would fit him. Joanna had long since sent Andy's things to a local clothing bank. Even if she was able to solve the basic issue of dressing Junior, what would she do with him after that? For one thing, there was the question of bedrooms. The house at High Lonesome Ranch was a modest two-bedroom affair with no guest room. Butch had slept fine on Joanna's cloth-covered sofa. With Junior that wouldn't be possible—for several obvious reasons.

On the seat beside her, an inconsolable Junior once again dissolved into tears. His despairing, muffled sobs were enough to break Joanna's heart.

"Hush now," she said. "Do you like to sing?"

Continuing to whimper, he didn't answer.

They were through Tombstone now, past the airport, and coming down the long curve into the upper San Pedro Valley. Off to the right—a good twenty miles across the valley—the combined lights of Sierra Vista and Fort Huachuca glimmered along the base of the mountains. Ahead of them, in the darkened sky over the Mule Mountains, a single star—the evening star—glittered brightly. Seeing it reminded Joanna of some of the trips she had made back and forth to Tucson when Jenny was a baby. Driving by herself, there had been no way to comfort her crying child but to sing. Would that same magic work on Junior?

"Twinkle, twinkle, little star," Joanna began. The familiar tune filled the night. At the sound of her singing, Junior quieted a little. He continued to sniffle and choke, but his heart-wrenching sobs eased.

By the time Joanna finished that first familiar ditty, Junior's breath was coming in long, ragged shudders, but at least he was quieter. And Joanna felt better, too. As the last notes of "Little Star" died away, she moved on to another equally familiar tune. For the next twenty minutes, she sang every childhood song she could remember. There were ones from Sunday school: "Zacheus," "Jesus Loves Me," "I'll Be a Sunbeam for Jesus." There were ones from kindergarten: "Eensy Weensy Spider," "I'm a Little Teapot," and "Do the Hokey-Pokey." By the time the Crown Victoria slid across the Divide and dropped down into Bisbee's Tombstone Canyon, Joanna had moved on to Girl Scout songs: "Make New Friends But Keep the Old" and "White Coral Bells."

By then it no longer mattered what she sang because Junior was sound asleep beside her. With the heater on, the smell of urine was thick in the air, but Joanna didn't dare open the window for fear the cold air would chill him. After all, he was wet. She wasn't.

Coming around Lavender Pit, she finally made up her mind about where she was going to go—straight to Butch Dixon's place in Saginaw. Picking up the phone, she dialed his number and breathed a sigh of relief when he answered right away.

"Where are you?" Butch asked. "Jenny and I are just now sitting down to eat."

"I'm coming through Lowell," she told him, speaking quietly, afraid that if she raised her voice she might disturb Junior, who was snoring softly beside her.

"Great," Butch said. "We set a place for you, but I didn't think you'd be here this early."

"Neither did I," Joanna murmured, wondering how she was going to break the news to him. "But I've got a problem, Butch."

"What kind of problem?"

"I've got a passenger with me. His name is Junior. At least that's as much of his name as we know. He's developmentally disabled. He peed his pants about the time we were leaving a crime scene in Tombstone, and now he's sound asleep."

"What's he doing in your car?" Butch asked. "Is he under arrest, or what?"

"He didn't commit a crime, so no, he's not under arrest. Somebody abandoned him at the weekend arts and crafts fair over in Saint David. It's hard to tell about his age. I'd say he's somewhere close to fifty, but we've got no identification to verify that. Mentally he's closer to three or four. Verbal, but only just."

"Not enough to tell you he needed to go to the bathroom."

"Right. He tried. I just didn't understand."

"So where are you taking him, to the jail?"

"I can't take him there, Butch. Some of those guys . . ."

"I know. I know. And you can't take him home, either."

"No," Joanna agreed. "I can't, but . . ."

"You want me to take care of him?"

Joanna's heart filled with a flood of gratitude. It was exactly what she had wanted, but she hadn't dared ask. By then she was less than half a mile from Butch's home in the Saginaw neighborhood. Driving around the traffic circle, she was tempted to go around several more times, just to give Butch time to adjust to the idea of taking in an unexpected house guest. It seemed, however, that Butch was already coping.

"Where are you now?" he asked.

"The traffic circle."

"I'll go out and move the Subaru so you can pull into the carport right next to the house. And I'll bring out a robe and some towels so we can get him out of his wet clothes before we try to bring him inside. How big is he?"

"Not very," Joanna responded.

"Will my underwear fit him?"

"He'll swim in it."

"No problem," Butch said cheerfully. "Sounds like he's swimming in something else at the moment. How bad is your car?"

"It's bad. Soaked."

"It'll have to wait. First things first," Butch said. "See you in a couple of minutes."

It wasn't much more than that when Joanna arrived at Butch's house. True to his word, Butch's new Outback was parked on the street. The chain-link gate to his driveway stood wide open, allowing Joanna access to a covered carport. Jenny stood at the back door clutching an armload of material that turned out to be the promised towels, a robe, and a pair of sweats with a drawstring at the waist.

For a change, Joanna was only too happy to stand aside and let someone else take charge. Butch knelt beside the car and untied Junior's high-topped tennis shoes. After removing the shoes, Butch gently shook Junior awake. Helping him out of the car, Butch stood him upright long enough to peel off the soaked khaki work pants, under-shorts, and shirt, all of which he allowed to fall into a sodden heap. After helping Junior step into the sweats, Butch wrapped the shivering and uncomplaining man in the ample folds of a thick terry-cloth robe.

"There you go," Butch said, taking Junior by the arm. "Come on in. It's cold out here, and dinner's on the table. I'll bet you're hungry."

Looking down at the terry-cloth robe, Junior ran his fingers across the soft, downy material in seeming delight. "Hungry," he said, nodding agreeably. "Junior eat."

As soon as Butch had begun unbuttoning Junior's shirt, Jenny had disappeared into the house. When Joanna followed Butch and Junior into the small, cozy kitchen, she was gratified to see that Jenny had made use of the time alone to set another place at the table.

"This is Junior, Jenny," Butch said.

"Hello, Junior," Jenny responded, as though welcoming someone like him was the most ordinary thing in the world. "What do you want to drink—milk, water, or soda?"

Junior's eyes fastened hungrily on the carton in Jenny's hand. "Milk," he said. "Junior like milk. Milk good."

Matter-of-factly, Jenny went to one of the places and filled the glass there with milk. "Here, Junior," she said, pointing. "You sit here."

Butch helped Junior onto the proper chair. Joanna wasn't sure how Butch had done it, but somehow he had managed to convey to Jenny exactly what was going on. Between the two of them, Butch and Jenny were handling Junior's afflictions with such easy grace and acceptance that they might both have been used to dealing with people like him on a daily basis.

Butch set a bowl of soup in front of Junior. Jenny seated herself next to their guest, picked up a piece of Butch's crusty, freshly baked bread, spread it with butter, and then laid it next to his place. Without a word, Junior picked up his spoon and buried it in the thick, steamy soup.

"Careful," Butch warned. "It's hot."

Nodding, Junior held the loaded spoon to his lips and blew on it noisily. Most of the soup slopped back into the bowl, but as soon as he put the remainder in his mouth, his face cracked into the same wide grin Joanna had seen when she had first pinned the sheriff's badge on his chest.

"Good!" he exclaimed happily. "Good, good, good."

Transfixed by all this activity, Joanna stood just inside the door and watched. She didn't know which was more gratifying—Butch's and Jenny's compassion toward Junior, or the total ease with which they dealt with his obvious abnormalities. Overcome by emotion, Joanna's eyes brimmed with tears. She tried to speak, but her voice caught in her throat.

Joanna was still struggling to find words when Butch took her gently by the shoulder and led her to a chair. "Will Madame be seated?" he asked with a comically formal bow. "And what are we drinking this evening? I can recommend the Cabernet . . ."

"Milk for me, too," Joanna said. "I may still have some work to do tonight."

Jenny made a face at that, but she didn't say anything to Joanna. Instead, she turned her wide blue eyes full on Junior's face. "Where are you from?" she asked.

Ladling his soup and blowing on each spoonful, Junior didn't answer. Jenny, however, seemed determined to draw him into conversation. "Is it near or far?"

Junior paused and looked at her. "Far," he said. A speech impediment made it difficult for him to pronounce the letter *r*, but Jenny wasn't fazed by that, either.

"How big is your family?" she asked.

Junior stopped eating. He put his spoon down and stared back at Jenny. Worried that any discussion of his family might provoke the same kind of outburst that had bruised Sister Ambrose's elbow, Joanna tried to interrupt, but Butch laid one hand on hers and shook his head, warning her to silence.

Junior held up one finger. "Mama," he said. Then he raised another finger. "Junior."

"So it's just the two of you," Jenny said. "That's like Mom and me. Butch here is our friend, and this is his house. But at home where we live, it's just Mom and me. Just the two of us, same as you."

A short silence settled over the table. "Do you like to play video games?" Butch asked.

Junior brightened. He reached for what would have been his pockets, then the smile faded. He knew enough to realize that video games required money and he had none.

"Don't worry," Butch told him. "I have some video games in the other room that came from my restaurant when I sold it. I've fixed them so they don't take quarters anymore. You can play them all you want, for free."

Junior's mouth dropped. "No quarters?" He started to push his chair away from the table.

"No," Butch said. "Soup first, then video games."

Without a murmur of objection, Junior settled back onto his chair and resumed eating. *If Father Mulligan thought the badge trick was impressive,* Joanna thought, *he ought to see this.*

When the soup was gone, Jenny led Junior into what had once been a small parlor but which was now a tiny video arcade. As soon as they were out of the kitchen, Butch turned a penetrating gaze on Joanna. "How are you doing?"

"Better now," she said. "Much better. How did you know how to handle him like that? You were great."

"I used to coach Special Olympics," Butch said. "The Roundhouse used to sponsor a team to the games over in Tempe every summer. I liked doing it, and I pride myself in thinking I was pretty good at it."

"I'd say very good," Joanna told him.

Butch stood up. "If you want to clear the table, I'll go outside, gather up his clothes, and stick them in the washer."

"Once we get him dressed again, though, what am I going to do with him?" Joanna asked.

"Leave him here," Butch replied. "I have an air mattress out in the shed. I'll blow that up and have him sleep right there on the living room floor. He'll be fine, and on the air mattress, if he has an accident overnight, it won't hurt anything."

"You don't mind?"

"Of course I don't mind. If I did, I wouldn't have offered. What do you expect me to do, leave you to handle this whole mess by yourself? No way!"

While Butch went to look after the clothes, Joanna cleared the table and loaded the dishwasher. Butch's house was a high-ceilinged, 1880s kind of place. It had once been part of a neighborhood called Upper Lowell. In the early fifties, this house and all of its neighbors had been loaded onto axles and hauled down out of the canyon to make way for the Lavender Pit Mine. When Butch had bought the place months earlier, it had been a run-down mess, with a bathroom so small that he claimed he'd had to stand in the kitchen to pee. It was Butch's own handiwork that had remodeled the place, reallocating the space, putting in new fixtures, appliances, and cabinets. Working in the small but convenient kitchen, Joanna couldn't help admiring his craftsmanship.

Joanna had finished loading the dishwasher and was just adding soap when Butch came back into the kitchen. "That took a while," she said.

"I know. I have a rug shampooer out in the garage. I took a crack at the upholstery in your car. It helped some, but it's not going to solve the whole problem. Unfortunately it had a chance to really soak in."

Reaching into his pocket, he pulled out Joanna's badge. "This looks like the real McCoy. It wouldn't happen to be yours, would it?"

Drying her hands, Joanna took the badge and returned it to the leather carrying case in her purse. Once she did that, she walked over to Butch and gave the base of his neck a nuzzling kiss. In the process his hand bumped against the elbow that had swatted up against the cholla. She winced.

"What's the matter?" Butch asked. "Are you hurt?"

"A little."

She rolled up her sleeve and looked. Her elbow was punctured by more than a dozen tiny pinpricks, all of them red and sore. "What happened?" Butch asked

"I had a run-in with a batch of cholla," she told him.

Shaking his head, Butch reached into a drawer and brought out a tube of Neosporin. "Maybe you'd better tell me the whole story," he said.

For the next forty-five minutes, she told him everything, starting with finding Alice Rogers' body and ending with Junior. When Joanna finished, Butch leaned back in his chair and folded his arms behind his head. "What's it going to take to find someone who doesn't want to be found?"

"I don't know," Joanna admitted. "I've never encountered a case quite like this before."

"I have," Butch said grimly. "Two years ago the family of one of my athletes took off out of town while Brad was away at Special Olympics. When the games were over and we tried to take him home, no one was there. One of the neighbors told us they'd packed up and left on vacation. In a way, you can understand it. It's got to be a terrible strain for the family members. For caregivers it's a never-ending, lifetime's worth of responsibility, with no hope and no respite. Still, abandoning ship like that is unforgivable. At least, that's how it seemed to me then, and it still does.

"But I'll bet the same thing that happened with Brad will happen with Junior. Somebody is going to notice that Junior isn't at home anymore, and they'll start asking questions. In the meantime, we're going to have to look after him, that's all."

"You mean that, don't you," Joanna said. "The 'we' part, I mean."

"Yes," Butch said. "If we don't, who's going to? And if you and Jenny and I all take a crack at this thing together, it won't be that big a problem. I'm sure Jeff Daniels will help out, and maybe even Marianne, if she's able."

"Did you hear from them today?" Joanna asked. "Has she turned in her resignation?"

"Not yet. According to Jeff, she's talking about maybe seeing a doctor. Talking, but she hasn't made an appointment yet. Jeff is afraid that if he pushes too hard, she'll give up on the idea of going at all."

Butch paused and grinned. "That's the trouble with women," he said. "They're totally unpredictable. You can never tell what will happen when you push."

They had been sitting at the kitchen table. Now Joanna stood up and walked over to Butch's chair. Taking his face in both hands, she leaned down and kissed him again squarely on the lips.

"That's right," she said. "Women *are* totally unpredictable."

EIGHT

As far as Joanna was concerned, Tuesday morning's briefing was more three-ring circus than anything else. Every officer came to the meeting bringing his own particular piece of the puzzle. The problem was, in addition to business as usual, there were far too many puzzles and not nearly enough people.

Frank Montoya, cut loose from Tombstone for the morning, came tapping on Joanna's back-door entrance, the private one that bypassed the main lobby and led directly into her office. "What's going on out there?" he demanded. "The lot is parked full of media vans. Don't tell me Clete Rogers' mother's death merits this kind of full-court press."

"They're here about Oak Vista Estates," Dick Voland said. "That's the current local hot button."

"What's happening at Oak Vista?" Frank asked. "Why don't I know anything about it?"

"Because you're so damn busy gallivanting

around Tombstone that you aren't tending to business here at home."

Before Frank could respond, Joanna came to his defense. "Lay off, Dick," she said. "Give the man a break. He's spent the last two days tied up on the Alice Rogers homicide. I'm sure you can bring him up to speed on Oak Vista. In fact, while you're at it, why don't you tell us all."

She glanced around her office. Since the waiting reporters were currently stashed in the staff briefing room, the morning briefing itself had been bounced into Joanna's private office. Usually Joanna, Dick Voland, and Frank Montoya were the only attendees. This morning they had been joined by Detectives Ernie Carpenter and Jaime Carbajal. In the far corner of the room sat Deputy Terry Gregovich. Peacefully sleeping at his feet lay Spike.

"I suppose you know all about the Monkey Wrench Gang," Voland said.

Frank nodded. "You mean those enviro-nuts from Tucson who used to go around the state trying to put developers out of business?"

"Forget 'used to,'" Dick Voland said. "They're back, or at least we've got ourselves a group that could be a carbon copy. Not only are they back, but they're here—in our very own Cochise County. They've been raising hell at Mark Childers' newest development, Oak Vista Estates. Just last week the contractor started clearing the area, the back side of which butts up against Forest Service land at the base of the Huachucas.

"The developer's no slouch. He has all his ducks

in a row on this one. He's properly permitted and has submitted all his environmental studies, but that doesn't mean diddly to some people. Twenty or so of them showed up yesterday afternoon armed with rocks and clubs and a whole bunch of tools which, from what we've been able to discover, they planned to use to take apart or disable Childers' fleet of bulldozers, front-end loaders, and dump trucks."

"Wait a minute," Frank Montoya said. "I remember now. Mark Childers is one of the movers and shakers out in Sierra Vista."

"Right," Dick Voland said. "As a matter of fact, he turned up at the board of supervisors meeting yesterday morning. At that point, all that had happened was what went on Friday, when the demonstrators formed a human chain to keep him from unloading equipment. Yesterday at the meeting, all he was worrying about was construction delays and wanting to know what we were going to do to protect him and his equipment. After what went down later on in the afternoon, my guess now is he's mad as hell.

"It turns out some of Childers' opposition came to the meeting as well. They wanted to know who it was who approved the project in the first place. Actually, for a board of supervisors meeting, it was pretty entertaining since they were the ones in the hot seat for a change."

"So, what happened?" Joanna asked.

"Nothing. Don't forget, those folks are politicians, every last one of them. It didn't take long for them to read the writing on the wall. Since a lot of people are obviously unhappy about the Oak Vista project, the board took about half a minute to pass the buck. They're blaming the whole mess on the head of Planning and Zoning Planning and Guessing, if you ask me. Looks like Lewis Flores is going to be elected scapegoat. He isn't going to like taking it in the shorts. I wouldn't be at all surprised if he ends up handing in his resignation over the deal."

"That's too bad," Joanna observed. "Lewis Flores has always struck me as a real nice guy."

"You know what happens to nice guys," Voland said. "Unfortunately, when the board finishes chewing him up and spitting him out, guess who's next in line? Us. The sheriff's department. With Childers pissing and moaning about the county having an obligation to protect his people and equipment, the board had to agree with him. Surprise, surprise! Which is why, when Deputy Gregovich called for help yesterday afternoon, I made sure he had it in a hurry."

Dick Voland stopped talking long enough to hand each attendee a sheaf of papers—incident reports from all of the deputies who had been summoned to Oak Vista. For the next few minutes, the group read through the reports in silence. Joanna was relieved to see that no one had been hurt in the melee. Twelve individuals had been arrested and hauled off to jail, but not before they had done considerable damage to Mark Childers' equipment.

Joanna's heart sank as she read through the

list: four punctured oversized tires; the track pried off one of the bulldozers; sugar in the fuel tanks of three dump trucks. She looked at Dick Voland. "This is going to be expensive," she said.

He nodded. "And you'll never guess who called me just a couple of minutes ago—Mark Childers' attorney. He's putting us on notice that we're being held responsible; claiming that we acted negligently in not providing adequate protection. According to him, we needed to have more and better-trained officers on the job."

Joanna had watched Terry Gregovich's shoulders slump lower and lower under the weight of Dick Voland's litany. Now, in the silence while everyone read through the various reports, he sat staring at his sleeping dog. Joanna supposed he was wishing he could be somewhere else—anywhere else!

Reading through the reports, Joanna couldn't see what could have been done differently. Her department didn't have nearly enough manpower to mount an armed guard around an entire subdivision. Not only that, the protesters had arrived at quitting time, having let most of the day pass without incident and lulling authorities into thinking there would be no further trouble.

When people finally looked up from their papers, Joanna turned to Deputy Gregovich. "Do you have anything to add, Terry?" she asked.

Gregovich leaped to his feet, and Spike did the same. Then, when no direct order was forthcoming from his master, the dog circled three times, heaved a huge sigh, lay back down, and closed his eyes. A part of Joanna envied the dog. She could have used a little more shut-eye herself.

"There were too many of them," Gregovich was saying. "There must have been ten carloads at least. When they showed up last Friday, it was just one of those nonviolent protests, with people lying down in front of the trucks and that sort of thing. I thought this time it would be the same thing, but it wasn't. Not at all. These guys came packing crowbars and sledgehammers and all like that. As soon as I saw they meant business, I called for backup, but there was only so much Spike and I could do. We weren't able to be everywhere at once. We did our best, but I'm afraid . . . ."

"It's all right, Deputy Gregovich," Joanna assured him. "I'm sure you did everything possible. It sounds as though you and Spike were outgunned and outmanned at every turn, so don't be too hard on yourself. Considering what was going on, we're lucky no one was hurt—you and Spike included."

"What about the dirty dozen who were arrested?" Frank asked.

"They're being arraigned right now, but I'm betting they'll all be bailed out this morning and back on the streets by early afternoon."

"Just in time for round three," Joanna said, shaking her head. "Who are they? Anybody we recognize?"

"Not really," Voland said. "From the booking sheets, it looks like they're mostly from Tucson. Professional demonstrator types. At least several of them have been arrested for this kind of thing before."

"If they're paid professionals," Joanna said, "who's writing the checks?"

"Good question," Dick said. "That's what we're trying to find out now. I've got three deputies working on it. If we can find out who's really behind the demonstrations, maybe we can talk them into calling them off."

"What do we do in the meantime?" Joanna asked.

"Spike and I are heading right back out there, ma'am," Deputy Gregovich said.

Voland nodded. "They'll be on-site this morning. By noon—about the time the last of our jailbirds gets bailed out—I expect to have several deputies patrolling on and around Oak Vista Estates."

"Are you worried about being sent there by yourself this morning, Deputy Gregovich?" Joanna asked.

Terry Gregovich was an awkward-looking young man with a shy, self-effacing way about him. He was immensely likable. The fact that Spike obviously adored him didn't hurt, either.

"Not at all, ma'am. Spike and me'll do just fine."

Joanna smiled. "I'm sure you will, but remember: If it turns out you need to call for reinforcements, I'd rather you did it sooner than later. Understand?"

"Will do, Sheriff Brady. Is that all?"

Joanna nodded.

"Come, Spike," Terry ordered.

Obediently, the dog rolled to his feet, and the two of them marched out the door. "All right now," Joanna announced to those remaining. "On to Alice Rogers."

Ernie Carpenter took the first turn in the barrel, reporting that Clete Rogers and Susan Jenkins had shown up at the Pima County morgue late the previous evening and had, together, positively identified their mother's body. The two of them were also due at their mother's house later that morning. There they would meet with Detective Carbajal and try to determine what items had been removed from Alice Rogers' home. Joanna couldn't help smiling at that bit of news. It pleased her to know that Susan had taken that much of Joanna's advice to heart.

"Do we know when Doc Daly has scheduled the autopsy?" Joanna asked.

"First thing this morning," Ernie replied. "What she told us at the scene was that she didn't think the body had been moved. If Alice died where we found her, that means the case belongs to Pima County, and we're out of it. Which is why Detective Lazier as good as told me that I'd be persona non grata at the autopsy."

"Went all territorial on you, did he?" Joanna observed.

Ernie nodded. "You could say that. Lazier is focused on getting the case pulled together enough to extradite those other three kids from Old Mexico but that's not going to be easy since so far the Mexican authorities aren't very keen on cooperating. They haven't even ID'd the suspects they have in custody."

Joanna nodded. "It's tough to extradite someone when you don't have a name to go by. Do the Pima County detectives know anything about Alice Rogers' house in Tombstone being ransacked?"

Carpenter shook his head. "Not that I know of. They didn't ask and I didn't tell. Actually, at the time I left to come home, I didn't know about it, either."

"Let's think about this for a minute," Joanna suggested. "Did Dr. Daly say anything about when Alice died?"

"Not exactly. Her preliminary estimate is sometime Saturday night or Sunday morning."

"All right, so the kids took the car—with keys?"

This time Frank was the one who answered. "Without. It was hot-wired."

"But they had Alice's identification along with her address. They could have gone to her place and taken it apart. Was there any sign of stolen goods in the car, anything that might be traceable back to Alice's house in Tombstone?"

"Not that I know of," Frank said.

"Here's my position then," Joanna said. "The murder may not have taken place in Cochise County, but it's possible that a burglary did. And until we see how all these dots are connected— Alice's death, the ransacking of her house, and the sudden disappearance of her boyfriend—our department is involved. Is that clear?"

There were nods all around the room. "I'll be in touch with Fran Daly's office and let her know that we're still in the game and need to be apprised of the postmortem results." She turned to Jaime Carbajal. "What's happening with the crime scene crews?"

"As I told you last night, there were fingerprints all over the place at Alice's house. We've collected a ton of them. It's going to take time to process them and feed them into the Automated Fingerprint Identification System. What's interesting, though, is the fact that while Alice's house is full of prints, we've hardly found any in the mobile home at Outlaw Mountain. We've dusted the whole place and haven't come up with more than one or two partials. There aren't any on the light switches or doorknobs or on the cans of soda in the refrigerator. How does that strike you?"

"Odd," Joanna said.

Jaime nodded. "It's odd, all right. Ernie suggested that I have them check the wall above the toilet in case the guy leans there when he's taking a leak."

"Right," Joanna said, hoping to forestall a blush. "Good thinking."

"We'll make sure that gets done today," Jaime continued. "The dresser drawers and closets are all empty. That means Farley Adams packed his bags and left, but before he took off, he must have raced through his house wiping every possible surface clean of fingerprints."

"Sounds like somebody with something to hide," Joanna suggested.

"That's what we thought," Jaime agreed. "So Ernie and I will be taking the crew back out there again this morning. Maybe in the clear light of day, we'll find something we missed last night."

"What about papers?" Joanna asked. "Did you happen to stumble across anything that looked like a marriage license?"

"A marriage license?" Jaime asked.

Joanna nodded. "Susan Jenkins thinks Farley Adams was about to marry her mother in a phony ruse to lay hands on Alice's money."

"So there is money then?" Ernie asked.

"Some, but I don't know how much. I have Alice Rogers' attorney's name out in Sierra Vista. Hogan, Dena Hogan. My thinking is if Farley figured he already had the money bagged, there must have been a reason. Either he and Alice had already tied the knot, or else she had rewritten her will in his favor."

Ernie frowned, once again beetling his thick eyebrows together until they formed a single rope-wide track across his forehead. "It sounds like you're saying Farley may be responsible for her murder instead of those kids in the lockup down in Nogales."

"What I'm saying is that there's more going on here than meets the eye. I'm not prepared to accept Pima County's slam-dunk clear until some of the strange stuff in our jurisdiction gets straightened out. That includes checking with Alice Rogers' attorney. You or Ernie can go talk to her. Or, if you guys are too busy with the crime scene investigators, I can handle Ms. Hogan myself."

"As far as I'm concerned, have a ball," Ernie said. "Jaime and I already have more than enough to do."

Avoiding looking at the burgeoning stack of mail Kristin had piled on her desk, Joanna added Dena Hogan's name to her To-Do list.

"Anything else?" Joanna asked.

"Not from us," Ernie said.

"All right then, you and Jaime go ahead and get with the program."

The two detectives stood up as one. "Wait a minute," Jaime Carbajal said. "What about that weird guy from Saint David, the one who was with you last night when you stopped by Alice Rogers' place? Whatever happened to him? Did you locate his family?"

"What guy?" Dick Voland asked.

Caught being less than candid with her subordinates, Joanna blushed to the roots of her bright red hair. She had thought about mentioning Junior's situation to the briefing as a whole but had decided against it—right up until Jaime's awkward question brought the issue out into the open.

"I guess I just haven't gotten around to telling you," Joanna replied. "His name is Junior. He's developmentally disabled. His family evidently drove off and left him behind when they finished up with the Holy Trinity Arts and Crafts Fair over in Saint David."

"Where's this Junior now?" Voland demanded. "You didn't take him home with you, did you?"

"No," Joanna replied. "I didn't. He's staying

with a friend of mine, someone who's had experience with people like Junior."

"Whoever he is, he'd better have experience," Voland growled. "If anything happens to that guy while he's in our custody, our ass will be grass. His family may not have wanted him last Sunday, but if he croaks out while we're in charge of him, you can bet they'll hit us with a million-dollar lawsuit so fast it'll make our heads spin."

"Nothing is going to happen to him," Joanna declared firmly.

"Who says, and how are you going to go about finding his family?"

"I don't know yet," Joanna admitted. "I still haven't decided."

"Let me remind you, Sheriff Brady," Voland said. "We're in the business of law enforcement, not social service. Considering what's gone on around here the last few days, we've got our hands plenty full playing cops and robbers without going out of our way to collect lost retards and drag them home."

Joanna sent her chief deputy a frosty glance. She was accustomed to that kind of comment from Voland. In the privacy of the morning briefing, where only she and Frank Montoya were present, she cut the man some slack. In front of her two homicide detectives, it was absolutely unacceptable.

"The proper term is developmentally disabled, Chief Deputy Voland, not retard," Joanna told him. "We're not calling Junior that in this office—not to his face and not behind his back, either.

And don't think for a minute this is some kind of mindless acquiescence to political correctness. It's called common decency. Is that clear?"

Voland backed down. "It's clear all right," he said.

Joanna turned back to the detectives. "You go on now. If we need your help on the Junior situation, I'll let you know."

As soon as the two detectives let themselves out of the office, Joanna zeroed in on Voland once again. "Don't pull that kind of stunt again, Dick. Understand?"

He nodded glumly. "Sorry," he muttered.

"And now," Joanna continued, "do either of you have any bright ideas about how to locate Junior's family?"

"Not me," Voland said.

"Frank?"

"You've checked his clothing for ID?"

"Right," Joanna said, "and found nothing. It looks suspiciously as though all the labels have been deliberately removed."

"So you're suggesting that whoever left him in Saint David did it on purpose, that they don't want to be found."

"Right."

Frank tapped a thoughtful finger on his forehead. "Maybe we should take a lesson from that television show, 'America's Most Wanted.' Let's try to spread the word on this. Maybe we could even hit the wire services. We'll show Junior's picture, tell where he was found, and all that. If we make a big enough splash, maybe someone will recognize him."

"That might work," Joanna concluded after a moment's thought. "Any ideas about how to go about it?"

"This is human-interest stuff. I think it's the kind of story Marliss Shackleford could really sink her teeth into."

"Not Marliss!" Joanna objected, setting her jaw. "After all, she's not even a reporter anymore. She's a columnist."

"Yes, but I bet she'd jump on this one, especially if it gives her a crack at national exposure."

Of all the people involved in the local news media, Marliss was Joanna's hands-down least favorite. However, if this really was the only way to help Junior get back home, Joanna knew she'd have to do it.

"All right," she agreed. "When you finish up with the Oak Vista Estates press conference, see if Marliss will play ball. Speaking of Oak Vista, what do you plan to tell the press?"

During the meeting Frank had continually thumbed through the sheaf of incident reports. "My usual media soft shoe, I suppose." He grinned. "What do you think they'll want to know?"

"Whether or not the county is under attack by a bunch of outside environmentalists who are going to try to bring the current building boom to a screeching halt. They're going to want to know the same things we do—where the protesters come from, what they're doing here, and who's behind them. Tell the reporters that when we have some answers, so will they."

Recovered from Joanna's reprimand, Voland took them through the other routine reports from the day before. Afterward, he pushed his chair back and heaved himself out of it. "I have *real* work to do," he announced. Even so, he paused at the door long enough to glower at Joanna one last time.

"I still think you'd better provide full documentation concerning anything and everything to do with your friend Junior since you took charge of him," he said. "That's the only way to go on a deal like that, otherwise you can pretty much count on the incident coming back and biting us in the butt."

"Dick," Joanna assured him. "I'll take care of it."

Mumbling under his breath, Voland left Joanna's office and slammed the door behind him. "He *is* right about that, you know," Frank said.

"About Junior?" Joanna asked.

"About the full documentation bit. Are you sure the person Junior's staying with is absolutely trustworthy?"

"I can tell you this," Joanna said. "Junior's a hell of a lot better off with somebody like Butch Dixon than he would be in a cell out back in the jail which, at the time, was my only other option."

"I'm sure that's true," Frank agreed.

They both fell silent. There wasn't much more to add. "So what are you going to do now?" Joanna asked finally. "Handle the press conference here and then head back to Tombstone?"

Frank nodded. "That's right. Back to my home away from home. What about you?"

"I plan to take a crack at the correspondence. When I finish up with that, I'm going to head out to Sierra Vista to talk with Alice Rogers' attorney."

"While you're out that way," Frank suggested, "you might consider stopping by to see Mark Childers."

Frank Montoya may have been a latecomer to the Oak Vista crisis, but already he had some helpful suggestions for handling the situation.

"How come?" Joanna asked.

"You do know who his girlfriend is, don't you?"

"No, who?"

"Karen Brainard."

Joanna was stunned. "As in Karen Brainard, member of the Cochise County Board of Supervisors?" she asked.

"None other. As a matter of fact, I've heard rumors here and there that Childers backed her to the hilt, that he even helped bankroll her campaign."

"And now, miraculously, he's gotten permission from the board of supervisors for a controversial construction project lots of other people around here hate."

"Have you looked it over?" Frank asked.

Joanna shook her head. "I haven't had time."

"Maybe the tree-huggers are up at arms for a good reason. I've never been much of an environmentalist myself, but I hate to see another section of the Huachucas get chewed up by un-controlled development."

"Your opinion and mine notwithstanding," Jo-anna said, "if the supervisors have already given Childers the go-ahead, what's the point of my go-ing to see him?"

"If he's somebody who can make or break a member of the board of supervisors, he could also make or break a sheriff—if he sets his mind to it, that is."

Joanna thought about that for a moment. "So you're advising me to do a little political fence-mending."

Frank nodded. "It couldn't hurt."

"Thanks," she said. "I'll think about it, but I'm not making any promises."

After Frank left, Joanna sat alone in her of-fice staring at the pile of mail on her desk. From the moment she had been sworn into office, there seemed to have been an unending ava-lanche of the stuff. It drifted in mountainous heaps from Kristin's desk to hers and back again. Joanna took the topmost sheet off the stack. Then, for the next five minutes, lost in thought, she stared uncomprehendingly at the piece of pa-per in her hand without the words ever sorting themselves into meaningful sentences.

What if what Frank had said was true? What if there was a far too cozy relationship between Karen Brainard and Mark Childers? She thought about what Dick Voland had said concerning the previous day's board of supervisors meeting. She couldn't help wondering if, besides chewing up a pristine desert landscape, Childers and his lady accomplice weren't also destroying someone else's life and career in the process.

"Kristin," Joanna said, picking up her phone. "Get Lewis Flores on the phone for me, would you? He's the head of Planning and Zoning. No, I don't know his number."

She put down the phone and then waited for it to ring again, which it did—a minute or so later.

"I talked to Linda, the secretary at Planning and Zoning," Kristin said. "She told me Mr. Flores is out sick today."

I'll just bet he is, Joanna thought grimly. *If I were in his shoes, I probably would be, too.*

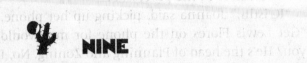

NINE

AFTER DOING what she could about reaching Lewis Flores, Joanna returned to the correspondence. She was making good progress when, after a light tap on the door, Marliss Shackleford let herself into Joanna's office. Marliss was a stout woman in her mid-forties with a mop of frosted hair that looked as though it had been permed with the help of a jolt of electricity.

"This is a first," the columnist said, casting an appraising glance around the room. "I've never been admitted to the inner sanctum before." She stopped in front of Joanna's oversized desk and ran a scarlet-enameled fingernail across the smooth grain of the polished cherry. "Very nice," she added.

"Thanks," Joanna said brusquely. "It's a hand-me-down. This desk used to belong to Walter McFadden. So did the rest of the furniture."

"But not that adorable picture of Jenny, I'll bet."

"No," Joanna agreed. "Not that. Come on, Marliss. Let's get down to business. I'm sure Frank already briefed you on the situation. What more can I tell you?"

"My, my. No time for polite chitchat around here. Just wham-bam, thank you, ma'am."

Joanna's jaws clenched. "I'm busy, Marliss," she said evenly. "If that's how you want to put it, yes."

"I'm looking for a personal angle," Marliss said. She sat down in one of the captain's chairs, dug around in her purse, and pulled out a small spiral notebook. "Frank tells me this young man . . . ."

"He isn't young," Joanna corrected. "His name is Junior, and he's somewhere in his mid-forties to mid-fifties."

"Junior was left—well, abandoned, if you will—at the Holy Trinity Arts and Crafts Fair over in Saint David. That ended on Sunday. Why are we just now hearing about it for the first time?"

"Because my department wasn't notified about the situation until late yesterday afternoon," Joanna said. "That's when Father Mulligan first contacted us."

"And where is he . . . What's his name again?"

"He calls himself Junior. No last name. If he knows what it is, so far he hasn't mentioned it."

"And where exactly is he staying? Deputy Montoya didn't say, but I take it you have him in custody of some sort?"

"He's not a criminal, Marliss," Joanna said with as much forbearance as she could muster. "He's developmentally disabled. So he's not in custody of any kind. He's staying with a friend of mine—with Butch Dixon, over in Saginaw. Of course, that is not for publication."

"Of course not," Marliss agreed. With a pen poised above her notebook, the columnist frowned in concentration. "But is it safe to have him loose in a neighborhood like that? Lowell School can't be more than a few blocks away. What if he was left unsupervised and ended up doing harm to one of the children? Would you ever be able to forgive yourself?"

Joanna's heart hardened even as her resolve melted away. Frank seemed to think that a drippy human-interest story from Marliss Shackleford was Junior's ticket home. As far as Joanna was concerned, dealing with the columnist made the price of that ticket far too high.

Pointing at her watch, Joanna stood up. "I'm sorry, Marliss. I can see this was a bad idea. It isn't going to work. I have another appointment. I have to get going."

"But wait," Marliss objected in dismay. "You can't just throw me out with nothing. I was led to believe that I'd have an exclusive from you on this. I'm sure that's what Chief Deputy Montoya said."

"Chief Deputy Montoya was mistaken, Marliss. The interview with me is over. Good morning."

"But—"

"No buts. Good-bye, Marliss. But let me warn you, if you go anywhere near Butch Dixon's house, you'll have me to deal with."

Marliss Shackleford's dismay turned to anger.

"Wait just a minute, Sheriff Brady. Are you threatening a member of the Fourth Estate? This is a free country, you know. We have a Constitution that guarantees freedom of the press. You can't get away with telling me what I can and can't do."

"Maybe not," Joanna agreed. "But in addition to freedom of the press, this country also makes allowances for private property. If you go where you're not welcome—and I can pretty well promise that you won't be welcome at Butch Dixon's house—then you can count on being arrested for trespassing."

"See there!" Marliss shrilled. "Another threat."

"No, it's not," Joanna said. "Not as long as you stay where you belong."

Slamming her notebook back into her purse, Marliss Shackleford rose from her chair and swept regally from Joanna's office. As soon as she was gone, Joanna picked up the phone and dialed Butch's number.

"How are things?" she asked.

Butch sighed. "If I'd known how much trouble it was going to cause, I would never have given you back your badge last night. Junior wants it—and he wants it bad. He's been searching all over the house for it, ever since he woke up."

"I'll find him another one," Joanna promised. "I'll come by later and drop one off. Right now, I'm calling to give you a storm warning."

"A storm? Are you kidding? I'm looking out the kitchen window right now. It's clear as a bell outside."

"Not that kind of storm," Joanna told him. "Remember Marliss Shackleford?"

"The *Bisbee Bee's* intrepid columnist?"

"None other," Joanna said grimly.

"What about her?"

"Frank Montoya suggested Marliss write a human-interest story about Junior in hopes that, if it was distributed widely enough, it might lead us to Junior's family."

"I suppose it could work," Butch said.

"It could but it won't," Joanna replied. "She came in to interview me about him and I ended up throwing her out of my office. In Marliss Shackleford's book, developmentally disabled and pedophile/pervert are all one and the same. She's afraid you'll turn Junior loose and he'll go attack some little kid from Lowell School."

"Are you kidding? I don't believe Junior would hurt a fly, not on purpose."

"You know that," Joanna said. "And I know that, but try convincing Marliss."

"What do you want me to do about it?" Butch asked.

"Fill the moat and raise the drawbridge. If she comes by the house and tries talking to Junior, don't let her near him. Period."

"With pleasure," Butch said. "I can hardly wait to see her try."

Reassured that Marliss wouldn't be hassling Junior, Joanna spent the next half hour concentrating on the correspondence. Then, when she had worked her way through the worst of it, she dropped a completed stack off on Kristin's desk for filing, duplicating, typing envelopes, and mailing.

"I'll be out of the office for the next little bit," she told Kristin. "Probably until late afternoon. I'm heading out to Sierra Vista to check on things."

"Will you be seeing Deputy Gregovich?" Kristin asked.

"Probably," Joanna said. "Why?"

Kristin sighed. "He's so cute," she said dreamily.

Cute? That was hardly the term Joanna herself would have used to describe Deputy Gregovich. He was tall, gangly, and moved with the loose-jointed jerkiness of a drunken marionette. There was nothing about the man that was remotely cute.

Frowning, Joanna studied her secretary. At twenty-four, Kristin Marsten was probably six or seven years younger than Deputy Gregovich. She was a good-looking, leggy, natural blonde who favored skirts with hemlines several inches above the knee. Although Kristin had never lived anywhere but in Bisbee proper, she was forever putting on airs of being worldly and sophisticated. Terry Gregovich came across as something of a small-town hick, even though he had done two separate tours with the Marine Corps, including time overseas and in the Gulf War, where he had served as an MP.

Had Joanna been picking out likely romantic pairings in her department, Kristin Marsten and Terry Gregovich would never have made the list. Furthermore, on a morning already overloaded with complications, the idea of a blossoming romance between Joanna's newest deputy and her secretary was almost more than she could handle. It wasn't just the idea of having two of her subordinates get involved that caused Joanna difficulty. There was always the distinct possibility that later they might become uninvolved, which could prove even worse.

"For a rookie," Joanna said, choosing her words carefully, "I think Deputy Gregovich is a pretty capable officer."

She made the comment in hopes of stressing the law enforcement nature of Terry Gregovich's job. She also wanted to make Kristin aware that, as sheriff, Joanna would have more than a casual interest in that kind of entanglement. Those subtleties, however, sailed over Kristin's smooth blond tresses without making any noticeable impact.

"And don't you just love the way Terry and Spike get along?" Kristin continued adoringly. "I mean—you know—it's like they really *like* each other."

Joanna knew all too well that the relationship between Deputy Gregovich and his dog represented hours, days, and weeks of grueling training as well as the expenditure of a big chunk of that year's officer-education budget. Joanna couldn't step back and see Terry Gregovich and Spike as a man and his dog. For her they were a K-nine unit—an important investment in her department's future.

While Kristin continued to gush, Joanna felt

suddenly old and wise and very, very official. "Terry and Spike are both still quite new at their respective jobs," she said finally. "We have to do our best to make sure nothing happens to disturb their concentration."

Kristin stopped short. "Are you telling me I shouldn't have anything to do with him?" she asked.

"No. What I'm saying is that at this time Deputy Gregovich really needs to have his mind on the job. He can't afford any distractions."

"Which I am, I suppose?" the secretary asked with a pout.

"Kristin," Joanna said. "You're young, you're blond, and you're very pretty. Of course you're a distraction."

Kristin had to think about Joanna's comment for a moment. She wasn't sure how to take it—as a compliment or as something else. "Thank you," she said stiffly, after a pause. "I think."

Joanna went back into her office, collected her purse and her To-Do list, and then headed for the car. She had arrived at the Justice Complex too late to stop by Motor Pool before the morning briefing. She had parked the Crown Victoria in her usual place. Now, the sun had spent two hours shining in through the window and onto the urine-soaked front seat. When Joanna opened the car door, the odor inside the vehicle was almost overpowering. Not wanting to leave the onerous job of moving the car to someone else, she got in and drove straight to the garage.

When Joanna walked into the cavelike service bays, at first she thought no one was there. "Anybody home?" she called.

About then she caught sight of a pair of work boots sticking out from under the midsection of the jail's utility van. Seconds later, Danny Garner, chief mechanic in charge of Cochise County Sheriff's Department Motor Pool, rolled out from under the van on a creeper. "Morning, Sheriff. What can I do for you?"

"I've got a little problem with my Crown Victoria."

"Not another water hose."

"Not a hose," Joanna told him, "but it *is* a water problem."

When Joanna left the garage a few minutes later, one of the jail trustees, armed with an upholstery shampooer, was already scrubbing away at the front seat. Joanna returned to the back parking lot and collected her Blazer. Heading for Sierra Vista, she had thirty minutes to organize her thoughts.

Other people claimed to see things in their mind's eye. Joanna exercised her mind's ear. Driving west on Highway 92, she rehearsed possible conversations with both Mark Childers, Oak Vista's developer, and with Dena Hogan, Alice Rogers' attorney. She wanted to let Childers know that members of her department would do what they could to protect his property and equipment while, at the same time, trying not to interfere with private citizens' rights to assembly and free speech. That meant that Joanna's people would be walking a tightrope between Childers' interests and those of the demonstrators. She also wanted to let him know that she wasn't about to be cowed by a cozy romantic relationship between him and a member of the board of supervisors.

As far as Dena Hogan was concerned, Joanna wondered how she could encourage the attorney's cooperation. She would have to finesse her way into the needed information and find out about Alice Rogers' newly written will or lack of same. Not only that, discovering a few pertinent details about Alice's financial situation would give everyone concerned a better idea of what the stakes were.

That was how far she had gone in her thinking process as she drove across the San Pedro at Palominas, where a blazing column of golden-leafed cottonwoods followed a meandering path through unexpectedly lush green river-bottom farmland in the middle of an otherwise parched desert.

Pulling out her cell phone, she dialed Fran Daly's office in Tucson. One of the things Joanna appreciated about Fran's down-to-earth way of doing business was that she usually answered her own calls.

"Daly here," the assistant medical examiner growled into the phone in her gravelly smoker's voice.

"It's Joanna—Joanna Brady."

"Should have known," Dr. Daly grunted. "You must operate on radar. I only finished the autopsy ten minutes ago. Detective Hemming was here during, but I haven't talked to Detective Lazier yet. He's going to be pissed as all hell when he finds out I talked to you before I talked to him."

"Tough," Joanna said. "Then again, on second thought, maybe you shouldn't tell him."

"There are some really good people working for the Pima County Sheriff's Department," Fran Daly told her. "Hank Lazier just doesn't happen to be one of them. He and I have gone nose-to-nose on several different occasions. But since I believe in picking my fights and this one doesn't seem worth it, I probably won't—tell him, that is."

"Thanks," Joanna said. "That'll make your life easier, and it should help Ernie Carpenter, too."

"Ernie. Isn't he the detective who was at the crime scene yesterday?" Fran asked.

"He's the one," Joanna replied. "He's also the same investigator Detective Lazier banned from attending Alice Rogers' autopsy this morning."

"Banned?" Fran repeated. "You mean Hank Lazier told someone he couldn't come to *my* morgue?"

"That's right."

"What a jackass!" Dr. Daly muttered.

Smiling to herself, Joanna knew that just like the Little Engine That Could, she had succeeded in finding another way over the mountain. Lazier had been hell-bent on shutting Cochise County's investigators out of the loop. Joanna had managed to open another channel.

"What did you find?" she asked, returning to postmortem results.

"Did you ever hang out with football players much?" Fran responded.

Joanna wished she could point out to Dr. Daly—as she often did with Jenny—that it wasn't polite to answer a question with a question. "No," she said. "I can't say that I ever did."

"I don't suppose Alice Rogers did, either," Fran continued. "But the bruises I found on her back, just over the kidneys, are consistent with the kinds of injuries you'd see in an emergency room on a Saturday morning after a hard-fought football game on Friday night. We're talking about bruises that would show up on someone's body after they were tackled from behind. That's the first thing I noticed—the bruising. And not just on the victim's back, either. There are definite fingertip-type bruises around her wrist—her right wrist. There's some additional bruising there as well that isn't obviously related to the handprints." Fran paused. "Wait just a minute, will you?"

Joanna expected Dr. Daly to go off the line, perhaps to take another call. Instead, she heard a rustle of paper and then, a moment later, the telltale click of a cigarette lighter. "There now," Fran said, inhaling deeply, "that's better. Where was I?"

"Bruising to the wrist."

"Right. So I'm thinking somebody knocked her down and then grabbed her by the wrist, which, considering the cholla spines in the back of her hands, was probably a little tricky."

"In other words, her attacker should have some cholla puncture wounds of his own."

"His or her," Fran Daly said. "Whichever. Most of the cholla puncture wounds are on her back, although there were also quite a few on her legs, arms, and both hands."

"Anything else?"

"She was drunk," Fran answered. "Point one-eight. And something else."

"What's that?"

"She was clutching a vial in one hand—an empty insulin bottle. Which makes me wonder if maybe that extra bruise on the inside of her wrist might have been caused by a needle—an injection."

"An insulin shot then," Joanna murmured. "You're saying Alice Rogers was diabetic?"

"Insulin isn't usually injected in arms," Fran Daly told her. "Since it's self-injected, it usually goes in the thighs. With long-term insulin use then, there's damage to the fat tissue in the legs—a puckering where the fat cells die due to repeated injections. I examined Alice Rogers' legs. There was no evidence consistent with long-term use. If she was on insulin, she hadn't been for long. We can find out for sure, once we locate her personal physician."

"Diabetics don't usually drink, do they?" Joanna asked.

"Alcohol?" Fran Daly asked. "It's not recommended."

"I talked to her daughter," Joanna said. "Susan Jenkins said her mother came to dinner on Saturday and that they had drinks before dinner and wine with the meal. It doesn't seem likely that a daughter, knowing her mother had diabetes, would serve drinks."

"Unless the daughter *wanted* to kill her," Fran put in.

"There is that," Joanna conceded. "But what if Alice didn't have diabetes? What happens to someone with normal insulin when they're given extra?"

"It depends on how much extra, what the person's physical condition is, and any number of variables."

"And if the person was already drunk?"

"Well," Daly said. "Again, it depends on how much insulin is administered. A hundred units of insulin or so, given to someone as drunk as Alice Rogers was, might cause her to pass out, but she'd wake up hours later and be fine, except for a hang-over, that is. With five or six hundred units, though, it could very well be lethal. In this case it might not have taken nearly that much, especially since there was already so much booze in her system, she was probably in shock from falling in the cactus, and she had almost no protection from the cold. I believe she passed out and her blood pressure dropped too low to sustain life. Whatever the cause, she died of heart failure. Still, I'm betting on insulin. If it's there, you can be sure we'll find it."

"What do you use, a blood test?" Joanna asked.

"A serum test, not blood."

"And how long does that take?"

"Two weeks, about. The thing is, without the presence of the vial, we wouldn't generally bother with an insulin test at all."

"What do you mean?"

"Just that. An insulin test isn't part of standard autopsy protocols. And that's what's so odd. It's as though the killer went out of his way to leave a calling card."

"Can batches of insulin be traced?" Joanna asked.

"Certainly. I'll get right on it."

"So where does this leave Detective Lazier and the joyriders he's planning on bringing back from Nogales?"

Fran Daly laughed. "Up a creek, if you ask me. This doesn't square with a bunch of gangster-wanna-bes. People who hot-wire cars don't go around armed with needles full of insulin. They use guns. Insulin is a prescription medication. For punks like that, nine-millimeter automatics are probably a whole lot easier to come by than insulin is."

Joanna heard another phone ringing in the background of Doc Daly's office. "Hold on a sec," Fran said. "I need to take this call." She came back on the line moments later. "Guess who?" she asked with a laugh. "None other than Hank Lazier himself. When he hears what I have to say, he's not going to be a happy camper."

"He didn't strike me as being that happy to begin with," Joanna said.

Fran allowed herself another deep-throated

chuckle, which was followed by a spasm of coughing. "Do you want a copy of my results?"

"Please," Joanna said. "Fax them along to Detective Carpenter."

"Will do."

She had ended the call but had not yet put down the phone when it rang in her hand. Shaking her head, Joanna Brady momentarily longed for the good old days when telephones were in houses and offices but not in cars. It wasn't so very long ago when she had been able to drive around southeastern Arizona without holding a cell phone to her ear.

"Hello."

"Hi, Joanna," George Winfield said. "Hope I'm not dragging you away from something important."

George Winfield, Cochise County's medical examiner, had been Joanna's stepfather for some time now, but her first supposition was that there was some official reason for the call. Perhaps there was some case—some other homicide she knew nothing about—that needed her immediate attention.

"No," she said. "I'm just driving from point A to point B. What's up?"

George Winfield paused before he answered. "It's about your mother," he said.

George most often referred to Eleanor Lathrop Winfield as Ellie, a loving nickname that had once been the private preserve of Joanna's father. The fact that George didn't use that name now, or even the more formal Eleanor, worried Joanna. The term "your mother" had a peculiarly ominous ring to it. In response, an orange warning light switched on in the back of Joanna's head.

"Is something the matter with her?" she asked. "Is Mother sick or something? Has she been hurt?"

"Not exactly." George said the words with such studied reluctance that Joanna's grip tightened on the steering wheel.

"George, for God's sake, tell me! What is it?"

"She's upset."

"Mother is always upset," Joanna countered in exasperation. "What is it this time?"

"It's you," George said. "You and Butch."

Not that again, Joanna thought. She took a deep, steadying breath. "What Butch and I do is none of Mother's business," she said. "I thought I made that clear when I talked to her yesterday."

"Well, yes," George said. "I suppose you did make it clear. She was quite disturbed about that conversation last night. In fact, after the Bodlemers left, we stayed up most of the night talking about it."

"Put Mother on the phone," Joanna said. "Let me talk to her."

"I can't do that," George returned. "I'm calling from the office."

"Hang up, then," Joanna said. "I'll call her at home."

"You can't do that, either. She isn't there."

"Where is she?"

"That's why I'm calling you right now—to let you know what's happening . . . where she is . . .

where she's going." George's voice, small and apologetic, was totally lacking the vitality of his usually booming, businesslike tone.

"So tell me, George!" Joanna barked. "Where is she going?"

"To Butch Dixon's house."

Joanna couldn't believe what she was hearing. "She went where?"

"You heard me. She told me this morning over breakfast that she was going to go see Butch and ask him whether or not his intentions are honorable. I did my best to talk her out of it, Joanna, but I just couldn't make her listen to reason. I tried calling her again just a few minutes ago, but she's not home, which makes me think she's already on her way. That's when I decided to go ahead and call you—to give you a little advance warning."

"Thanks, George," Joanna said, meaning it. "I'm going to hang up and call Butch."

As she punched Butch Dixon's number into the keypad, Joanna tried to unravel the hard knot of anxiety that was forming in her gut. After all, it hadn't been that many minutes ago when she had called Butch from her office. How much damage could have been done in such a short period of time?

"Butch?" she breathed in relief when he came on the phone. "Thank God you're there. George just called me. He says my mother's on her way over to see you."

"She's already here."

Joanna felt sick. "I'm calling too late then. She's already done it."

"Done what?"

"Asked if your intentions are honorable. My mother's pushy, but still, I can't believe she'd do such a thing. Butch, I'm sorry . . ."

"You're in luck," Butch said. "She just drove up, but she hasn't made it into the house yet. She's still outside. She and Marliss Shackleford met up at the end of the driveway. Marliss was pulling away as your mother arrived. They're still out there chewing the fat—chatting away like long-lost buddies."

"No," Joanna moaned. "Say it isn't so."

"Well," Butch said, "it is, but don't sound so upset. I didn't let Marliss in, and I won't let your mother in, either, if you don't want me to. Although, I have to say, I don't have a problem with seeing her."

"You don't?"

"Not at all. Because my intentions are honorable, you see. Completely. What about yours?"

"Mine?" Joanna stammered stupidly.

"Yes, yours," Butch said. "We can either go on having what they call a totally meaningless relationship—which, I have to tell you, isn't half bad. Or we can get married. If you'll have me, that is."

"Wait a minute. You're asking me to marry you?" Joanna returned. "On the telephone?"

"Well, I admit it's not the best possible arrangement. But it seems like I'd better do it now. Otherwise, your mother will do it for me."

"Butch. I don't know what to say."

On the other end of the phone, Joanna heard a doorbell chime.

"Say yes," he urged.

"But you promised. You told me you wouldn't push."

"That was before your mother rang my doorbell. So, will you or won't you?" The doorbell chimed again. "Well?" he pressed.

Joanna took a deep breath. "Yes, dammit. All right. I will."

"Good answer. Good answer," Butch said. "Now I've gotta run and answer the door. Otherwise Junior will beat me to that."

Butch Dixon hung up then. Twenty miles away, across the San Pedro Valley, Joanna Brady stared at her cell phone in stunned silence.

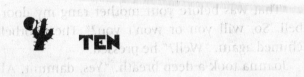

TEN

FOR THE next several minutes, Joanna was so thunderstruck by what had happened that she barely saw where she was going. How could it be? Butch had asked her to marry him and she hadn't said no. She hadn't said "I need to think it over." She had simply said yes. And not even very graciously at that.

She wanted to call him back, to say something—anything, but she couldn't do that. Not with her mother there! Her mother! How dare she! And yet . . . Try as she might, Joanna couldn't be angry with Eleanor Lathrop Winfield right then. She was happy in a way she had never thought to be happy again. Giddy, almost.

When Joanna was growing up, a place called Nicksville—little more than a bar and a couple of scattered mobile homes—had been civilization's last visible outpost along Highway 92 between Sierra Vista and the cutoff to Coronado Pass. The isolated mountain pass overlooked the route Coronado and his men once followed as they came north in search of the Seven Cities of Gold. Nicksville was where Joanna finally came to her senses. She realized then that she had overshot the turnoff to Mark Childers' Oak Vista Estates without even noticing.

Laughing now, Joanna made a U-turn in the bar's parking lot and headed back the way she had come. On the way she made a conscious effort to put her life-changing phone call to Butch aside. She was going to Oak Vista on business—on police business. She understood how vitally important it was for her to keep her mind on the job. Inattentive cops too often become dead cops.

Just north of the cutoff to Coronado Pass, the sweeping majesty of the Huachucas was marred by several moving columns of dust and by the thick smoke of a slash-burn fire that spiraled skyward above the grassy foothills. Gigantic bulldozers had left behind red earthen scars through the tall yellow grass and knocked down grove after grove of sturdy scrub oak.

Seeing the damage, Joanna shook her head. *Welcome to urban blight,* she thought. No wonder people were offended by Mark Childers' grandiose plans and thundering equipment. By the time his dozer-wielding construction crews were done with their work, people buying homes in Oak Vista would be lucky if there were any viewable oak left standing for miles around.

Three miles back down the highway she came to a huge billboard. WELCOME TO OAK VISTA ESTATES, the sign read. MODELS OPENING SOON. Underneath, on the far side of a cattle guard, a narrow road wound off into the desert. Next to the cattle guard, propped against one of the uprights, was an orange-and-white hand-lettered sign. NO TRESPASSING, the sign announced. CONSTRUCTION VEHICLES ONLY.

Switching the Blazer into four-wheel drive, Joanna bounced across the cattle guard. She followed the narrow dirt track for the better part of a mile. By then she noticed that, although smoke from the slash burns was still rising in the brisk autumn air, the moving columns of dust she had spotted from farther up the road were no longer visible. She drove up to a construction shack behind which sat a row of transportable chemical toilets.

It was only when she arrived at the shack that Joanna realized why the earth-moving equipment was no longer moving. It was lunchtime. One whole wall of the construction shack—the shady side—was lined with dusty, hard-hat-wearing workers, all of whom sprawled in the shade, eating lunches out of lunch pails and brown paper bags.

One of the men, a muscular blond in his early thirties, stood up and sauntered toward her. He was stocky with the broad, bulging shoulders and bull neck of a chronic weight lifter. He swaggered up to Joanna's unmarked Blazer, buttoning the top several buttons of a faded flannel shirt and grinning suggestively. Joanna rolled down her window.

"Hey, red," he said, referring to Joanna's bright red hair, "can't you read, or didn't you see the sign? It says 'no visitors.' Mr. Childers doesn't want people who don't belong hanging around here."

Joanna pulled out her ID wallet and opened it. As soon as she did so, the extra badge she had picked up from the storeroom—the one she had planned to drop off for Junior—plummeted out of the wallet. It landed in the dirt with a tinny *thunk*. Bent on retrieving it, Joanna bounded out of the truck. As she hit the ground, her ears were assailed by a series of approving catcalls from the other workers. Meanwhile, Mr. Weight Lifter beat her to the punch. When he handed the fallen badge back to Joanna, she was blushing furiously and still trying to offer him a glimpse of the other badge as well as her picture ID.

He chose to ignore both. "What's the matter, little lady?" Mr. Weight Lifter asked with a leering grin. "Are Crackerjacks having a ran on badges these days?"

At five feet four inches tall, Joanna Brady had spent a lifetime being self-conscious about her height—or lack thereof—and being teased about it as well. Consequently, there were few terms that raised her ire more than a derisive "little lady," although sarcastic comments about her hair color came in a close second.

"No," she said frostily. "As a matter of fact, this badge came out of a box of Wheaties right along with my Colt 2000, my Glock, and my handcuffs. Care to tell me where I can find Mr. Childers?"

The leer retreated slightly but it didn't disappear altogther. "He's not here," the man answered. "He went into town to grab some lunch."

"Do you know what time he'll be back?"

Mr. Weight Lifter raised his hard hat and swiped a grimy forearm across his forehead, leaving behind a muddy track on a sweat-stained brow. "Probably not before two-thirty or so. He believes in long lunches."

Joanna dug in her pocket and pulled out a business card. "Tell Mr. Childers Sheriff Brady stopped by to see him," she said. "Now then, one of my deputies is out here somewhere. Any idea where I'd find him?"

"The guy with the dog?"

Joanna nodded.

Taking her card, the man stuffed it into a shirt pocket that was scarred with the round telltale brand of an ever-present can of snuff. "Hey, you guys," he called back to his fellow workers. "Anybody here know where that deputy went—the one with the big dog?"

One of the other men tossed a soda can past Joanna into a trash can a few feet away. Dregs of soda sprayed out of the can, missing her dry-clean-only suit by mere inches. Evidently pleased with himself the guy favored Joanna with a gap-toothed grin as she dodged back out of the way.

"Up on the back forty," he said. "Youse go straight up here and turn right at the barbed wire. It'll take youse right to him."

Dismissing her, the first guy ambled away. As

he turned his back, Joanna noticed a sickeningly familiar bulge in his hip pocket. "Wait a minute," she said. "What's your name?"

He stopped, turned, and stared back at her disdainfully. "Are you talking to me?" he asked.

"Yes, I am."

"It's Rob. Rob Evans. Why? I notice you're not wearing a ring. You interested in a date, maybe?"

Hoots of laughter erupted among Rob Evans' fellow workers. Joanna didn't smile. "I'm interested in knowing whether or not you have a permit to carry that concealed weapon," she said.

Surprise spread over Evans' face—surprise followed by dismay. He turned and looked down at his pocket, then back at her. "It's not concealed," he said.

"It is," Joanna said. "It's not readily displayed in a holster. It's in your pocket and out of sight. That means it's considered a concealed weapon and you're required to have a permit. Hand it over."

"My gun?"

"Either the gun or the permit, take your pick."

For several long seconds, Joanna couldn't tell whether or not Evans would comply. Finally he did. Reaching into his pocket, he pulled out a .22 handgun. Holding it gingerly by the barrel, he gave it to her. The Saturday-night special—a cheap knockoff—was such a non-brand name that Joanna didn't recognize the label.

"It's for protection," Evans explained. "The jobsite was attacked by rioters yesterday afternoon.

We've got a right to defend ourselves. It says so in the U.S. Constitution—the right to have guns."

Joanna wondered why it was that suddenly everybody in Cochise County was busy quoting the Bill of Rights to her.

"I'm familiar with the right to bear arms," she said. "And while federal law allows for that, the criminal code of the state of Arizona specifically forbids the carrying of concealed weapons. Let me ask you again, Mr. Evans. Do you have a permit?"

"No," he said, as his face turned beet-red. Seeing it, Joanna couldn't tell if the heightened color came from anger, embarrassment, or both.

"How about a holster, then? Do you have one of those?"

"Sure. It's in my truck."

"Suppose you go get it," Joanna said. "I can wait."

Evans' face turned that much redder. "It's not *here*," he hissed under his breath. "I came to work in a car pool this morning."

While the other workmen watched in stony silence, Joanna expertly emptied the weapon of bullets. Then she slipped both the gun and the ammunition into her purse.

"Tell you what, Mr. Evans," she said. "Here's the deal. You can have your gun back as soon as you show up at my office in Bisbee with either a permit or a holster. Until then, I'm keeping it."

"You can't do that!" Evans bawled. "That's unlawful search and seizure."

"I haven't written you up yet," Joanna reminded him. "And I won't, either, as long as you show up at my office within the next twenty-four hours to retrieve your weapon. In the meantime, I need to see some ID."

Still grumbling objections, Evans dug out his wallet and handed over his driver's license. While Joanna made a note of the number, she continued talking, speaking loud enough for everyone else's benefit.

"As for the rest of you—" she told the gawking and fascinated onlookers, all of whom had long since given up any pretense of eating lunch. "I'm sure you all know from what happened yesterday that we have a pretty volatile situation on our hands. How many of the rest of you brought guns along to work today—for protection?"

No one raised a hand. Still, Joanna could tell from the uneasy shifting back and forth and from the surreptitiously exchanged glances that she had hit a nerve, that she had landed on something important. Guns were present, all right—present, unaccounted for, and potentially lethal. And that was the very last thing Sheriff Joanna Brady needed on a Tuesday—for a fully armed construction crew to go after a collection of equally armed environmental activists. She could already imagine a banner headline blazing across the front page of the *Bisbee Bee*. MASSACRE AT OAK VISTA LEAVES X DEAD. The only thing lacking right then was filling in the number of victims.

"After yesterday," she continued evenly, "I'm sure tempers are running high on both sides of this issue. We don't yet know for sure whether or not the demonstrators will be back this afternoon, but I promise you this: There will be a group of deputies here to keep the peace. Not only will they be here on the Oak Vista property, they will also be under orders to confiscate any and all weapons—especially concealed weapons—found to be in the possession of people who do not have valid permits to carry.

"Furthermore, for any of you who may have had run-ins with the law on previous occasions, let me remind you that guns are strictly off-limits for most convicted felons. In fact, in some circumstances, the very act of carrying a weapon may result in a one-way ticket back to the slammer. If that applies to anyone here, I won't hesitate to help your parole officer ship you straight back to Florence."

"But, Sheriff," Mr. Soda Can objected. "Youse weren't here when it happened, so youse didn't see it, but yeste'day when them people came after us, we wus nothin' but a bunch of sittin' ducks. They could'a creamed us."

"Could have, but they didn't," Joanna pointed out. "And in case you haven't heard, several of those demonstrators ended up spending the night courtesy of Cochise County. Some were arrested for simple assault; others for assault with a deadly weapon. So listen up. If anyone here goes after demonstrators with guns, the same thing will happen to you. You'll end up in jail—at least overnight—and you'll lose your weapons besides. You can count on the fact that, if you happen to be arrested by one of my deputies, your weapons will be confiscated and you won't be getting them back anytime soon. Understood?"

No one spoke aloud. For an answer, Joanna had to content herself with a series of grudging nods.

"All right, then," she said. "Which way to find my deputy?"

"Bitch," Bob Evans muttered under his breath. "I hope you go to hell."

She looked back at him and smiled. "Not today," she said. "For right now, I only have to go as far as the barbed-wire fence. See you in my office, Mr. Evans. Either late this afternoon or first thing tomorrow morning. You might want to call, though, first. Just to be sure the little lady is in."

Back in her vehicle, Joanna breathed a sigh of relief as she switched on the ignition. As soon as the Blazer was in motion, she reached for her radio. "Patch me through to Dick Voland," she told the dispatcher.

"What's up?" he asked.

"We've got a big problem out at Oak Vista," she told him. Over the next several minutes, she brought him up-to-date. "We've got to have people out here," she urged as she finished. "If the demonstrators show up again today, they'll be walking into an armed camp. They're likely to be met with a hail of bullets. As I said, I don't know how many more guns are involved over and above the one I took off Rob Evans, but I'm willing to bet money that he isn't the only one who came to work today packing a weapon."

"Do you think Mark Childers encouraged it?"

"He sure as hell didn't *dis*courage it," Joanna replied. "Which means in effect that he's fomenting a modern-day range-war-type mentality where people are going to get hurt and/or killed."

"Have you talked to him about it?"

"Not yet. According to his work crew, he's in town having a long lunch. I wasn't going to bother hanging around here and waiting for him, but now I think I'd better. In the meantime, I want you to assemble that squad of deputies. Take them from whatever sectors you have to. Since demonstrators showed up around quitting time yesterday, we should have our people here no later than two. That way, if there *is* going to be trouble, they'll already be on site."

"Great," Voland said. "By the way, have you talked to Deputy Gregovich yet?"

"Not so far. I was just on my way to look for him. According to Childers' work crew, Terry's out here somewhere, but I haven't managed to spot him yet. What about Ernie and Jaime? I don't suppose they've found any trace of Farley Adams."

"Nope," Voland told her. "The last I heard, Carpenter and Carbajal were both still over in Tombstone. But I do have a little bit of good luck to report. Jaime's in charge of the crew working Farley Adams' mobile home at Outlaw Mountain. About an hour ago, one of his investigators opened the dishwasher. Guess what?"

"They found a dead body inside?" Joanna suggested.

"Ha, ha!" Voland said without humor. "The dishwasher was full of dirty dishes. The guy forgot to run it."

A jolt of excitement coursed through Joanna's body. "If he forgot to turn on the dishwasher," she said, "does that mean he also forgot to wipe the dishes for prints?"

"You've got it," Voland told her. "Once the techs finish dusting the dirty dishes, we should have a good set of prints—a complete set—to input into AFIS."

"Great. While we're on the subject of Alice Rogers, you might let Ernie know that I've spoken to Dr. Daly up in Tucson. She's got some preliminary autopsy information for him that she'll be faxing down to us. He'll want to stay on top of it."

"Daly says it's murder then?" Voland asked.

"Looks like. The Pima County detectives continue to hang tight to their neat little theory that Alice Rogers got herself falling-down drunk and then went staggering off into that grove of cactus to die, helped along by a convenient bunch of teenaged car thieves. From what I've seen of Hank Lazier, he may not let the facts get in the way of his pet theory. That's why I want Ernie and Jaime to keep after it."

"They already are," Dick said. "I think you'd be hard-pressed to convince them otherwise."

Just then Joanna came to the end of the newly bladed road. Across an expanse of tinder-dry, knee-high grass she could see an old firebreak meandering off to the right along a drooping barbed-wire fence that evidently marked the boundary of the

Oak Vista development. With the Blazer already in four-wheel drive, Joanna bounced easily across the intervening desert and turned north on the old dirt firebreak. It was rough, slow going. Joanna was grateful she was behind the wheel of the Blazer rather than driving the lower-slung Civvy.

Half a mile north, she topped a slight rise and had to slam on the brakes to avoid hitting a white Subaru Legacy parked directly in her path. Had the circumstances been different, she might have simply assumed that the car belonged to a hiker off on a day-long jaunt in the Huachucas. Considering the ongoing problems at Oak Vista, however, Joanna couldn't afford to ignore the possible threat of that parked vehicle. She had just told Dick Voland that the demonstrators probably wouldn't show up at the job site much before quitting time. Now, though, she wondered if, in fact, some of them weren't already there and wandering around undetected.

Using her radio, Joanna ran a check on the license plate. The results came back with gratifying speed.

"The car belongs to Elvira and Luther Hollenbeck," the records clerk told her. "The address listed is 6855 Paseo San Andreas in Tucson."

"The Hollenbecks didn't happen to get picked up along with the rest of our crew of born-again monkey wrenchers yesterday, did they?" Joanna asked.

"No," the clerk said. "I don't see anything at all at that address in Tucson. No police or criminal activity, anyway. There've been several nine-one-one calls, but those all turned out to be medical emergencies of one kind or another. The last one was three months ago."

While Joanna had the Records clerk on the line, she asked for any available information on Rob Evans as well. That check, too, came up empty.

After Joanna finished with Records, she sat for the better part of a minute staring at the Legacy. Although there was nothing to say that Elvira and Luther Hollenbeck were connected to the monkey wrenchers, there was nothing that said they weren't, either.

Keeping one hand on her Colt and holding her breath, Joanna exited the Blazer and made her way to the driver's side of the Subaru. Only when she discovered both the front and back seats to be empty did she take another breath.

She returned to the Blazer and to her radio. "Dispatch," she said. "Try to raise Deputy Gregovich for me."

Moments later, Terry's voice came hiccuping through the radio. There was so much static in the transmission that he might have been in Timbuktu rather than a mile or so away. "What can I do for you, Sheriff?" he asked.

"Have you been on the firebreak this morning?"

"I've been up and down it two or three times. Spike and I have been going around the perimeter to make sure no one tries to come in via the back door."

"I think someone has come in that way now

anyway," Joanna said. "I drove due west from the construction shack to where the road ends. I'm about half a mile north of there now, parked behind an empty Subaru Legacy that's sitting in the middle of the road."

"That's strange," Terry said. "I didn't see it an hour ago when I was by there last. Anyone around?"

"Not that I can see, but I'd appreciate it if you'd come down and give me some backup, just in case."

"You bet, Sheriff," Terry said. "Spike and I will be there just as soon as we can."

While she waited, Joanna got back out and walked up to the Legacy once again. In the fine dust behind the vehicle she saw several sets of footprints. All the prints seemed to have been made by the same pair of shoes. It looked as though the same person had come and gone several different times.

Joanna was crouched down examining the prints when a woman walked up behind her. "Who are you?" she asked.

The woman, a spare gray-haired lady in her late sixties or early seventies, had approached in such complete silence that Joanna almost jumped out of her skin. "Elvira?" she stammered, lurching to her feet. "Elvira Hollenbeck?"

"Yes. That's right. Who are you? What do you want?"

"My name is Brady, Sheriff Joanna Brady. What are you doing here?"

"It's a nice day," Elvira answered. "I'm taking a walk."

But not up in the mountains, Joanna thought, noting Elvira's dusty hiking boots and thick leather gloves. Joanna also noticed that the woman had approached from the direction of Oak Vista rather than across the fence in the Coronado National Forest. Still, she didn't appear to pose any threat. With her iron-gray hair pulled back in a bun and a broad-brimmed sun hat shading her face, Elvira Hollenbeck looked like the most ordinary of grandmothers. She didn't seem to be the least bit upset or agitated.

In fact, the woman seemed so totally harmless that Joanna began to feel a little silly for having summoned Terry Gregovich. "You're not from around here, are you?" Joanna asked.

"Tucson," Elvira answered.

"Well, then, you may not be aware that we're currently having some difficulties at this location. Some people object to the construction of this new subdivision. In fact, there was a near riot on this property yesterday, and there's likely to be another one this afternoon. I'm afraid I'm going to have to ask you to leave."

"All right, then," Elvira said. "I'll go."

Elvira Hollenbeck was moving toward the car door just as Terry Gregovich drove up from the opposite direction. Stopping with the front of his Bronco nose-to-nose with the Legacy, the deputy jumped out. Then he opened the Bronco's back door and Spike bounded out after him.

Terry turned and started toward Joanna and Elvira, walking along the passenger side of the Subaru.

"Everything under control?" he asked.

Joanna was just nodding yes when a sudden transformation came over Spike. He stopped dead. His long ears flattened against his head. A low growl rumbled in his chest.

Terry froze too and stared down at the dog. "What is it, boy?" he asked. "What's wrong?"

"Get him away from me," Elvira yelled. "That dog is vicious. Get away! Shoo."

But instead of going in the other direction, she charged toward the dog, screeching and flapping her arms. Spike stood his ground. In fact, the dog paid no attention to the flailing woman. His whole being seemed focused on the car—on the back of the car.

Joanna looked at the vehicle, too, and saw nothing. Just inside the window was a cloth shelf that seemed to conceal a small covered trunk space. Other than that, the backseat appeared to be totally empty. Spike, however, continued to growl.

Not knowing the dog well enough, Joanna turned to Spike's handler. "What does it mean, Deputy Gregovich?" Joanna asked.

"I don't know, ma'am," he replied. "Spike's never done this before. What is it, boy? What are you trying to tell me?"

Joanna turned to Elvira. "What's in the vehicle?"

"Nothing," she snapped. "You can see for yourself. There's nothing there."

"The dog seems to think otherwise. Open the trunk."

"I won't," Elvira Hollenbeck declared. "You can't make me. You don't have a warrant, and I haven't done anything wrong."

"Yesterday this site was the scene of a riot, Mrs. Hollenbeck," Joanna observed. "The dog's unusual behavior is enough to suggest that you have something dangerous concealed in your vehicle. In other words, probable cause. Now, are you going to open that trunk, or are we?"

"I won't."

"All right. Fair enough. Deputy Gregovich, if you'll check in the backseat of my Blazer, you'll find a toolbox with a crowbar in it. Go get it, please, and then come back and pry this thing open."

"But my car," Elvira objected. "You'll wreck my car."

"Then open it yourself," Joanna told her. "It's your choice."

Leaving Spike where he was, Terry walked to Joanna's Blazer and brought back the crowbar. He was just starting to place it between the hatch and the frame when Elvira stepped forward. "Don't," she said. "Someone will get hurt."

"Why?" Joanna asked. "What's in there?"

She expected Elvira to answer "Dynamite," or "Blasting caps." Something explosive. Something that would blow pieces of Mark Childers' earthmoving equipment to kingdom come. What

Joanna didn't expect was Elvira Hollenbeck's one-word answer.

"Snakes," she said.

"Snakes?" Joanna echoed.

Elvira nodded. "Rattlesnakes. Fifteen or so. I had another one that I was bringing back to the car, but when I saw you parked here, I had to let him go."

Joanna was dumbfounded. "You have a carful of rattlesnakes? How come?"

"I collect them," Elvira said. "They're worth a lot of money these days. When a developer comes through and clears land like this, they're here for the picking. Besides, with their habitat all torn up and with winter coming on, they'll all die anyway."

"You collect snakes and sell them?" Joanna asked. "Isn't that illegal?"

Elvira looked Joanna directly in the eye. "It may be," she said. "But it shouldn't be. What should be against the law is this." She gestured off across the great expanse of yellowed grassland with its wide gashes of bulldozed red earth where not a single tree or blade of grass had been left standing. "We don't leave homeless dogs and cats to die long lingering deaths," she continued. "The SPCA sees to that. Snakes are God's creatures, too."

"So that's what you're doing?" Joanna asked. "Operating a one-woman humane society for the benefit of displaced snakes?"

Elvira clamped her lips shut and didn't answer.

"Open the trunk, Mrs. Hollenbeck," Joanna ordered. "I want to see for myself what you have inside."

Elvira moved forward and unlocked the hatch. As soon as she began to raise the lid on the inner trunk, Joanna heard the telltale buzzing. As the hairs rose on the back of her neck, Spike's low-throated growl turned to a frenzied bark.

"That's enough," Joanna said. "I don't need to see any more."

Elvira shut the lid. "What happens now?" she asked. "Am I under arrest, or what?"

For a moment Joanna didn't know what to say. "Deputy Gregovich," she said finally. "Why don't you take Mrs. Hollenbeck over to your vehicle and let her have a seat."

While Terry and Spike led Elvira back to the Bronco, Joanna returned to her Blazer. Knowing the radio was out of the question, Joanna used her cell phone instead. "Dick," she said, when Chief Deputy Voland answered the phone. "Any suggestions about what to do with a Subaru full of rattlesnakes?"

"I beg your pardon?"

"We've picked up a woman whose trunk is full of rattlesnakes. What do we do with them?"

"How would I know?"

"Get on the horn and check with somebody from Arizona Fish and Wildlife," Joanna ordered. "Tell whoever you talk to that the snakes were picked up from a construction site at the base of the Huachucas and that their habitat's pretty well destroyed. Ask if we should turn them loose, or what."

"Don't tell me, let me guess." Dick Voland groaned. "The Subaru's on Oak Vista Estates."

"Right you are," Joanna told him cheerfully. "Where else would it be?"

ELEVEN

IT TOOK almost an hour and a half for the ranger from Fish and Wildlife to show up and take charge of both Elvira Hollenbeck and her snakes. By then Joanna was sick to death of Oak Vista Estates. She had hung around with the snake lady longer than necessary in hopes Mark Childers would finally return from his endlessly long lunch. Finally, Joanna left Deputy Gregovich and the ranger to sort things out and drove on into Sierra Vista. After locating Dena Hogan's office on Fry Boulevard, Joanna was told by the receptionist that Mrs. Hogan was in court—in Bisbee.

Frustrated, Joanna gave up and decided to head back there herself. On the way, her phone rang once again. "Where are you?" Butch Dixon asked.

"Just over the Divide."

"Since we seem to be engaged, don't you think we should meet for a late lunch?"

"What about Junior?"

207

"I'll bring him along. Not very romantic, I know, but that's the way it is."

"How's he doing?" Joanna asked.

"All right. Once I got him started on video games, he finally stopped driving me crazy about the badge."

"I have one for him," Joanna said. "Remind me to give it to him at lunch." She paused, needing to ask and not wanting to. "Well?" she said.

"Well what?"

"What happened with Eleanor?"

"We had a nice chat."

"Butch, when it comes to my mother, there's no such thing as a nice chat. What did she say?"

"She asked if I was going to marry you, and I said yes. End of discussion."

"Just wait," Joanna predicted. "She isn't going to let me off that easy."

"Of course not," Butch agreed. "You're her daughter. Maybe we could work out a deal. You talk to my mother, and I talk to yours."

"I don't even know your mother."

"It's just as well."

"You never talk about her."

"For good reason."

"Is she going to be happy about this?"

"About our getting married? Sure."

"Then why don't you want to talk to her about it?"

"Probably for a lot of the same reasons you don't want to talk to yours," Butch admitted. "That's why I know how to handle Eleanor. It's familiar territory. Those two women are birds of a feather. My mother and yours could be twins."

"Oh, great!" Joanna said. "That should make for a really interesting wedding."

"Right," Butch said. "We'll turn our mothers loose on each other. Bisbee, Arizona, will never be the same. When it comes time for the rehearsal dinner, your mother can complain about having a sheriff for a daughter, and mine can gripe about having an ungrateful son who left Chicago—where they're currently having an early winter ice storm, by the way—and won't come back. Speaking of which, have you thought about it at all—about what kind of wedding you want? Where? That kind of thing?"

"Butch, give me a break. I've had my hands full with a gun-toting construction crew and a Gray Panther who evidently supplements her Social Security checks by illegally collecting rattlesnakes. I haven't exactly had a chance to pick up the latest copy of *Bride* magazine."

"Well," Butch said. "Maybe we can talk about it at lunch."

WALKING INTO Daisy's, Joanna hurried to the back booth where Butch and Junior were already seated. Both of them seemed overjoyed to see her. Joanna planted a kiss on the top of Butch's smoothly shaved head. "'Yes, dammit' isn't a very good answer," she said.

Butch grinned up at her. "It works for me," he said.

It turned out, however, that Daisy's Café in the early afternoon was neither the time nor the place to discuss wedding plans. For one thing, the addition of a very noisy Junior to the mix made Butch and Joanna's presence the object of more than the usual amount of curiosity. Several people stopped by to chat, but talking was merely a subterfuge to check out what was going on in their booth.

Hoping to quiet Junior, Joanna finally gave him his new badge. He greeted the gift with exuberant glee. When Daisy Maxwell showed up to take their order, Junior was so delighted that he practically bounced out of the booth.

"What have you got there?" Daisy asked, pulling a stubby pencil out of her stiffly lacquered beehive hairdo.

"Mine!" Junior announced triumphantly, waving the badge before her eyes. "Put on," he begged. "Put on, please."

Before Joanna could do as he asked, Daisy had slapped her order pad and pencil down on the table. "All right, I will," she said. "But you'll need to stand up, and you'll have to be very still."

Grinning, Junior bounded out of his seat and then stood ramrod-straight while Daisy Maxwell carefully pinned the badge to his shirt pocket. "There now," she said, patting it in place. "Isn't that something!"

Joanna was touched by Daisy's easygoing kindness and also by the fact that Junior's khaki shirt and slacks had been washed and neatly pressed. The people who lived in Bisbee—even new arrivals like Butch—were generally pretty good folks, and Sheriff Brady was proud to be one of them.

"You from around here?" Daisy asked as Junior resumed his seat.

Junior's face clouded. The grin vanished. He shook his head sadly, then he pointed at Joanna. "Take Junior home," he said. "Me go home."

"Well," Daisy said, "lunch first. What'll you have?"

Junior looked at her in bewilderment.

"How about a hamburger," Daisy coached. "You like hamburgers?"

He nodded. "Like."

"And to drink. What about a milk shake? Chocolate, maybe?"

The grin returned. Junior beamed. "Yes. Junior like."

After Joanna and Butch placed their orders, Daisy started away from the table. Then she turned back. "So where's he from really?" she asked.

"We don't know," Joanna admitted. "He was left behind at the arts and crafts fair in Saint David over the weekend. His name is Junior, but that's all we know about him. No last name. No idea of where he's from. Nothing. He's staying over at Butch's house for the time being—until we find out where he belongs."

"How are you going to do that?"

Joanna shook her head. "I have no idea. If we had some clue about where he was from, it would be a big help. But we don't. He could be from somewhere in Arizona or from someplace out of state as well. It's snowbird season again. According to Father Mulligan at Holy Trinity, the arts and crafts fair drew visitors from all over the country."

"So he could be from almost anywhere," Daisy said with a thoughtful frown. "That would make it tough."

Joanna smiled at her obvious concern. "If you come up with any bright ideas, we're open to any and all suggestions."

"I'll think about it," Daisy said. "But before I do that, I'd better turn in your order or you won't ever get any lunch."

Daisy disappeared into the kitchen, and Joanna turned back to Butch, who seemed suddenly subdued. "That does take some getting used to," he said.

"What's that?"

"The fact that you're always on duty," he said seriously. "The fact that your pager can go off anytime of the day or night and you have to go. You're like a doctor on call, and it's the same way for Marianne. She's always on duty, too. I think the only time she ever lets her hair down is when she's around you. Look what happened to her and Jeff after Esther died. Grief should be private, but it seems like theirs is everybody else's business. It'll be exactly the same thing when it comes to our wedding, Joanna. You think your mother is bad, but just wait. You're a public person around here. Everybody in town—no, make that everybody in the whole county—is going to have a vested interest in what happens to you. To us. Are you going to be able to handle it?"

Over time Joanna had gradually grown accustomed to the constant attention. For Butch it was a new phenomenon. "I think so," she said. "What about you?"

Butch shrugged. "Like I said. It'll take some getting used to."

Daisy came back with their drinks. Coffee and water for Joanna and Butch and the milk shake for Junior. "I'll bet chocolate is your favorite," she said, as she placed the whipped-cream-topped shake in front of him.

Nodding and beaming, Junior reached for the paper-wrapped straw on the plate beside the shake. In his eagerness, his hands trembled so much that he wasn't able to free the straw from its wrapper. After watching him struggle for the better part of a minute, Butch reached across the table, unwrapped the straw, and stuck it into the drink.

"There you go, Junior," Butch said. "Have a ball."

Halfway through lunch, Junior once again announced the fateful word, "Go." This time there was no mistaking the message. Butch instantly hustled him off to the rest room. When they returned after successfully completing the mission, Joanna met Butch with a smile.

"You're right," she said. "This isn't the most romantic of engagement lunches, but I have to say, from where I'm sitting, the prospective groom is making a very good impression on the prospective bride."

"Thanks," he said.

When it was time to leave, the three of them gathered around the cash register near the front door while Daisy rang up their bill. "You know," she said, "I was thinking. A couple of years ago for Christmas, our kids gave us one of those big coffee-table books, *America the Beautiful*, I think it's called. It's full of pictures from all over the country. You know, the kind of stuff people recognize—like San Xavier Mission in Tucson or the Space Needle in Seattle. I wonder if we showed it to Junior, would he recognize anything?"

"He might," Butch said. "It's a long shot."

"Well, Moe's at work up at the post office right now," Daisy said. "As soon as he gets off, I'll have him drop the book off here at the restaurant. That way, you can stop by and pick it up whenever you like." She looked at Junior. "Moe's my husband," she explained. "He has a book—a very pretty book—with all kinds of pictures in it. Do you like pictures?"

Junior smiled and nodded. "Like pictures," he said.

"Good, then. The book will be here waiting for you, and you can look at it however much you like."

Some other people came in the door, and Butch led Junior out to his car. "He's just as sweet as he can be, isn't he," Daisy commented, looking after them.

"Yes," Joanna said, thinking of Butch. "He is sweet."

"What do you suppose happened to his family? And why haven't they come back for him? Surely they didn't leave him on purpose, do you think?"

"It looks that way," Joanna said.

"That's awful," Daisy said. "What kind of a low-down snake would do such a thing?"

Joanna thought about the trunk of Elvira Hollenbeck's Subaru. "Actually," she said, "I don't think snakes would. They're probably more honorable than that."

Back in her office, Joanna settled down to work. Dick Voland had taken charge of the squad of deputies patrolling Oak Vista Estates. Since he was perfectly capable of handling the situation, there was no need for Joanna's added presence. Not only that, after spending two days on the road, there was plenty of work for her to catch up on.

She had labored in peace for the better part of an hour and felt that she was starting to make some real progress when the phone rang. "Yes, Kristin. What is it?"

"Someone to see you, Sheriff Brady. She says her name's Monroe. Jessie Monroe. She wants to talk to you about her sister."

"Who's her sister?"

"Alice Rogers," Kristin answered.

With a swipe of her arm, Joanna cleared the remaining clutter of paperwork from her desk. "Show her in," she said.

The woman Kristin ushered into her office was a stooped, bird-boned woman who leaned almost bent double on a walker. She was tiny and frail, but the piercing eyes she focused on Joanna were sharp and uncompromising. "Sheriff Brady?" she said, peering out crookedly from under a permanently ducked head.

"I'm Sheriff Brady," Joanna said. "What can I do for you?"

"You're in charge here?"

"Yes."

"And you're investigating my sister's death— Alice Rogers' death?"

"I'm not doing that personally," Joanna said. "I have two detectives who are handling the case."

"I suppose they've already spoken to that worthless niece and nephew of mine."

"Susan Jenkins and Clete Rogers?" Joanna said. "Yes, they've both been spoken to, but I doubt they've been interviewed in much detail so far. It's still too early in the investigation for that."

"But you will be talking to them."

"My detectives will."

"Well, then," Jessie Monroe said. "I want you to give them a piece of my mind."

Jessie's walker had what looked like a bicycle basket attached between the two handles. At that point, Jessie reached into the basket, pulled out a clothbound book and dropped it onto Joanna's desk.

"What's this?"

"What does it look like?" Jessie demanded. "It's a book."

Joanna picked it up and examined the cover. *"My Life and Times,"* it said. "By Alice Monroe Rogers."

"Your sister wrote this?" Joanna asked.

Jessie Monroe nodded. "Paid good money to have it printed, too. She wanted people to know about her, about who she really was. I watch all those programs on TV," Jessie continued. "You know the ones—'Law and Order' and all those other things they call police dramas. It seems to me, the dead people never get to tell their side of the story. The people in authority only learn what the people who are left want to tell them, which may or may not be the truth. I wanted someone to know what Alice thought instead of hearing what her kids *think* she thought. There's a big difference, you know. A big difference."

"Won't you please sit down," Joanna said, motioning Jessie Monroe toward one of the captain's chairs on the far side of her desk. "Would you care for something to drink? Coffee? A soda?"

"A glass of water would be nice. I am feeling a bit parched."

Joanna summoned Kristin and asked her to bring water. Then she turned back to her guest. "You don't sound particularly fond of your niece and nephew."

"Fond? Absolutely not. They're both next thing to worthless. Cletus never amounted to a hill of beans. How he ever got himself elected mayor is more than I'll ever know. Susan always drank like a fish. Still does, as far as I know. And then she went and married that long-haired freak who sells cars out in Sierra Vista. Have you ever seen him?"

"I've met him," Joanna said.

"He doesn't do a thing for me," Jessie Monroe announced. "Thinks he's something of a ladies' man—like that weird guy who does all those margarine commercials on TV. Stringy hair all the way down to his shoulders. Girl's hair. Twice as long as Susan's. Wears it in a ponytail some of the time. For the most part, it just hangs loose around his ears. One of those guys with a Custer complex."

"Custer?" Joanna asked.

"General George Armstrong Custer. Except I don't suppose *he* ever wore earrings," Jessie sniffed. "Ross Jenkins does, you know. Two or three to an ear."

Kristin came in with water. Jessie took the glass, emptied it with several long unladylike gulps, and then handed it back. "Thank you," she said. "Much obliged. Now, then, to get back to Alice. She was the baby of the family. I'm the oldest. Eleven years difference between us. But even with the age difference, we were always friends and I always looked out for her. Some of my brothers and sisters I can pretty much take or leave, but Alice and I were good friends. You know what I mean?"

Joanna nodded. "I think so," she said.

Suddenly, unexpectedly, Jessie Monroe's eyes misted with tears. She groped in her pocket and found a hankie. "You'll have to excuse me. I still haven't quite accepted the idea that she's gone. I always assumed I'd be the one who'd go first, you see. Anyway, Susan called me this morning. She's the 'full of business' one in the family. She called to let me know what had happened. She said Alice had been killed up near Tucson. She said the authorities seem to think some young Mexican boys did it, although Susan seems to have her own ideas on that score."

"Hispanic boys," Joanna corrected. "They're from Tucson, not Mexico. And yes, that is the theory the Pima County investigators are working on at the moment—that they're the ones responsible for your sister's death."

Jessie blew her nose. "Well," she announced, "Susan doesn't believe that, and I don't either. Not for a minute. If Alice has been murdered— and that's the word Susan used, she said murdered—then that's where I'd start looking for her killer, if I were you. Right there in Alice's own backyard, as it were. You know what they say. 'How sharper than a serpent's tooth,' and all that? Well, it's true. Clete and Susan are two of a kind that way. I wouldn't trust either one of them any further than I can throw them."

"When did you last see your sister, Mrs. Monroe?"

"Miss," Jessie corrected. "I'm the old maid of the family. And the last time I saw Alice was about three months ago, when she came down to Douglas to show off that new beau of hers. Seemed like a nice enough chap to me. And I could see he thought the world of her, too, opening and closing doors for her, helping her in and out of chairs.

A regular gentleman. You don't see too many of those around anymore. Nope, they're scarce as hen's teeth."

"Farley Adams?" Joanna asked.

"Alice's beau? That's right. Farley Adams was his name. Is his name. I should imagine he'll be devastated, losing her so soon after like this. It's a tragedy—a terrible tragedy, and, as I said before, I'm sure those selfish kids of hers are behind it one way or the other."

"You said, 'losing her so soon after,' Miss Monroe," Joanna put in. "So soon after what? What exactly did you mean by that?"

Jessie Monroe heaved a sigh and then fumbled a black satchel-sized purse out of the basket on her walker. Once she snapped it open, she spent several long minutes sorting through the contents. At last she withdrew a stiff piece of paper—a postcard—which she handed over to Joanna. It was addressed to Jessie Monroe c/o Golden Agers Home and Convalescent Center, 816 G Avenue, Douglas, Arizona. To the left of the address was a neatly written note: "Having a wonderful time. Wish you were here. Love, Ali."

The picture side of the card showed a smiling couple posing inside an enormous heart-shaped wreath of flowers. The woman was holding a small bouquet. The man wore a suit complete with a boutonniere. The caption at the bottom of the picture said: "Greetings from Mr. and Mrs. Farley Adams. Laughlin Chapel of Love. Specializing in Weddings to Go. All-inclusive."

"Didn't they make a handsome couple, though?"

Jessie Monroe was saying. "Alice was always the prettiest little thing. And she managed to keep her looks, even if she didn't keep her own teeth."

Holding the picture, Joanna was painfully aware that Jessie's "handsome" wedding portrait was actually a study in motive. If Farley Adams and Alice Rogers were already married at the time of her death, Farley would have a good deal to gain from his wife's death. Even without a rewritten will, he would have been able to go against an existing one, demanding his spousal share of Alice's estate. The fact that Farley was Alice's husband bumped Susan Jenkins and Clete Rogers down a notch on the list of suspects. Had they been able to prevent the marriage, the children could have split the take two ways. Afterward, it would most likely have to be divided differently, with half going to the husband and a quarter to each of the children.

Studying the picture closely, Joanna noted that Farley was probably twenty years younger than his bride. She remembered hearing something about his being stone-cold broke when he had arrived in Tombstone a year ago. For someone coming from that kind of straitened circumstances, an estate of any size would come as a bonanza. And even if he had to split the take with Alice's children, Farley Adams would still be walking away with far more than he'd had when he started.

Joanna turned the postcard over and studied the canceled stamp. The year was illegible, but the date wasn't. October 18. Susan Jenkins' worst nightmare had been realized. Clearly, the road trip to Laughlin, Nevada, had been for purposes other than throwing money away on one-armed bandits.

"May I make a copy of this, Miss Monroe?"

"Of their wedding picture? I suppose so. I don't see what it could hurt. But I want it back. As a remembrance, you see."

"It'll only take a minute or so. Let me call my secretary."

Kristin was summoned once more. She took the picture down the hall and returned a few minutes later with the original and with color copies of both sides of the postcard. Joanna placed the two copies face-up on her desk and returned the original to Jessie. The old woman leaned forward and peered across the desk.

"Remarkable," she said. "I remember all those years with Ditto machines. Do you remember those? The purple ink?"

Joanna looked at her blankly.

"Oh, well, I suppose not. There were probably mimeograph machines by the time you came along, or maybe even Xerox. But I used Dittos for years when I was teaching school. The idea that you can just make a copy of something like this is astonishing. Why, you almost can't tell the difference between the original and the copy! I guess that's progress for you. I'm glad I've lived long enough to see it."

As she spoke, Jessie carefully filed the postcard back away in her purse. "Have you spoken to Farley?" she asked. "I've tried calling his number out at the mobile, but there wasn't any answer, and he doesn't seem to have a machine. Alice did, but not Farley. I wanted to give him my condolences and find out about arrangements and all. I do hope he'll have something to say about that—about the funeral, I mean. By rights, he should, since he's her husband and all. But I wouldn't be surprised if Susan and Clete didn't cut him out of it. That's the way they are, you see. Both of them selfish as the day is long. Both of them wanting to run the whole show. You have no idea how their constant bickering bothered Alice. There were times when she considered disowning them both."

Cramming her purse back into the basket on the walker, Jessie Monroe struggled to her feet. "I'd best be going," she said.

"Will you be needing a ride back to Douglas?" Joanna asked. "If you do, I can get one of my deputies . . ."

Jessie waved the offer aside. "Oh, no," she said. "I have my own wheels. Not really mine, of course. I turned in my license when I hit eighty-five. Seemed like the responsible thing to do because my reflexes were getting so bad. But Helen Dominguez, one of the attendants from the home, drove me here. I'm paying her, of course. That's only fair. But she can't get home too late. She's a young person, you see, and still has children that will be coming home from school soon. I've always felt that mothers should be at home when their children get out of school, don't you?"

"Oh, yes," Joanna agreed. "I certainly do."

By force of will she managed to keep herself from casting a guilt-ridden glance at her own watch. Jenny would be out of school by now and on her way to Butch's house where there would be no at-home mother in attendance.

Jessie started toward the door. "By the way," she added, "when you read Ali's book—Alice's book—don't expect it to be great literature. It was done by one of those self-publishing outfits. Vanity presses, I think they call them. I don't know how much she paid for it—probably way too much—but the company who did it certainly didn't squander any of what she paid on editing. My sister was a great gal, but she never was much of a writer, so the book's a bit rough in spots. You'll get the picture, though. Or your detectives will."

"Thank you," Joanna said, following her guest to the door. "By the way, is your address in the book, so I'll be able to return it to you when I finish reading it?"

"You can keep it if you like," Jessie said. "Alice gave me ten copies for my birthday last year. Even with this one gone, I still have seven. That should be plenty. It's not like I have any children of my own to leave them to. I did give one to the Douglas Historical Society and another to the historical society over in Tombstone. Alice lived both places, you see. Both towns are in the book."

"I'm looking forward to reading it," Joanna said. "I'll get to it just as soon as I can."

As the door closed behind Jessie Monroe, Joanna picked up Alice's book and began to read.

The first chapter was a charming childhood remembrance of playing hide-and-seek with her older brothers and sisters. Halfway through the second chapter, though, Joanna could no longer hold her eyes open.

With the book lying open on her desk, Joanna laid her head on her arms and fell fast asleep. She had no idea how much time had passed when Kristin tapped on the door. "Yes," Joanna managed, rubbing the sleep from her eyes and hoping she sounded more wide awake than she felt. "What is it?"

"Casey down in AFIS needs to see you right away."

"What about?" Joanna asked.

"All I know is she said it's urgent."

Before Joanna could stand up, she had to find the shoes she had kicked off under her desk. It took several tries before she was able to force her aching feet back into them. "All right," she said. "Tell her I'm on my way."

TWELVE

CASEY LEDFORD, the gifted young technician who ran Cochise County's Automated Fingerprint Identification System, was a Bisbee girl who had gone off to college on a full-ride Veterans of Foreign Wars scholarship. She had enrolled in the University of Arizona's College of Fine Arts, where she had planned on becoming a commercial artist. Smart, but not smart enough to avoid all the treacherous pitfalls of young adulthood, she had returned to her parents' home two years later, with no degree, but with a four-month-old baby—a daughter named Felicity—in tow. Back in Bisbee, Casey had taken whatever work she could find, including stints waiting tables in the dining room at the Copper Queen Hotel while she continued to attend college-level classes on a part-time basis.

Like a lot of other things, the AFIS equipment had fallen into Cochise County hands through a law enforcement, War Against Drugs grant that paid for hardware and software, but no "liveware"— the people necessary to make the other two work. Prior to receiving the equipment, Joanna had mistakenly supposed that automated fingerprint identification meant just exactly that—automated. With the arrival of the equipment and the technical documentation that accompanied it, Joanna learned that fingerprints usually had to be augmented by hand before they could be fed into the computer. That meant that the department was going to need to hire someone who was not only artistically inclined but also more than moderately computer-literate. When the position was advertised in the paper, only one applicant had responded—Casey Ledford.

"What's so urgent?" Joanna asked, poking her head in Casey's lab, where dozens of images of Felicity Ledford—most of them framed pastels— covered the walls.

"It's the Rogers case," Casey said.

"You got a hit?"

Casey Ledford nodded, but she didn't look any too happy about it. Joanna perched on a lab stool. "So tell me," she urged. "What did you find?"

"The hit resulted from prints we found at the mobile at Outlaw Mountain."

"Farley Adams' place," Joanna murmured. "The ones left on the dirty dishes?"

Casey nodded again. "Right," she said. "None of the guys thought to look there. They had dusted the outside controls, but they hadn't bothered to check inside."

"Good work," Joanna said with a grin "That's what it takes around here sometimes—a woman's touch. Go on."

"I actually brought the dishes back here to process them," Casey continued. "It was easier that way. And the prints I lifted were good ones. They didn't need all that much augmentation or anything. And once I fed them into the computer, the hit came back almost right away."

"So what's the problem then?"

"The computer spits out the person's name and the name of the jurisdiction that's looking for him. We usually have to call that department by phone in order to get the original fingerprint card as well as details on the criminal activity in question. I'm the one who does that. It's just a bureaucratic formality. I get the information and pass it along to whoever's working our end of it."

"You did that, then?"

"Yes. The hit was from North Las Vegas, up in Nevada."

"Let me guess," Joanna said. "Farley Adams' name isn't Farley Adams."

"Right," Casey agreed. "It's Jonathan Becker."

"What's he wanted for?"

"He *was* wanted for conspiracy to commit murder."

"You said was," Joanna said. "You mean he isn't anymore?"

"Jonathan Becker is dead," Casey said. "At least that's what the first person I talked to up in Nevada told me. He said Becker's prints should have been pulled from the system because he's deceased. According to the guy I talked to, Becker died in a one-car roll-over accident on the road between Vegas and Kingman. And that's where he's supposedly buried—Kingman, Arizona. The problem is, Becker obviously isn't dead. If he were, he couldn't have left fingerprints for us to find."

"There has to be some kind of mixup," Joanna suggested.

Casey shook her head determinedly. "There's no mixup," she said. "Not ten minutes after I get off the phone with the first detective, somebody else was on the line, calling me from North Las Vegas and pumping me for any and all information we might have on this case. It just didn't sound right, Sheriff Brady. There's something weird about this, and I don't know what it is."

"I don't know either," Joanna said, taking the fistful of computer printouts Casey handed her. "But I'm going to make it my business to find out."

She went straight back to her office and shut herself inside. There she studied the papers and tried to make sense of the conflicting bits of information. The more she examined the materials, the more she agreed with Casey's assessment. Something was wrong there. Obviously Becker and Farley Adams were one and the same. If Jonathan Becker really were dead, then the detective in North Las Vegas would have no possible interest in what was going on in Cochise County.

Joanna Lathrop Brady had learned the art of the full frontal attack at her mother's knee. Eleanor Lathrop's approach to life had often served her daughter well, and Joanna applied it now. Searching through Casey Ledford's thorough paperwork, Joanna located the notes she had made concerning the incoming call from North Las Vegas. The inquiring detective's name was listed as Garfield—Detective Sam Garfield, but he hadn't left a phone number. There was one, however, listed with Jonathan Becker's AFIS printed record.

Joanna dialed it and reached the non-emergency number for the North Las Vegas Police Department. "Detective Sam Garfield, please," she told the operator who answered.

"Who?"

"Detective Garfield," Joanna repeated, enunciating clearly. "Detective Sam Garfield."

"I'm afraid we don't have anyone here by that name. This is North Las Vegas. Have you checked with Las Vegas Metropolitan PD? Detective Garfield probably works there. People are always getting the two cities mixed up. Would you like me to give you that number?"

Joanna took the number, jotting it down mechanically, even though she knew in advance that she wasn't going to call. Casey Ledford's "weird" feeling had just become a whole lot weirder. Something was more than wrong, and Joanna knew the answers she needed wouldn't be coming through regular channels in Vegas, or North Las Vegas, either.

After only a momentary delay, she dialed Frank Montoya's number at the marshal's office in Tombstone. "How are things?" she asked.

"Pretty quiet. I guess you heard about the fingerprints they found at Outlaw Mountain," Frank said.

"I heard," Joanna told him. "And that's why I'm calling."

Over the next few minutes she explained about Casey's call from the mysteriously nonexistent Detective Garfield. "So here's the deal, Frank," she finished. "I'm hoping you can tune up that hotshot computer of yours, go on the Internet, and find out anything and everything you can about someone named Jonathan Becker. Look for articles about the accident, obituaries, whatever."

Frank Montoya, a self-taught technophile, had created a totally mobile and wonderfully hightech office for himself that was usually based in his departmental Crown Victoria. The fact that he was always more than willing to go online in search of esoteric pieces of information made it unnecessary for Joanna to do so.

"I'll get on it right away," he said. "By the way, did you hear about Alice Rogers' funeral?"

"What about it?"

"Clete stopped by just a few minutes ago. He said it's going to be Friday afternoon. The funeral itself will be at the Episcopal Church, with burial afterward in Tombstone Cemetery."

"Did he say what time?" Joanna asked, pulling out her calendar.

"Early afternoon. Two, I think."

"I'd better plan on going." Joanna made a note of it. In the process she saw the notation for Wednesday, November 11. "Kiwanis," it said. "Seven

A.M., Tony's in Tintown, guest speaker." She had almost forgotten about the speaking engagement. That would have been embarrassing.

"What's happening out in Sierra Vista?" Frank asked, changing the subject. "Any word on the Oak Vista situation?"

"None so far," Joanna told him. "I'm hoping that means no news is good news. It's about quitting time, and this is when the trouble started the other day. As soon as I get off the phone with you, I'll call and check."

Moments later she was on the horn with Dick Voland. "Any sign of monkey wrenchers revisited?" she asked.

"None whatsoever," he growled back at her. "Here I am with half the deputies for this shift stuck out here in the middle of nowhere with nothing happening. Meanwhile, big chunks of the county are totally without patrol coverage."

"Any more weapons turn up among the workers?"

"No. But that's hardly surprising. As much hell as you raised earlier, if they brought guns to work with them, they've stowed them out of sight. I'm guessing they're in tool chests and glove boxes. At the moment, though, we've got no probable cause, so they'll most likely stay there."

"What happened with the snakes?" Joanna asked. "When I left, Ranger Brooks from Fish and Wildlife was just getting ready to write up a citation for hunting without a permit and taking wildlife for profit. She didn't need to keep the snakes for evidence, did she?"

"No. She let them go."

"Right there?"

"On the spot," Voland answered. "Elvira had a snake stick hidden back up in the brush behind her car. Ranger Brooks used that to remove the snakes from the trunk and put them back where they belonged, more or less. According to Brooks, snakes are real homebodies, and they don't like to be moved around at all. Naturally, it wasn't possible to return them to exactly the places where they had been found. Which means the construction site is going to have snakes milling around for the next few days, looking for a way to get out of the cold once the sun goes down. That should make life interesting for Childers' work crews. I wouldn't be surprised if one or two of the workers gets bitten."

"I'm voting for Rob Evans," Joanna said. "If one of those displaced snakes has to go after someone, I hope it's him. It couldn't happen to a nicer guy."

"Is there anything else?" Dick Voland asked. "Deputy Pakin just radioed me that Marliss Shackleford is down by the gate on the highway. She evidently wants to talk to me about something. I told him to tell her that Frank Montoya is in charge of media relations and she should talk to him, but that had absolutely no effect. She still wants to talk to me. Any idea what it's about?"

Joanna knew exactly what it was about—Junior. She felt a stab of regret that she hadn't played the game better. "Remember Frank's idea about having Marliss help find Junior's family by writing a human-interest piece about him?" she asked.

"Right," Voland growled. "Another one of Frank's cockeyed ideas. But why is she coming to see me about it? Shouldn't she be talking to you?"

"We tried that," Joanna said. "I threw her out of my office."

"That's probably not the best way to treat one of our local newsies."

"I'm sure that's true," Joanna agreed. "So do me a favor, Dick. Talk to her. Try to smooth things over."

"I'll see what I can do," Voland replied. "But I'm not making any promises."

Knowing Dick was about to be interviewed— make that grilled—by Marliss Shackleford, Joanna wasn't at all eager to let him go. "By the way," she asked, "did Mark Childers ever show up?"

"As a matter of fact, he didn't," Voland replied. "That's what happens with high-rollers, though. They can afford to take lunches that last all afternoon, and nobody gives a damn."

"If you do see him," Joanna said, "let him know that we're not going to tolerate his encouraging a range war. Pass along the message that his workers had better show up unarmed from now on."

"I'll spread the word," Voland said. "First chance I get."

Cringing at the thought of what Marliss would have to say to Dick Voland, Joanna put down the phone just as Kristin came into the office. "Jenny called," she said.

That was the first Joanna noticed that she had used the private line for her calls to Dick and to Frank Montoya. That left Jenny no option but to call in through the switchboard. "I'll call her right back," Joanna said.

But she didn't. Not right away. Instead, she sat staring at the phone and wondering how and when she was going to get around to telling Jenny what was going on with Butch. Obviously she couldn't delay too long. If she did, Eleanor would steal a march on her and tell Jenny herself.

When Joanna finally did pick up the phone, she didn't find it at all surprising that Jenny answered the phone at Butch Dixon's house. "What are you up to?" Joanna asked.

"Me and Junior are playing video games."

"Junior and I." Joanna had tried to cut down on the reflexive grammatical corrections, but it was useless. It was one of those inevitable traits that had been passed down the DNA chain on her mother's side.

"Well, we are," Jenny said. "He's pretty good. Not as good as me . . . I am. How are you?"

"Busy, but things are beginning to get better," Joanna said. "How would you like to go out to the Pizza Palace for dinner tonight?"

"Do you think Junior likes pizza?" Jenny asked.

"I wasn't asking Junior," Joanna told her. "I was asking you."

"You mean, just us? Not even Butch?"

"Not even."

"How come? Am I in trouble or something?"

Joanna shook her head in exasperation. "Why

would you be in trouble? And what's the matter with just the two of us going out for pizza?"

"I guess that'll be okay," Jenny's acquiescence was less than enthusiastic. "When?"

Joanna looked at her watch. "In about an hour," she said. "I'll come by to pick you up."

Kristin came in again, this time bearing a stack of documents that had come through the inter-departmental mail. Topmost on the stack were the transcribed minutes from the previous day's board of supervisors meeting. Curious about what exactly had been said concerning Oak Vista Estates, Joanna scanned through several pages. Reading the actual quotes, Joanna could see that Dick Voland had given her a pretty accurate report about what had gone on. If anything, Voland had underplayed Mark Childers' vehement criticism over how the sheriff's department had handled the first set of demonstrators the previous Friday afternoon. Joanna hated to think what he would say at the next meeting, when the property damage to his equipment had all been properly tallied. Idly Joanna wondered if there wasn't some out-of-town event—a law-enforcement seminar somewhere—that would cause her to miss the next meeting, the one where her department would inevitably be stuck on the hot seat.

After Mark Childers gave up the podium, several of his critics had stepped forward to voice their dismay and outrage over the fact that, with very little advance warning and with only negligible public notice, Mark Childers' company was being allowed to tear up one of the last untouched tracts of Cochise County grassland. Childers' critics were far more vociferous and adamant than the developer had been. As the tenor of their comments became more and more negative, so did the mood of the board. But rather than turning their wrath on Childers, the board members instead focused their ire on poor Lewis Flores. He was the one who had signed off on the Environmental Impact Statement. His was the signature on Mark Childers' building permits.

Joanna knew Lewis Flores. He had been in Andy's class in Bisbee High School. His wife, Carmen Rojas, was a year younger than Joanna. After graduating from Arizona State University, Lewis had worked in county government in both Pima and Pinal counties before he and Carmen had come home to Bisbee. He had accepted the job as head of the Planning and Zoning Department while Carmen taught first grade at Greenway School. The two of them had taken up residence in Carmen's parents' old home on O.K. Street up in Old Bisbee.

Reading through the comments made in the meeting, including an especially vituperative one from none other than Karen Brainard, was upsetting. In his discussion of the meeting, Dick Voland hadn't gone into much detail about the verbal confrontation between the board and Lewis. Joanna suspected that Dick didn't have nearly the eye and ear for political intrigue that Frank Montoya did. It was entirely possible that Dick had no idea that there was a romantic relationship between the developer and the lady supervisor.

Thanks to Frank, Joanna did know, and the out-
rageousness and unfairness of Karen's attack on
Flores made Joanna see red. She picked up the
phone book and paged through until she found
the Flores' home number.

Carmen answered almost immediately. "Hello."

"Hi, Carmen," Joanna said. "It's Joanna Brady.
May I speak to Lewis?"

"He's not home from work yet," Carmen said.
"Have you tried his office?"

For a second or two, Joanna had no idea what
to say. She remembered Kristin's message from
earlier in the day. Linda, the secretary in Planning and Zoning, had said that Mr. Flores was
out sick. Sick but not at home. That was worrisome. Joanna wondered if she should tell Carmen that she had already tried reaching Lewis at
the office. In the end she decided not to. Considering what had gone on the day before, Lewis
Flores probably needed some space. He'd come
home when he was good and ready.

"I haven't but I will," Joanna said. "If I miss
him or if you hear from him before I reach him,
have him give me a call. Here's my cell-phone
number. I'll be leaving the office right around
five. I won't be home until later, but I'll have my
phone on and with me."

"This sounds urgent," Carmen said. "Is anything wrong?"

Joanna scrambled for something to say that
would sound reasonable and not too alarming.
"It's about that mess out at Oak Vista. Nothing

serious, but I wanted to have the benefit of some input from Lewis—from someone who saw how this whole deal came together. You know, historical perspective, cover-your-butt kind of stuff."

Carmen laughed. "Lewis is good at that. I'll have him give you a call."

Joanna hung up. She finished sorting through her papers and straightened her desk until it looked half civilized. Then she packed her briefcase—including her copy of Alice Rogers' autobiography—and walked out the door promptly at five o'clock.

She drove into town and stopped at Butch's house. While Jenny finished gathering up her things, Butch came outside and motioned for her to roll down the window. "What's up?" he asked. "Jenny was a little upset that Junior and I weren't invited to dinner."

"I need to talk to her," Joanna said. "Alone."

"Are you going to tell her?"

"If I don't, you-know-who will, and Mother will put her own particular spin on the story when she does. I'd like to give Jenny my side of the story—our side—minus Eleanor's editorializing. In the meantime, how's Junior doing?"

"We're fine. Jenny's really great with him. She did her homework as soon as she came home, and the two of them have been playing video games ever since. If anything, I think Junior's a little overstimulated. I thought later on this evening, after dinner, we'd go for a ride and stop by the café to pick up Daisy's book."

Jenny darted out of the house, followed by

Junior. "Me go, too," he said, following Jenny around to the passenger side of the Blazer.

"No," Butch said, "We have to stay here."

"Go with Jenny," Junior said as his face screwed up. "Go too. Go too. Go too."

He was so heartbroken and forlorn that Joanna started to relent. "No, you don't," Butch said with a smile. "If Eleanor sends the message to Garcia first, you'll be mad as hell, and my life won't be worth living. You and Jenny go have your pizza. Junior and I will manage just fine. Come on, Junior. Jenny and Joanna have to leave now. Let's you and I go into the house."

"No. Won't."

"Come on. I have something to show you."

Junior stood rooted to the ground, balefully shaking his head. "No! No! No!"

"Do you like videos?" Butch asked. Junior continued to shake his head.

"Movies, then?"

The head-shaking stopped. "Movies?" Junior asked.

"Yes. I have movies. Lots of them. Have you ever seen *The Lion King?*"

Junior brightened a little. "Lions," he said. "Grrrrr."

"That's right," Butch said. "That's how lions sound when they growl. Come on. Let me show you."

Taking a now uncomplaining Junior by the hand, Butch led him into the house while Joanna backed out of the driveway.

"Butch is really good with Junior, isn't he," Jenny observed.

"Yes, he is," Joanna agreed.

"Did you already know that when you brought Junior here?"

"No," Joanna said. "It turns out it was just a lucky guess."

That should have been her opening. A discussion of Butch's strong points could have led naturally and easily to the topic she needed to bring forward, but at that moment, Joanna's considerable courage failed her. It seemed as though it might be better to wait until they were safely ensconced in the Pizza Palace and downing slices of pepperoni-dotted pizza before she ventured into that emotional minefield.

And it almost worked. They ordered root beers and ate salad while they waited for the pizza to cook. Jenny's chatter was all about school and her homework while, for a change, Joanna did nothing but listen. Their freshly baked pizza was out of the oven and being sliced by the Pizza Palace owner, Vince Coleman, when Joanna's cell phone crowed its distinctive ring.

Jenny made a face. "Not again," she grumbled.

"You go get the pizza," Joanna told her. "This will only take a minute."

"Joanna?" her caller said. "This is Carmen Flores."

The undisguised anxiety in Carmen's voice put Joanna on edge. "It's me, Carmen. What's wrong?"

"I just found out Lewis never went to work today. And he still isn't home."

Joanna felt a stab of guilt. She had already known that. Should she have told Carmen about her husband's absence immediately, or had Joanna been right in letting the woman find out the truth in her own good time?

"He didn't?" Joanna stammered.

"No. I just drove down to Melody Lane to check."

"Do you have any idea where he might have gone?"

"No. Not really. But when I came home from his office, I checked the gun cabinet. His guns are both missing, Sheriff Brady. One's a hunting rifle—a Remington thirty-ought-six. The other's a shotgun, a twelve-gauge Browning pump action."

Jenny, having secured the pizza, had slid one slice onto her plate and was gingerly chewing the first piping-hot bite.

Carmen Flores continued. "I knew he was upset about what happened at the board of supervisors meeting yesterday, but I didn't think he was *that* upset. I'm scared, Joanna. He's never done anything like this before. What am I going to do?"

"What kind of car is he driving?" Joanna asked.

"Our old station wagon—a Taurus, a silver-gray Taurus. He left me the Escort today. I drove that to school. Joanna," Carmen added after a pause. Her voice sounded as if she was close to tears. "What if he's done something awful?"

That was Joanna's fear as well, but she couldn't say so. "Don't panic, Carmen," she said reassuringly. "You stay right there at the house. Call me immediately if you hear from him. In the meantime, I'll get someone to go to work on this right away."

Jenny was already on her way to the counter. "Mr. Coleman," she said. "My mom has a problem. We'll need to have this boxed up to go."

THIRTEEN

ON THE way back to Butch's house and at Jenny's insistence, Joanna ate a single piece of pizza. Butch came out to the carport to greet them as Jenny scrambled out of the Blazer and darted into the house, calling Junior's name as she went.

"What's going on?" Butch asked.

Joanna told him. "See there," he said when she finished. "You don't want a husband; you just want a baby-sitter."

The phone call from Carmen Flores had erased all Joanna's playfulness. "If it's a problem, Butch, I can take her to Jim Bob and Eva Lou's."

"Come on, Joanna. I was teasing. You know Jenny's welcome to stay here. How long do you think you'll be?"

"I don't know."

"Since tomorrow's a school day, why don't Junior and I give Jenny a ride out to the ranch a little later. That way, he can meet the animals,

244

and Jenny can get to bed at a halfway decent hour."

"It might be late," Joanna hedged. "Are you sure you don't mind?"

"Not at all. It's fine. Junior and I don't have school tomorrow. It won't matter if we get in late."

"All right then," Joanna said. "I'll see you out at High Lonesome later on." She put the Blazer in gear and started to back away.

"Did you tell her?" Butch asked, pacing beside the Blazer down the driveway.

"I didn't have time. The call came in and—"

"It's okay. You'll have another chance. In the meantime, I'll do my best to keep her out of your mother's clutches."

"Thanks," Joanna said.

On the way uptown from Butch's Saginaw neighborhood, Joanna used her cell phone in an attempt to call both Mark Childers and Karen Brainard. When there was no answer at either place, Joanna's sense of unease heightened. Her next call was to Dispatch, where Tica Romero was on duty. Joanna gave the dispatcher both names and phone numbers. "I don't have the addresses, but I'm sure you can get them. I want officers sent to each address to check things out."

"Any idea of what they should be looking for?" Tica asked.

Joanna was afraid she did know—a possible kidnapping and/or homicide. Maybe even two. "I'm not sure," she said. "Signs of struggle, maybe. Warn the investigating officers to be careful. Have them keep a lookout for a silver Taurus station wagon that belongs to Lewis Flores. Run a DMV check and broadcast the license. Flores is to be considered armed and dangerous."

Tica seemed stunned. "Are we talking about the same Lewis Flores I know?" she asked. "The one from O.K. Street up in Old Bisbee?"

"That's him," Joanna said. "He's been caught in the middle of this Oak Vista controversy. After the board of supervisors took him to task yesterday, I'm afraid he may have gone off the deep end. He may be out to get Childers or Brainard, or he may end up taking his frustrations out on himself."

"Armed and dangerous," Tica repeated. "And maybe suicidal to boot."

"That just about covers it," Joanna said.

Parking on O.K. Street and setting the emergency brake against the steep incline, Joanna climbed out of the Blazer. Next to a narrow concrete stairway marked "116" was a sturdy wooden lean-to that passed as a garage. Inside was a blue Ford Escort, but a silver Taurus station wagon was nowhere in sight.

Climbing the flight of thirty-two steep stairs took stamina. Joanna was breathless by the time she reached the top and found herself standing in a postage-stamp-sized yard perched on the flank of the mountain. Inside the yard stood a small frame house. Carmen Flores came to the door before Joanna raised her hand to knock.

"Come in," she said. "Lewis still isn't here."

"Have you found a note or anything that might

give us a clue about what he's up to or where he went?"

Carmen shook her head. "Nothing," she said.

"Can you tell what he was wearing?"

"His work clothes are all in the closet. I checked."

"He goes hunting, doesn't he?" Joanna asked.

Carmen's face suddenly brightened. "Maybe that's it," she offered eagerly. "It's whitetail season right now, isn't it? That's probably what happened. Lewis went hunting and just forgot to tell me about it. I don't know why I didn't think of that on my own."

The woman seemed to be grasping at straws, but Joanna didn't want to be responsible for snatching away Carmen Flores' last vestige of hope. "Where does he keep his hunting gear?" Joanna asked.

"In a little shed out back," Carmen said. "He keeps everything out there in a trunk except for his guns. Not as much clutter that way. Come on. I'll show you."

The shed out back had an open padlock hanging from a hasp. Inside was an empty steamer trunk. "See there?" Carmen said triumphantly. "It's all gone—his vest, boots, cap, everything. I'm sure one of his buddies must have called to invite him on a hunting trip, and he didn't have time to let me know."

"Doesn't he carry a cell phone?" Joanna asked.

"He left it home or else he forgot it," Carmen said. "He does that sometimes. I found it just a little while ago, still on the kitchen counter, sitting in its charger."

Joanna was sure the phone had been left behind deliberately, and she was equally convinced that the hunting trip Lewis Flores was on had nothing to do with whitetail deer. But she couldn't bring herself to tell Carmen Flores what she feared to be the truth. Not just yet. She also knew she couldn't afford to wait around the Floreses' house to find out if she was right. Too many lives were at stake.

"I'll tell you what," Joanna said as she watched Carmen carefully replace the lid on Lewis' empty steamer trunk. "Why don't I leave you to handle things here. I have one or two other matters to clear up. Is there anyone who could come stay here with you tonight—your folks, maybe?"

Carmen shook her head. "Mother can't get up and down the stairs anymore. That's why she and Daddy moved out of the house to begin with. I might call my sister, though. Rose could probably come over. But really, there's no need. I'm sure Lewis is out hunting. Just wait. He'll turn up around midnight with a big buck strapped to the luggage rack. I'll spend the whole weekend making tamales."

"All the same," Joanna insisted, "I think you'd better have someone here with you."

"Okay," Carmen agreed. "I'll call Rose and see if she can stop by."

Mulling over what to do next, Joanna made her way down the long stairway. As soon as she was back in the Blazer, she called Tica on the radio. "What's the word?"

"I got those two addresses and dispatched deputies to both. They reported that no one answered the door at either place. There were no lights on and no sign of struggle, but the afternoon papers were still in the driveways."

"Afternoon but not morning," Joanna observed.

"Right."

"That probably means both Brainard and Childers were home this morning, but they haven't come back tonight. Are the deputies still there?"

"Yes."

"Have them check with neighbors and see what time Childers and Brainard usually arrive home. Also have them ask if there have been any unusual goings-on around either address earlier today."

"Where will you be?" Tica asked.

"In the car. I'm going to head on out to Sierra Vista myself. I have a bad feeling about this one, Tica. Flores went out dressed to go hunting, but I'm afraid he isn't looking for whitetail deer. Where's Dick Voland, by the way?"

"He called in a little while ago after he and the other deputies left Oak Vista. He said he was going home and to call him only in case of a crisis."

"Nothing happened out there today?" Joanna asked.

"Nothing at all," Tica responded. "The monkey wrenchers didn't show. Once Chief Deputy Voland told me he was taking the rest of the evening off, I put Frank Montoya on notice that he's on call. He's standing by his radio."

"Can you patch me through to him?"

"Sure. Hang on."

Seconds later, Frank Montoya's voice came through the radio. "Glad to hear from you," he said. "I was just going to give you a call. It took me most of the afternoon, but I finally managed to track down that Becker stuff. Want to hear it now or later?"

"Go ahead."

"Jonathan Becker was a police officer in North Las Vegas. It's a separate entity from Las Vegas proper, sort of like the city of Tucson and South Tucson. Becker had put in eighteen years when his son signed on as a rookie. The son and some of the other North Vegas cops got caught up in some bad stuff. What the son thought was a sting turned out to be the real thing. The kid went to his dad and told Becker what he was into. There was a big internal-affairs investigation and supposedly the kid was going to break blue and testify. Before that happened, though, he was found dead, floating face-down along the shores of Lake Mead. After that the IA investigation went nowhere, and the other dirty cops skated.

"Sometime after that, Becker quit the force and went after the other guys on a freelance basis. He finally found out enough that he was able to blow the whistle on them. They fought fire with fire and tried to frame him for attempted murder. That's where the conspiracy-to-commit deal came from. He was picked up, arrested, printed, but never charged. The next thing anybody knew, the Internal Affairs investigation was reinstated.

Four officers in all left the force. Two of the dirty cops went to prison for murdering Becker's son after Jonathan Becker testified against them in court. Shortly after their guilty verdicts, Becker reportedly died in that one-car roll-over. According to the obituaries, his remains were cremated. There was a memorial service for him in Kingman, his hometown."

Frank paused. "That's it?" Joanna asked.

"That's it. What does it sound like to you?"

"Phony as a three-dollar bill," Joanna replied. "My guess is he disappeared into the Federal Witness Protection Program."

"Bingo," Frank agreed. "And that's what I've been doing all evening—pulling strings to find out whether or not that's what happened. It turns out we're right. Becker went into the program and stayed for the better part of a year. Then he let himself right back out again—a little over a year ago."

"Which is about the time Farley Adams showed up in Tombstone. That means he's pulled two disappearing acts instead of just one."

"If you take what happened Sunday into consideration," Frank said, "it sounds more like three."

"Let's go back to the Witness Protection Program. Don't they pull prints once someone goes undercover?"

"Usually. At least, they're supposed to. I'm guessing, though, that some wise-ass up in North Las Vegas—one of the dirty cops' pals—figured things the same way we did—that the Feds were hiding him. Whoever it was had enough pull to put Becker's prints back into circulation on the off-chance that one day Becker's prints would show back up in the system."

"And now they have," Joanna mused. "When Alice Rogers turned up missing, he must have realized that we'd come to him looking for answers. He also knew that if we did even the most limited of background checks, it would lead to more and more questions. And straight back to North Las Vegas, where someone is still harboring a grudge and looking to kill him. Which brings us right back to the mysterious Detective Garfield."

"Exactly."

"So here we have someone who was once suspected of conspiracy to commit murder. That might make him prime-suspect material in this case, but the problem is, he didn't take off until *after* you and Susan Jenkins came to see him. Which means that until you both showed up, he probably didn't have an idea that anything was wrong."

"Which would mean that he isn't our killer after all."

"May not be our killer," Joanna corrected. "But even if he himself didn't kill Alice Rogers, he may know something that would help lead us to whoever did. And we have to find him before someone else gets to him first. Or else we have to find Detective Garfield."

"Did the call to Casey come in through the regular switchboard?"

"As far as I know."

"Well, then," Frank said. "How about if I work

with the phone company and try to find out where that call came from?"

"Can you make inquiries like that after hours?"

"Watch me," Frank replied.

The radio was quiet for a moment as Joanna considered her next move. "Do that if you can," she said at last. "In the meantime, we've got another problem."

"I gathered that much from what Tica said. What's going on?"

Joanna reeled off everything she knew as well as what she suspected concerning the disappearance of Lewis Flores. "What's the next step then?" Frank asked when she finished. "If you've got deputies at both Childers' house and at Brainard's, what else is there to do?"

"I'm on my way out to Sierra Vista right now," Joanna told him. "I want to talk to the deputies in person and find out what, if anything, they've discovered. If it goes bad, though, I'm going to need you on the double."

"Okay," Frank said. "I'll stand by. Call if you need me."

Going back to Tica, Joanna asked for detailed directions to the two houses in question. Karen Brainard lived near Huachuca City. Childers' house, in Sierra Vista Estates, was far closer, so Joanna headed there first. She was about to turn off the highway when she was hit by a sudden stroke of inspiration. All of Lewis Flores' difficulties seemed to stem from the controversy swirling around Oak Vista Estates. Maybe that's where the answers lay as well.

Switching off her turn signal, Joanna continued on down Highway 92. At the entrance to Oak Vista, she found that a makeshift barbed-wire gate had been pulled across the road and stretched between the two upright posts of the cattle guard. There was a padlock hanging on a chain around one end of the gate, but when Joanna checked, she found it wasn't fastened. If the lock was supposed to keep monkey wrenchers out, it wasn't going to do much good left open.

Joanna opened the gate, drove across the cattle guard, then doused the Blazer's lights and turned off the engine. "Tica," she said into the radio. "I'm out at Oak Vista Estates right now. I'm stopped just inside the entrance, and I think I'd better have some backup."

"I'll get someone right there. What's happening?"

"I'm not sure. The gate has a chain and a padlock, but it wasn't fastened shut. I'm afraid someone may be here ahead of me."

"The monkey wrenchers?" Tica asked.

"Maybe, but I don't know. That's why I want backup."

"I'll send the deputies who are already at Mark Childers' house. They should be able to get to you in under ten minutes."

"Have them come ASAP," Joanna said. "But no lights or sirens. I don't want to advertise our arrival."

"Got it," Tica said.

Joanna stepped out of her car. A raw autumn

wind was blowing down off the Huachucas. Shivering against the cold, Joanna returned to the Blazer and pulled on her sheepskin jacket—the one with the bullet hole still in the pocket. Fingering that hole and remembering how the weapon she had carried there had once saved her life, Joanna pulled the Glock out of her small-of-the-back holster. She was just putting it in her pocket when she heard first one shot, then another and another. The shots were followed by something else—a woman's terrified scream that floated down to Joanna carried on the icy wind. The sound of it raised the hairs on the back of her neck and sent her scrambling into the Blazer.

Waiting for backup to arrive was no longer an option. The deputies summoned from Mark Childers' house were still minutes away. The terror and desperation in the woman's scream left no margin for delay.

"Shots have been fired," Joanna declared into her radio microphone. "I'm going in, Tica. Tell my backup to use the hell out of their sirens. I want Flores to know we're coming. I want all of them to know we're coming."

With the gas pedal shoved to the floor and with her own siren screaming, Joanna tore up the freshly bladed road that wound uphill to the construction shack. And that's where Joanna's headlights zeroed in on a silver Taurus station wagon. Lewis Flores sat on the hood, leaning back against the windshield. One weapon lay across his lap. From a distance, Joanna couldn't make out if he was holding the shotgun or the rifle, but it didn't really matter. Either one of them was sufficiently lethal.

She parked, cut the lights, and opened the window, but she didn't step out of the Blazer. If it came to a shootout, she wanted the benefit of whatever cover the engine block might provide.

"Lewis," she called as she drew the heavy-duty Colt 2000 out of her shoulder holster. "That's enough. Lay down your weapon."

For an answer, Lewis Flores reached out. Joanna thought he was going for his other gun, which lay beside him on the hood. Instead, he picked up something else. By then Joanna's eyes were adjusting to the lack of light and she was able to make out that he had picked up a bottle—a tequila bottle perhaps—and was taking a swig.

"Lewis." Joanna tried to make her voice sound authoritative but calm. "More deputies are on their way. They'll be here in a few minutes. You'll be surrounded. Give up before someone gets hurt."

"I already am hurt," he said.

Joanna breathed deeply. She had him talking. That was a good sign. "Where are Mark Childers and Karen Brainard, Lewis? What have you done with them?"

There was a sudden pounding. It seemed to be coming from one of the Porta Potties. "I'm in here," Karen Brainard yelled. "I'm locked in the toilet. He's been shooting at me. He's crazy. Get me out of here."

Relief spilled over Joanna. At least one of the

two was still alive, still safe. "Where's Mark Childers?" she asked.

"Why don't you ask him?" Lewis responded.

But Joanna didn't want to talk to Mark Childers. She didn't want to take her focus off Lewis Flores. He was the one with the guns. "Why are you hurt, Lewis? What's happened?"

"They lied to me," Lewis answered. "They told me that it wouldn't matter if the process got hurried up a little. They said they'd make it worth my while, and no one would care. But people do care, and as soon as there was trouble, they turned it all on me. Tried to make out that it was all my fault—all my responsibility."

"That's not true," Karen responded from her prison. "We didn't do any such thing, did we? Tell her, Mark. Tell Sheriff Brady that Lewis is lying."

But if Mark Childers had anything to add to Karen Brainard's denial, he wasn't saying. In the distant background, Joanna heard the sound of at least one siren. Reinforcements were on their way. The cavalry was about to ride to the rescue.

"Please, Lewis," she begged. "Think about Carmen. Put down your weapons. Move away from the car with your hands in the air."

"I am thinking about Carmen," Lewis Flores replied. "I was thinking about her and all those steps and her having to climb them every day. Of her having to carry groceries home just the way her mother did. I wanted a better place for her, something really nice. And Mark Childers was going to help me get it. But it's not worth it. I finally figured that out. I've lost everything now—my job, my family, my self-respect. They've taken it all away."

"You have to let us out of here," Karen Drain ard pleaded. "He locked us in here, and he's been using us for target practice. Please let us out."

Half a mile away across the desert, a patrol car rumbled across the cattle guard and then roared up the roadway.

"Do you hear that, Lewis?" Joanna asked. "The other deputies are coming right now. Please, put down your weapon so no one gets hurt."

His hand shot out again. Joanna thought he was reaching for the bottle again, which was out of her sight line on the other side of the hood. But what Lewis Flores raised to his lips that time wasn't tequila. Joanna saw the flare of light as the gun was fired, heard the explosion, and saw him flop backward against the windshield.

"No!" she heard herself screaming as she ran toward the Taurus. "Nooooooo!" But Lewis Flores was dead long before she reached him.

"Oh, God. What's he doing now?" Karen screeched. "Make him stop. He's going to kill us. The man is crazy. He's going to kill us all."

Joanna stopped at the Taurus long enough to grab Lewis Flores' limp wrist. Briefly her fingers searched for a nonexistent pulse. One look at the bloody carnage that had once been the back of Lewis Flores' head told her there was nothing to do. Dropping his lifeless arm, Joanna raced to the line of Porta Potties just as a patrol car skidded to a stop behind her Blazer.

Unholstering his side arm, Deputy Dave Hollicker jumped out of the vehicle. "What's the status, Sheriff Brady?"

By then Joanna was at the door to the Porta Potty. It wasn't just closed. It had been nailed shut. The top of the door was riddled with bullet holes. From inside, she heard the sound of hysterical weeping.

"Bring a crowbar, Dave," she ordered. "And make it quick. There's one in the back of my Blazer."

Leaving the first Porta Potty, Joanna went down the line until she found another one that had been nailed shut. Again, the top of the door was riddled with bullet holes. Lewis had been firing at the Porta Potties all right, but high enough not to hit anyone inside—scaring hell out of them but not necessarily trying to kill anyone.

"Mr. Childers," Joanna called through the door. "Are you in there? Are you all right?"

There was no answer, not even a whimper. Behind her Joanna heard the sound of running footsteps and, off across the ghostly starlit grassland, another siren. Dave was headed toward the first Porta Potty, but Joanna stopped him.

"Open this one first," she ordered. "The woman's all right, but I'm not so sure about Mark Childers."

It took several tries before Dave Hollicker finally pried open the door. When he did so, Mark Childers' limp body cascaded out onto the ground.

"He may have been shot," Joanna said, kneeling beside the stricken man and checking for a pulse. There was one. It was faint and erratic, but it existed. Nowhere on his body, however, was there any sign of blood.

"Call for an ambulance, Dave," she said. "We'll have to have him airlifted out of here. And bring blankets." About that time Mark Childers' pulse disappeared altogether. Without even thinking about it, Joanna began to administer CPR.

"Please," Karen Brainard pleaded from her prison. "What are you doing? Can't you let me out? What's taking so long?"

Joanna wanted to tell the woman to shut up and wait, but she didn't. Couldn't. She was too busy concentrating on what she was doing—too busy keeping track of the rhythmic and life-saving breathing and pushing. In the end, Joanna didn't have to say a word. Dave Hollicker did it for her.

"Quiet in there," he yelled as he came racing back to Joanna's side with an armload of blankets. "We're trying to save a man's life out here. Be patient. We'll get to you in a minute."

FOURTEEN

IT WAS almost three o'clock in the morning before Joanna finally made it home to High Lonesome Ranch. She had stayed long enough for the Air-Evac ambulance to load Mark Childers' ominously still body onto a stretcher and carry it away. She had stayed long enough for Ernie Carpenter to arrive on the scene.

"What do we do with her?" the detective asked, nodding in the direction of a no longer hysterical Karen Brainard, who had taken refuge in the back of Dave Hollicker's patrol car. "Do we book her and haul her off to jail?"

"Not yet," Joanna said. "We don't know enough. Have someone take her home for now, but tell her that she'd better not leave the county."

After that, and with a heavy heart, Joanna drove to Bisbee and made her way up the steep steps to what had been Carmen and Lewis Flores' home. As she climbed them, one at a time, it hurt Joanna to think that those very steps—the ones Lewis had wanted to spare his wife from climbing—were at the root of all the trouble.

When she arrived in the tiny yard, Joanna was dismayed but not really surprised to see that all the interior lights were off. Convinced her husband had merely taken off on a hunting trip without bothering to tell her, Carmen Flores had evidently gone to bed and to sleep. Roused by Joanna's knock, Carmen flung open the door before she finished tying on her flannel robe.

"Joanna!" she exclaimed when she saw who was standing in the glow of the porch light. "What is it? What's happened?"

And so Joanna told her story. This time she waited until Carmen's sister Rose actually arrived on the scene before she left the Flores house. Then, knowing there was nothing else to be done, Joanna headed home. On the way, she called the department and left word for Dick Voland. She told him she was scrapping that day's morning briefing and that she probably wouldn't be in the office much before noon.

It warmed Joanna's heart to drive into the yard of High Lonesome Ranch and see lights glowing at the window; to see Butch's Outback parked in front of the gate. He and the two dogs, Sadie and Tigger, bounded out the back door to greet her before she managed to park the Blazer and turn off the ignition.

"Rough night?" Butch asked, opening the door.

"You could say that. But you didn't wait up for me all this time, did you?"

"No. I dozed on the couch. Junior's asleep on the living room floor. Jenny hauled an air mattress and bedroll down from the attic for him. She said you wouldn't mind."

"I don't," Joanna replied. "Come on. Let's go inside. It's cold out here."

"Have you eaten?"

"I had a piece of pepperoni pizza," she told him. "But I think that was several hours ago."

"Do you want me to fix you something?"

Butch's questions contained all the familiar words and phrases. Not only had Joanna Brady heard them before, she had actually said them as well. Once she and her mother had been on the other end—the solicitous end—of those carbon-copy conversations. When Andrew Roy Brady had come home after a long and grueling nighttime shift—once Joanna had finished being scared for him, once she had moved beyond being irritated with him for coming home so late—she had always offered to fix him a meal no matter what time it was, no matter how late. And Eleanor Lathrop, in her turn, had done the exact same thing for her husband, Sheriff D. H. Lathrop. It felt strange for Joanna to be the recipient of those ministrations—a receiver rather than a giver—and in her own home as well.

"All I want is a drink," Joanna said. "A drink and some sleep."

"It must have been bad then," Butch said.

He wrapped one arm around her shoulder and led her inside. In the kitchen, he mixed her a vodka tonic, using some of the leftover stock of liquor he had moved down to Bisbee after the sale of the Roundhouse Bar and Grill up in Peoria. Due to a lack of storage space in his own house, he had used some of it to create what he called a respectable bar at High Lonesome Ranch.

While Joanna sipped her drink and told him what all had happened overnight, he fixed her a tuna sandwich. By the time she finished both eating and telling, Butch was standing, leaning against the counter. "Weren't you afraid?" he asked.

"Of course I was afraid," Joanna told him. "I was scared to death."

"Flores could just as well have shot you instead of himself," Butch observed. "What would have happened then?"

"I was careful," Joanna said. "I was wearing my vest. I stayed in the Blazer. I used it for cover."

"A vest will work for everything but a thick head," Butch replied. "And you still haven't answered my question. What would happen to Jenny if something happened to you? What if you hadn't come home tonight at all? Are you sure this is what you want to do? Do you want to spend your whole life going to someone's home in the middle of the night, waking up some poor sleeping woman, and telling her that her husband has just blown his brains out?"

Joanna felt her eyes welling with tears. "Please, Butch," she said. "Not now. I'm too tired to fight."

"I'm not fighting," he said. "I'm talking. That's why . . ." He stopped.

"Why what?"

"Never mind," he said. "It doesn't matter. Go on to bed. I'll clean up here. Then I'll wake Junior up and we'll head home."

"Don't go," Joanna said. "I don't want you to go. I need you here."

He took her glass and plate and put them in the dishwasher. "I don't suppose a night on the couch will kill me," he said.

"I don't mean for you to sleep on the couch," she told him. "We're engaged. I want us to sleep in the same bed."

"What will Jenny think?" Butch asked. "She doesn't know we're engaged. You didn't tell her, remember?"

"I didn't have a chance. I'll tell her in the morning."

In the end, it didn't take all that much convincing to get Butch to give up the idea of sleeping on the couch and to come join Joanna in her bed. Still chilled from spending so much of the night outdoors, she snuggled up against the warmth of his body and felt her own muscles begin to relax.

"By the way," Butch told her, "we picked up that book from Daisy—*America the Beautiful.*"

"Did you have a chance to look at it?"

"Jenny and Junior did. They spent at least two hours poring over every page."

"Find anything?" Joanna asked, but she had to struggle to frame the words. She was fading fast. It was difficult to concentrate.

"I think so."

"Tell me."

Butch did, but Joanna Brady didn't hear a

word of it. She was already sound asleep, and she was still asleep the next morning when the phone rang at five past seven. Joanna was so groggy that even the jangling of a phone next to her bed didn't wake her. Butch answered the call in the kitchen and then came into the bedroom.

"Phone," he said, shaking her awake. "Something about a meeting you're supposed to attend."

"I called the department last night and canceled the briefing," Joanna mumbled, turning over and burying her aching head in a pillow. "Tell them to forget it. Tell them I'll come in when I'm good and ready."

"I don't think it's that kind of meeting," Butch said. "Jeff Daniels is on the phone. He says you're supposed to be the guest speaker at a Kiwanis meeting this morning. When you weren't there by the time they finished the Pledge of Allegiance, he was afraid you'd forgotten."

Groaning, Joanna rolled out of bed. "I forgot all right. Tell him I'm on my way. But what about Jenny?"

"Don't worry. Junior and I will get Jenny off to school," Butch assured her. "You go do what you need to do."

After showering and throwing on her clothes, and with only the barest attempt at putting on makeup, Joanna pulled into the parking lot of Tony's in Tintown some twenty minutes later— less than five minutes before she was scheduled to speak.

Slipping into the dining room, she dived as

unobtrusively as possible for the open seat next to Jeff Daniels. "Where's Marianne?" Joanna asked, her eyes searching the room as she poured herself a much-needed cup of coffee.

"At home," Jeff said. "She's really feeling rotten. I'm afraid it's something serious, Joanna. What if it's stomach cancer or something like that?"

"Has she been to see a doctor?"

"No. I guess she doesn't want to know."

"What about her resignation? Did she hand that in?"

"No. Not yet," Jeff admitted. "It's like she's paralyzed, Joanna. Emotionally paralyzed. She's just going through the motions. Ruth keeps asking me what's the matter with Mommy. I don't know what to tell her. Would you try talking to her, Joanna? She won't listen to a word I say, but maybe you can get through to her."

"I'll see what I can do."

By then the business portion of the meeting was winding down and Joanna knew it would only be a matter of seconds before she would be called upon to speak. She had been invited to discuss the county-wide DARE program. But, in view of what had happened at Oak Vista the night before, Joanna had already scrapped her planned speech and was busily constructing another in her mind. No doubt people would have heard rumors about Lewis Flores' suicide. The story had hit too late to make the morning edition of the *Bisbee Bee*, but sketchy reports had probably been aired on Tucson television and radio news broadcasts. Once again, unfortunate events in Cochise County were providing headline fodder for the rest of Arizona.

It wasn't until Joanna stood up to speak—until after she had launched off into her rendition of what had happened the night before—that she noticed Marliss Shackleford seated at a table on the far side of the room. An openly smiling Marliss Shackleford. *What's she so happy about?* Joanna wondered.

She made it through her speech by operating on remote control. Her whole body ached with weariness. Her head hurt. Her mouth felt dry. All she wanted to do was fall back into her warm bed. When the speech ended and Joanna opened the subject up to questions, she expected Marliss to be among the first to raise her hand. Instead, Marliss slipped out of the room early without asking a single query. That struck Joanna as odd, but she was too tired to be anything but grateful about having dodged a public firefight with her most vocal critic.

Leaving the meeting, Joanna sat in the car for a few minutes and rested her head on the steering wheel. She felt rotten—almost as if she had the flu. *So stop being a martyr,* she told herself. *Go home and go to bed.*

After all, she was allowed ten days of sick leave per year. So far she had used only two days total. In the past few weeks, Cochise County had exacted far more than its pound of flesh from its lady sheriff. With that realization, she called in to the department and told Kristin that she wasn't feeling well. She was taking the day off and going back to bed.

"You and Chief Deputy Voland must have caught the same bug," Kristin told her. "He called in sick, too."

"If Voland is out, maybe I should come in after all," Joanna began.

"No. Don't bother. Chief Deputy Montoya is here this morning. He says he has everything under control. He offered to hang around all day if need be. You go on home."

Joanna was too tired to require any more persuasion. "Good," she said. "I'm on my way."

When she turned onto the road to High Lonesome Ranch, she was surprised that Sadie and Tigger didn't come racing to meet her. Their raucous greeting was so much a part of any homecoming that Joanna worried about it as she came up the road. Maybe Butch and Jenny had gone off to town that morning without remembering to put the dogs outside. In that case, it was a good thing Joanna hadn't gone to work. No telling what mischief those two scoundrel dogs would get into if left to their own devices inside the house.

Joanna came through the last stand of mesquite, then jammed on the brakes when she saw a vehicle parked by the gate. Dick Voland's Bronco sat there with someone slumped against the driver's window. On the ground nearby lay Sadie and Tigger, both of whom now bounded to their feet and came running toward Joanna, barking their tardy greeting. Inside the Bronco, the slumping figure stirred and then moved. As soon as he straightened into an upright position, Joanna recognized that the driver really was Dick Voland.

Parking beside him, Joanna jumped out of her Blazer and walked up just as Dick rolled down his window. A cloud of boozy air erupted from the enclosed cab. The smell was so thick and pungent that it almost made her gag.

"What are you doing here, Dick?" she asked. "I thought you were sick."

"I am sick," he returned. "Why didn't you tell me?"

"Tell you what? About Lewis Flores? I tried. At least I think I did. But you had already put in a full day by then. You had gone home."

"About Butch Dixon," Voland said doggedly.

Joanna was dismayed. "There was no reason to tell you," she said. "Butch and I are—"

"I know. You're engaged," Voland finished, although that wasn't close to what Joanna had intended to say. "I know all about it. Marliss told me. She heard it from your own mother. How could you do that to me, Joanna? How could you?"

"Dick," she said reasonably, "I didn't do *anything* to you. Butch and I have fallen in love. What do you expect—"

Again Dick Voland cut her off. "I expected you to have the decency to tell me, that's all. You must know how I feel about you. It's been like that since you first came to the department. I've been waiting and waiting for you to give me some sign that it would be okay for me to ask you out. For

you to say that you had spent enough time grieving over Andy and that you were ready to move
on with your life. I didn't see this coming. I didn't
think you'd do an end run around me and take
off with someone else."

He paused long enough for Joanna to say something, but by then she was too floored to speak.

"When Marliss came out to Oak Vista yesterday afternoon and told me all about it, I didn't
believe it. I was sure it was a lie—that she was just
being Marliss. But she made it sound real enough
that I had to know for sure. So I came out here to
see for myself. I parked out on High Lonesome
Road and waited. And sure as shit, the first person to show up is Butch Dixon in that little Outback of his. Jenny was in the car with him, and
somebody else I didn't recognize. Probably that
cretin you dragged home from Saint David."

"Dick," Joanna said warningly. "I told you—"

"I don't care what you told me," he said. "I saw
it with my own eyes. First he drove up and then,
hours later, who should show up? You, Sheriff
Brady—you and nobody else. Come home to shack
up. If you didn't care any more than that about
yourself, it seems to me that you'd at least care
about Jenny."

"That's about enough," Joanna said. "I think
you'd better go now."

"No, it isn't enough. Not nearly. Here." He
reached in his shirt pocket and fumbled out a
wrinkled, much-folded piece of paper.

"What's this?" Joanna asked.

"My letter of resignation. I quit. As of now."

Dick Voland had tried to quit once before—right after Joanna's election. Back then she had talked him into staying because she needed his help, his expertise. Even now, she still could use his experience, but not without respect. Lacking that, there was no way they could continue to work together. She unfolded the letter and glanced at the contents.

"All right," Joanna said when she finished reading. "Considering what's happened, that's probably for the best. I'll expect you to turn in your vehicle and your departmental weapons before the close of business today."

"Don't think this is the last you're going to hear from me," Voland warned as he turned his key in the ignition. The Bronco's engine roared to life.

"No," Joanna said. "I don't suppose it is." As soon as the heater fan caught hold, another cloud of rancid air blasted into Joanna's face. "Are you sure you should be driving?" she added. "It's possible you're still drunk."

"I'm not drunk," he insisted. "Besides, who's going to stop me? You? I don't think so."

Voland rammed the Bronco into reverse and then stepped on the gas. Joanna had to sidestep out of the way in order to keep from being creamed by the outside mirror. He drove off, leaving Joanna in a cloud of dust.

Fleeing into the house, it was all she could do to press her door key into the lock. She dropped the letter on the dryer and then ran weeping through the house. She threw herself across the bed and buried her face in the covers. Joanna hadn't cried that way for months. A wild fit of racking sobs came from deep inside her and shook her whole body. Her tears didn't have their source in any one thing. It was everything: Dick Voland quitting. Eleanor bossing her around. Butch asking her if being sheriff was what she really wanted. Lewis Flores blowing his brains out right in front of her. And that was not all. There was also the fact that Joanna had lost her nerve and hadn't actually told Jenny what was really going on with Butch. Now, thanks to Marliss Shackleford, everyone else in town already knew about it or soon would.

Eventually the combination of tears and exhaustion caught up with her. Joanna fell asleep. The next thing she knew, she and Butch were standing together at the altar of Canyon United Methodist Church. Butch, wearing a tuxedo, was grinning from ear to ear. Junior, standing beside him, was evidently best man, although the badge he wore in place of a boutonniere looked a little out of place on his tux.

Looking down, Joanna discovered that she, too, was dressed for the occasion. She was wearing her wedding dress—the same dress she had worn years earlier when she and Andy were married. Beside her, as maid of honor, stood Angie Kellogg, the ex-hooker Joanna and Marianne Maculyea had rescued from the clutches of a sadistic drug-enforcer. Living in Bisbee, Angie had achieved a certain kind of respectability, but in

Joanna's dream she had regressed. Standing in front of the church, the lushly voluptuous Angie looked anything but prim. One hip was cocked at a suggestive angle. She looked like a hustler standing on a street corner and waiting for her next trick to show up and make her an offer.

In front of them a smilingly oblivious Marianne Maculyea looked past the bridal party toward the rest of the congregation. "If anyone here present knows of any reason why these two should not be joined in holy matrimony," Marianne intoned, "let them speak now or forever hold their peace."

Behind them, at the far end of the aisle, the church door slammed open. Joanna turned and looked back, but in her dream Canyon Methodist's beautifully varnished mahogany doors had vanished. In their stead, separating the sanctuary from the entryway vestibule, was a shabby swinging door straight out of the Blue Moon Saloon and Lounge in Brewery Gulch, where Angie Kellogg now worked as relief bartender. And in front of the door, posing with his feet apart like some latter-day gun-slinging John Wayne, stood Dick Voland.

"I object," Voland said. "I saw her first and that makes her mine. If anybody here disagrees with that, I'll be happy to meet him outside and settle this man to man."

That was all it took. Butch Dixon turned and strode down the aisle, leaving Joanna standing alone. "Come back," she called after him. "This is stupid. Don't do this." But he just kept on walking. He didn't even look back.

Joanna awakened with a start. One hand, trapped under her cheek, felt as though it were made of wood. As soon as she moved her weight off it, circulation began returning, sending a painful tingling all the way from her fingertips up to her elbow.

Turning over, Joanna glanced at the clock. It said one-thirty. That meant she had been out of it for over four hours. Her clothing was wrinkled. There was a wet spot on the bedspread where she had drooled in her sleep. She was thinking about getting up and maybe making herself something to eat when the phone rang.

"Mrs. Brady?" a voice asked.

That was strange. Joanna wasn't used to being called Mrs. Brady anymore. Most people addressed her as Sheriff. "Yes," she said. "Who's this?"

"Enid Sutton," was the reply. "I'm the principal at Lowell School."

Enid Sutton was new to Bisbee, but Joanna remembered meeting her once at a school open house. She hadn't been particularly impressed one way or the other.

"I'm afraid you're going to have to come pick up your daughter," Mrs. Sutton continued.

"What's wrong? Is Jenny sick? Hurt?"

"She's not hurt, but I am putting her on a three-day suspension."

"Suspension!" Joanna gasped. "What on earth for?"

"For fighting, Mrs. Brady. I've tried to get to the bottom of it. She claims that some of the boys were teasing her at lunch. Apparently it was something about your upcoming marriage. I can certainly understand how a child might feel upset and threatened at having to deal with that sort of thing, but I'm sure you can see my position. We have a zero-tolerance policy when it comes to violence on the school grounds. Jenny bloodied one boy's nose and tore the other one's shirt right off his back."

Drowning in Enid Sutton's words, Joanna closed her eyes and let the guilt wash over her. Once again she had failed her daughter. She had been so busy trying to save the world—trying to rescue people like Lewis Flores and Karen Brainard from their own foolishness—that she had left Jenny, her own precious daughter, vulnerable to attack from none other than the likes of Marliss Shackleford. It wasn't at all a fair contest, and the awful realization of Joanna's own culpability left her shaken.

How could I have done such a thing? she wondered. All it would have taken was a few minutes on her part—a few minutes and a few meager words of explanation to Jenny—and none of this would have happened. Jenny would be sitting in class at the end of her school day instead of being locked up in disgrace in the principal's office.

How could I have been so cowardly and neglectful? Joanna demanded of herself. Instead of giving Jenny what she needed, Joanna had thrown her child to the wolves. It was unthinkable. Inexcusable. And totally unacceptable.

"I'll be right over to get her," a repentant Joanna Brady whispered into the phone. "Tell my daughter I'll be right there."

FIFTEEN

"I'M SORRY, Mom," Jenny said as she climbed into the Blazer. "I know you don't like me fighting, but I couldn't help it. They made me so mad!"

"I'm the one who should be sorry," Joanna returned. "I should have told you that Butch had asked me to marry him, Jenny. I never should have left you hanging like that. You should have heard it from me, and not through some second-hand newspaper story. I meant to tell you about it last night. That's why I wanted just the two of us to go out for pizza—so we could talk. Then the call came in. Rather than make a bad job—a rushed job—of telling you, I decided to wait until a better time."

"You mean it *is* true then?" Jenny demanded.

Joanna nodded. "It's true."

"You and Butch really are getting married?"

"Yes. But Marliss had no business putting it in

278

the paper before we were ready to make an official announcement."

"Why did you tell Marliss before you told me?" Jenny asked.

"I didn't tell her, and neither did Butch."

"How did she find out then?"

Jenny's pointed questions made Joanna feel as though she were in the hands of some trained interrogator. Jennifer Ann Brady would make a hell of a detective someday if that was what she chose to do.

"Grandma Lathrop told her," Joanna explained. "She found out because she rode over on her broom yesterday morning and put the question to Butch. She wanted to know if his intentions were honorable."

"What does that mean?"

"Whether or not he planned to marry me."

"Why?" Jenny asked. "Because he slept over?"

Joanna was taken aback by the perceptiveness behind the question. Once again a well-thought-out talk with her daughter wasn't going at all the way Joanna had intended, but she wasn't prepared to tell any more half-truths, either. "Yes," she said.

"It's my fault then," Jenny said. "I'm the one who told Grandma that Butch was there the other day when she called—the other morning. I didn't mean to. As soon as I did, I could tell it made her mad. Now Grandma thinks Butch has to marry you?"

"Well, yes. Grandma's a little old-fashioned that way."

"But do you want to marry him?" Jenny asked. "I mean, really, really want to?"

Another direct question that deserved an equally direct answer—one that came from the heart. "Yes," Joanna said. "I really do."

Jenny sighed. "All right then, as long as you want to. Just don't do it because Grandma says. She can be pretty bossy, you know."

Joanna laughed outright at that. "I know," she said. "And so can a few other people I could mention."

"You're not mad at me then?" Jenny asked.

"No. I'm not."

"You won't mind if I tell you a secret, then?"

"What's that?"

"I asked Butch if he'd go with me to the Father and Daughter Banquet next week. You know the one. For Scouts. You don't mind, do you?"

In Bisbee the Girl Scouts' annual Father and Daughter Banquet was a traditional affair. After the death of Joanna's father, she and her mother had gone to war over the next scheduled banquet. Eleanor had insisted that Joanna attend alone, and had gone so far as to drive her to the high school and drop her off. Instead of going into the cafeteria, Joanna had bugged out on the festivities, walked for hours in the cold November wind and rain, and had ended up with a case of pneumonia for her pains. Jenny, it seemed, had taken charge of a similar situation in her own fashion.

"No," Joanna replied. "I don't mind at all. Of course not. Why would you think I would?"

"You know," Jenny said. "Because of Daddy. I

was afraid it was too soon. That you'd think I was forgetting him. I didn't want to hurt your feelings."

Joanna reached over and patted Jenny's leg. "My feelings aren't hurt," she said. "I'm thrilled. You must like Butch almost as much as I do. But that doesn't mean we're forgetting Daddy. Or being unfair to him. Okay?"

"Okay," Jenny said. And then, after a pause, "Where are we going?"

"Well, since you're out of school an hour and a half earlier than anyone else will be and earlier than Butch is expecting you, I thought we'd go uptown and see what Marianne is doing. And Ruth, too, if she isn't spending the afternoon at Jeff's garage."

"Don't you have to go back to work now?"

"No," Joanna replied. "It turns out I'm taking the day off, too."

With temperatures in the fifties, the weather was cool and crisp. The sky overhead was a clear cobalt-blue. As Joanna drove up through Old Bisbee, she noticed that the red-and-gray hills, dotted with scrub oak, stood out in stark relief against the distant sky. The contrasts between earth and sky were so sharp that they reminded Joanna of the three-dimensional pictures she remembered from her father's treasured old View Master.

When they pulled up to the parsonage, Joanna was relieved to see Marianne Maculyea's old VW Bug parked out front. It was bad manners to show up unannounced like that, but most of what Joanna wanted to discuss with her friend wasn't telephone-conversation material. In the past few days, telephones had intruded in her life far too much. She craved the comfort of human companionship, of looking someone in the eye and pouring out her heart.

"Run up and knock on the door," Joanna told Jenny. "Ask Marianne if it's all right for us to come in, or would it be better if we came back later?" Jenny clambered out of the Blazer, slamming the door behind her. "And if you can avoid it," Joanna added, "don't tell her what you're doing out of school so early. I want to tell her myself."

"She probably already knows about it, Mom. Doesn't Marianne read the paper?"

Damn Marliss Shackleford anyway!

Jenny bounded up the steps and rang the doorbell. Marianne opened the door, and the two of them spoke briefly before Jenny turned and motioned for Joanna to follow. Then the child disappeared into the house while Marianne waited on the porch.

"Sorry I missed your speech at Kiwanis this morning," Marianne said. "I was feeling so rotten that I told Jeff to go on without me."

"How are you doing now?"

"A little better," Marianne said.

"But not much, from the looks of you," Joanna observed. "Jeff tells me you haven't seen a doctor yet, either."

"Come on in," Marianne said. "Is that all you came by for—to chew me out? Tommy's been out of town on vacation for the last two weeks. He went home to visit his family back in Taiwan.

He's due back tomorrow. I have an appointment scheduled for Friday afternoon."

Tommy was actually Dr. Thomas Lee, a Taiwanese immigrant doctor who had come to Bisbee's Copper Queen Hospital as a way of paying off his medical-school loans. Once the loan obligation was repaid, he could easily have gone elsewhere. Instead, he had decided to make Bisbee his permanent home.

After Jeff and Marianne brought their adopted twins home from mainland China, Dr. Lee had become Esther's primary physician. In the process of caring for the seriously ill child, he had become a close friend—an uncle almost—to the rest of the family. In order to help Ruth stay connected to her roots, he was teaching the family to speak two separate Chinese dialects. He was also helping turn Jeff Daniels into a passable expert in home-cooked Chinese cuisine.

"Well," Joanna said, "that's a relief. I'm surprised he didn't insist on you seeing him long before this."

"I didn't tell him," Marianne said, smiling wanly. "But I thought you'd be glad to hear that I was taking some of your advice, and not just about seeing the doctor, either. I was supposed to do housework today, but I've spent most of the morning working on the Thanksgiving sermon."

The parsonage's once pristine living room was a shambles. Toys, books, and papers were scattered everywhere. The couch was almost invisible beneath a mound of unfolded laundry. On the floor, smack in the middle of the debris field, lay Ruth and Jenny. Frowning in concentration, the two girls were building a structure out of a set of pre-school sized Legos, Joanna and Marianne picked their way through the mess as far as the couch. There they took seats on opposite ends of the couch and heaped the clothing into an even higher mound between them. Once seated and without a word of discussion, they both began folding clothes.

"If you're working on a Thanksgiving sermon," Joanna said, "that must mean you plan to stick around long enough to deliver it. What's the title?"

"'Stop Digging.'"

"'Stop Digging,'" Joanna repeated. "What does that mean?"

"You should know," Marianne said. "You're the one who told me to talk about the black hole. To stop digging is the first rule for getting out of holes."

"You really are taking my advice."

Marianne smiled. "I told you," she said. Glancing at her watch, she frowned. "What's Jenny doing out of school so early? She's not sick, is she?"

"She's been suspended," Joanna replied matter-of-factly. "For fighting. Have you read today's newspaper?"

"The *Bee?*" Marianne asked. "No. I just didn't feel like it. Why? What's in it?"

"Do you happen to have a copy?"

"It's probably still in the box down by the street. I'll go get it."

"No," Joanna said. "Let Jenny."

Minutes later, Joanna unfolded the paper, opened it to the page containing Marliss Shackleford's "*Bisbee* Buzzings" column, and began to read aloud:

A reliable but unnamed source tells us that Co- chise County Sheriff Joanna Brady, a widow, will soon tie the knot with Bisbee newcomer Frederick W. Dixon. Dixon, a former tavern owner, is cur- rently unemployed.

"That witch!" Joanna exclaimed, carefully choosing one word over another because of the listening children playing on the floor. "How dare she say he's unemployed. Butch spends at least four hours every morning working on his book, and he looks after Jenny every afternoon after school. Not only that, he's spent the better part of the last three days taking care of Junior."

"Who's Junior?" Marianne asked. "You didn't adopt another dog or horse, did you?"

Briefly Joanna brought Marianne up-to-date on the Junior dilemma.

"And who's the unnamed source?" Marianne asked, looking at the newspaper column again when Joanna had finished telling the Junior story. "Your mother, I presume?"

Marianne and Joanna's friendship—a relation- ship that dated all the way back to junior high— held very few surprises for either of them.

"You guessed it," Joanna said. "And that's why Jenny got in a fight at school today. Some of the boys were teasing her about my getting married. She didn't think it was true because I hadn't got- ten around to telling her."

Marianne smiled a genuine smile then. "Naturally she beat them up. Given that kind of provocation, I probably would have, too. So it is true then? You and Butch really are getting married?"

"He asked me yesterday," Joanna replied, "and I said yes."

"That's wonderful. Congratulations."

"Thanks. That's one of the two things I came by to discuss with you. If you're going to quit the ministry, you can't do it until at least after the wedding."

"Which is when?"

"I don't know. We haven't had a chance to talk about that yet. I've been too busy."

"And the other thing we need to discuss?" Marianne asked.

"Marliss Shackleford. How do I keep from killing her the next time I see her?"

Marianne glanced toward the children. Jenny and Ruth both seemed totally engrossed in their building project, but Marianne knew better than to trust to appearances. "Maybe we'd better go into the kitchen," she said. "I'll make a fresh pot of coffee."

An hour later, feeling as though an interior pressure valve had been released, Joanna packed up Jenny and headed home. "We'd better stop by Butch's house and let him know you won't be there after school today."

But Butch Dixon wasn't home. Parked in the Outback's spot in his carport was a decrepit bronze Honda.

"Hey, look," Jenny crowed in delight. "The Gs are here. Grandpa's still in the car."

The Gs were Jenny's paternal grandparents, Jim Bob and Eva Lou Brady. For two cents, once Joanna spotted the car, she would have kept right on driving. The possibility of her remarrying was something she had long avoided discussing with her former in-laws. Unfortunately, by the time Joanna saw the Honda, Jim Bob had seen the Blazer as well. He was already climbing out of his car.

"What's the matter?" Jenny asked, glancing at her mother's face. "Aren't you glad to see Grandpa Jim Bob?"

"I'm glad all right," Joanna said, but her voice didn't sound the least bit convincing.

As soon as the Blazer stopped, Jenny shot out of the passenger seat. Jim Bob caught her, scooped her into his arms, and swung her high in the air.

"There's my girl," he said. "How's tricks?"

"I got suspended from school," Jenny replied at once. "For three whole days. I can't go back clear until Wednesday."

"Suspended, eh?" Jim Bob said. "Maybe you'd better come home with me tonight. That way you can tell Grandma and me all about it."

"Can I go, Mom?" Jenny begged. "Can I, please?"

"May I," Joanna corrected automatically. "And yes, I suppose you may."

"And should I tell them about you-know-what?"

While Joanna sent her daughter a withering look, Jim Bob looked questioningly from Jenny to her mother. "Tell us what?" he asked.

"Butch and Mom are going to get married," Jenny blurted. "Marliss Shackleford said so in the paper."

Jim Bob Brady waved one hand as if swatting at a pesky fly. "Oh, that," he said. "All I can say is, it's high time."

And that was all there was to it. Joanna had gone to great lengths to avoid telling Jim Bob and Eva Lou Brady that there was a new man in her life, someone who wasn't their son. And yet, here was Jim Bob accepting the news at face value and giving every indication that not only did he approve but also that he couldn't see why it had taken Joanna so long to make up her mind. He seemed to accept her decision with the same kind of aplomb Jenny had.

Joanna swallowed hard. "You and Eva Lou don't mind then?"

Jim Bob put Jenny down and then gathered Joanna into his arms. "Of course we don't mind, honey bun. Why would we? When Andy was alive, you were the very best wife a man could ask for, but he's gone now. You have the whole rest of your life ahead of you, Joanna. You're young and bright and you deserve some happiness. In fact, I can't think of anyone who deserves it more."

Joanna squeezed her eyes shut to keep the tears from spilling out. "Thank you," she whispered.

Jim Bob pushed away and held her at arm's length. "You're welcome," he grinned. "And congratulations." Then he turned to Jenny. "Come on now, you little hellion. Let's get going. Grandma was putting a batch of corn bread in the oven as I was leaving the house. On the way home you can tell me all about who you were fighting with and how come."

Joanna felt a bit left out. "Wait a minute. You mean to tell me that Eva Lou's making some of her world-famous corn bread and I'm not invited?"

"No, ma'am," Jim Bob said. "Butch called a little while ago and asked if I could come pick Jenny up right after school. He said the two of you had a date tonight—that he was taking you out to dinner."

"He is, is he? Funny he never mentioned it to me," Joanna returned. "Which reminds me, where is he?"

"Said he had a bunch of errands to run. That he wouldn't be able to be here right when school let out. That's why he wanted me to be Johnny-on-the-spot to meet Jenny."

Moments later, Jim Bob loaded Jenny into his Honda Civic, and the two of them drove away. Unexpectedly relieved of her parental responsibilities for the evening, Joanna decided to stop by the department on her way back home. After all, it wouldn't hurt for her to check out what had happened during her absence and try to get a head start on the next day's business.

Pulling into her reserved parking place, Joanna noticed Dick Voland's Bronco parked in its usual place. During her long talk with Marianne Maculyea, Joanna had neglected to mention her conflict with Dick Voland, and she wasn't sure why. Maybe she was ashamed and worried that she herself had somehow, unwittingly, brought on the whole mess. Now, though, seeing his parked car, she knew she would have to face the music. She hadn't brought the situation up in the privacy of Marianne's living room. Now, though, she would have to do so in public.

She paused briefly at her private entrance and thought about letting herself into the office that way. Then she changed her mind. People might think she was so upset by her chief deputy's sudden defection that she was sneaking in and out of her office in hopes of avoiding seeing anyone. No. The only way to handle this was to go in by way of the lobby entrance and simply brazen it out.

Dick had tendered his letter of resignation, and she had accepted. Period. That was all there was to it. And since his letter stated no specific reason for his departure, there was no reason for discussion on Joanna's part, either.

On her way through the lobby, Joanna heard several conversations stop abruptly as she passed by. She also noted several sidelong questioning glances. Stiffening her spine, she smiled, greeted people by name, and marched right on past.

Let 'em talk, she told herself firmly. *All I've got to do is show them it's business as usual. Everything will be fine.*

But everything wasn't fine. In the reception area outside Joanna's office, a red-nosed and tearful Kristin Marsten barely acknowledged Joanna's greeting. "Your messages are on your desk," the overwrought secretary told her boss.

A glance into Dick's office showed that the place had been stripped bare of every personal item. Relieved, Joanna turned back to Kristin. "Did Mr. Voland drop off the keys to his Bronco?"

"Yes, he left them," Kristin snapped back. "Those are on your desk, too. Why don't you go look for once instead of asking me!"

That outburst brought Joanna to a full stop in front of Kristin's desk. Never one to raise her voice when she was angry, she didn't do so now.

"Let's get something straight, Kristin," she said in a voice just barely above a whisper. "Chief Deputy Voland left of his own volition. I did not ask him to leave, but I didn't ask him to stay, either. There are certain basic requirements for working around here, and mutual respect is one of them. If you're not happy with my personnel changes, then you have three choices. One: You can learn to live with them. Two: You can quit. Three: You can ask for a transfer to some other duty station inside the department.

"It's your choice, Kristin," Joanna continued, "but those are the options. Let me warn you, however. If the choice you make is to continue working as my secretary, you'd better be prepared to give me the respect I deserve. Understood?"

Ashen-faced, Kristin nodded bleakly and said nothing.

"All right then," Joanna finished. "I'm going into my office to return some calls. Is Frank Montoya still around?"

"He's in his office."

"Good. Ask him to come see me when he has a minute."

With that, Joanna stalked off. She knew she had lashed out at Kristin, probably harder than the young woman deserved. After all, Kristin had worked with Dick Voland for years, and she obviously liked him. Still, Joanna had to make the point so word would get around. If there were any other die-hard Dick Voland loyalists in the office—and he had worked for the Cochise County Sheriff's Department long enough that there were bound to be some—then those people needed to know exactly how the wind was blowing. Joanna Brady was in charge and she wasn't going to be stepped on. That was the way it was, by God, and she had to let people know!

Dick Voland's keys sat on top of the stack of messages in the middle of her desk. Putting the keys to one side, Joanna sorted through the messages. On her way home from the Kiwanis meeting, when Joanna had decided that she was going home for the day, she had shut off her pager and shifted her cell-phone calls to the office. As a consequence, all of that day's calls had been routed through the office and had been transcribed by Kristin.

Sorting through them was a bit like dealing out a hand of solitaire. There were sixteen in all. Three of them were from Butch. The first one from him contained an invitation to dinner. The second set the time and neglected to tell her where, while the third worried about whether or not she had received either of the first two. Seven were congratulatory calls from people around town who had read about her expected engagement and who were calling to wish Joanna well. Two of the remaining six were from Marliss and two were from Eleanor, with one each from George Winfield and Dr. Fran Daly.

Deciding to return the congratulatory calls later, Joanna set those aside. The messages from Marliss and Eleanor went straight into the circular file under her desk. The calls from the two medical examiners were the only ones she actually tackled.

"Oh, it's you," George said, when he recognized her voice. "When I didn't hear from you, I called Ernie Carpenter. He sent Jaime Carbajal up here to pick up the preliminary report on Mark Childers."

That was Joanna's first hint that Mark Childers hadn't survived the night, but she didn't let on. "So what was it?" she asked.

"Heart attack," Dr. Winfield answered wearily. "His heart was already badly diseased to begin with. And I'm sure the drugs didn't help."

"Drugs?" Joanna repeated.

"You bet. I'll bet Mark Childers was a long-time recreational drug user—cocaine and/or heroin. He was a heart attack waiting to happen. And sitting locked in the dark in a crapper with somebody outside taking pot shots at the door was enough to do him in. I did that one first thing this morning, and just finished up with Flores a little while ago. I'll be sending that paperwork along as well, but since you were right there when it happened, I suppose that one is pretty self-explanatory."

"Right," Joanna said. "But Ernie and Jaime will need a copy all the same."

An awkward pause followed. "I'm sorry as hell about the way things worked out," George Winfield said finally "That bit in the newspaper was ridiculous. I told your mother—well, never mind. Suffice it to say, we've had words about this. She had no right to do that to you, Joanna, or to Butch, either. I've always given Ellie the benefit of the doubt where you were concerned. To hear her tell it, you were always a handful from the day you were born and always a step or two out of line. Now—what can I say?"

He sounded so genuinely upset that Joanna felt sorry for him. "You don't have to say anything, George. It's all right. Butch asked me to marry him and I said yes. That's all there is to it. An item in Marliss Shackleford's column certainly wouldn't be my first choice for letting the world know, but now the word's out, and it's all right."

"Really?"

"Yes."

"Have you talked to your mother then?"

"Not yet." Joanna laughed. "I talk a good game, but maybe not quite that good."

"I understand," George Winfield said with obvious relief. "But do call her as soon as you can. For all our sakes."

"All right," Joanna said. "I will."

As soon as she ended that call, Joanna tried returning Fran's call, only to be told that the assistant medical examiner was unavailable. *Well,* Joanna thought, *it turns out so am I.*

She stood up and started into the lobby to tell Kristin she was leaving. Frank Montoya met her at the lobby door. "For someone who didn't come to work today, you've had yourself quite a day," he observed.

"Is everything under control?" she asked.

"As much as it can be."

"Good. I may not look sick, but I'm having a sick day nonetheless. Since you've done a great job of handling things so far, keep right on doing it. We'll talk about all this tomorrow morning. What do you say?"

"You're the boss," Frank replied. "Tomorrow it is."

✿ SIXTEEN

WITH THAT, Joanna left the office and rushed home, where she showered for the second time that day. This time she worried over her makeup and spent the better part of half an hour trying to get her hair just right. When it came time to dress, she chose with care, settling at last on her pearl-gray suit with an off-white silk blouse. She liked that outfit especially. It made her seem taller, and it showed off her red hair and green eyes to good effect.

Pausing in front of her dresser after spraying on one final spritz of perfume, she opened the top drawer and pulled out a tiny velvet-covered jewel box. She opened it and stared at the contents for some time before dropping the box into her pocket. Minutes later, the dogs' frantic barking announced Butch's arrival.

She hurried out to the car before he had a chance to come inside. "So, Mr. Unemployed," she said, getting into the Outback. "Are you sure you can afford to take me out to dinner?"

Butch grinned at her. "At least Marliss spelled my name right."

Joanna rolled her eyes. "What did you do with Junior?"

"Moe and Daisy Maxwell," Butch answered. "As soon as I told them what kind of a bind I was in, they offered to take him, and I accepted. Besides, Junior knows Daisy and he likes her. She promised him another chocolate shake."

"And where are we going? Not Daisy's, I presume."

"The Rob Roy, of course," Butch said, naming a recently built golf course out near Palominas. The clubhouse contained an upscale dining room that had quickly become one of the hot-spot dining places in all of Cochise County.

"Since I'm a sentimental slob, where else would I take you? After all, that's where we had our first real date. You look beautiful, by the way."

"Thanks," she said.

Their table was in a secluded corner of the elegant dining room. A chilled bottle of Veuve Clicquot was waiting for them when they arrived, as was a beautiful bouquet of roses—a dozen of the delicately colored apricot ones that were Joanna's favorite.

"There's only one thing missing," Butch apologized, as they sipped their first glass of champagne. "I love you. I'm thrilled that you've said yes, regardless of whether or not it was under duress because your mother was holding a gun to our heads. But you were so damned busy today that I couldn't catch up with you long enough to drag you to a jeweler. Which I'm sure I should have. After all, with our engagement already public knowledge, you'd better turn up with a ring pretty damned soon or we'll be in even more trouble."

Joanna fingered the stem of her champagne flute. "Have you priced engagement rings lately?" she asked.

"Well, yes. I have. But I'm fearless," he added. "I'm sure I can handle it."

"What would happen if I told you I already have an engagement ring?"

His face fell. "You don't mean that there's someone else . . ."

Had Butch not been so serious, it might have been comical. Reaching in her pocket, Joanna fished out the tiny box. She flipped it open to reveal the diamond engagement ring that lay inside, then she slid the open box across the table.

For a long moment Butch stared at the ring with its glittering emerald-cut stone. "What's this?" he asked finally.

"Andy gave it to me," Joanna explained. "I never had a diamond before we were married. We couldn't afford it. And with Jenny coming along so soon, we couldn't afford one for a long time afterward, either. Andy bought it for me for our tenth anniversary, but by the time it arrived, he was in the hospital dying. I tried wearing it for a while. But finally I just put it away in a drawer and left it there. Andy gave it to me, Butch, and it was exactly the kind of ring I would have chosen for myself. But it never meant what it was supposed to mean. Or what it can mean now—for us."

"It's very beautiful," Butch said. He was still staring at the ring with downcast eyes.

"Yes, it is," Joanna agreed.

"And you're suggesting that we use this ring— Andy's ring—for our engagement, yours and mine?"

"It was Andy's anniversary present," Joanna said. "It would be our engagement ring. Don't forget, you and Andy are both a part of my life now, Butch. You always will be."

For what seemed an eternity, he continued to stare at the ring. Then, carefully, he pried it out of its velvet-covered bed. When he looked up at her, he was grinning.

"One thing about me, I'm smart enough to know a good deal when I see one. As far as the world is concerned, even though I have money in the bank, I am currently unemployed. It was nice of Marliss to point that out, by the way. So, since Andy already bought this and since I can be pretty well assured that the size is right, once and for all, Joanna Lathrop Brady, will you marry me?"

"Yes, I will," she returned. With that, he slipped the ring on her finger.

Myron Thomas, co-owner of the Rob Roy, had been observing them from a discreet distance. "Bravo, bravo!" he exclaimed. "Let me be the first to congratulate you. What an extraordinarily beautiful ring," he added, as he refilled both their flutes. "Did you choose it all by yourself?"

Myron's question was addressed to Butch, who looked at Joanna and smiled. "No," he said. "I believe you could say we picked it out together."

Dinner passed quickly. They skirted around the when-and-where wedding questions in favor of less difficult subjects, only one of which was Jenny's suspension from school. Joanna would have been content to keep on talking the night away, but at nine o'clock sharp, Butch looked at his watch and signaled for the check. "Daisy has to be in to open the restaurant by five o'clock in the morning. I promised it wouldn't be any later than ten when we stopped by to pick up Junior."

While the waiter headed for the cashier's station, Butch turned back to Joanna. "Which reminds me. We haven't talked about that at all. Did you make any progress on the Junior situation today?"

"No. How could I?"

Butch seemed perplexed. "But we talked about it last night, and I thought—"

"Talked about what?"

"About checking with the authorities in South Dakota."

"Butch," Joanna said. "I have no idea what you mean."

"You don't remember my telling you about Mount Rushmore?"

"Not at all. Are you sure you're not making this up?"

"It was after we went to bed last night. I told

you how there was only one picture in the whole book that got Junior all excited, and that was the one of Mount Rushmore. When Jenny asked him if that's where he lived, he nodded his head up and down and said, 'Home. Home. Home.' He was so excited, I was afraid he was going to pee his pants again. Yesterday it was Junior and his sheriff's badge. Today it was Junior and his book. Whenever anyone came near him, he'd open the book to the Mount Rushmore page and make them look at it."

"You told me all this last night?"

"Yes, and you said you'd call South Dakota today to see if anyone there has reported him missing."

Joanna shook her head. "Sorry, Butch, but I don't remember any of that. I must have dozed off and been talking in my sleep. Which also means that I didn't do a thing about it today. But I will tomorrow. I promise."

They drove back to Bisbee. Moe and Daisy Maxwell lived on Quality Hill uptown in Old Bisbee. When Junior came out to the car, he was wearing his badge and carrying his book, one well-worn page of which he insisted on showing to Joanna. "Home," he announced proudly with one of his wide grins. "Home. Mine."

"Pretty convincing, wouldn't you say?" Butch asked.

"Definitely convincing. Daisy Maxwell is one smart woman."

Behind her, Junior tapped on her shoulder. "Daisy," he said. "Me like."

"Yes, Junior," Joanna agreed. "I like her, too."

Driving around the abandoned black hole that was Lavender Pit Mine, Joanna had a thought. "What time is it?" she asked.

"Nine-thirty. Why?"

"Would you mind making a stop along the way?"

"What kind of a stop?" Butch asked.

"I think we should go by the house and show George and Eleanor the ring."

"What a good idea," Butch said. "That might go a long way toward getting us both out of the dog-house with her. But what do we do with Junior?"

"Take him along in and introduce him," Joanna said. "That'll give Mother something else to talk about the next time she runs into Marliss Shackleford."

Minutes later, they pulled up in front of the house on Campbell Avenue that had been Joanna's home when she was a girl. The porch light was on. A purple glow behind the living room windows showed that the television set was on.

"Joanna!" Eleanor Winfield said when she opened the door. "What are you doing here?"

"Now that I have a ring, I thought you'd want to be among the first to see it."

Joanna held out her hand. Taking it, Eleanor pulled her daughter into the living room and switched on the overhead light. "George," she called over her shoulder. "You have to come look at this. Frederick has given Joanna a ring."

As usual, Eleanor's insistence on using Butch's given name irked Joanna. Eleanor was of the opinion that the name "Butch" wasn't nearly a dignified enough name for a grown man.

"It's beautiful," Eleanor was saying, "although it does look a little like the one Andy gave you. It isn't, of course."

"Of course not," Joanna agreed, and let it go at that.

Butch and Junior stepped inside long enough for Butch to be congratulated and for Junior to be introduced; then they climbed back into the car and drove out to High Lonesome Ranch. "We can come in for a while," Butch offered hopefully.

Joanna looked in the backseat, where Junior was nodding off. "No," she said. "Your charge looks pretty worn out. You'd better get him home and to bed."

Butch shrugged. "You can't blame a guy for asking," he said.

He waited outside in the Subaru until Joanna had unlocked the door and taken the dogs into the house. As the car drove away, Joanna was touched by a feeling of being alone but not necessarily of being lonely. It was a sign that slowly, over time, she was getting better, and that knowledge made her almost giddy. She wanted to call people and tell them what had happened—that she was in love and engaged—but it was too late. It was also too late to return the phone calls of the people who had called her office during the day. She went out to the kitchen, thinking she'd squander some of her excess energy on cleaning up the mess out there. Only the kitchen was spotless. The dishwasher had already been loaded and run. That was the way Butch always left any kitchen—clean and ready to use.

Looking for something to do and hoping for an occupation that would calm her down and help her sleep, Joanna pulled open the briefcase she had brought home the day before and hadn't opened since. There, on top, sat *My Life and Times* by Alice Rogers.

It worked yesterday, Joanna told herself. She had read one chapter and been out like a light. Maybe it would work the same way now. Undressing, she took the book to bed with her. Skimming, Joanna scanned through the rest of Alice Rogers' childhood remembrances. Jessie Monroe was right. The book wasn't written in smoothly flowing prose. Some of the sentences careened dangerously off track without ever coming up with something so simple as a subject and a predicate. Alice's free-form punctuation also made for tough going.

Joanna's eyes were growing heavy when she reached the part where the mine supervisor's headstrong fifteen-year-old daughter met a handsome, fast-talking man-about-town named Calhoun Rogers. The unlikelihood of their pairing was enough that it roused Joanna to attention once more. And then it happened.

When my father could see that Cal and I were determined to get married, he offered Cal a job. I know Daddy could have found Cal a good position with Phelps Dodge. After all, Daddy was the superintendent of the smelter by then. It wouldn't have been any trouble, but Cal didn't want to be

*beholding. He liked being his own boss and doing
his own thing, so we said no and went our own
way. But sometimes now I wish we hadn't done
that and wonder what would have happened if
we had accepted Daddy's offer. For one thing, we
would have had medical insurance and maybe
the company doctors would have caught Cal's diabetes before it got so bad that he had to go and lose
his leg. That's what the doctors said happened.
That it went untreated for so long that by the time
they figured out what was the matter with him a
lot of the damage was already done.*

Joanna finished reading that paragraph and
went on to the next before she realized what she
had read. Diabetes. Wasn't that hereditary? And
if so, who else might be diabetic in the family—
diabetic and a user of insulin? Of course, Joanna
realized with a jolt of excitement. Calhoun Rogers' son, Clete.

She remembered the bad spell he had suffered
up on Houghton Road after Susan arrived and
raised such hell with him. What was it he had
said? Something about having medication in his
truck. She remembered, too, how concerned he
had been that he have food along with him on
the drive to Tucson. That had to be it. Cletus Rogers was an insulin-dependent diabetic, and his
mother may have been murdered with an over-
dose of insulin.

Too excited to sleep, Joanna jumped out of
bed, threw on a robe, and paced the floor. It was
after midnight now—too late to call any of the

detectives involved—too late to try contacting Dr. Fran Daly up in Tucson. No, the only thing to do was to go to bed, try to sleep, and go to work on the whole mess first thing in the morning.

Eventually she did go back to bed and to sleep. Long before her alarm sounded the next morning, Joanna's eyes popped open of their own accord. She was up, dressed, and drinking coffee by the time Clayton Rhodes came to feed the livestock at six. By six-thirty she was on the phone to Fran Daly in Tucson.

"Well," Fran said, "if we aren't a pair of early birds—worms and all. What's got you up and going so bright and early?"

"The insulin," Joanna answered.

"Pharmaceutical companies aren't to be rushed," Fran Daly said. "I spoke to at least half a dozen people yesterday. They all assure me that they should be able to trace the batch number to its distribution point, but so far the computer guru who's supposed to make that happen can't be bothered with returning my calls."

"I think I can help," Joanna said. "Is it possible that Clete Rogers is diabetic?" Breathlessly she went on to explain what she had learned.

"It certainly sounds plausible," Fran said, when Joanna finished. "And with that kind of direction, it shouldn't be too difficult to get the supplier to confirm that the insulin container we found on Alice Rogers' body was actually part of her son's prescription. In fact, the druggist who sold it might even be able to do it."

"What about fingerprints on the vial?" Joanna asked. "It was made out of glass, wasn't it? Shouldn't there have been fingerprints left on it?"

"Probably, as long as the killer didn't use gloves. I sent the vial over to the crime lab," Fran said. "But the results from that don't come back to me. They go directly to the detectives working the case."

"To Hank Lazier, in other words."

"Right," Fran said. "And since he and Tom Hemming are working like hell to extradite those three kids from Mexico, Hank's not going to be ecstatic when you show up with another suspect altogether, along with a whole new theory about what went on."

"Tough," Joanna said. "He'll have to learn to live with it."

Finishing that phone call left Joanna energized and ready to take on the world. She drove into the office and went straight to work. By the time Kristin Marsten and Frank Montoya showed up at eight o'clock, Joanna had already mowed through most of the previous day's correspondence and was starting to return the congratulatory phone calls.

Frank Montoya stuck his head in the door. "Is it safe?" he asked. "Word is out that Her Majesty—meaning you—is lopping off heads right and left."

"Dick Voland quit; I didn't fire him," Joanna said. "And I gave Kristin a clear choice of either shaping up or shipping out. In other words, I don't think you're in any danger of having your head lopped off. Come on in."

"Won't it be boring having our morning briefing without Voland here sniping at us?" Frank asked. "A little like coffee with no cream?"

Joanna gave him a rueful smile. "I'm sure we'll manage. First off, you need to know that I'm engaged to Butch Dixon, and here's the ring to prove it." She waved her hand and flashed the diamond past Frank's face. "That's all I'm saying about it," she continued. "If you receive any questions from the media regarding my engagement, I will expect you to deliver a very firm 'No comment.' Is that clear?"

"Very."

"I've been on the phone to Fran Daly this morning. She's tracking the insulin vial that was found on Alice Rogers' corpse. That trail may lead us straight back to Clete Rogers. Do you happen to know whether or not he's diabetic?"

Frank shook his head. "Nobody's ever talked about specifics, but I do know he's had some long-term health difficulties. I remember Nancy, the hostess at the Grubsteak, making some allusion to it. It probably wouldn't be all that hard to find out. If nothing else, I can ask her."

"Do it," Joanna said. "Also, is there a chance Clete Rogers' fingerprints are on file anywhere?"

"I doubt it. As far as I know, he's never been involved in anything that requires prints. He runs a restaurant, Joanna. It isn't like he's a securities dealer or something."

"Would it be possible for you to get his prints?" Joanna asked. "Casually, of course. I'd want you to do it in a way that wouldn't necessarily arouse suspicion. Maybe you could have him sign some phony-baloney form and then bring the pen back to Casey down in AFIS."

"That shouldn't be too hard," Frank said. "How soon do you want it?"

"ASAP."

"It figures. I'll handle it." Frank paused. "What about Karen Brainard? I understand she resigned from the board of supervisors as of yesterday morning. What, if anything, are we doing about her?"

"I've assigned Ernie Carpenter to the Mark Childers/Lewis Flores cases," Joanna said. "I told Ernie that if he finds any evidence of wrongdoing on her part, we should go after her for it."

Frank raised a questioning eyebrow. "Ernie Carpenter investigating white-collar crime? That's a long way from his usual area of expertise, isn't it?"

"Not that far," Joanna replied. "After all, two men are dead as a direct result of what was happening at Oak Vista. If there were bribes or payoffs involved in that mess, Ernie's going to find them."

"Fair enough," Frank agreed. "Now, tell me. With Dick gone, have you given any thought as to who should be your next Chief Deputy for Operations?"

"As a matter of fact I have," Joanna said. "You're it."

"Really?" Frank Montoya beamed. "Thanks, but who's going to be in charge of Administration, then?"

"You again," Joanna answered. "I've decided that from now on, I'm only going to have one chief deputy, and you're it. That means you'd better find someone to take over the Tombstone marshal job, because I'm not going to be able to spare you. Any ideas?"

"Not right off the bat," Frank said. "I'll have to think about it. I'm sure I'll come up with someone. Anything else?"

"Yes. I want you to get on the phone with authorities in western South Dakota. Check out all the jurisdictions within spitting distance of Mount Rushmore to see if they have a reported missing person whose first name is Junior."

Montoya beamed again. "So my suggestion did work then. I haven't had a chance to see the article yet, but if you've already got results this fast, Marliss must have written a dandy."

"Marliss Shackleford had absolutely nothing to do with it," Joanna replied. "If this pans out, we owe it all to Daisy Maxwell."

"Daisy, over at the café?" Frank marveled. "I had no idea she was a writer."

"She isn't," Joanna answered. "She's just a woman with a whole lot of common sense, which is far more than I can say for Marliss Shackleford. Now then, what about that phone call from the fictitious Detective Garfield?"

"The call came from a pay phone located in North Las Vegas. That's all I've been able to come up with so far."

"And what about the rogue cops, the ones who

went to prison?" Joanna asked. "Do we have any idea where they're incarcerated?"

"Not so far, but I'll check it out. Anything else?"

"Yes. What about yesterday's incident reports? Do you have them?"

"No. I didn't know I was supposed to have them. No one gave them to me."

"That figures. I want you to make an official announcement about the change in personnel. We'll need to issue a statement to the media saying that Dick Voland has resigned for personal reasons and announcing that from now on the department will have only one chief deputy. We'll also need to let people inside the department know that those incident reports are to be routed to you from now on. Once you have them in hand and have a chance to go over them, come back and we'll finish up."

Frank had been making notes all along. Now he stopped. "What's the real story behind Dick's leaving?" he asked. "One minute the man is his usual charming self, throwing his weight around and giving people all kinds of grief. The next minute his office is empty and he's out of here. What's going on?"

Joanna had planned to keep her personal problems with Dick Voland strictly to herself, but Frank Montoya deserved a straight answer. "This is for your information only," Joanna said, "and it's not to leave this room. But it seems Dick Voland had some mistaken ideas about the relationship between us, some seriously mistaken ideas."

"You're kidding! As in romantic ideas?"

"That's right."

"What made him think that?" Frank asked. "He's got to be a good fifteen years older than you are. In fact, I'm a lot closer to your age than he is."

"Don't *you* go getting any weird ideas." Joanna grinned at him. "Otherwise, I'll be running this department with no chief deputy at all."

Frank Montoya jumped out of his chair. "Yes, ma'am," he said, grinning back. "Forget I even mentioned it. I'm sure Dick has plenty of time in grade, so he can afford to retire. Not me. I'm too young."

"Get out of here then," Joanna told him. "I've got work to do, and so do you."

Seconds after Frank returned to the lobby, Kristin entered Joanna's office. She slapped a pile of mail down on the edge of Joanna's desk. Next to the stack of mail she placed a cup of coffee.

Joanna looked up at Kristin. "Does that constitute a peace offering?" Joanna asked.

Without looking her boss in the eye, Kristin shrugged. "I guess," she said.

"Does that mean you've decided you want to keep working here—that you want to continue being my secretary?"

"Yes."

"Good, then," Joanna said. "I'm glad to hear it, and thanks for the coffee."

SEVENTEEN

AS SOON as Kristin had left her office, Joanna picked up the phone and dialed Butch. "How's it going?" she asked when he answered.

"Slowly," he replied. "Very slowly. Junior slept so much in the car that by the time we made it home, he was wide awake and wired. Now he's asleep again, and I wish I were, too. But I've got to get going today. I've spent days without touching my computer, and it's time to get back on the horse. If I'm ever going to finish my book, I've got to sit down and work. Otherwise, I'm going to remain what Marliss Shackleford calls unemployed forever. The word's out that unpublished novelists are worth a dime a dozen."

Joanna had worried that leaving Junior with Butch was imposing on the man's good nature. Now she felt certain those worries were justified. Junior's presence was most likely exacerbating an already raging case of writer's block.

"Maybe I could bring Junior to the office for the day," she suggested. "He'd probably get a kick out of it. At least it would give you some time to work."

"He'd get a kick out of it right up until you got called out on a case," Butch replied, "on something where he couldn't go along. He'd end up being stuck in your office all by himself. No, that's already happened to him once, and it's not going to happen again, not if I can help it."

"Speaking of that," Joanna said, "you'll be happy to know that Frank Montoya is tracking the South Dakota connection."

"Good."

"And I'm sitting here admiring my ring," she continued. "I still can't quite believe it, Butch. I said 'yes.' We are actually engaged."

"I'll believe it more when I can corral you into setting a date," Butch replied. "But don't get me wrong," he added quickly. "I'm not pushing."

Joanna laughed. "The hell you're not. I'm going to work now. You do the same. I'll let you know the second Frank hears something."

Without even putting down the phone, Joanna dialed her in-laws. When Eva Lou Brady answered the phone, Joanna had to pause momentarily and gather her nerve before she spoke. "Good morning," she said.

"Good morning yourself," Eva Lou returned. "How are you today?"

"Engaged," Joanna said with a gulp. She had already sampled Jim Bob's reaction, but Eva Lou was Andy's mother. Would she manage the same kind of grace and generosity in the face of what she might well regard as her daughter-in-law's defection?

"Did you think I didn't know? Jim Bob and I had already discussed it with Jenny, and then Eleanor was on the phone to us last night, probably before the door closed behind you. I'm pleased at the news, Joanna, pleased for all of you. I really am. It means that Jenny's going to have a daddy after all. From the sound of things, I think she needs one. Maybe Butch will be able to teach her not to fight all the time. Eleanor is all bent out of shape because she doesn't think fighting is ladylike, which, of course, it isn't. I'm more worried that one of these times Jenny's going to pick a fight with the wrong bully and end up getting hurt."

Now that word was out, Joanna breathed a little easier. "Speaking of the little truant, how is she this morning?"

"Fine as frog's hair. She and Jim Bob are out back raking leaves."

"Has she told you about Junior?" Joanna asked.

"She certainly has. Bubbling over with it. She seems to like him a lot. And it's so nice of Butch to lend a hand that way. Most men wouldn't."

"But it is keeping him from doing any of his own work," Joanna said. "And I was wondering if . . ."

"If we'd take him for a while?" Eva Lou asked. "Of course. I know Jenny gets bored hanging around with just us old folks. And with all the kids in school . . ."

"I believe that's the whole idea of a school suspension," Joanna observed. "She's supposed to be bored. And miserable."

"Well, I still think having Junior for the day will be fine. I'll call Butch a little later and make arrangements. Come to think of it, maybe the whole bunch of you could come to supper tonight. I might even ask George and Eleanor. We could have a little engagement celebration. It'll give me a chance to see your ring."

Joanna's breath caught. She had been able to pass off the ring as new with her own mother, but not with Andy's. "You've already seen it, Eva Lou," Joanna said quietly. "It's the same one Andy gave me for our anniversary, just before he died. Since I already have a ring that I love, it just didn't make sense to have to go out and buy another one."

"What a perfectly lovely thing to do," Eva Lou said at once. "I know Andy paid an armload for that ring. Of course I understood why you put it away, but it seemed like such a waste to me to have a beautiful piece of jewelry like that hidden away in a dresser drawer. This makes far better sense."

"You don't mind then?" Joanna asked. "You don't think I'm being disloyal to Andy's memory?"

"Disloyal? The only way you could be disloyal to Andy, Joanna, is to not go on with your own life. He loved you. All he ever wanted was for you and Jenny to be happy. If Butch Dixon makes you happy, he's exactly what Andy would want for you too. And he'd be delighted that you didn't have to go out and spend money on a ring when you already had one that was bought and paid for."

"Thank you for saying that," Joanna murmured. "Thank you so much."

"Don't mention it," Eva Lou said. "I'm hanging up now. I need to call Butch and let him know about dinner. I'll also find out when he wants Jim Bob and Jenny to come by and pick up Junior."

"One more thing," Joanna said hurriedly before Eva Lou could hang up.

"What's that?"

"Don't tell my mother where the ring came from. She'll never understand."

"She'll never know then, will she?" Eva Lou said. "At least not from me."

Holding the receiver after ending that call, Joanna knew there was one more that she needed to make. It was after nine by then—time enough for Hank Lazier to have shown up at his office in the Pima County Sheriff's Department.

"Joanna Brady here," she said when he answered.

There was a noticeable chill in his voice when he replied. "To what do I owe the pleasure?"

Pleasure, my foot! Joanna thought. Knowing there was no love lost between them, she dispensed with the usual pleasantries. "I'm calling about the crime lab results," she said briskly. "Any hits on the fingerprints from the insulin vial?"

"None," he replied.

"You ran them through AFIS?"

"Sure did."

That meant Farley Adams' prints weren't there, because they would have come up with a hit. That also held true for the three young men still sitting in the Nogales, Sonora, jail, as well as for Joaquin Morales, the boy who had aided searchers in finding Alice Rogers' body.

Sitting on his end of the telephone line, Detective Lazier must have been reading Joanna's thoughts. "The lack of fingerprints means nothing," he said. "When we searched the Buick, we didn't find any gloves, but they could have used them and then ditched them somewhere between Houghton Road and Nogales."

"It could mean they didn't do it," Joanna pointed out. "It could mean you and Detective Hemming are barking up the wrong tree."

"Right this minute, Detective Hemming is out tracking down some search warrants." Lazier told her. "We've ID'd the three suspects now and we'll be executing those warrants as soon as we have them. In the meantime, stop sticking your nose in where it isn't wanted or needed."

"You have a nice day, too," Joanna returned pleasantly. But it was too late. By then Hank Lazier had already slammed the phone down in her ear.

Joanna's first and second cups of coffee disappeared along with the stack of mail. Next, Joanna went to work on the duty rosters. As she tried in vain to make sense of the complicated graph Dick Voland had devised to create shift schedules,

Kristin buzzed Joanna's intercom. "Someone to see you, Sheriff Brady," she announced.

"Who is it?"

"Monica Childers," Kristin said. "She's Mark Childers' wife."

Widow, Joanna thought. She said, "Ernie Carpenter is in charge of that case. I'm sure he's the one she needs to see."

"I told her that already," Kristin said. "She insists on seeing you."

"All right," Joanna agreed, shoving the graph aside. "Send her in."

The door to Joanna's office swung open and a tall woman strode into the room. At nearly six feet, Monica Childers was an imposing yet slim forty-five-year-old with fair skin and startlingly blue eyes. Her gray hair was cut short enough to resemble a crew cut. She was wearing jeans, a flannel work shirt with the sleeves rolled up to her elbows, and a pair of dusty work boots. She stopped in front of Joanna's desk.

"How long is that detective of yours going to keep us shut down?" Monica demanded.

"Pardon me?" Joanna asked. "I'm not sure I understand what's going on."

"That makes two of us," Monica said. Uninvited, she sank into a chair. "My work crew showed up this morning. A deputy met them at the gate and sent them packing, which means I have to pay at least an hour's worth of show-up time, even though I didn't get a lick of work out of them. The deputy claimed your office isn't finished investigating yet. Lewis Flores shot Mark and then he shot himself. They're both dead. This isn't rocket science, Sheriff Brady. How much investigation can it take?"

"You're talking about the Oak Vista work crew?"

"Of course. What else?"

"First off, your husband wasn't shot. He died of a heart attack. And secondly, investigations take as long as they take. When it comes to crime scenes, I encourage my people to take all the time they need."

"Whatever," Monica said dismissively. "All I know is, two of the Porta Potties are plugged full of holes. If the detectives need to, have them pack 'em up, put 'em on a flatbed, and haul them away to wherever you take stuff to hold as evidence. But let my crew come back to work. We lost all of yesterday, and now today, too. I can't afford it, Sheriff Brady. Delays like this are going to throw the whole project behind schedule."

"Mrs. Childers, does this mean that you're taking over as project manager in place of your husband?"

"Ex-husband," Monica Childers corrected. "Or at least he would have been ex in a matter of weeks. And you're damned right I'm taking over. It was my father's company long before it was Mark's. I watched Daddy run it for twenty-five years, but he wasn't willing to leave it to me. No, it was sort of like that lady at the *Washington Post*— the one whose father turned the newspaper over to her husband even though she had worked there for years. The same thing happened to me.

"Before Mark came along, I spent fifteen years handling the books and doing the paperwork for Foster Construction. But when the time came for my father to bow out of the business, he was far more willing to hand the company over to my husband than to me. The two of them put my name on the paperwork, but only when affirmative action came along and they thought that would help corner the market on some of those minority contracts. That was back in the old days, of course, when we were still struggling. Once things really started to click and Mark didn't need me anymore, he went looking for greener pastures. Ever since then, he's been doing his best to cheat me out of what's rightfully mine."

"When you say greener pastures, do you mean someone like Karen Brainard?" Joanna asked.

"Meaning any number of Karen Brainards," Monica Childers replied bitterly. "A whole string of them. When we got married, I was considered a 'trophy wife.' Over the years, Mark worked his way down the food chain. Karen wouldn't even qualify as a brass plaque. If I'd had guts enough, I would have taken a potshot at the man myself. But now that Lewis Flores has done my dirty work for me, I intend to make the most of it. Mark swore he was going to make a ton of money out of the Oak Vista project. All he would have owed me is whatever pittance Dena could have wrangled out of the property settlement. Now I end up with the whole shebang."

"Dena?" Joanna interrupted. "Do you mean Dena Hogan, by any chance?"

"Yes," Monica answered. "She's my attorney. The one who was handling my divorce. Do you know her?"

"Not personally," Joanna said. "But I've heard the name. Go on."

"She's a good friend of mine. We went to school together. Anyway, luckily for me, the divorce wasn't final yet, which means that now the company passes to me right along with the ongoing projects, Oak Vista included. Believe me, I intend to make it work. I'm also going to meet those deadlines if it kills me. The first models are due to be open by the middle of January. I intend to see to it that they are."

"Mrs. Childers," Joanna began.

"Call me Monica Foster," the other woman corrected. "I'm done with being Monica Childers. I've decided to go back to using my maiden name."

"Ms. Foster then," Joanna corrected. "I can see why you'd be eager to get the Oak Vista project back under way, but there are certain investigative steps that must be taken. Furthermore, I'm not sure you're aware of what all happened out at the construction site in the past few days. There were protesters—"

"I know all about the protesters," Monica interjected. "They won't be back."

"I don't know how you can be sure of that. Just because your husband—your former husband—is dead doesn't mean the protesters won't make trouble for you."

"They'll stop all right," Monica Foster said confidently. "I just won't pay them anymore. Not one of them is so committed to saving the world that he'll show up for nothing."

"Wait a minute," Joanna said. "You mean you're the one who was paying them?"

"Who else?" Monica returned. "I was prepared to do anything that would make Mark's life miserable. Having protesters screw up and delay his project was the least I could do. Now that it's my project, however, protesters are no longer necessary and delays aren't acceptable."

Joanna crossed her arms. "What's unacceptable is faking protests and deliberately creating situations where my officers could have been in danger," Joanna shot back. "My department had to pull patrol officers away from other sectors in order to deal with what was going on at Oak Vista. That left whole areas of the county without any law enforcement coverage at all. Not only that, your husband's attorney called yesterday and said they would be suing my department for negligence due to the damage caused by the alleged protesters."

"Things did get a little out of hand," Monica Childers admitted. "Some of my hired help may have been a bit too enthusiastic. But believe me, there won't be any lawsuit. All I want to know is when my crew will be able to go back to work."

"The plain answer is, I don't know," Joanna said. "And I'm not about to give you the go-ahead without checking with my detectives first. And speaking of your work crew, that reminds me. I was out at your job site the other day and had a run-in with one of your workers—a fellow by the name of Rob Evans. He came to work armed. In fact, I'm holding his twenty-two revolver right here in my desk. I told him he can have it back as soon as he shows up with either a holster to carry it in or else a concealed-weapons permit. So far he hasn't turned up with either one."

"I wouldn't hold my breath if I were you," Monica observed. "For him to come pick it up, I mean."

"Why not?"

"Because he's long gone. I fired his ass. First thing yesterday morning. In fact, that was my first official duty upon assuming command. I can't tell you how much pleasure it gave me."

"Why?" Joanna asked.

"Why did I fire him or why did it give me such pleasure?"

"Both," Joanna said.

"Rob was a jerk," Monica replied, "and no more of a construction foreman than my Aunt Betsy. He never should have been given that job in the first place."

"Why was he?"

"Probably as a favor to one of Mark's drug-dealing cronies. That would be my first guess anyway."

"So you knew about the drugs?"

"I knew about all of it," Monica returned darkly. "I made it my business to find out. That worm thought he was just going to dump me and walk away whole, taking the contracting company and the development companies with him. He thought Sierra Vista was a small enough town that I'd just shut up, go quietly, and spare myself the humiliation. He thought I'd be too embarrassed to stand up and fight. When he found out otherwise, it must have come as a bit of a shock."

"How did you do that?"

"Fight him?" Monica shrugged. "My attorney hired a PI to get the goods on him and his collection of heroin-sniffing honeys. And she subpoenaed all his financial records. By the time we were scheduled to go to court, Dena swore she would know more about Mark's financial dealings than he did himself."

Joanna was still trying to listen, but she found herself hung up on one particular word. "Did you say heroin-sniffing?" she asked.

Monica gave a short, mirthless laugh. "You don't think Mark would inject the filthy stuff, do you? Into his beautiful body? None of them do. They're all far too good-looking for that. And too upstanding. They're all part of the country-club set. They may party like hell on Friday and Saturday, but they shape up and go to church on Sundays, attend Rotary on Tuesdays, and show up for their Chamber of Commerce meeting first thing Wednesday mornings. Needle tracks wouldn't go over very well with the Chamber of Commerce. So they import top-quality Mexican heroin— pure stuff—and sniff it the way some people used to sniff cocaine. It took me a long time to figure out that a big chunk of our money was going straight up Mark's nose. Call me a slow learner, but I finally wised up."

When Monica Foster fell silent, Joanna Brady stayed that way. She had been in several filthy and impoverished crack houses. She had donned Haz-Mat gear to walk through the moldering ruins of a mobile home turned meth-lab. For her, drug addicts existed in a lawless, shadowy, and poverty-stricken world. She didn't want to hear that Cochise County harbored an invisible collection of high-flying, well-connected heroin users. That unwelcome news was enough to leave her shaken.

"Can you give me names?" Joanna asked at last.

"I can't," Monica answered. "I wasn't part of the gang. Karen Brainard was."

"You're saying Karen Brainard uses heroin?"

"Why don't you ask her? In fact, I'm tempted to ask her myself. Poor baby. She and Mark were an item for a good six months. I'd guess she's pretty broken up about now."

"Which you're not," Joanna observed.

Monica Foster's bright blue eyes hardened to flint. "No, I'm not," she agreed. "I did my grieving a long time ago—*before* I filed for a divorce. Back then I kept hoping something would happen so I wouldn't have to go through with it. Maybe Mark would die, or else I would. And now that he's dead, I don't feel anything but alive, goddammit! I'm alive and getting on with my life and nobody's going to stand in my way! Which brings me back to why I came to see you this morning, Sheriff Brady. I need to know what to tell my crew. Should they come to work tomorrow morning or not?"

"As I said," Joanna assured her. "I have to check with my detective first. As soon as I do, I'll get back to you. Can you leave me a number?"

Reaching out, Monica Foster snagged a yellow Post-it pad from Joanna's desk and scribbled a series of phone numbers on it—home, work, and cell phone.

"What about your husband's financial records, the ones your attorney has?" Joanna asked. "Before Lewis Flores killed himself, he claimed that your husband—your soon-to-be former husband—and Karen Brainard were mixed up in some kind of payoff scheme. I don't know whether or not any money actually changed hands. If we could get a look at his records, we might be able to—"

"Talk to Dena," Monica said. "I'll put her number down here too. Tell her I told you to see her."

"Because of attorney-client privilege, she may not agree to talk with me," Joanna said.

"I don't see why not," Monica said. "I haven't committed any crime, and I don't have anything to hide. And Mark is dead, so it shouldn't matter to him. But if she needs my permission to release the records, she can always call me and check."

Monica pushed the notepad filled with phone numbers across the desk to Joanna, then she stood up. "I guess I'll be going then," she said.

"No," Joanna said. "Wait just a minute." Since

Monica Foster seemed more than willing to help, Joanna decided to try returning the favor.

She picked up the phone. "Kristin," she said. "Have Dispatch put me through to Ernie Carpenter."

Smiling slightly, Monica Foster settled back in her chair. It took several long minutes before Ernie Carpenter finally came on the line. "What's up?" he asked.

"How long before you'll be ready to release the crime scene at Oak Vista? Monica Foster, Mark Childers' widow, is here in my office. She needs to know when her construction crew can get back to work."

"Her again!" Ernie exclaimed. "That woman's nothing but trouble. She was out here this morning raising hell with the deputy I left at the gate. I told her these things take time, but obviously she's gone over my head and is raising hell with you."

"In a manner of speaking," Joanna said. "But she's also given us some important information. If her permits are all in order, I think we should cut her some slack."

"All right, all right. We're pretty much finished up now. Tell her she can have her work crew in here first thing tomorrow morning."

"If you're almost finished now, why does she have to wait until tomorrow?" Joanna asked.

"Well," Ernie said. "To tell you the truth, I was hoping to hang around long enough to see if we could get another shot at those damned tree-huggers. If I were in their shoes and wanted to damage a whole bunch of construction equipment, this is exactly the time I'd show up—when no one is here working."

"I don't think you need to worry about that," Joanna said. "I'm relatively sure the demonstrators won't be back."

"What are they doing, broadcasting their scheduled stops on NPR?"

Joanna laughed. "I think we've got a case of domestic environmentalists."

"No news there. Whoever said they were foreigners?"

"Not that kind of domestic, Ernie. As in hotly contested D-I-V-O-R-C-E. I have it on good authority that the Oak Vista tree-huggers-for-hire were on Childers' ex-wife's payroll. Now that she's running the company, she's called off the dogs." Joanna glanced at Monica Foster, who nodded.

"Nice lady," Ernie observed. "That being the case, I suppose we can release the crime scene anytime. By the way, was Lewis Flores on her payroll, too?"

"I don't think so, but we'll talk more about that later," Joanna said. "In fact, I'll probably be out that way before long. Where will you be?"

"When I leave here, Jaime and I had planned to rendezvous at Clete Rogers' place in Tombstone at noon to finish up our paperwork and figure out what the hell to do next."

"Sounds like a good idea," Joanna said. "Maybe I'll join you. Then we'll all be able to get a handle on what's going on."

Joanna put down the phone and turned back

to Monica Foster. "Your crew will be able to go back to work this afternoon—if you can find them, that is."

"I can locate most of them," Monica said, as she stood to leave. "Thank you. I appreciate it."

"Thank you, too," Joanna returned. "You've been a big help. We'll be in touch with your attorney and with Karen Brainard as well."

At the mention of Karen Brainard's name, Monica winced visibly. "Maybe I should send the bitch a sympathy card."

There was a catch in the woman's throat when she said the words. The sound of it was enough to make Joanna realize that underneath all of Monica Foster's hard-nosed bravado was a soft center of residual hurt. Monica may have been divorcing Mark Childers, but she was a long way from being over him. And despite the fact that Joanna was still angry by the trouble caused by Monica Foster's hired protesters, she couldn't help feeling sorry for her.

"Let it go," Joanna advised. "Who's doing the funeral arrangements?"

"Wetherby's out in Sierra Vista," Monica replied. "They handled both my folks' funerals. I know they'll do a good job."

In other words, Monica still cared enough to send the very best—to want her philandering husband's funeral arrangements to be dignified.

"I'm sorry," Joanna said. "This must be terribly painful for you."

For the first time, Monica Foster softened. Her

eyes welled with tears. "It is," she said. "It hurts like hell." And then she was gone.

As soon as Joanna was left alone, she picked up the phone and dialed Dena Hogan's number. A receptionist answered. "Dena Hogan, Attorney at Law."

"This is Joanna Brady, Sheriff Joanna Brady," Joanna said. "I was wondering if it would be possible for me to see Ms. Hogan early this afternoon. Say between one-thirty and two?"

"Sure," the receptionist said. "I can pencil you in, but I don't have access to her official calendar. There could be a conflict that I don't know about."

"That's all right," Joanna said. "Since I'm coming out that direction anyway, I can afford to take my chances."

Just then Joanna's call waiting sounded, telling her there was another caller on the line. "Hello."

"Joanna? Fran Daly here. I hope I'm not interrupting anything."

"No. What's going on?"

"I just had a call back from Al Paxton, the computer nerd at Holloway/Rimblatt Pharmaceuticals."

"And?"

"We are, if you'll pardon the expression, a couple of smart cookies. That particular numbered batch of insulin went first to a distributor in L.A. who ships to drugstores all over the Southwest. From there it went to the O.K. Pharmacy in Tombstone, Arizona, where Cletus Rogers just happens to have his insulin prescription filled on a regular basis."

"How very interesting," Joanna said. "I'll have one of my detectives go have a chat with Hizzoner the Mayor. Do you suppose Detective Lazier would be interested in being in on that interview?"

"Wait just a minute," Fran Daly complained. "I no sooner finish telling you you're smart when you start acting like a complete fool. You don't mean that, do you?"

"No, I don't mean it at all," Joanna said with a laugh. "I was just checking to see if it would get a rise out of you. And it worked."

"I'll say," Fran agreed. "That man bugs the daylights out of me. Don't you dare invite him along."

"Believe me," Joanna said. "I wouldn't think of it."

EIGHTEEN

IT WAS high noon when Joanna stepped through the swinging doors into the dim and shabby interior of Clete Rogers' Grubsteak. The bottle-blond hostess, looking nervous and out of sorts, led Joanna to a table for four, where Jaime Carbajal and Ernie Carpenter were already waiting. Considering the relative distances involved, Joanna should have beaten Ernie there by a good ten minutes. Around the department, the detective was sometimes called "Lead-foot Carpenter," and for good reason.

"I can see Ernie didn't let any grass grow under his steel-belted radials," she said pointedly as she sat down.

"When the boss offers to meet for lunch, I figure it must be important," Ernie countered.

"Important," Joanna agreed, picking up her menu. "But not a matter of life-and-death."

Nancy returned to the table and sloshed a

brimming coffee mug onto the table in front of Joanna.

"Is the mayor around?" Joanna asked.

The hostess responded with a narrow-eyed glare. "Mr. Rogers wasn't here five minutes ago, when he asked," Nancy said, jerking her head in Jaime Carbajal's direction. "And he still isn't."

With that the hostess turned and flounced away from the table.

"What's the matter with her?" Joanna asked.

Jaime shrugged. "Who knows? I asked about Clete when I first showed up, and the woman nearly bit my head off."

Whoever had designed the menu for the Grubsteak had been cute enough to create entrée items with names that matched a selection of local mining claims. When the waitress came around with her pad, Joanna ordered a Lucky Cuss hamburger and coffee. Jaime settled for the Tough Nut steak sandwich, while Ernie decided on a bowl of Contention stew. When the food came, Joanna's hamburger and Ernie's stew were both fine, but from all the knife-sawing and necessary chewing, it was clear the steak in Jaime's Tough Nut sandwich lived up to its name.

During the course of the meal, Joanna had to endure some good-natured ribbing about her "doorknob" diamond, followed by a discussion of Dick Voland's abrupt departure. Later on, Joanna brought the two detectives up-to-date with everything she had learned that morning, and they did the same. Susan Jenkins had turned up for the inventory meeting at Alice Rogers' house, but Clete hadn't appeared. Susan had verified that Alice's television set and a VCR were missing along with several pieces of antique jewelry. In view of Clete's possible involvement in his mother's death, his failure to show up for the inventory seemed far more ominous.

Ernie pushed back his chair. "I suppose we'd better get with it. Do one of you want to ask the lady where Clete Rogers is, or should I?"

"You go right ahead," Jaime said with a smile. "I believe in taking turns. This Bud's for you."

The third time around, Nancy's reaction was downright explosive. "What the hell's the matter with you people? I've already told you, Clete isn't here!"

"How about telling us where he is then?" Ernie prodded gently. "It's about his mother, you see. That's why we need to talk to him."

To Joanna's surprise, Nancy immediately collapsed onto the fourth chair at their table, buried her face in her hands, and then sobbed into them. "That's just it," she wailed. "I don't know *where* he is! I haven't seen him all morning. He's usually here when we open for breakfast. I've called the house at least a dozen times now, but he doesn't answer. I even went over there looking for him. His car's there, but he isn't. Or, if he is, he wouldn't come to the door.

"I'm scared to death something awful has happened to him. I thought about breaking the window in the door and letting myself in to see. But the thing is, if nothing's wrong, he'll be furious. He hates it when I fuss over him or when I do something he calls fussing. But what if he's passed out, or even worse? What if he forgot to take his medicine?"

"His insulin?" Joanna asked, innocently.

"Yes. His insulin. Ever since that business with his mother, he's been so upset that his whole system has been out of whack. He hasn't been able to stabilize his blood sugar. What if he forgot to give himself an injection and he's gone into a diabetic coma or something? Or maybe he got mixed up and gave himself too much. Either way, it could be bad for him—real bad. I know he'll be all bent out of shape with me for telling on him like this, especially if it turns out to be a false alarm. He hates it when people treat him like an invalid. But you people are all cops, aren't you? If you break into his house to check on him, it'll be all right. It's not like you'd be going in to steal something. I just want to know that he's okay."

When Nancy finally stopped talking long enough to draw a breath, Joanna and Ernie exchanged discreet glances. The last thing they needed was to enter a prime suspect's home without the benefit of a search warrant. Here in the restaurant, with a tearful Nancy begging them to go check on her boss's well-being, the idea of breaking and entering seemed perfectly reasonable—necessary, even. But Joanna knew that if Clete Rogers was ever brought to trial for his mother's death, even the most dim-witted of defense attorneys would be able to make hay out of what would then be considered an illegal search.

"What do you think?" Ernie asked.

It was a tough call. On the one hand, a man's life might be at stake. On the other, a conviction. "We'd better go check," Joanna said. "In and out. In the meantime, Jaime, how about if you streak back to Bisbee and pick up a search warrant. Just in case."

Ten minutes later they were standing in front of Clete Rogers' modest tin-roofed house. It was a white clapboard affair that clearly dated from Tombstone's mining heyday. On three sides the house was surrounded by a thicket of agave. Some of the cacti had done their century plant performance, leaving behind long skeletal stalks that still held shriveled and blackened seed pods while all around a new generation of tiny plants sprouted from the hardened earth.

Seeing the dying cacti gave Joanna a weird feeling, as did spotting Clete Rogers' much-dented F-100 Ford. The pickup, parked almost out of sight in a narrow-faced, one-car detached garage, had a forlorn, abandoned air about it.

Joanna and Ernie stepped up onto the porch and Ernie knocked on the front door. It was an old-fashioned piece of antique craftsmanship with a glass window at the top. Etched into the window was a magnificent stag, standing on a promontory in the middle of a forested glade.

Joanna and Ernie waited for several long moments before Ernie knocked a second time. This time, the old door shuddered under the force of his blows. Still no one answered.

"I guess we'd better break it," Ernie said.

"Let's try the back door," Joanna suggested.

"This one looks too much like a valuable antique for my taste."

The back of the house contained a shaky but fully enclosed utility porch. The door with its horizontal panels dated from the same era as the one at the front of the house, but here the etched glass had long since been replaced by a single pane of ordinary window glass.

"Break away," she told Ernie. "At least this one won't cost as much when it comes time to replace it."

Seconds after shattering the glass, Ernie unfastened the inside latch, opened the door, and let Joanna into the house. "Hello," she called. "Anybody home?" But there was no answer.

With Joanna leading the way, they walked through the makeshift laundry room that had once been a back porch and on into the kitchen and living room. The whole house couldn't have been more than eight hundred square feet. The tiny rooms all had the enormously high ceilings of houses built before the age of air-conditioning. The furnishings were threadbare, but everything about the place—from the worn linoleum to the brass push-button light socket—was spotlessly clean. Joanna had expected typical bachelor-pad debris—with clothing and trash littering the floor and with dirty dishes stacked on the counters and attracting bugs in the sink. She had visited several pits like that during her tenure as sheriff. It surprised her a little to see that Cletus Rogers didn't play to type.

While Joanna stood in the middle of the living room peering around, Ernie disappeared into what was evidently a bedroom. "Hey, boss," he called. "I think you'd better come take a look at this."

The bedroom was crammed with furniture. Not only did it contain a bed, a huge mirrored dresser, and a nightstand, it also held a frail cherry-wood dining room table that evidently functioned as a desk. Here there were papers—neatly stacked and/ or assigned to folders. In the middle of the desk sat a computer, an old desktop model that looked old-fashioned and clunky even to Joanna.

"What?" she asked.

"Come around here and look. The screen's so bad that you'll have to stand directly in front of it before you'll be able to read it."

Joanna squeezed her way between the table and the foot of the bed until she was standing beside Ernie. From that vantage point she could read the only two words printed on the sickly-green screen. "I'm sorry."

"Sorry for what?" Joanna asked.

"Doesn't say."

"What does that sound like to you?" Joanna asked.

"Well," Ernie said. "Taken with our suspicions about what happened to Alice Rogers, my guess would be it's the beginning of a suicide note. Or else it's a complete suicide note."

"That's what I'm thinking," Joanna agreed. "And since his car is here, he didn't go far. Let's go check the garage."

The pickup was not only unlocked, it was also empty. The single-car garage, most likely built in the era of the Model Ts, was too small for the whole of the truck to fit inside. Only the front hood and fender nosed into the garage's darkened interior. At the front of the garage the two officers found a series of wooden shelves, sagging under burdens of neatly labeled boxes and paint cans. Paint and boxes, but no sign of the missing Cletus Rogers.

Back out in the yard, Joanna and Ernie made their way around the whole of the agave hedge, but there was no sign of a body there and no hint that anything had been disturbed. Once back in the front yard, Joanna stopped and looked back. "I think it's time to call in Search and Rescue," she said.

"Good," Ernie replied. "That makes two of us."

From the moment Joanna called Dispatch and summoned Mike Wilson and his Search and Rescue team, she knew it would be at least an hour, maybe even an hour and a half, before the team could rendezvous at Clete Rogers' house. Forced to wait outside lest they be accused of doing anything improper, Joanna found herself frustrated with the idea of just standing around. Finally she opened the small suitcase she kept in the back of the Blazer. From her selection of "just-in-case" crime scene clothing, she removed a pair of tennis shoes, put them on, and laced them up.

"I'm going to walk around a little," she told Ernie. "You don't need a search warrant for that."

Tombstone may have been the Town Too

Tough to Die, but the same couldn't be said for municipal infrastructure. Within three blocks on either side of the main drag, thin layers of long-ago-laid asphalt had now reverted to pot-holed gravel trails. As Joanna set out walking, she had to keep her eyes glued to the disintegrating pavement in order to avoid falling in one of the holes and twisting her ankle. The necessity of watching her feet meant she didn't necessarily notice where she was going. Two blocks from the house, a large shadow intersected with hers. Glancing up, she saw a huge buzzard riding the updrafts.

In the desert, a circling buzzard carries its own ominous message of death and dying. Sighting in on the bottom of the bird's lazy circle, Joanna found herself staring at a small concrete complex carrying an identifying sign that said, TOMBSTONE MUNICIPAL SWIMMING POOL. Joanna made her way toward the pool, suspecting in advance what she might find there.

The fully clothed body of a man lay sprawled facedown on the bottom of the deep end of an empty swimming pool. There was no question about whether or not he was dead. Joanna could tell from the rag-doll way his head canted off to one side that his neck had been broken.

"Ernie," Joanna yelled over her shoulder. "Come here. Quick!"

Moments later, the detective came huffing down the hill. "What is it?" he demanded as he caught up with her. "What's going on?"

"Call Dispatch and cancel Search and Rescue. I'm pretty sure we've found Clete Rogers."

For Joanna, the next part of the scenario was achingly familiar. George Winfield had to be summoned. The crime scene investigation team had to be called out once more. As curious onlookers gathered around and as the screen of crime scene tape went up, Joanna sat in her Blazer and waited for the wheels of bureaucracy to grind. Watching all the activity, she felt terribly sad.

Alice Rogers was dead and now so was her son. *What does it take*, Joanna wondered, *for a son to kill his mother? How much money could stimulate that much greed? And after the deed was done, how much regret would cause a remorseful killer to take his own life?*

Sitting in the Blazer, Joanna realized that answers to some of those questions were well within her reach. All she had to do was talk to Dena Hogan, the attorney who had handled the writing of Alice Rogers' will. Dena Hogan most likely would know the general amounts of money and other assets that were part of Alice Rogers' estate. Glancing at her watch, Joanna saw there was still plenty of time to make it to Sierra Vista for her tentative appointment with Dena Hogan.

Joanna's purpose in making the appointment had been to discuss the Mark Childers' case—to see if any of the financial records subpoenaed in Monica Foster's divorce case would shed light on what had happened at Oak Vista Estates. But since Dena Hogan was connected to both investigations, one excuse for seeing her was as good as another. Besides, with the two homicide detectives already at the scene of Clete Rogers' appar-

ent suicide, there was no need for Joanna to hang
around.

"I'm leaving," Joanna told Ernie Carpenter.
"I'm going to go out to Sierra Vista and see Dena
Hogan. While I'm at it, I may even pay a call on
Karen Brainard."

"Do you want some backup on that?"

Joanna thought about it. "I don't think so," she
said. "For right now, I think what I have to say to
Karen Brainard is best said in private."

Ernie looked at her and shook his head. "You
go on ahead," he said, "but don't say I didn't warn
you."

By two o'clock Joanna was out of her tennies,
back in her heels, and standing in front of the
receptionist's desk in Dena Hogan's office on Fry
Boulevard in Sierra Vista. The receptionist was
young and vague.

"She's not in," Joanna was told when she announced her name.

"Not in," Joanna echoed. "I called this morning. I made an appointment."

"Ms. Hogan went home sick at lunchtime. She
said she may not be back before Monday," the
receptionist added. "I probably should have tried
to call, but I didn't know where to reach you."

"You might have tried the sheriff's department," Joanna said icily. "I did give my name as
Sheriff Joanna Brady. That's usually where sher-
iffs hang out."

Steamed, Joanna made her way out of Dena
Hogan's office. Standing in the cold but sunny
November afternoon, she decided to disregard

Ernie's advice and go see Karen Brainard after all. If nothing else, the drive from Sierra Vista to Huachuca City would give Joanna a chance to cool off.

It turned out that Karen Brainard didn't live in Huachuca City proper. The Brainard place was on Sands Ranch Road in the foothills of the Whetstones. Her house was a sprawling adobe affair—new construction with carefully contrived landscaping that made it look far older and more well-established than it was. A FOR SALE sign sat next to the mailbox.

The silver-haired woman who answered the door resembled Karen Brainard. "I'm Sheriff Brady," Joanna said. "I'm looking for Karen."

"She isn't here right now," the woman said uneasily. "I don't know when she'll be back."

The wary way the woman responded put Joanna on guard. "And you are?" she asked.

"I'm Maureen," the woman said. "Maureen Edgeworth. Karen's mother." She opened the door wider. "Won't you come in?"

Stepping inside, Joanna was surprised to see that the house was almost entirely devoid of furniture. All that was left in the living room was a single end table with a lamp. "There are chairs in the kitchen," Maureen explained. "If you don't mind sitting there."

Following Maureen Edgeworth through the house, Joanna could see shadows on the walls where paintings had once hung. It looked as though someone was in the process of moving out. The kitchen, too, was missing artwork, although a table and chairs remained. Maureen Edgeworth motioned Joanna into one of those.

"You say you don't know when your daughter will return? You are aware that with the ongoing investigations into Lewis Flores' and Mark Childers' deaths, your daughter was told not to leave town."

"But she had to," Maureen Edgeworth replied. "She didn't have a choice."

"Where is she?"

Maureen Edgeworth bit her lip. "I don't want to tell you," she said. "She hasn't gone far, and she will be back eventually. I promise. Her father and I are taking care of Derek and the house in the meantime."

"Who's Derek?" Joanna asked.

"Karen's son. Our grandson," Maureen said. "He's only sixteen, you see. This has all been awful for him. It was all I could do to get him to go to school today. He didn't want to, and I don't blame him. He's embarrassed. I feel the same way when I have to go to the grocery store. I don't know what I'll do when Sunday comes around and I have to go to church. That's the most difficult thing—seeing people you know and knowing they know. It's so hard—so very, very hard."

"Where is your daughter?" Joanna persisted.

"In Tucson."

"Where in Tucson?"

"Ed drove her there. Ed's my husband—Karen's father. He's checking her into a treatment center—a drug treatment center. We knew some of this when Paul left. Paul's our son-in-law, you see.

When he moved out, he tried to tell us what was going on—that Karen was mixed up in some pretty wild stuff. But Ed and I didn't want to believe it. Not Karen. Not our own daughter.

"But when she called last night and told us what had happened and that she'd had to resign from the board of supervisors, there wasn't any choice. We had to believe her then. And Ed did the only thing that made sense. He made arrangements to check her into the center first thing this morning. She'll be there for six weeks. We've talked to Paul—we're on very good terms with him, you see—but he's doing a consulting job and is out of the country for the next three weeks at least. Ed and I assured Paul that we'll look after Derek at least until he gets back."

Maureen Edgeworth stopped speaking and seemed to become aware that her hospitality was somehow lacking. "Can I get you a cup of coffee?"

"No, thank you," Joanna told her. "I just had lunch."

"If you don't mind, I'll fix some for myself."

As Maureen moved around the kitchen, Joanna wrestled with her conscience. The poor woman was clearly devastated by what was going on with her daughter. She needed someone to talk to right then, and Sheriff Joanna Brady was the only person who happened to be there.

"Karen's fortunate to have you and your husband for parents," Joanna said tentatively. "Not everyone would be willing to step in and handle things in a situation like this."

Maureen shrugged. "What choice do we have?"

she asked. "What choice do parents ever have? Karen was always a handful—she and those wild pals of hers, Dena and Monica. They were all smart and they all got good grades, but they were always getting into mischief together, always walking the fine edge."

"Dena Hogan and Monica Foster Childers?" Joanna supplied.

"Dena James then," Maureen said. "And yes, Monica Foster. I thought it was just because they were teenagers. I told myself that it was just a phase they were going through and that they'd grow out of it eventually. And I guess Monica did, but Karen and Dena are both in their mid-forties now. That's a little late for them to keep falling back on that old 'just-a-phase' excuse."

"Did Karen say anything to you about her dealings with Mark Childers?"

"More than we wanted to know," Maureen Edgeworth said sadly. "She had more than 'dealings' with the man. And to think he was her best friend's husband!"

Maureen shuddered, and her voice rose with indignation. "You have to understand, Sheriff Brady. I tried to raise my daughter to have good morals and high standards. I tried to teach her about right and wrong. I thought wife-swapping went out with the AIDS virus, but I guess not. These days all the kids learn about safe sex in junior high. Somebody needs to teach the parents. They're the ones who need to grow up. I don't blame Paul for leaving, not at all."

"From the sound of it, I'd say your daughter

was involved with a whole group of people," Joanna said gently. "Did she give you any names?"

"Other than Dena? Not really. I'm sure you can ask her yourself if you need to, but I don't know how soon that'll be. According to Ed, the first thing that happens at the center is the addicts go into detox for a while—for several days at least. They can't have any visitors at all until they complete that portion of the treatment. Do you need the address?"

Joanna nodded. "And a phone number," she added. "Both would be helpful."

"Just a minute. I wrote them down, but I put the piece of paper in my purse."

While Maureen went to get the information, Joanna sat considering her next move. Dena Hogan was handling Monica Foster's divorce from Mark Childers, but she was also palling around with someone who was Mark Childers' drug-using mistress. This sounded very much like a conflict of interest. Dena Hogan may have left work sick that day, but it seemed to Joanna that it was time someone paid the woman a visit at home.

"Do you happen to know where Dena lives?" Joanna asked when Maureen returned to the kitchen.

"Kino Road," Maureen replied. "Just south of Ramsey. You're not going to go see her, are you?"

"I may," Joanna hedged.

"If you do, please don't tell her I said anything. I don't want to cause any more trouble than I already have."

A car—an old T-Bird—pulled into the yard and stopped. "That'll be Derek," Maureen said. "He drives himself to and from school. Please go now, Sheriff Brady. I hope you won't mind if I don't introduce you. I'm sure you understand. I just can't upset him any more right now."

"Of course," Joanna agreed, standing up to leave. "I understand completely."

In the end, there was no problem with introductions, because once Derek Brainard came into the house, he slammed the front door and disappeared into the depths of the house without ever showing his face in the kitchen. Joanna let herself out, climbed into the Blazer, and headed back for Sierra Vista. She used her cell phone to get Dena and Rex Hogan's exact address on Kino Road. Half an hour later, Joanna approached the Hogan address just as a woman, blond and carrying two suitcases, exited the house.

Driving slowly and checking house numbers, Joanna stopped to watch. The woman heaved two massive bags into the open trunk of a car parked in the driveway. It was only when she turned around to reenter the house that Joanna realized she wasn't a woman at all. The long blond locks and the missing trademark buckskin jacket had fooled her. No, the person returning to Dena Hogan's house was none other than Ross Jenkins. The car the suitcases had been loaded into was the same Chrysler Concorde Joanna had seen Jenkins driving on Houghton Road three days earlier. In front of that was a pearlescent-white Lexus.

All at once, the threads of the two separate cases came together for Joanna like crosshairs in the sights of a rifle. She felt an eerie prickling at the back of her neck and knew that Ernie Carpenter had been dead-on right. She never should have come here alone.

NINETEEN

AS ROSS Jenkins disappeared into Dena Hogan's house, Joanna switched off the Blazer's engine. From a discreet distance two houses away, she grappled with what to do. Other than instinct and moral indignation, she had very little to go on. Despicable behavior wasn't criminal. If Dena Hogan was screwing around with Susan Jenkins' husband, that was the business of the four people most closely involved. It certainly wasn't Joanna's. And standing someone up for an appointment while claiming to be sick but really heading out of town couldn't be considered criminal either.

Sure, there were clear conflicts of interest involved. Even in small-town legal circles people would frown on an attorney who, while representing one party in a divorce proceeding, was also best friends with the opposing spouse's mistress. But that called for disciplinary action from a bar association and nothing more, especially since wife, mistress, and attorney were all long-term friends with a supposedly "close" relationship that dated all the way back to girlhood.

All those things were bothersome—worrisome, even—but not cause for involvement by a local law enforcement agency. Still, Joanna knew instinctively that whatever was going on right then was more than morally wrong. Dena Hogan had been privy to the contents of Alice Rogers' will. More than privy, she was the attorney who had drafted the damned thing. Alice's two children, as well as her Johnny-come-lately husband, would have benefited to some extent from Alice's premature death. With one of those beneficiaries dead and the other among the missing, that left only one, Susan Jenkins—and her husband Ross, who had just loaded a pair of suitcases—Dena's, presumably—into his car.

What's the relationship between these two? Joanna wondered. *And how much of this is Susan Jenkins in on?*

The door opened once more and again Ross Jenkins emerged from the house. This time he crammed one more, smaller, suitcase into the trunk, then slammed the lid shut before he tossed a heavily loaded garment bag into the backseat. As he returned to the house once again, Joanna realized she didn't have much time. The car was full. When it was completely loaded, Ross and Dena would most likely drive away from the house. When that happened, Joanna wouldn't have sufficient probable cause to pull them over.

She wanted to confront them sooner than that,

without the necessity of what might later be characterized as an illegal traffic stop. The problem was, she was there by herself. Approaching a pair of suspected killers alone was downright foolhardy.

After first slipping her cell phone into the coat pocket of her blazer, she thumbed the talk button on her radio. "Dispatch," she said. "Sheriff Brady here. I need backup."

"Where are you?" Tica Romero asked.

"Kino Road, just south of Ramsey. It's a residence that belongs to Rex and Dena Hogan."

"That's the same address I found for you a few minutes ago, isn't it?"

"Yes. Two suspects are loading a vehicle. I want to keep them from leaving. How long before you can have another unit here?"

"We're short-staffed in that sector right now, Sheriff Brady. The closest county unit is over at Palominas, finishing investigating a multi-car accident. Deputy Pakin can probably be there in half an hour or so. Do you want me to ask for mutual aid from Sierra Vista PD?"

"Yes," Joanna agreed at once. "Better safe than sorry."

The door to Dena Hogan's house opened again. This time two people walked out and headed for the Concorde. The woman was wearing a coat and carrying a purse. That meant the loading was done. The suspects were leaving. There would be no time to wait for backup, none at all.

"I'm going to have to go in alone," Joanna said. "But when I do, I'll leave my cell phone turned on. That way, you'll be able to monitor what's happening."

Quickly Joanna punched up Tica's direct number and then waited for the dispatcher to answer before stowing the phone itself inside the cup of her bra. By then, Ross Jenkins and the woman were standing on either side of the Chrysler. Switching on the ignition, Joanna sent the Blazer roaring forward. Once it was astraddle the driveway and blocking the Concorde's exit, Joanna slammed the Blazer into neutral and then stepped out onto the parking strip.

"Hi there, Ross," Joanna said. "Do you have a minute?"

From the dismayed look that passed across his face, it was clear that Ross Jenkins was startled to see her. He recovered quickly, however.

"Well, hiya there, Sheriff Brady," he said easily. "We were just leaving. If you don't mind, we're a little pressed for time at the moment."

"I'm sure you are," Joanna replied. "I only have a few questions. I presume this is Dena Hogan?"

"Yes, I'm Dena." The woman's answer was chilly and wary at the same time. "What do you want?"

Joanna wavered momentarily. She could play it cool and pretend that all she was looking for was a copy of Mark Childers' financial records. Or she could go for broke. She could take a page from her father's old poker-playing days and bluff like hell.

"I'm curious where you both were last Saturday night," she said quietly. "Where you were after Alice Monroe left Sierra Vista to drive back home to Tombstone?"

Glances might not be admissible in a court of law, but the dagger-filled look Dena Hogan shot across the top of the car toward Ross Jenkins spoke volumes.

"We were together," Ross said with a dismissive shrug, as though the fact that he was sleeping around behind his wife's back was an unimportant detail too insignificant to bother denying. "Right here. I came over after dinner and was here until late—until two or three in the morning."

"With no witnesses, of course," Joanna said.

Ross smiled. "I should hope not. I don't think Susie would like it much if she found out. She's been through so much lately. I wanted to spare her feelings."

"We both did," Dena said.

"How very thoughtful of you," Joanna observed. "And I suppose you're also sparing your husband's feelings at the moment, Ms. Hogan? I'm assuming Rex isn't home. Otherwise he'd be the one lugging your suitcases out to the car, not Mr. Jenkins here. And speaking of suitcases, from the size of them I'd say you're planning on being gone for some time. Maybe even longer than next Monday morning, which is when your receptionist said you might be recovered enough to return to work."

There was no way for Joanna to tell if her cell phone was picking up any of the conversation. It was buried under both her bra and the Kevlar material woven into her soft body armor.

Dena looked at her watch. "Come on, Ross. It's getting late. Let's go. She's got no reason to hold us. If you have to drive across the grass to get around her, do it."

Ross Jenkins made no effort to comply, and when he didn't get in the Concorde, neither did Dena Hogan.

"Look, Sheriff Brady," he said, turning on a gratingly wheedling tone, the persuasive one that could have been dubbed straight into one of his auto dealership's radio commercials. "You may not be able to understand this or believe it, but Dena and I are in love. Neither one of us planned for it to happen quite this way, but it did. And yes, we are leaving town. We're going away to try to get some perspective on things—to try to figure out what we should do about it. Maybe you've never been trapped in a loveless marriage, but we both have. We feel like we owe it to ourselves to salvage whatever bit of happiness we can."

Angered by his phony-baloney excuses, Joanna crossed her arms. "As they say in rodeo, Mr. Jenkins, nice try, but no time. This isn't about love or lack of it. It's about murder—your mother-in-law's first and now, quite possibly, your brother-in-law's as well."

Dena's jaw dropped. A dumbfounded expression flitted across her face. The look caught Joanna's eye and her attention wavered momentarily. That was all the opening Ross Jenkins needed. His attack came without warning. One moment the man was standing at ease beside the Concorde, with one arm draped casually across the vehicle's roof. The next moment he sprang at Joanna in a flying tackle that caught her smack in the midsection and sent her flying backward.

The force of the blow knocked her to the ground and drove the wind from her lungs. Before a gasping Joanna knew what had happened or could inhale another breath, the man was on top of her, sitting astride her waist. He wrestled Joanna's Colt 2000 out of her shoulder holster and stuffed it in his pants pocket. Then he grabbed both her arms, twisted them behind her, and threw her facedown in the dirt.

"For God's sake, Ross, what are you doing?" Dena demanded. "Are you crazy?"

"I'm not crazy. I'm saving our lives. Do you have any duct tape in the garage?"

"Yes."

"Go get it then. Hurry. No, on second thought. I'll bring her into the garage. There's not much time."

Wrenched to her feet, Joanna looked up and down the street, hoping there would be someone around to see what was happening. But there was no one. No children were outside for an afternoon bike ride. No retirees took advantage of the crisp afternoon to rake leaves or do other yard work. Ross Jenkins might as well have launched his attack in a completely deserted village.

When he hauled her to her feet, Joanna was afraid the phone might have been jarred loose or turned off. She worried that it would fall out of its hiding place, but it remained where she had put it, the battery warm against her breast as he hustled her past the two parked cars and up the driveway. Moments later, with the whir of an electric motor, the door of Dena's garage moved slowly open. Jenkins didn't wait for it to rise all the way before he ducked underneath and pulled Joanna into the garage with him. Immediately the door whirred shut again.

"Dena's right, you know," Joanna managed when she was finally able to speak. "Assaulting a police officer is a bad idea. I've already called for backup, Ross. Other cars will be here momentarily."

Still slightly dazed, Joanna tried to assess her situation. Jenkins was far bigger than she was, and his attack had caught her so much by surprise that she hadn't been able to utilize any of the countermeasures Andy had taught her. Her Colt was gone, but in his haste to hustle her into the garage and out of sight, Ross Jenkins had failed to discover Joanna's reserve weapon. Her Glock 17 still rested securely in her small-of-back holster. And, as long as he was busy keeping her arms pinned to her shoulder blades, he might still miss it.

"Don't listen to her, Dena," Ross admonished as the woman reappeared with what looked like a brand-new roll of duct tape. "And don't worry. We'll be gone momentarily. Here. Wrap the tape around her wrists. When you finish that, tape her ankles together as well."

With a rip, a length of tape tore loose from the

roll. Behind her back, Joanna felt the sticky stuff wrap around her wrists, lashing them together. Any second, Joanna expected one of Dena's hands to fall against the Glock, but that didn't happen. When Dena had finished with the wrists, she knelt to tape Joanna's ankles.

"You can't kill her, Ross," Dena was saying. "Aren't we in enough trouble already?"

"Shut up and tape. Ankles first and then her mouth. I'll go outside and juggle cars."

"What are you going to do with her, Ross?"

"You'd be surprised. Right now I'm going to move the luggage from my car to hers. Then we'll load her into my trunk. If she isn't bluffing and if cops are on their way, we sure as hell can't leave her here. All we have to do is make sure that by the time reinforcements show up, we're long gone."

With that, Ross let go of Joanna's arms and moved away, leaving her standing unsteadily, trying to maintain her balance. With her feet taped together, that was almost impossible. Meanwhile, Dena closed in on Joanna's face with her roll of tape once more firmly in hand.

Joanna noticed that she and Dena Hogan were fairly evenly matched in size. Had Joanna's arms and legs been free, Joanna no doubt could have taken the woman in a fair fight. But for now, all Joanna could do to defend herself was to hop away, with the ungainly crooked hop of a drunken Easter bunny. As she did so, she looked around the virtually empty two-car garage, trying to get her bearings.

At the far end of the garage was a door that opened into the house. Lining the front of the garage were recycling baskets, a refrigerator/freezer, and a workbench. The right-hand wall of the garage, from workbench to corner, was lined with a collection of garden tools and equipment—rakes, hedge trimmers, grass shears—hanging on a series of wall-mounted hooks.

Having her feet bound was like being caught in a life-and-death sack race. Hopping along, Joanna made for a small open space between the freezer and workbench, all the while dodging away from Dena and her tape and trying, at the same time, to drive a wedge between the two conspirators.

"Don't do this, Dena," Joanna pleaded. "Don't let Ross talk you into it. Once you load me into that car of his, it's kidnapping. Add that to murder and conspiracy to commit, you're talking capital offenses. In case you haven't noticed, executions are back in style in Arizona, and being a woman is no excuse."

"Shut up," Dena said, following doggedly behind Joanna, with the roll of duct tape still in her hand. "Just shut up."

She was so focused on taping Joanna's mouth that she clearly wasn't thinking of anything else. She didn't notice that Joanna was leading her into the foot and a half of confining space between the freezer and the workbench, a space so small that there would be almost no room for maneuvering—for either one of them.

"Think about a plea bargain, Dena," Joanna said. "If you'll agree to testify against him, I'll do whatever I can to help you."

"I said, shut up," Dena insisted. "I don't want to hear it."

By then, Joanna had backed herself against the wall. Just as she expected, Dena charged after her. There wasn't much time. Joanna knew that her only chance was to make her move now, while it was still a one-on-one contest, while Ross Jenkins was still outside the garage. Once he finished transferring the luggage, it would be too late.

Pressed up against the wall and using that to help maintain her balance, Joanna ducked her head until her chin was resting on her breastbone. Then she flexed her knees. As Dena moved in with the tape, Joanna sprang forward. The top of her head caught Dena Hogan square on the chin. The head butt hit Dena hard enough that Joanna herself saw stars. She stood there reeling while Dena Hogan, groaning in surprise, fell to the floor and lay still.

Joanna didn't bother looking at her. Hopping again, she made her way around the fallen woman. She had noticed grass shears among the collection of tools. Seeing them again, she noted the sharp blades glinting wickedly in the light from the garage-door opener. If Joanna could get to the shears, maybe she could hack through the tape enough and free her hands long enough to wrest her Glock from its holster.

The distance from where she was to the shears

was only a matter of a few feet, but it might as well have been the length of a football field. Hopping and with her heart hammering in her chest, Joanna was almost there when the automatic garage light hit the end of its timer and went off, plunging the place into total darkness.

Crashing a rib against the corner of the workbench as she made her way past it in the dark, Joanna knew she was close. Turning, she felt along the wall. She remembered that a long-handled rake had been next to the workbench and the shears had been next to the rake, hanging with the handle up and the closed blades down. Joanna had found the blades and was just beginning to saw through the tape when the garage door opener whirred once more. As the light came on again, Ross Jenkins reentered the garage.

"Come on," he was saying as he came. "I heard the talk on her police radio. The cops are on their way. Let's go, Dena." Just then, catching sight of Dena on the floor, he stopped short. "What the hell!" he exclaimed.

Huddled against the wall of tools with her hands still not freed from the tape, Joanna saw him turn on her. With his face distorted by rage, Ross Jenkins charged forward. There was no time to finish cutting through the tape; no hope of prying the hidden Glock loose from its holster. There was only time enough for her to register that he was hurling himself toward her with both of his hands visible and empty.

Standing on tiptoes, Joanna managed to wrench the shears loose from the hook that held it to the wall. Then, with a half-jump, she spun around so that she was facing the wall with the handle of the shears clutched in both hands behind her.

Ross never saw the danger or, if he did, the warning came too late for him to check his head-long attack. Momentum carried him forward and onto the upthrust blades of the shears. The force of the blow to her back sent Joanna smashing face-first into the wall. The other tools hanging there crashed to the floor around her. Meanwhile, as Ross fell back, Joanna felt something hot and sticky ooze onto her hands.

"Why, you bitch!" he howled, rolling on the floor and clutching his bleeding abdomen. "You incredible bitch!"

Joanna tried to move out of the way, but hopping on both feet together didn't make for maneuverability. He caught her by the leg and pulled her down on top of him.

"You're going to help me," he hissed. "You're going to help me get up and out of here."

Somehow, though, through it all—through being knocked down and then dragged on top of him—Joanna had managed to keep hold of the shears. Twisting in his grasp, she plunged the shears into him a second time. This time the blade went deep into his thigh. As Ross squirmed and howled in pain, Joanna managed to roll away from him and go slithering across the cold cement floor.

Joanna had heard Ross say that help was on its way. All she had to do was keep him there and keep herself out of harm's way until the promised backup units arrived. Unable to regain her feet, Joanna scooted out of the garage and onto the driveway. The cold and rough cement tore through her nylons, rubbing her legs raw. With every inch of forward motion, Joanna kept looking back over her shoulder, expecting him to come lunging after her once more.

Joanna moved past the Lexus without stopping, but when she reached the Concorde, she used the car's fender as a brace and hauled herself up into a sitting position. There, she dropped the shears and wrested the Glock out of her holster. It wasn't a matter of taking aim. She simply held the barrel of the gun against the rubber tire and pulled the trigger.

Then, after retrieving the shears and with both them and the Glock in hand, she made her way back to the Blazer. There was always a chance that Ross Jenkins' vehicle was equipped with those new expensive tires, the ones you were supposed to be able to drive on for fifty miles even if they were plugged full of holes. Joanna knew it would be a long time before Frank Montoya would agree to buy them for the sheriff department's fleet of vehicles.

When she finally reached the front of the Blazer, she did the same thing to the right front tire there, shooting it twice for good measure and sighing with satisfaction as the confined air came rushing out.

"Lady," a voice directly behind her said. "What are you doing? Are you crazy or something? And what's on that shears? It looks like blood."

Joanna turned. There, scowling at her from the seat of a bicycle, stood a young boy of eleven or twelve. "I'm not crazy," she said. "There's a killer loose in there—a killer with a gun. Here. Take the shears and cut my hands loose before he comes after us."

The boy hesitated, but for only an instant. Dropping his bike, he grabbed the bloody shears and snipped through the tape. First he freed Joanna's hands and then her legs, not without nicking her in the shin. In the distance Joanna heard the welcome swell of a siren announcing the arrival of at least one patrol car.

"Thank you," she said. "Now go. Get out of here before you get hurt."

The boy scrambled for his bike.

"What's your name?"

"Andrew," he said. "Andrew Styles."

"Where do you live?"

He pointed. "Two houses down," he said.

"Go!" Joanna ordered. "Get inside the house and stay there. Don't come out until I come and tell you it's okay."

"But what about you?"

"I'm okay now. I'll be fine."

She slipped into the Blazer and was reaching for the radio. Just then, as Andrew Styles went wheeling away, two people emerged from the garage. With one hand, Ross Jenkins leaned heavily on a rake handle. His other arm was wrapped around the supporting shoulder of Dena Hogan.

"Stop right there," Joanna ordered. "I'm placing you both under arrest. Put down your weapons."

Dena raised her hands. "Don't try to stop him," she warned. "He's got a gun. He says he'll shoot me if you do."

By then Joanna could see that her Colt 2000 hung loosely in Ross' hand, inches from Dena Hogan's right ear. And now the arriving sirens—two of them at least—were that much closer. The patrol cars couldn't be more than a block or two away, far too close to be outrun by a Blazer with a flattened tire. And the blood on Ross Jenkins' trousers had its own tale to tell. It was possible he still had no idea of how badly he was hurt, but Joanna knew exactly where the blades had plunged into his body. Without swift medical help he was likely to bleed to death. Even then, it would take all the skill of modern medicine, along with powerful antibiotics, to keep the wounded man from succumbing to the ravages of peritonitis.

With that understood, it was easy for Joanna Brady to be gracious—as long as no one stooped to inspect the tires. "All right," she agreed. "I don't want anyone else to get hurt. I'll get out. I'm stepping away from the vehicle. Here are the keys. I'll leave them right here on the seat. But you're not going to get far, Ross. You're going to need a doctor."

"Don't listen to her," Ross said to Dena. "Help me get in. You drive."

They hobbled as far as the Blazer's passenger door. Ross moaned in pain as Dena helped him up onto the seat. Then she closed the door. But instead of walking to the driver's door, Dena

Hogan left Ross Jenkins sitting in the car and walked straight over to Joanna.

"Can you help with a plea-bargain?" she asked.

"I'll do whatever I can," Joanna replied.

"I surrender then," Dena Hogan said. "Ross is on his own."

Joanna grabbed Dena and propelled her around the corner of the garage just as the first arriving Sierra Vista patrol car roared through the intersection on Ramsey and came barreling down Kino. That was when a blast from Joanna's Colt shattered the still autumn air and sent a cloud of safety glass blowing out of the Blazer's windshield.

"Damn you, Dena!" Ross Jenkins raged. "Don't you dare do that. This was your idea, remember? It was all your idea."

"No, it wasn't," Dena countered. "You don't believe him, do you?"

"I don't have to," Joanna told her. "That'll be for the prosecutors and courts to decide."

By then one of the Sierra Vista officers sprinted around the back of the house and arrived at the spot where Joanna was fastening Flexi-cuffs on Dena Hogan's wrists. Joanna pulled out her ID and flashed it in his face. "Are you all right?" he panted, gasping for breath.

"We are, but he's not," Joanna said nodding toward the Blazer. "He's wounded. In the gut and the leg both. You take her, and I'll see what I can do about him."

The arriving officer took charge of Dena. "You heard her, Ross," Joanna called to him. "Dena wants to make a deal. If you don't want her to have first dibs, you'd better throw my Colt out the window and come out with your hands up."

There was a long silence after that. In the background there was some radio chatter as two sets of dispatchers tried to make sense of what was happening. Joanna waited. Time seemed to stand still. What she really expected to hear was another roar of gunfire. What she heard instead were two distinct clicks as the Colt misfired—twice. Finally, after what seemed like an eternity, the Colt came whirling out through the driver's window. It spun across the browned grass like a deadly metal Frisbee and landed some fifteen feet away.

"Help me," Ross Jenkins said. "It hurts real bad. I need a doctor. Now."

"Right," Joanna said, moving forward and wrenching open the door. "We'll get you one right away."

When we damned well get around to it.

TWENTY

AFTER THE danger was over, Joanna felt weak and half sick to her stomach. While the EMTs loaded Ross Jenkins into an ambulance and Dena Hogan was hustled into the backseat of a Sierra Vista patrol car, Joanna made her way to the front step of the house and weakly sank down on it. That's where she was when Frank Montoya arrived. He had been in Palominas supervising the automobile accident and had arrived at the scene only minutes behind the officers from Sierra Vista.

He came over long enough to check on her and then went to confer with the other officers. After a few quiet moments, Joanna heard voices that seemed to be coming from inside her body rather than outside it. For a scary moment or two, she was afraid that the blow to her head when she crashed into Dena's chin had caused a concussion or some other kind of head injury. Then, finally, Tica Romero's voice came into audio focus.

"Can you hear me, Sheriff Brady? Are you all right?"

Feeling foolish, Joanna extracted her cell phone from the cup of her brassiere. "Sorry, Tica," she said into it. "In all the excitement I forgot about the phone. And yes, I'm fine."

"I heard most of it. It's awful to listen when something like that is going down and not be able to help."

"You helped, all right, Tica," Joanna said gratefully. "Believe me, you helped. Those backup units got here without a moment to spare."

"What's the situation with the two suspects?"

"Ross Jenkins is being airlifted to Tucson for abdominal surgery. Frank Montoya is taking charge of Dena Hogan. He'll bring her back to Bisbee. We'll question her there and then book her into the jail."

"Are you sure you're all right?" Tica asked. "You still sound a little shaky."

"I'm fine. I've got a cut on my leg. It's not bad enough that I'll need stitches or anything, but since I got it from a grass shears, one of the medics told me I should have a tetanus shot. Which reminds me. I need to go find Andrew Styles."

"Who's he?" Tica asked. "One of the Sierra Vista cops?"

"No, he's the little kid who put the hole in my leg. He's also the one who cut me loose. I need to let his parents know what a brave, quick-thinking son they've got."

Joanna stood up and looked at herself. As usual, her new pantyhose were wrecked. In addition to the cut from the shears, her knees and shoulders were scraped and bleeding from scrambling along the cement. Another perfectly good set of work clothes—a two-piece suit and matching blouse—were done for.

Still, not wanting to delay talking to Andrew Styles, Joanna patted her hair into place as best she could, pressed on a new layer of lipstick, and started down the street to the Styles' house. A woman answered the door.

"Mrs. Styles?" Joanna asked.

"Yes."

"I'm Joanna Brady—Sheriff Joanna Brady. I had to come by and tell you a terrific thing your son did this afternoon. I'm sure you're aware that we've had a serious police incident just up the street. Two escaping suspects had caught me unawares and duct-taped my feet and hands together. Andrew came by, saw that I needed help, and cut me loose. He saved my life. I just wanted you to know how much I appreciated it. Would it be possible for me to talk to him? I'd like to thank him again."

"Andrew's in his room," Mrs. Styles said. "He's grounded, but I suppose you can talk to him if you like."

"Grounded? How come?"

"For riding his bike without permission, that's how come," Mrs. Styles returned. "Last Saturday he came home an hour and a half later than he was supposed to, and he lost his biking privileges for the whole week. But he's home from school before his dad and I get off work, and—grounded or not—he went bike riding today anyway. One of the reporters came here wanting an interview. Having her show up blew the whistle on him and Andrew decided to come clean. That's why I sent him to his room, and I expect him to stay there."

"I don't want to get in the way of family discipline, Mrs. Styles," Joanna said. "But please don't be too hard on him. Andrew's a hero. I was between a rock and a hard place. There wasn't a soul around to help me until he rode up on his bike."

Reluctantly, Andrew Styles' mother opened the door. "Come on in," she said. "I don't suppose your talking to him will make that much difference."

She pointed the way across a narrow living room. "His room's down that hall, first door on the left."

Joanna went to the closed door and knocked. When no one answered, she knocked again, louder this time. Finally, she opened the door and stepped inside.

Everything about the room screamed little boy. The walls were plastered with posters of cars and athletes. A squadron of model airplanes dangled from the ceiling on strings. In front of the window sat a low bookshelf that was covered with model cars. Andrew himself lay on his back on the bed, staring up at the ceiling and listening to music. Even though he was wearing earphones, Joanna could still hear the pulsing bass.

"Andrew?" Joanna said. She had to speak to

him twice before he finally turned in her direction. He slipped off the earphones.

"Whaddya want?" he asked.

"First, I wanted to introduce myself. I'm Sheriff Joanna Brady." She extended her hand. Gravely, Andrew Styles reached out and shook it. "I also wanted to say thank you once again," she continued. "Maybe a little less hurriedly this time. Staying around long enough to help me was really brave, Andrew. That man had a gun, and you could have been badly hurt. I want you to know how much I appreciate it."

"I got in trouble for it," Andrew Styles said. "I wasn't supposed to be riding my bike. I didn't think Mom would find out, but when that reporter came to talk to me, I knew she would, so I decided I'd better tell the truth."

"That's always the best idea," Joanna said.

"What about those people up the street? Are they really bad guys?"

"Yes. Really bad."

"What did they do?"

"We don't know for sure."

"Did they kill somebody?"

"We think so, although they're not considered guilty until after a judge and jury say they are. What I can tell you for sure is that they're not the kind of people who tell the truth. They're not like you, Andrew. If they had been out riding their bikes when they weren't supposed to, they wouldn't have admitted it, especially not if it was going to get them into trouble."

Andrew rolled over onto his side, planted one

bony elbow in his pillow, and cushioned his chin in the palm of his hand. "Are you really the sheriff?" he asked.

"Yes."

"How come?"

"Because the people elected me. I ran for office and I won."

"I wouldn't mind being sheriff," he said. "But I don't think I'd like it if people tied me up with duct tape."

Joanna smiled. "Fortunately that doesn't happen very often. Thanks again, Andrew, and remember, if there's ever anything I can do for you—"

"Would you come speak to my social studies class sometimes?" Andrew asked. "The DARE officer is at school all the time, but I think it would be cool to have the real sheriff come talk to us."

Joanna reached into her pocket and pulled out a card. "I'll be glad to. Have your teacher call me to set up a time."

She started toward the door. "One other thing," Andrew said.

"What's that?"

"Are you going to get in trouble for shooting a hole in those tires?"

"I could, but I doubt it," Joanna said. "I had to make a choice, Andrew, between public property and public safety. If the crooks had made it to the cars, it would have been a lot harder for them to get away in a vehicle with one flat tire than it would have been in one with four good tires. My deputies sometimes have to make those kinds of choices as well. As long as what they do is justified, no one gets in trouble."

"Who decides whether or not they get in trouble?"

"I do."

"How come?"

Joanna smiled. "Because I'm the boss. I'm going now, Andrew. See you later."

As she walked back out to the crime scene, she hoped her explanation of the bullet hole in the Blazer's right front tire would make as much sense to Danny Garner in Motor Pool as it had to Andrew Styles. Then there was the matter of the broken glass.

Out on the street, Chief Deputy Montoya was waiting for her. "What took you so long?" he asked.

"I had to see someone, Frank—the little boy who saved my neck. And I need some badges."

"What kind of badges?"

"Some I can keep in my purse and hand out as necessary."

"Fake ones, you mean. For little kids?"

"And grown ones."

"I'll see what I can do," Frank said, jotting down a note. "Anything else?"

"Remind me to look into a new gun. The Colt misfired twice this afternoon. Both times when a crook was using it instead of me, but twice is two times too many."

She paused and looked around. "Now, where are we?"

"Deputy Pakin is just finishing changing your

flat. The Blazer's drivable, even though part of the windshield's blown, or we can have it towed."

"Tape the windshield," Joanna said. "I'll drive."

"Meantime, we have Dena Hogan all loaded up in my Civvy and ready to go. I mirandized her, but she's waiving her right to an attorney. She claims to be representing herself. She wants to see the prosecutor about a plea bargain, and she wants to do it right away. Now. Tonight."

"Of course she does," Joanna said. "She's got to hurry and strike a deal *before* Ross Jenkins gets out of surgery, otherwise he may beat her to the punch."

"You know what they say," Frank said with a smile. "No honor among thieves."

"Or killers," Joanna said. "Any idea where Ross and Dena were headed when I was lucky enough to interrupt them?"

"She had two tickets to Mexico City in her purse—one for her and one for Ross Jenkins. But I'm sure Mexico City wasn't their final destination."

"What was?"

"Rio. Brazil doesn't have capital punishment. Authorities there won't extradite someone if it looks like they're going to come back to the States and face a possible death penalty."

"Fortunately, neither one of them made it that far. What kind of a deal do you think old Arlee will strike?" Joanna asked.

Arlee Campbell Jones, Cochise County's aging prosecutor, had his own peculiar way of doing things—one that didn't seem to stand in the way of his winning reelection time after time.

"Dena Hogan's pretty enough," Frank Montoya observed. "And she's got nice legs. Nice legs always seem to count for something when it comes time for Arlee to wheel and deal."

"Tough luck for Ross Jenkins," Joanna said.

Just then, a car—this one a silver-gray Camry—wheeled around a blocking patrol car and surged up the street. Despite three different officers signaling for the vehicle to stop, the driver refused to slow down until he was directly behind Joanna's Blazer, then he jammed on the brakes. A balding, paunchy, middle-aged man jumped out of the car and slammed the door.

"What's the meaning of this?" he demanded. "What's going on here?"

"I'm Sheriff Joanna Brady," she told him. "Who are you?"

"Rex Hogan," he said. "What are all these people doing here? Why's the street blocked off? And what's the meaning of all these cars parked in my driveway?"

Looking at the man, Joanna sensed that Rex had no idea what was going on. She felt a stab of empathy. His face was flushed. He looked as though he was already a candidate for a coronary even *without* hearing what Joanna was about to tell him. Before opening her mouth, she glanced in the direction of Frank Montoya's Crown Victoria. From where she and Rex Hogan stood, it looked as though the Civvy's backseat was empty. Dena

Hogan had ducked down in the seat, concealing herself from her husband's view.

"I'm sorry to tell you this, Mr. Hogan. I'm afraid I have some bad news."

Rex Hogan's face crumpled. "Not Dena. There's been some kind of an accident, hasn't there! Please, God, don't tell me something's happened to Dena. I couldn't stand it. She's not hurt, is she? Not dead?"

"Your wife's not dead," Joanna said quietly. "She's under arrest."

"Arrest? Did you say under arrest? For what? You can't be serious. This has to be some kind of joke."

"I can assure you, Mr. Hogan, it's no joke. Your wife is under arrest on suspicion of murder—for the murder of a woman named Alice Rogers. There may be other charges as well, but for right now, that's how things stand. She's waived the right to an attorney and insists she wants to represent herself."

Rex Hogan staggered backward and rested against the fender of Joanna's Blazer. For the space of almost a minute he seemed to be hyperventilating, and Joanna was afraid an ambulance would have to be summoned to care for him next. Eventually, though, he settled. "This can't be," he gasped when he was finally able to speak. "It's utterly impossible. Preposterous. Where is she? Let me talk to her."

"She's in that car over there, Mr. Hogan. If you want to, I suppose you could exchange a word or two, but once we take her away, you won't be able to talk to her again until after she's been questioned and booked into the Cochise County Jail. At that point, you'll be able to speak with the jail commander and make arrangements for visitation."

Taking Rex by the arm, Joanna led him to Frank's Crown Victoria. Frank unlocked the front door and got inside. By then Joanna and Rex were close enough to the vehicle that they could see Dena Hogan through the Civvy's tinted glass windows. Frank said something to the woman and was answered with a decisive shake of the head. Frank spoke again and was answered with another head shake. Finally, the chief deputy stepped back out into the street.

"I'm sorry, Mr. Hogan," he said. "Your wife refuses to speak to you."

Rex walked up to the car, bent down, and put his face directly in front of the window. "Please," he mouthed. His plea was answered by another adamantly negative response.

"Why?" Rex asked. He turned back to Joanna. His face screwed up and his eyes threatened to fill with tears. "What have I done? Why's she so mad at me?"

"I don't think she's mad at you," Joanna said softly. "I think she's mad at herself."

"But I don't understand," Rex Hogan said. "I don't understand at all. You said Dena murdered someone—someone I've never even heard of. How can that be? Won't someone please tell me what's going on?"

Joanna looked at the broken hulk that was

Rex Hogan and felt her heart swell with pity. If his and Dena's marriage had been as loveless as Ross Jenkins had claimed, it had been a very one-sided lovelessness. Rex Hogan obviously adored his wife, but Joanna suspected that there was a lot he didn't know about Dena. Joanna had done her official duty in telling Rex what legal charges were pending against his wife. She refused to tell him the rest of it. If the poor man knew nothing of his wife's liaison with Ross Jenkins, he wasn't going to learn about it from Joanna Brady. Dena Hogan was going to have to do that much of her own dirty work.

"You'll have to ask your wife," Joanna said quietly. "Maybe she can explain what's happened to you. Now is there anyone who can come be here with you tonight, Mr. Hogan? You probably shouldn't be here alone."

"I can call my daughter, I suppose," he said. "She's married and lives up in Tucson, but I'm sure she'll come down."

"I hope so, Mr. Hogan. Come on, Frank," Joanna added. "We need to get going."

She didn't mention that one of the reasons she needed to leave right then was that she couldn't bear being around Rex Hogan's pain for even a moment longer. Gratefully Joanna observed that Frank and Deputy Lance Pakin had finished fixing her flat tire and had duct-taped a piece of clear plastic sheeting over the bullet hole and the accompanying cobweb of cracks that criscrossed the rider's side of the Blazer's windshield. Joanna climbed into the truck and shifted it into gear.

She was barely back on Highway 92 when her cell phone rang.

"What is it now?" she asked wearily, expecting the caller to be Tica Romero.

"It's me," Butch said. "I came by your office a few minutes ago and found out all hell has broken loose. Are you all right?"

"I'm fine. I'm not so sure I'm proud to be a member of the human race at this point, but I am alive."

"And lucky to be so, from what I've heard," Butch said grimly.

"Yes," Joanna agreed. "Very lucky. But the good news is, we've caught ourselves two killers."

"I don't believe there was any *we* involved," Butch said. "People tell me you took it all on yourself—single-handed. Are you—"

"Butch, please. I did the best I could, and I kept two murderers from getting away. I'm not hurt, although I must say my clothes have seen better days. So let's not fight. Let's just be grateful that we're both alive. Is that why you called me? To chew me out? Or to tell me that you love me?"

"Well, not exactly. I do love you, of course, but that's not why I called."

"Why did you then?"

"Ellen Dowdle," Butch replied.

"Who?"

"Dowdle," Butch said, then he spelled out the name. "D-O-W-D-L-E."

"Who's that?" Joanna asked.

"Junior's mother," Butch said. "She lives in a nursing home in Rapid City, South Dakota."

"So Frank found her!" Joanna exclaimed. "We've both been so busy with this other deal that we haven't had a moment to talk about it."

"Frank, nothing," Butch said irritably. "He may have called a few law enforcement agencies looking for a missing person, but no one back there knew Junior was missing because no one had bothered to report it. *I'm* the one who found her, and I demand full credit."

"You did?" Joanna asked in amazement. "That's wonderful. How did you do it?"

"I called the Special Olympics headquarters in Yankton. They keep track of special athletes by both first and last names. Once I got hooked up to their database, I had what I needed in less than sixty seconds."

"But how did you even know to look there? Did Junior tell you about Special Olympics?"

"Well," Butch said reluctantly, "I suppose I have to give some credit where it's due. Jim Bob and Jenny came by this morning to give me a break and take Junior off my hands for a little while— which I appreciated, by the way. Anyway, Jim Bob asked if I had any other picture books they could take along, since Junior clearly got such a hoot out of that copy of *America the Beautiful*. All I had to offer were some old photo albums. I didn't think anything of it, but it turns out there were some pictures of me in there with some of the Roundhouse's Special Olympics teams from over the years. And once again, as soon as Junior saw something he recognized, he went ballistic. When that happened, Jim Bob called me, and the rest you know."

"So have you talked to her?" Joanna asked. "Or has Junior? How soon can we make arrangements for him to go back there?"

"We can't," Butch said.

"What do you mean, we can't? Maybe Junior isn't capable of flying home by himself, but one of us could travel with him."

"He doesn't have a home," Butch said.

"How can that be? You just said—"

"I said I found his mother. Ellen Dowdle is in a nursing home. She had a stroke and is totally incapacitated. Long before that happened, she sold off all her assets, including a family farm, and put them in trust so Junior would be properly taken care of. A niece and her husband, Chuck and Irene Johnson, agreed to take Junior in and look after him."

"And where are they?"

"Supposedly in Mesa somewhere. The nursing home gave me their name, address, and phone number, but when I tried calling I found out that the phone has been disconnected with no forwarding message. They've skipped, Joanna. My guess is that those sons of bitches have disappeared. I'm sure they thought they could just walk off and leave him and no one—including Junior's mother—would ever be the wiser."

"Sort of like the people who come by and drop off baby chicks and rabbits once Easter is over."

"Exactly!" Butch agreed. He sounded utterly outraged, and Joanna loved him for it.

"There's a big difference, though," Joanna said. "We can't do much about people who abandon baby chicks, because chickens don't have money. That's not the case here. And, if there's money involved—most likely including social security as well as the private funds—then my guess is the guardians have made mail-forwarding arrangements so they can continue receiving Junior's checks. That all adds up to fraud and embezzlement. Did the nursing home have the name of the attorney who set up the trust and handled the guardianship arrangements?"

"I'm sure they do, but they wouldn't give that information to me."

"They'll give it to someone with the word 'sheriff' in front of her name," Joanna said. "I have to go by the hospital and get a tetanus shot. As soon as I get back to the office, though, I'll get right on it."

"See you at dinner then?" Butch said. "Remember, we're all supposed to meet at the Bradys' for dinner tonight. I believe Jim Bob was threatening to go out and buy some champagne."

"I don't know for sure what time I'll get there," Joanna said, "but I'll show up as soon as I can."

TWENTY-ONE

AN HOUR after returning to the department, Joanna was sitting at her desk, resting her aching head in her hands. Her whole body hurt from her collection of scrapes and bruises and from being slammed against the wall of Dena Hogan's garage. She had ditched her torn clothing in favor of some of her crime scene duds, but the denim jeans were rough and uncomfortable on her chafed knees.

Ernie and Jaime had come in to perform the interview honors with Dena Hogan and to confer with Arlee Jones. Meanwhile, Joanna had tried to deal with the Junior issue. She was right. Having the word "sheriff" connected to her name had enabled her to extract the information she needed from Ellen Dowdle's nursing home. Armed with the name of Ellen's attorney, Drew Gunderson, she had tried calling, only to fall victim to the time-zone difference and to the fact that Gunderson had no answering machine at his office and an unlisted number at home.

Joanna had just decided to wait until morning to call when someone tapped on her door. "Anybody home?"

She looked up to see her stepfather, Dr. George Winfield, standing in the doorway. "Come on," he said. "Ellie just called me at the office and gave me my marching orders to come pick you up. We're late for dinner and it sounds like we're both in the doghouse."

Looking at her watch, Joanna was dismayed to see that it was already after seven. She stood up and reached for her jacket. "I'll have to run down to Motor Pool and see if they have a car I can use," she said. "My Crown Victoria still isn't fixed. Between a damaged windshield and a flat tire on the Blazer, that won't really be usable until sometime tomorrow."

"I heard rumors about that," George said. "The word is out that you're tough on the county's rolling stock. First you shot the tire, and then somebody else blew out the window. Or are those just vicious rumors?"

Joanna scowled. "They're true."

George Winfield grinned. "I thought so. Come on. Don't bother checking with Motor Pool right now. I'll give you a ride over to the Bradys' place. I'm sure someone there—" he gave Joanna a conspiratorial wink—"some certain someone—will be only too glad to give you a ride back."

Joanna started to argue, but she was too tired to object. She realized it would be good to be driven for a change—good to be pampered. "Let's go," she said.

She picked up her purse and started toward the door. "You may want to fix your face," George suggested.

"My face? What's the matter with it?"

"A matched pair of shiners, for one thing," George replied. "How'd you do that?"

Joanna ducked behind Kristin's desk and examined her face in the mirror that hung there. George was right. Both eyes had distinct shadows under them, shadows that weren't yet purple but they would be.

"I had to head-butt my way out of trouble today," Joanna said.

George grinned. "Was that before or after you shot the tire?"

"Before," Joanna replied, digging through her purse to retrieve her compact. She rubbed some of the powdery cake makeup onto her face and added a dash of lipstick for good measure, but another check in the mirror proved that her makeup efforts had done little to disguise the damage.

"That's as good as it gets," she said, closing the compact. "I'm not a very good example, am I?" she added. "Jenny's been suspended from school for fighting. I'm her mother and supposedly a grown-up, but just look at me. Not only that, Mother's going to have a fit."

"Let her," George said. "It won't be the first time. Besides, you were only doing your job."

Joanna settled into the front seat of George's new county-owned car, a Dodge Caravan with temporary plates and the new-car smell of new leather. How he had managed to finagle leather out of a tight-fisted county budget was more than Joanna could understand. When he switched on the ignition, however, none of the dash lights lit up. He had to lean forward and squint to read the shift dial as he moved the van into gear.

"Brand-new car," George complained. "The dealer made me a good deal—maybe even a little too good. But here it is less than a week after I drove it off the lot, and I'm having some kind of mysterious problem in the electrical system. It's probably just a fuse. I was supposed to take it into the dealer today, but I ended up having to go to Tombstone instead. So this afternoon, I tried calling to switch the appointment to tomorrow, and the place is closed."

"On Friday?" Joanna asked. "Is it a holiday or something?"

"No, according to the message on the answering machine, it must be more serious than that. The announcement says the dealership is closed until further notice. For service work, there's a referral number to a dealer up in Tucson."

"Wait a minute," Joanna said. "Where did you buy this vehicle?"

"Fort Apache Motors in Sierra Vista."

"From Ross Jenkins?"

"Do you know him?"

"Know him! He's the guy who took a shot at me today—the one who's in the hospital right now having his bowel sewn back together."

"Small world," George marveled. "Well, small county, anyway. But still, why would they close the dealership?"

"He was on his way out of town," Joanna replied. "To Rio de Janeiro. I'll bet he stripped the dealership clean of money before he went."

Once the two detectives and the prosecutor had locked themselves in the interview room with Dena Hogan, Joanna had deliberately stayed away. If and when it came time to testify about what had happened on Kino Road that afternoon, Joanna didn't want to have muddied the waters by being involved in the interview. She had written up a full report of what had happened from her point of view and would let that stand on its own. Still, it seemed that this new bit of information was something Ernie and Jaime needed to know.

"I need someone to go tap on the interview room door," she told the desk clerk who answered her phone call. "I need to talk to either Detective Carpenter or Detective Carbajal." "The double Cs," as the two detectives were sometimes called.

Ernie came on the phone a few moments later. "What's up?"

"You may want to find out if Dena knows what happened to Ross Jenkins' auto dealership," Joanna suggested. "According to George Winfield, it's shut down until further notice."

"Will do."

"How's it going with Arlee?"

"Sounds to me as though he's going to strike a deal. I think Dena will cop a plea for Alice Rogers.

By the time Ross Jenkins gets out of the hospital, he'll wish he hadn't."

"If she's ready to admit to Alice Rogers, what about Clete? Has she said anything about that?"

"Not so far. If Ross Jenkins took out his brother-in-law, maybe he did that one on his own. I'd better get back in there so I don't miss something important. Anything else?"

"No," Joanna said. "That's all. See you in the morning." She turned off the phone.

"You sound tired," George said after a moment. "It's been a rough week around here, even without getting engaged."

"Have you done the Clete Rogers autopsy yet?" Joanna asked.

George shook his head. "That'll have to wait until tomorrow morning."

"Any initial observations?"

"Yes," George Winfield said. "Some readily visible contusions. Those are always possible signs of a struggle. Been dead since sometime last night. It sounds to me like you're thinking that whoever killed Alice also killed her son."

"That's the way it looks," Joanna told him. "Right up until Ross Jenkins tackled me, Clete was our prime suspect in Alice's death. So now Cletus Rogers is innocent, but he's also dead."

"Who stood to benefit most from Alice's death?"

"Her children," Joanna said. "Clete and his sister, Susan. There's also a brand-new husband, if he's still alive, that is. Farley Adams disappeared sometime Sunday afternoon and hasn't been heard from since."

"Her husband!" George exclaimed. "I was under the impression that she was a widow."

"So was everybody else, including her kids. According to Alice's sister, Jessie Monroe, Adams and Alice were already married. Jessie even has a wedding picture to prove it. But when Alice talked to her daughter and son-in-law about Adams on Saturday night, she didn't exactly play straight with them. At that point Alice claimed she was only *thinking* about marrying the man."

"Let me get this straight," George Winfield mused. "If Alice Rogers died prior to marrying again, her two kids would have split the take fifty-fifty. And if Clete had been fingered for Alice's murder, then Susan and Ross Jenkins would have taken the whole wad."

"That's about it," Joanna agreed.

"Ungrateful kids. Do you think the daughter was in on it?"

"Susan Jenkins?" Joanna thought about it. "Maybe, but it doesn't seem likely that she'd throw in with her husband and her husband's mistress in a plot to murder her own mother. Still, stranger things have happened. And this is a strange bunch. I feel like we kicked over a rock and a whole den of vipers came slithering out from underneath. These are people who took bribes, cheated on their spouses, used drugs, and didn't blink an eye when it came time to kill someone. They're a dishonorable, despicable lot without a conscience among them. Just knowing that people like that exist makes me sick. Makes me feel dirty."

George pulled over behind Butch Dixon's Subaru

and switched off the engine. "Look, Joanna," he said, "the fact that people like that *do* exist is the reason you have your job and I have mine. If there weren't any bad people in the world, there wouldn't be any need for cops, or for medical examiners, either. Now come on. We're here. Let's go have dinner."

Eleanor Lathrop Winfield lived up to her reputation. She was appalled by her daughter's black eyes and didn't mince any words in saying so. The fact that Joanna had earned her injuries in the process of apprehending two possible murderers did nothing to mitigate Eleanor's tongue-clicking disapproval. Jenny thought her mother looked neat—like somebody wearing a Halloween costume. Butch stayed close, held Joanna's hand and said very little.

Joanna tried to let herself be caught up in the celebration, but it didn't work. For the first time in his life, Jim Bob Brady had gone out and purchased champagne, although, when it came time for the before-dinner toast, he and Eva Lou joined Jenny and Junior in drinking sparkling cider. Still, even the champagne failed to lift Joanna's mood.

The things that had happened to her in the past few days—the evil and greed she had seen at work in other people—had changed her somehow, had set Joanna apart. She was no longer sure she could accept anyone at face value. When she walked in the door, Junior had greeted her with effusive delight. Now his greeting itself was tinged with sadness. After all, Junior was stuck in Bisbee for one reason and one reason only—he, too, had been betrayed by someone who should have been trustworthy and wasn't.

After dinner, as Jenny passed around slices of Eva Lou's incomparable pumpkin pie topped with mounds of homemade whipped cream, Joanna's cell phone rang. Eva Lou looked at it as Joanna dragged it out of her purse. "If I had a rooster that sounded like that," she said, "he'd be looking to get turned into Sunday dinner."

Excusing herself, Joanna went into the living room to take the call. "Joanna," Ernie Carpenter said, "I think we have a problem."

Not another one. "What now?" Joanna demanded.

"Dena Hogan's starting to go gunny-bags on us."

"Gunny-bags? What does that mean?"

"I think she's coming off drugs," Ernie said. "We found a bag of white powder in her purse that may be heroin. If she's an addict, we don't want her going through detox while she's locked in a cell in the Cochise County jail. What do you suggest?"

Joanna was still haunted by the mentally disturbed woman who had taken her own life in a county jail cell several months earlier. If Dena Hogan was crashing after months of heroin use, she might well be a danger to herself and others. Joanna didn't know the medical ramifications of heroin detox, and she didn't want to find out, either—not firsthand.

"We put her in a hospital under guard."

"Which one?" Ernie asked. "County? The Copper Queen?"

This was one of those situations where Dick Voland would have known exactly what to do, but Dick wasn't around to ask anymore. This time Joanna Brady was on her own.

"If it's going to be on the department's nickel, it better be County," she decided. "No matter what, it's going to be expensive. I guess we'd better see if they have a bed available."

"And what about transportation?" Ernie asked. "Do we send her there by ambulance or have a deputy drive her in a patrol car?"

Damn Dick Voland anyway! Joanna thought. "Look," she said. "I'm at my in-laws' house right now. I'll have somebody give me a ride back over to the department, and I'll sort all this out from there."

"Do you want Jaime or me to stay on it?"

"No. You've already put in a full day. Did Arlee and Dena strike a deal?"

"Yes. Murder two, immunity from everything else, and she agrees to testify against Ross Jenkins in the Alice Rogers case."

"What everything else?"

"It sounds like we've landed smack in the middle of a whole slew of recreational drug users. Dena says she can give us dealer info, provided she serves her time under an assumed name at an out-of-state facility."

"I don't understand," Joanna said. "She's a lawyer. Why is she so willing to cop a plea? Why's she turning state's evidence?"

"She's broke," Ernie said.

"Broke!" Joanna echoed. "How can she be? She drives a Lexus."

"It's leased and she's behind in the payments. Same goes for her house and the rent for her office."

"What about her husband?"

"I don't think he has a clue, at least he didn't before today. She says he's always turned his paycheck over to her and left her to handle the bills. Sounds like she's been handling them all right. Her drug habit has been eating up every penny they both made, and then some. The same is true for Ross Jenkins. He's broke, too. He was looking for a quick influx of cash from Alice's estate to bail him out of the hole. Then, presumably, he and Dena would have ridden off into the sunset."

"Nice guy. What about Mark Childers and Karen Brainard? Did Dena tell you anything about them? Were they in a financial bind as well?"

"Same deal."

"And Monica Foster?"

"Apparently she's not in on it. Dena referred to Monica as Miss Goody Two-shoes. Monica doesn't do drugs. Paul Brainard and Rex Hogan don't either. What I can't figure out is how come straight-shooters end up getting stuck with people who aren't? What is it, wishful thinking?"

"That, or out-and-out stupidity."

Jenny tiptoed into the living room. "Mom," she whispered, "are you going to come have your pie or not?"

"I have to go, Ernie," she told him. "You go on

home. I'll come by in a little while and handle the Dena Hogan paperwork. You don't need to worry about it. And tomorrow—"

"Tomorrow Jaime and I will both go straight to Tombstone," Ernie told her. "In the morning we'll finish interviewing Clete Rogers' neighbors. Since Dena Hogan denies any involvement in that case, we need to find something that will link Ross Jenkins to Clete's death. Then, in the afternoon, we'll attend Alice's funeral. That'll take place at the Episcopal church in Tombstone at two tomorrow afternoon. Visitation is tonight at Garrity's, down in Douglas. One of us had planned to make an appearance there as well, but there are only two of us, and Jamie and I can only be in so many places at once."

"Mom!" Jenny insisted.

"I'll see you tomorrow, Ernie. I've got to go." Joanna ended the call while Jenny skewered her with an accusing stare.

"Are you going back to work?"

"Yes. I have to."

"Well, can I stay here then? I know the Gs will let me."

"I suppose," Joanna said. "I don't want to wear out your welcome, but we'll ask."

"Well," Eleanor sniffed as Joanna resumed her seat. "What is it now? Another crisis, I suppose?"

Joanna looked around the table. Everyone else was finished with dessert. Hers was the only piece of pie left on the table. She took a bite. It was delicious, but she felt self-conscious eating after everyone else had finished.

"Mom has to go back to work," Jenny announced. "So can I—may I stay here again? Please?"

"It's fine with us," Eva Lou said.

"Thanks," Joanna said, then she turned to Butch. "Do you mind giving me a ride over to the department? I need to pick up a car. Both the Crown Victoria and the Blazer are out of commission at the moment."

"Sure," Butch said. "Finish your pie and we'll go right away. Maybe Junior can stay here until I get back."

"That'll be fine, too," Eva Lou said.

Butch and Joanna left the Bradys' house a few minutes later. At the stop sign at Cole Avenue and Arizona Street, Butch Dixon stopped, reached over, pulled Joanna as close as the seat belt would allow, and kissed her on the cheek.

"Are you all right?"

"I'm fine," she said. "I'm sure I look awful, but really, I'm fine."

"You were amazingly quiet during dinner. You barely said a word. I was afraid you were upset about something."

"I am upset," she admitted. "I've spent a week dealing with people who are liars and cheats at best; druggies and murderers at worst. George gave me a little buck-up talk in the car, but it didn't help very much. I still feel like the world is full of dirtbags, and they're winning. People like Eva Lou and Jim Bob Brady never lied or broke a promise in their lives, but they're the exception, Butch. They're not the rule. The problem is, how do I bring

Jenny up in a world where people like Dena Hogan and Ross Jenkins may end up running things?"

"We already live in that kind of world," Butch said. "And the only thing you can do to change it is to keep on doing what you're doing."

"Even if it keeps me out late at night? Even if it makes me feel betrayed?"

"Even if it means you have to keep on taking chances. I don't want to lose you, Joanna. And the idea that you had to go toe-to-toe with those creeps today drives me crazy. But I also know what'll happen if you quit. You'll be in exactly the same kind of fix as Marianne Maculyea. So where are you going now?"

"Down to Douglas to make arrangements to check a prisoner into the mental ward at County Hospital. She's coming off drugs of some kind, and I don't want her detoxing in one of my jail cells."

"Can't somebody else handle that?" Butch asked. "What about Frank Montoya or Dick Voland? Isn't that what they get paid to do?"

"Frank has gone home, and Dick Voland doesn't work for me anymore," Joanna said quietly.

"He doesn't? Since when?"

"Yesterday."

"What do you mean? How did that happen?"

"He was waiting for me out at the ranch when I got home after Kiwanis," Joanna explained. "He was drunker 'an nine hundred dollars and pissed because I had gone and gotten myself engaged to you when all the time he was waiting for me to give him the go-ahead so he could ask me out."

"Why didn't you tell me about this earlier?" Butch asked.

"I didn't have a chance." Joanna paused. "No, that's not true," she added. "I didn't want to tell you. I was afraid you'd be upset, and I didn't want to worry you."

"You fired him?"

"He gave me his resignation, and I accepted it."

"At the ranch," Butch said. "While you were there alone."

"I handled it," Joanna said.

"What if he comes back tonight? What if he's there now, waiting for you?"

Joanna grinned. "He'll have a long wait, then, won't he?"

Her lame attempt to diffuse the sudden tension didn't work.

"You know what I mean, Joanna," Butch continued. "If Voland is so obsessed over losing you that he quit his job, it's serious. You may think he's just going to go away and leave you alone, but he won't. I know how these guys work—how they think."

"Butch, please—"

"No. You shouldn't be out at the ranch by yourself. You should come stay at my house, or else Junior and I can come there."

"That isn't going to work."

"At least let me ride down to Douglas with you. Or let me follow you down and back. That way I can be sure you're all right."

"Wait a minute, here," Joanna objected. "You're

talking to a woman who already has two black eyes. I can take care of things, Butch. I'm not some helpless little woman, you know. If push comes to shove, I think I qualify under the heading of armed and dangerous."

"Armed and bull-headed is more like it," Butch said.

A stiff silence fell over the car. Thinking back, Joanna couldn't quite figure out how the quarrel had started, but she did know that by the time Butch whipped the Outback to a stop beside her private back-door entrance, it still wasn't over.

"I'll call you as soon as I get home," she said.

"Sure," he muttered.

"And I'll be all right, Butch. Honest. Don't worry."

"Right."

Once Joanna stepped out of the car and slammed the door, he sped away, leaving her standing in a hail of gravel. *Great*, she told herself. *Another perfect ending to another perfect day.*

TWENTY-TWO

IN THE office, it took only a few minutes to formalize the paperwork to have Dena Hogan admitted to Southeastern Arizona Medical Center. Once Joanna had managed to locate the necessary forms, she typed them up herself. Twenty minutes later, she was part of a two-car caravan headed for Douglas. Handcuffed and shackled both, Dena rode in a patrol car accompanied by two deputies. Joanna drove the aging white Bronco that had, for years, been assigned to Deputy Dick Voland.

S.A.M.C., was still called County Hospital by locals, situated just outside the town of Douglas. As Joanna drove there, she couldn't help thinking about Alice Rogers and those first few chapters of her memoirs—the ones that dealt with her happy childhood years spent in Douglas. Reflecting about Alice inevitably led Joanna to the missing Farley Adams.

Her investigation had determined that Adams

wasn't his real name. That meant that he, like some of the other people Joanna had encountered in the past few days, had played fast and loose with the truth. If there were people in North Las Vegas who were looking for him and wanting to kill him, maybe Jonathan Becker had good reason to lie about his name. What Joanna wondered was, had he lied to his wife or not? Had he told Alice the truth about his past, or had Becker been as dishonest with Alice as Dena Hogan had been with Rex? Had he married Alice in hopes of inheriting a portion of her estate, as Susan Jenkins believed? Or was it possible that the man who called himself Farley Adams had really loved Alice Rogers and that the look captured on his face in Jessie Morgan's postcard wedding portrait had been one of real affection rather than a supreme job of acting?

Keeping one eye on the road, Joanna dug around in her purse until she located the copy of that picture she had stowed there. Switching on the reading light, she held the picture close to the light and glanced at it several times. There was no getting around it. Both people pictured looked incredibly happy. Neither of them seemed to be faking it.

Joanna put the piece of paper down on the seat. *Supposing he really did love her and supposing he's still alive,* she wondered, *what will he do now?*

Joanna suspected that the people looking for Jonathan Becker were prepared to go to a good deal of trouble to find him and get rid of him. And there was always a chance that they had already succeeded in doing so. But if they hadn't, and if he had really loved Alice Rogers, would he simply turn his back and walk away, or would he be there for her—even in death?

Once at the hospital, Joanna turned Dena Hogan over to the emergency room people and directed the deputies to take turns guarding her. Meanwhile, Joanna went to work on the admissions process. Even though she had come armed with all the necessary information and documents, it still took the better part of an hour before Dena Hogan's admission was complete. And all the while the watch on Joanna's arm and the clock over the admission clerk's head continued to tick.

Free at last, Joanna raced out to the Bronco. It was eight-thirty. No doubt Alice Roger's visitation at the funeral home would end at nine. With no time to lose, Joanna started the Bronco and switched on the pulsing blue emergency lights for the next several miles. Once she hit Douglas proper, she turned off the flashing lights and slowed to a more reasonable pace. By the time she drove under the railroad underpass, she was actually driving at the speed limit.

Garrity's Funeral Home had once been a massive old house on G Street. It was situated only a few blocks from Jessie Monroe's Golden Agers Nursing Home, and only a few more blocks from where Alice Monroe Rogers and her brothers and sisters had played hide-and-seek as children.

Joanna shivered as she stepped out of the Bronco and walked toward the mortuary. It was

a cold, brisk night, but the chill she felt was more
than that. Joanna knew from reading Alice's
own words that she had lived her whole life trying to escape Douglas. Now, at the end of her life,
here she was again, mere blocks from where she
had started. To Joanna, it all seemed pointless
somehow, and, at the same time, inevitable.

With her copy of the wedding picture folded
into a small square in her hand, Joanna walked
into the plushly carpeted lobby of the mortuary.
A man in a suit and tie met her at the door. "Are
you here for Mrs. Rogers?" he asked.

"Yes."

"Second door on the right," he directed. "But
the visitation is almost over," he added. "I'm not
sure if you're aware of it or not, but there's been
another tragedy in the family today. As a result,
most family members had to leave earlier than
expected. There are only a few stragglers left."

The man's politely unspoken message was
clear: *It's over, lady. All the important people are gone
already, so don't hang around and waste my time.*

"That's fine," Joanna said. "I won't be long."

She walked into the room. Like the lobby, the
small, chapel-like room was plushly carpeted. An
open casket, eerily lit, sat at the front. Glancing
around the room, Joanna realized that the man
in the lobby was wrong. Besides Alice, there was
only one person left in the dimly lit chapel—a
man, seated near the front. His head was bowed.
He appeared to be deep in prayer.

Walking silently, Joanna moved forward. She
took a seat three rows back from the man and

waited. For a long time, he continued to sit there without moving. Finally he stood up. As he turned to walk toward the aisle, Joanna recognized him. She also saw that he was carrying something—a flower, a single rose. Once in the aisle, he walked to the casket and placed the rose inside.

It was such a simple, moving gesture, that Joanna felt her heart squeeze. *He does care*, she thought. *The look on his face in the wedding picture isn't a lie.*

Knowing the man known as Farley Adams still thought himself alone, Joanna waited for him to turn. She had no idea what he would do when he saw her. Was he armed? Would he think she was someone sent to kill him?

As soon as he saw her, Joanna saw the look of dread that passed briefly over his tear-stained face. His eyes shifted desperately from side to side, as if searching frantically for some other way out of the room. Realizing there was none, he turned back. For a long moment, the two people stared silently at one another. Finally Farley Adams shook his head. The look of fear on his face was replaced by one of profound resignation. His shoulders sagged, then, slowly, he raised his hands.

"All right," he said. "It's no use. I can't run anymore. You've got me. Go ahead and get it over with."

"It's all right, Mr. Becker," Joanna said softly. "I'm not one of them. My name's Joanna Brady, Sheriff Joanna Brady. We need to talk."

"But you called me Becker," he objected. "You must know all about me then?"

"And about your son," Joanna replied. "And about the dirty cops from North Las Vegas who killed your son and who want you dead as well."

Becker dropped into one of the rows of seats and covered his face with his hands. "If you could find me this easily, they will, too. I knew better than to go to the funeral, but I thought I could take a chance on coming here. There were so few people. Nobody recognized me—except you. I know it's all my fault. That's why Alice is dead. The people who are looking for me must have thought she would lead them to me, although I don't know how they found out."

"They didn't," Joanna said.

"They didn't?" Joanna saw the smallest flicker of hope register on the man's haunted features. "You mean somebody else killed her?"

"Yes," Joanna said. "Her son-in-law."

"Ross Jenkins? But why?"

"For money," Joanna replied. "We found evidence at the scene that made us think Clete Rogers was responsible. But since Ross Jenkins' accomplice has already confessed to her part in Alice's murder, I suspect that was a frame job."

"Clete would never do such a thing," Becker declared. "He thought the world of his mother. In fact, I'm surprised he wasn't here tonight. I was hoping to get a chance to tell him how sorry I am."

For the first time Joanna realized Jonathan Becker hadn't yet heard the rest of the news. "Clete Rogers didn't come to the visitation because he couldn't," Joanna said softly. "He's dead, too."

"Clete? No. What happened to him? The stress was probably too much."

"It wasn't stress," Joanna said. "Somebody threw him in the deep end of an empty swimming pool and broke his neck. It happened last night."

"Did Ross do that, too? I knew Ross and Susan didn't get along with Clete, but I never thought they'd do something so—"

"How did you first meet Alice Rogers?" Joanna interrupted.

"I suppose you've figured out about the Witness Protection thing," Becker ventured.

"Yes. Nobody told us for sure, but we've pretty well pieced it together."

"Well, I couldn't stand it. It was too confining— a jail with no bars on the walls, but a prison nonetheless. When I couldn't take it any longer, I split. I was on my way through Tombstone headed God knows where—Mexico, probably—when I heard Clete complaining that he couldn't get anybody to come help him patch his roof. I offered to help out. I ended up hanging around town doing odd jobs. It was summer, so the rents were cheap. Clete introduced me to Alice because she needed some work done, too. So I started doing handyman jobs for her, but it turned out we liked each other— really hit it off. One thing led to another, and before long—well, you know how it goes. Some people thought Alice was cantankerous, and maybe she was. But she also had an independent streak. I liked that about her."

"Going back to you and Clete Rogers. Would you say the two of you were close friends?"

"No. Clete was a good guy, and he was nice to Alice—a lot nicer than Susan and Ross. But no, we weren't really close."

"Still, though, since Clete was really your first point of contact in Tombstone, mightn't someone think you were good friends? If someone came to town looking for you, might they assume that of all the people in town, Clete Rogers would know where you'd gone off to?"

Joanna's question was followed by a long silence. "You think that's who killed him?" Jonathan Becker asked. "The people who are looking for me?"

"The only other possibility would be Ross Jenkins," Joanna said. "He's undergoing surgery in Tucson at the moment, so he's in no condition to tell us one way or the other. But his accomplice says not."

After a long moment Jonathan Becker nodded thoughtfully. "They'd do it in a minute," he said. "They swore they'd get to me, and they probably will. As soon as I knew Alice was missing, I was afraid it was them. That's why I took off. But how did you find me?"

"Your prints," Joanna said.

"The Witness Protection people said they had pulled my prints, but still I worried about that. That's the reason I tried to wipe down everything in the house. Where did you find them, at Alice's?"

"No, at Outlaw Mountain," Joanna said. "They were on the dirty dishes in the dishwasher. You forgot to run it. I think it's possible that the Witness Protection folks did pull your prints, but somebody came behind them and put them back into the system. Have you ever heard of a Detective Garfield?"

"Who's he?"

"A phony detective who called my AFIS tech claiming to be a North Las Vegas detective. He called within minutes of her getting the hit on your prints when the regular clerk had already told her you were dead. It was enough to arouse suspicion, especially since Detective Garfield doesn't exist and the phone call placed to my tech came from a North Las Vegas pay phone and not a police department."

Behind them in the chapel, the man from the lobby cleared his throat. "Excuse me," he said. "The visitation is over. I really do need to lock up now."

"Fine," Joanna said. "We were just leaving."

"I'm sorry I've caused so much trouble," Jonathan Becker said. "I guess I'll just head on down the road. Although there doesn't seem to be much point. It won't matter where I go. They'll just track me down again."

He sounded so beaten—so defeated and alone—that Joanna ached for him. And in that instant, she had an idea. "What if we let them find you?" she asked.

Becker frowned. "What do you mean?"

"What about if we lay a trap for them, tomorrow, at Alice's funeral?"

"How?"

"I'm not sure. I'd have to check with some

friends of mine, including Adam York, the local agent in charge at the DEA. I'm sure he could point us in the right direction."

"I don't know . . ."

"Excuse me," the man from the funeral home insisted. "I really must close up now."

"Come on," Joanna said, taking Becker by the arm and pulling him from his chair. "We'll talk more about this outside."

"Do you think it would work?" Becker asked once they were outside the mortuary.

Joanna looked up and down the street, but there was almost no traffic. G Avenue seemed completely deserted.

"It might," she said, "but it could also be very dangerous. We'd need to have you in body armor, of course. And we'd have the whole funeral laced with plainclothes officers."

Becker shook his head. "Even if we succeed—even if we catch whoever they've sent this time—who's to say they won't try again? They'll just turn around and send someone else."

"Maybe not," Joanna said. "Maybe if we nail the messenger, he'll lead us back to whoever sent him, and we'll get those guys, too."

A long silence followed as Jonathan Becker seemed to consider Joanna's idea. At last he sighed. "Tell me what to do," he said. "I'm tired of running. I don't want to do that anymore. When Alice let me move into her little place at Outlaw Mountain, I finally started feeling like I was alive again. For the first time since my son died, I felt like life was worth living. Maybe someday I'll feel that way again, but not if I'm forever on the run."

"Come on, then."

"Where are we going?"

"Back to my office at the Justice Complex. I need to make some calls. Where's your car?"

"I ditched it. It was too distinctive. I drove it into a wash out east of town, right along the border. I thought maybe I could trick people into believing that I'd crossed the line into Old Mexico. All I have left is this." Becker held up a small single suitcase Joanna hadn't noticed before. "When you're on foot," he added, "you have to travel light."

Joanna smiled. "You're not on foot now. We'll go in my Bronco." She pointed. "It's over there on the corner."

Leading the way, Joanna climbed in the driver's door and then used the electronic lock to let Becker in on the other side. Once they were both strapped in, she started the engine and eased into the sparse late-evening traffic on G Avenue. She had barely started up the street when a car pulled out of an alleyway and fell in behind them.

Concerned but unwilling to show it, Joanna made at least three separate turns, following the old truck route back to the highway and keeping her eye on the narrow pair of headlights that duplicated her every maneuver. By the third turn, Joanna knew she was in trouble. She realized that the men tracking Becker must have worked their way through the same assumptions Joanna

had and decided that they, too, would attend
Alice Rogers' visitation. The question now was:
What to do about them?

Had Joanna been in her own Blazer, she would
have had a spare Kevlar vest for Jonathan Becker
to slip on and wear. As it was, she didn't.

"Don't turn around, Mr. Becker," she said
evenly, "but someone is following us. I'm going to
call for backup. As soon as we have another car or
two to make a squeeze play, I'm going to pull over
and try to trap this guy. When I do, you're to hit
the floor and stay there. Is that clear?"

"Yes."

Calling into Dispatch, Joanna learned there
were no county units available anywhere in the
near vicinity, other than the two deputies who
had been left guarding Dena Hogan at the hospital. One could be spared, but at best he would be
a good ten minutes away.

"What about Douglas cops, then?" Joanna
asked. "Are any of them available?"

Two minutes later, just after Joanna had
crossed the road to Pirtleville, a city of Douglas
patrol car met Joanna. The cop flashed his lights
briefly, and then pulled a U-turn as a second car
came sliding to a stop in the left-hand lane and
cut off all means of escape. Joanna jammed on
the brakes, and so did everyone else. Within seconds, the desert lit up with the glare of flashing
red lights.

Joanna remained in the Bronco long enough to
make sure Jonathan Becker had hit the floorboard and would stay put. By the time she stepped

out of the vehicle, the Douglas cops had already wrestled the suspect out of his vehicle and had him pinned flat on the pavement. One of them was just snapping shut a pair of handcuffs when Joanna arrived on the scene.

"Here he is, Sheriff Brady," one of the Douglas cops announced proudly, shining a flashlight down on the suspect's shiny bald head. "He never had a chance."

"I'll say!"

Joanna recognized Butch's voice the moment he spoke. Finally, without the headlights glaring in her eyes, she recognized his Outback, too. "Butch, what on earth are you doing here?" she demanded.

"I was following you," he said sheepishly. "I was worried. I wanted to make sure you were all right."

"You know this guy?" one of the Douglas officers asked.

"Unfortunately, yes," Joanna Brady said. She was grateful that in the pulsing glow of lights it was impossible for anyone to see the vivid blush that had flooded her face. "His name's Butch Dixon. He's my fiancé."

"I guess that means we should let him up?" the patrolman asked.

"I guess so," Joanna said.

Furious and embarrassed both, Joanna turned on her heel and marched back to the Bronco to tell Jonathan Becker that everything was under control. Meanwhile the two Douglas officers helped Butch to his feet and removed the cuffs.

They were still apologizing and brushing the dirt off Butch's clothing when Joanna returned.

"It's all right," Butch said to them impatiently. "I'm fine."

"You only *think* you're fine," Joanna corrected. "What the hell were you thinking of?"

"What were *you* thinking of?" Butch returned. "You said you were going to the hospital, but when you left there, instead of going home you took off in the opposite direction. What was I supposed to think?"

"That I was doing my job."

"And I suppose that includes laying a trap for me—having a whole squad of cops pull me over, handcuff me, and throw me on the ground?"

"I happen to have an endangered witness in my car," Joanna told him. "A witness somebody's gone to a lot of trouble to get rid of. When I saw your car, I thought someone had followed me and was going to try to kill him."

"So who is he?" Butch grumbled. "Shouldn't I at least get to meet the guy?"

Something in the way he said the words touched Joanna's funny bone. She stopped being mad and started to laugh. The release of tension was catching. Within moments, Butch was laughing uproariously too, as were the two Douglas cops.

Holding her sides, Joanna staggered up to the door of the Bronco and opened it. "Jonathan Becker," she gasped. "I'd like you to meet Butch Dixon—the man I'm going to marry."

Butch temporarily stifled his laughter. With

dead-pan seriousness he shook Jonathan Becker's hand. It was enough to make Joanna giggle
that much harder. Only when two cars came by,
passing carefully and gawking, did Joanna realize how ridiculous they all must have looked.

"We'd better get out of the road before someone does get hurt," she said.

"Where to?" Butch asked.

"Let's go to High Lonesome Ranch instead of
my office," Joanna said. "And if Dick Voland happens to be there, it'll make it that much more interesting."

✤ TWENTY-THREE

FRIDAY DAWNED clear and cold. Joanna awakened bone-tired and completely alone. After hours of strategic planning, Butch had taken Jonathan Becker into town and booked him into a room at the Copper Queen. Both Junior and Jenny had spent the night with Jim Bob and Eva Lou.

During the contentious discussions that followed their arrival at High Lonesome Ranch, Butch Dixon hadn't been shy about voicing his opinions. With Becker and possibly Joanna in danger, Butch had been in favor of scrubbing the whole idea. To be fair, Joanna herself had wavered back and forth a dozen times. On the one hand, using Becker as bait seemed like a daring enough plan that it just might work. On the other, if Alice Rogers' funeral was stocked with cops on loan from jurisdictions all over southeastern Arizona, how would it be possible to tell all the strangers apart? How would anyone be able to separate good guys from bad guys?

The drug-selling activities of the rogue North Las Vegas cops were enough to justify calling in the DEA, and in the end it was Adam York, Joanna's friend at the DEA, who tipped the scales in favor of mounting the operation when he offered Joanna the use of one of his crack squads of undercover agents. That way, all the visiting officers would be known to one another and, hopefully, unknown to whatever bad guys might show up.

At one o'clock in the morning, when Butch and Jonathan Becker had left, the outlined game plan had seemed feasible enough. At seven-thirty that same morning and in the cold, harsh light of day, it didn't seem like nearly such a good idea.

Stiff, sore, sluggish from lack of sleep, and with her two black eyes glowing like purple beacons despite a dusting of Coverup, Joanna straggled into the office at ten after eight. When she tore off the topmost sheet on her desk calendar, it didn't help her mood when she saw that the date was Friday the thirteenth. Leaving her purse on her desk, she hurried out into the lobby in search of a cup of coffee. She found Frank Montoya waiting by Kristin's desk, a cup of coffee in one hand and a stack of paperwork in the other.

"Whoa," he said when he caught sight of Joanna. "That's a matched pair of shiners if I ever saw one."

"Thanks," she said. "That's not exactly what I wanted to hear."

By the time Joanna returned to her office with her own cup of coffee, Frank was already seated at the conference table and sorting through copies of incident and contact reports. Joanna stopped by her desk and picked up two messages. Drew Gunderson's name and telephone number was on one. The other was from Detective Hank Lazier with the Pima County Sheriff's Department.

"What's this?" Frank asked when she set Gunderson's message in front of him.

"The name and number of the lawyer who set up Junior Dowdle's guardianship arrangement."

"Junior Dowdle?" Frank repeated. "You mean we've figured out Junior's last name? We know where he lives? How did you do that?"

"I didn't," Joanna admitted. "Butch did. He located the mother with the help of some people from Special Olympics. Her name is Ellen Dowdle, and she's in a nursing home in Rapid City, South Dakota. Because Ellen has been left incapacitated by a stroke, Junior was placed in the care of relatives—Ellen's niece and the niece's husband, Chuck and Irene Johnson. Last known address on them was in Mesa, but they've skipped. My guess is they're the ones who ditched Junior at the arts fair. I'd also be willing to bet that just because they're no longer caring for Junior doesn't mean that they've stopped cashing the checks that were supposed to go for his care and upkeep. I want someone to start skip-chasing on them right away. I tried calling the lawyer, Drew Gunderson, last night, but he had already gone home for the day."

"Would you like me to call him?" Frank asked.

"No," Joanna said. "I will, but not until after I drink at least one cup of coffee and get my head screwed on straight. In the meantime, I need to bring you up to speed on the Jonathan Becker situation."

"What about him? He's still missing, isn't he?"

"No, he's not. I found him last night. Becker's going to be at his wife's funeral this afternoon, along with several other people."

"What people?" Frank asked. "What all went on last night?"

"You'd be surprised," Joanna told him. Half an hour later, Frank Montoya left Joanna's office with a whole series of marching orders which included checking with the attending physicians for both Ross Jenkins and Dena Hogan as well as coordinating the joint operation which would include Adam York's DEA squad along with Detectives Carpenter and Carbajal.

By ten o'clock that morning, Joanna was on the phone with Drew Gunderson in Aberdeen, South Dakota. "I wish I could say I'm surprised," he said, when Joanna finished reeling off her story. "I never did like the man Irene Wilcox married. Smiles all the time, but smarmy. Tried to tell Ellen as much, but she insisted it would be all right. It was either let Irene and Chuck have Junior or send him to a home. Ellen's kept her son out of a home all her life. In fact, I'm sure the strain of it is part of why she ended up having that stroke. She's not very old, you know, only seventy-five."

Listening to him, Joanna wondered how old

Drew Gunderson was—probably some years older than Ellen Dowdle.

"I'll have to make arrangements to go over to Rapid to see Ellen this weekend," he continued. "I had other plans, but I'll change them. Ellen and I will talk it over and try to decide what to do, although talking isn't quite the right word. I talk and Ellen blinks—one for yes and two for no. I'm not sure what to do with Junior in the meantime. Is there someplace down there where you can send him to be cared for until I can make arrangements to have someone come get him?"

"Sure," Joanna said. "That won't be a problem. Junior's staying with a friend of mine right now—Butch Dixon. He won't mind keeping him for a few days longer." *I hope.*

As soon as Joanna had finished that call and put down the phone, it rang. That was the story of her life. It seemed she spent most of her waking hours with a phone held to her ear.

"Joanna? Ernie."

"What's up?"

"A couple of things. Have you talked to Hank Lazier?"

"I hadn't gotten around to calling him. I've been too busy."

"And I guess he couldn't wait any longer. He called to let us know that one of the search warrants paid off. They found a television set and a VCR that match the makes and models missing from Alice Rogers' house. They also found a paper bag stuffed with jewelry and savings bonds made out in Alice Rogers' name."

"Where did they find them?" Joanna asked.

"You'll never guess. In Joaquin Morales' mother's garage."

"Joaquin Morales?" Joanna repeated. "The guy the Pima prosecutor cut a deal with?"

"That's the one."

"What's Hank Lazier going to do about that?" Joanna asked.

"Beats me," Ernie replied. "That's his problem."

"Is that all?" Joanna asked.

"Not quite. I just talked to Doc Winfield about Clete Rogers' autopsy. According to the doc, Clete put up quite a fight. He's got flesh and fiber scrapings from under Clete's fingernails. That means that if we ever find the guy, we may not have any fingerprints, but we should have DNA."

"That's good news, Ernie," Joanna told him. "As far as it goes. Now what?"

"Jaime and I are about to head over to Tombstone to meet up with Adam York's guys from DEA. I just heard Frank's already there. You're bringing Becker?"

"That's right. He's still up at the hotel. The funeral starts at two. I told him I'd pick him up around one."

"All right," Ernie said. "See you there. I hope this works."

So do I, Joanna thought.

A few minutes later, when Joanna's private line rang, she wasn't at all surprised to hear Butch on the phone.

"Am I forgiven about last night?" he asked.

"Pretty much," Joanna conceded.

"Lunch, then?"

Joanna had planned to tell Butch about Junior right away and ask if he'd mind keeping his charge a little longer. On second thought that request seemed like something best discussed in person.

"As long as it's soon," Joanna said. "I'm famished."

They met at Daisy's. "Beautiful pair of shiners," Daisy announced as Joanna slid into the booth where Butch was already seated.

"Thanks," Joanna said. "I forgot and left my sunglasses in the car. From now on, I'm keeping them in my purse. For the next few days, I'm going to be wearing them inside and outside both. Now, what's for lunch?"

"Fresh Welsh pasties today," Daisy replied. "Just out of the oven ten minutes ago. Big, though. I'd think about splitting one if I were you."

"Good idea," Joanna said. "Sold."

Butch grinned as Daisy reached into her apron pocket and pulled out a one-dollar bill which she slapped down on the table in front of him.

"What's that all about?" Joanna asked.

"I told her that's what you'd say," Butch said. "And she bet you wouldn't."

Daisy, after writing down their order, stuck her pencil back into her beehive hairdo and picked up their menus. "If I were you, honey," she advised Joanna, "I'd try not to be so predictable. If he already knows you this well and you've only been engaged for two days, think what'll happen after you've been married twenty years. It's better to keep 'em guessing."

"I'll see what I can do about that," Joanna said.

"And where's Junior today?" Daisy continued. "I didn't see him at all yesterday. Isn't he about due for another chocolate shake? Have you done anything about finding his people yet?"

"We've found them all right," Joanna said. "Butch here is the one who located his mother in a nursing home in Rapid City, South Dakota. I just talked to her attorney a little while ago. The news isn't good."

There were other noontime customers coming into the restaurant, but Daisy Maxwell didn't leave Joanna and Butch's booth until she had heard the whole story. "Don't that just beat all," she said, shaking her head. "Some people are such low-down worms they don't hardly deserve to live!" With that, an irate Daisy stalked off to the kitchen.

"So do you mind?" Joanna said to Butch after Daisy left.

"Mind what, keeping Junior a few days longer?" Butch asked. "No. Not at all. I suppose we could think about offering to take him permanently. I mean, if the only other alternative is to put him into a home . . ."

Butch's voice trailed off. Joanna heard the plaintive tone in his voice and knew they were in real danger. Neither one of them could resist a needy stray, human or otherwise. But Joanna was living a life that was already filled to capacity.

She shook her head. "No," she said firmly. "Absolutely not. Our world is complicated enough already. Besides, we're not even married."

"That could be fixed," Butch suggested with a grin.

"No," Joanna said. "We're not going to bring that up. Period."

They ate lunch. "So what's going to happen then?" Daisy asked, as they stood in front of the cash register after lunch, paying their bill. "Is Junior going to end up being put in a home somewhere?"

"That's how it looks," Joanna said, avoiding Butch's eye. "According to Drew Gunderson, there's no other alternative."

Daisy shook her head. "That's what I call criminal," she said. "Plain and simple."

Butch reached for the door and held it open. Before Joanna had a chance to step outside, Marliss Shackleford walked in, followed by none other than Dick Voland.

"Why, Sheriff Brady," Marliss said brightly. "Imagine running into you this way! Whatever happened to your face?"

"I ran into a door," Joanna said. Nodding curtly in Dick's direction, she and Butch stepped outside, where Dick's old Bronco was parked next to the door.

"What the hell is that all about?"

"I don't know," Joanna said. "If those two have their heads together, you can bet it isn't good. Right this minute, though, I don't have time to think about it. I need to get uptown and pick up Jonathan Becker."

Butch leaned inside the car window and gave Joanna a peck on the cheek. "You'll be careful?"

"I'll be careful," Joanna said, "as long as you promise to stay home where you belong."

"In other words, I'm not quite forgiven."

Joanna smiled. "Close," she said, "but not completely."

The death of the mayor's mother, followed days later by that of the mayor himself, was more excitement than Tombstone had seen since the gunfight at O.K. Corral. The street outside Tombstone's Episcopal Church—billed as the oldest Protestant church in Arizona still operating in its original location—was filled to capacity, with excess mourners spilling out onto the street where people from Garrity's Funeral Home were busy erecting a bank of temporary speakers.

Adam York and Butch both had suggested that someone besides Joanna escort Jonathan Becker to the funeral, but she had insisted otherwise. This had been her harebrained idea, and now she was going to see it through to its inevitable conclusion.

With Joanna holding tightly to Jonathan Becker's arm, the two of them were escorted down the aisle. She heard a few whispers as they passed—noticed a few discreet coughs and knowing nods—but nothing out of the ordinary. With each wary step, Joanna glanced from side to side, trying to sort out who was who. Adam York himself stood by the guest book, but if his men were there, they blended in with the locals well enough to be completely invisible. That also went for the killers. If they were there in what was fast becoming an overheated oven of a sanctuary, they too had melted invisibly into the congregation.

The front two pews of the crowded church had been reserved for family members, but when Joanna and Jonathan Becker arrived, only one person was seated there—Alice Rogers' sister, Jessie. As soon as she caught sight of Jonathan Becker, she reached out one gnarled hand to him, beaming as she did so.

"I'm so glad you came," she said. "People have been saying such awful things, but I knew you cared too much to let Ali down."

"Where's Susan?" Joanna asked, sliding into the pew beside Jessie.

"She isn't coming," the old woman answered. "She's up in Tucson, staying at the hospital with Ross. If he did even half the things they're saying he did, I can't see how she could tolerate being in the same county with the man. I wouldn't waste another breath on him, but then Susan's always been different. And I can see how even Susan might not have nerve enough to show up here in town and face people. I doubt I could."

The funeral had been scheduled to start at two, but it was actually two fifteen before the ushers finished moving people around and cramming rows of extra chairs up and down the side and middle aisles. Once the service finally started, it seemed to take forever. Joanna kept sitting there, waiting for something to happen, and nothing did. It was almost an hour and a half before Alice Rogers' friends and neighbors finished eulogizing her. By then, Joanna was convinced she had been completely wrong. No one was going to come looking for Jonathan Becker. The Kevlar vest she had lent him was probably completely unnecessary.

At last the service ended. When it came time to walk back down the aisle, Joanna tried to place herself between Jonathan Becker and Jessie Monroe. "Let me walk with him," Jessie insisted. "If there's any ugly talk, this should put an end to it."

And with that, a dignified Jessie Monroe, leaning on her walker, led the procession out of the church. When they reached the door, Joanna took charge of Becker once more, leading him toward the waiting limo that would follow the hearse to the cemetery.

Once Becker was safely in the car, Joanna straightened up in the clear, cold afternoon sunlight just as Adam York moved in beside her. "Got him," he whispered in her ear. "In fact, we've got them both."

"Are you kidding?"

He smiled. "Nope. The man from Garrity's told us how many motorcycles were supposed to show up to escort the cortege to the cemetery. As soon as an extra cycle showed up, we took that guy out and handed him over to Ernie Carpenter. Ernie said to tell you he's got a Nevada driver's license, two long scratches down the side of his neck, and a nine-mm automatic. He also had an accomplice with a van parked up on Tough Nut Street. As soon as the motorcycle guy did the job, they would have loaded the cycle into the van and disappeared."

Joanna was both dumbfounded and relieved.

"You mean it's over? That's all there is to it?" she demanded.

Adam York grinned. "Isn't that enough?" he returned. "What were you looking for, another shootout à la O.K. Corral? From the sound of things, I'd say Cochise County has already had more than its share of excitement this week. Good work."

"But I didn't do anything," Joanna objected.

"On the contrary," Adam said. "You found the dots. All we did was connect them."

Carried forward by the crowd behind them, Joanna and Adam York moved on into the street. Now, as people spilled toward their vehicles, Joanna caught sight of a photographer moving purposefully toward her, camera in hand. Behind the photographer stood Marliss Shackleford.

Quickly Joanna reached into her purse, grabbed her sunglasses, and slapped them on her face, deftly covering her blackened eyes.

"Sheriff Brady," Marliss said. "I understand there's been some police activity here this afternoon. What's going on?"

Joanna looked up at Adam York before she answered. "No comment," she said.

TWENTY-FOUR

DINNER THAT night was at Daisy's, too. On Friday nights the place stayed open until ten o'clock, and it was usually jammed. Nonetheless, Eva Lou had told her husband that she was tired of cooking, so the whole group—Jim Bob, Eva Lou, Jenny, Junior, Butch, and Joanna—trooped into the restaurant and waited until Moe Maxwell, Daisy's husband, was able to clear a table for six.

While they waited for their order, Jenny and Junior—still wearing his sheriff's badge—played tic-tac-toe, and Joanna summarized the day's events. "So what will happen to Jonathan Becker now?" Butch asked when she finished.

"I don't know. He has what appears to be a valid marriage license that proves he and Alice Rogers were man and wife. The fact that he used a different name doesn't matter as long as use of that name wasn't done to defraud anyone. Since Farley Adams is the name the Witness Protection

429

Program assigned to him, I guess he has a right to use it."

"So he's likely to inherit something then?" Jim Bob asked.

"If the only will found turns out to be the one drawn up by Dena Hogan, that one won't stand up in court, so the state of Arizona will most likely end up divvying up Alice Rogers' estate, depending on whether or not Susan Jenkins was involved in the plot against her mother. If she was, Farley Adams could turn out to be Alice's sole heir."

"If he does inherit," Butch said, "will he stay in Tombstone or not?"

"I think he'd like to," Joanna said. "Especially if he'd be able to stay on at Outlaw Mountain. He says he's tired of running. He wants a place he can call home, but it will depend on whether or not what happened today really clears the books on what happened up in Nevada."

"I hope he can stay then," Butch said.

Joanna nodded. "So do I."

Daisy's was busy enough that Moe Maxwell, Daisy's husband, had been drafted into waiting tables as well as busing them. He came over to the table carrying a tray of drinks.

"All right," he said. "I've got four coffees and two chocolate shakes. Who gets the shakes?"

"Me!" Junior shouted. "Me. Me. Me."

"Me, too," said Jenny.

Once again Junior was so excited that he needed help unwrapping his straw. Once again Butch did the honors. As Jenny and Junior slurped away on their shakes, Moe shook his head. "They're not really going to put him in a home, are they?" he asked.

"That's what the attorney told me," Joanna said guardedly. "According to him, the mother is incapacitated, and there aren't any other relatives who can step in."

"But does it have to be relatives?" Moe asked. "Couldn't somebody else take care of him? It's the only thing Daisy talked about all afternoon. She says to me, 'Moe, we're just rattling around in this big old house. Couldn't we take him in?' I tried to tell her it was the wildest-haired scheme she's ever come up with, but if that's what the woman wants . . . ."

"Daisy wants you two to take Junior?" Joanna asked.

"She's determined to talk to that lawyer and see if she could convince him to let us look after Junior. I'm about to retire, you see. Two weeks from yesterday, as a matter of fact. She says to me, 'Moe, what the hell are you going to do with all your spare time?' And you know what? I didn't have a good answer."

"But you barely know him," Joanna objected. "And you have no idea how hard it would be."

"Daisy knows," Moe Maxwell said. "Daisy had a baby sister once that was just like Junior here, only she died when she was just fourteen—two months after some state busybody convinced Daisy's folks to put the girl in a state-run home. Believe me, Daisy knows exactly what we'd be up against, and that's why she wants to do it: it's for her little sister. Daisy and me may seem like we're over the hill, but we're neither one of us afraid of hard work. Besides, like I always say, 'Whatever Daisy wants, Daisy gets.' Once't that woman gets some damn-fool notion in her head, I know better than to argue. So if you could see your way clear to put us in touch with that lawyer guy, we could at least talk about it. See what he has to say."

"Sure," Joanna said. "I will. First thing Monday morning."

At that precise moment, Joanna's cell phone—buried in her purse—began to ring. For a second or so, Joanna was tempted to ignore it—simply not to answer and let whatever new crisis was at hand handle itself. But when the irksome crowing made people turn and stare, the unwelcome attention got the better of her.

"Hello," Joanna said.

"Joanna? It's me, Marianne. Where are you?"

Marianne's voice sounded odd. "We're at Daisy's," Joanna told her. "We're waiting for our food. Why, is something wrong?"

"Wrong?" Marianne babbled. "What could be wrong? I just got off the phone with Tommy. He told me what's going on. I'm pregnant, Joanna. Jeff and I are going to have a baby! Do you believe it? I can't!"

Joanna was stunned to silence. After all the years of Jeff's and Marianne's trying to have children and failing, after finally adopting the girls and then losing Esther, it didn't seem possible.

Feeling her eyes fill with tears, Joanna tried to stanch the flow by shutting them. But it didn't work. The tears leaked out anyway. They ran down her face and dripped off her chin. With her eyes still closed, Joanna felt Butch's hand reach over and cover hers.

"What is it?" he asked. "Is something wrong?"

Opening her eyes, Joanna gave Butch a teary but radiant smile. "It's Marianne," she said. "She's pregnant. She and Jeff are going to have a baby!"

That announcement was followed by a burst of cheering and clapping. Junior, caught up in the excitement, joined in as well, cheering louder than anyone. There was so much noise that Joanna could hear Marianne was speaking but she couldn't make out the words. Joanna signaled for people to quiet down. Eventually they did.

"Sorry, Mari," she said. "I couldn't hear. What were you saying?"

"Tommy really let me have it for not seeing a doctor sooner," Marianne said, "but I was scared it was going to be bad news. After what happened with Esther, I didn't think Jeff could stand another disaster, and I *knew* I couldn't. I'm already almost two months along, Joanna. Two whole months! By next June, Ruth will have a little brother or sister. What do you think of that? What are the people at Canyon United Methodist going to think?"

"Does that mean you're not quitting?" Joanna asked.

Marianne laughed. "Of course I'm not quitting,

but the first thing I have to do is rewrite my Thanksgiving sermon once more. The bulletin's going to be out of date, but that's all right, too."

"Hold on a minute, Mari," Joanna said. "I have to ask someone a question." She turned to Butch. "What do you think about having a pregnant minister?" she asked.

"It doesn't bother me," he said.

"But for a wedding?" she asked. "What about that?"

Butch shrugged. "That's fine, too."

"What about April then?"

Butch's face split into a wide grin. "April would be just fine, but what pushed you over the edge? I thought you weren't ready to think about setting a date."

"Daisy," Joanna said, holding the phone away long enough to give Butch a brief kiss.

"Daisy?" he asked.

"That's right," Joanna said. "You heard her. She told me not to be too predictable."

When dinner ended, Joanna's Bronco and Butch's Subaru were the last two cars in the parking lot. With an almost full moon rising overhead, Butch gathered a shivering Joanna into his arms.

"Any plans for the weekend?" he asked.

"No. Why?"

"I had thought we'd be going to Tucson this weekend to look for a ring, but now that the ring situation is under control, I've decided to spend my ring money on something else."

"What?" Joanna asked.

"Don't you want it to be a surprise?"

"Tell me."

"After you told me about your Colt misfiring, I did a little research. It turns out Colt 2000s are notorious for doing just that—misfiring. You need a new gun—another Glock maybe."

"But, Butch," Joanna objected, "I paid a ton of money for that gun."

"And it doesn't work," Butch replied. "If you're going to be my wife and sheriff, too, you're going to have a gun that works."

"Right," Joanna said. "It looks like we're going shopping."

Here's a sneak preview of
J. A. Jance's new novel

BETRAYAL OF TRUST

Coming soon in hardcover from
William Morrow
An Imprint of HarperCollins*Publishers*

I WAS sitting on the window seat of our pent-house unit in Belltown Terrace when Mel came back from her run. Dripping with sweat, she nodded briefly on her way to the shower and left me in peace with my coffee cup and the on-line version of the *NYTimes* Crossword. Since it was Monday, I finished it within minutes and turned my attention to the spectacular Olympic Mountains view to the west.

It was June. After months of mostly gray days, summer had come early to Western Washington. Often the hot weather holds off until after drowning out the Fourth of July fireworks. Not this year. It was only mid-June, and the on-line weather report said it might get all the way to the mid-eighties by late afternoon.

People in other parts of the country might laugh at the idea of mid-eighties temperatures clocking in as a heat wave, but in Seattle where the humidity is high and AC units are few, a long June afternoon of sun can be sweltering, especially since the sun doesn't disappear from the sky until close to ten PM.

I remember those long miserable hot summer nights when I was a kid, when my mother—a single mother—and I lived in a second story, one bedroom apartment in a blue-collar Seattle neighborhood called Ballard. We didn't have AC and there was a bakery on the floor below us. Having a bakery and all those ovens running was great in the winter, but in the summer not so much. I would lie there on the couch in the living room, sleepless and miserable, hoping for a tiny breath of breeze to waft in through our lace curtains. It wasn't until I was in high school and earning my own money by working as an usher in a local theater that I managed to give my mom a pair of fans for Mother's Day—one for her and one for me. (At least I didn't give her a baseball glove.)

I refilled my coffee cup and poured one for Mel. She grew up as an army brat. Evidently the base housing hot water heaters were often less than optimal. As a result she takes some of the fastest showers known to man. She collected her coffee from the kitchen and was back in the living room before the coffee came close to reaching drinking temperature. Wearing a silky robe that left nothing to the imagination and with a towel wrapped around her wet hair, she curled up at the opposite end of the window seat and joined me in examining the busy shipping traffic criss-crossing Elliott Bay.

A grain ship was slowly pulling away from the massive terminal at the bottom of Queen Anne Hill. Two ferries, one going and one coming, made their lumbering way to and from Bremerton or Bainbridge Island. They were large ships, but from our perch twenty-two stories up, they seemed like tiny toy boats. Over near West Seattle a collection of barges was being assembled in advance of heading off to Alaska. Nearer at hand, a many-decked cruise ship had docked overnight spilling a myriad of shopping intent cruise enthusiasts into our Denny Regrade neighborhood.

"How was your run?" I asked.

"Hot and crowded," Mel said. "Myrtle Edwards Park was teeming with runners off the cruise ships. I don't like running in crowds. That's why I don't do marathons."

I had another reason for not doing marathons— two of them, actually—my knees. Mel runs. I walk or, as she says, I "saunter." Really, it's more limping than anything else. I finally broke down and had surgery to remove my heel spurs, but then my knees went south. It's hell getting old. I talked to Doctor Bliss, my GP, about the situation with my knees.

"Yes," he said, "you'll need knee replacement surgery eventually, but we're not there yet."

Obviously he was using the royal "we," because if it was his knee situation instead of mine, I'm sure "we'd" have had it done by now.

I glanced at my watch. "We need to leave in about twenty, if we're going to make it across the water before traffic stops up."

Since we were sitting looking out at an expanse of water, it would be easy to think that's "the water" I meant when I spoke to Mel, but it wasn't. In Seattle, however, that refers to several different bodies of water, depending on where you are and where you're going. In this case we were looking at Elliott Bay, which happens to be our "water view," but we worked on the other side of Lake Washington, in this instance, the "traffic" water in question. People who live on Lake Washington or on Lake Sammamish would have an entirely different take on the matter when they used the same two words. Context is everything.

"Okie dokie," Mel said, hopping off the window seat. "Another refill?" she asked.

I gave her my coffee mug. She took it, went to the kitchen, filled it, and came back. She handed me the cup and gave me a quick kiss in the process. "I started a new pot for our travelers," she said then added, "Back in flash."

I had showered and dressed while she was out, not that I needed to. There are two full baths as well as a powder room in our unit. When I married Mel, rather than share mine, she took over the guest bath and made it her own, complete with all the mysterious vials of makeup and moisturizers she deems necessary to keep herself presentable. I happen to think Mel is more than presentable without any of that stuff, but I've gathered enough wisdom over the years to realize that my opinion on some subjects is neither requested nor appreciated.

So we split the bathrooms. As long as we share the bed in my room, I don't have a problem with that. Occasionally I find myself wondering about my first marriage to Karen who is now deceased. Most of the time we were married, we had two bathrooms—one for us and one for the kids. Would our lives have been smoother if Karen and I had been able to have separate bathrooms as well?

No, wait. Denial is a wonderful thing, and I'm going to call myself on it. Despite my pretense to the contrary, the warfare that occurred in Karen's and my bathroom usually had nothing to do with the bathroom. Karen was a drama queen and I was a jerk, for starters. Yes, we did battle over changing the toilet paper rolls and leaving the toilet seat up and hanging panty hose on the shower curtain rod and leaving clots of toothpaste in the single sink, but those were merely symptoms of what was really wrong with our marriage—namely my drinking and my working too much. All the squabbling in our bathroom— the only real private place in the house—was generally about those underlying issues rather than the ones we claimed we were fighting about.

For years, Karen and I never showed up at the kitchen table for breakfast without have spent the better part of an hour railing at one another first. I'm sure those constant verbal battles were very hard on our kids, and I regret them to this day. But I have to tell you that the pleasant calmness that prevails in my life with Mel Soames is nothing short of a dream come true.

And we are married, by the way. Mel is my third wife. She didn't take my name, and I didn't take hers. As for the single day Anne Corley's and my marriage lasted? She didn't take my name, either, so I'm two for one in the wives-keeping-their-own-names department. Karen evidently didn't mind changing names at all—she took mine, and later, when she married Dave Livingston, her second husband, she took his name as well. So much for the high and low points of J. P. Beaumont's checkered romantic past.

When the coffee pot—an engineering marvel straight out of Starbucks—beeped quietly to let me know it was done, I went out to the kitchen and poured most of the pot into our two hefty stainless traveling mugs. This is Seattle. We don't go anywhere or do anything without sufficient amounts of coffee plugged into the system.

I was just tightening the lid on the second one, when Mel appeared in the doorway looking blonde and wonderful. Maybe the makeup did make a tiny bit of difference, but I can tell you she's a whole lot better looking than any other homicide cop I ever met.

On our commute, she drives. Fast. It's best for all concerned if I settle back in the passenger seat of my Mercedes S-550, drink my coffee, and do my best to refrain from back seat driving. One of these days Mel is going to get a hefty speeding ticket that she won't be able to talk her way out of. When that happens, I expect it will finally slow her down. Until that time, however, I'm staying out of it.

And don't let all this talk about making coffee fool you. Mel is no wizard in the kitchen, and neither am I. We mostly survive on take-out or by going out to eat. We have several preferred restaurants on our list of morning dining establishments once we get through the potential bottleneck that is the I-90 Bridge.

The people who planned the bridges in Seattle—both the 520 and the I-90—were betting that the traffic patterns of the fifties and sixties would prevail—that people would drive into the city from the suburbs in the mornings and back home at night. So the lanes that were built into the I-90 bridges, have express lanes that are westbound in the morning and eastbound in the afternoon. Except there are almost as many people working in the 'burbs now as there are in the city, and "wrong-way" commuters like Mel and me, on our way to the east side of Lake Washington to the offices of the Attorney General's Special Homicide Investigation Team, pay the commuting price for those decisions every day.

If we make it through in good order, we can go to the Pancake Corral in Bellevue or to Li'l Jon's in Eastgate for a decent sit down breakfast. Otherwise we're stuck with Egg McMuffins at our desks. You don't have to guess which of those options I prefer. So we head out a good hour and fifteen minutes earlier than we would need to without stopping for breakfast. Getting across the lake early usually makes for lighter traffic—unless there's an accident. Then all bets are off. A successful outcome is also impacted by weather—too much rain or wind or even too much sun—can all prove hazardous to the morning commute.

That Monday morning we were golden—no accidents, no stop and go traffic. By the time the sun came peeking up over the Cascades in the distance, we were tucked into a cozy booth in Li'l Jon's ordering breakfast. And more coffee. Because our office is across the freeway and only about six blocks away from the restaurant, we were able to take our time. Mel had pancakes. She's a runner. She can afford the carbs. I had a single egg over easy with one slice of whole-wheat toast.

We arrived at the Special Homicide Investigation Team's east side office at five minutes to nine. We don't have to punch a time clock. When we're on a case, we sometimes work extraordinarily long hours. When we're not on a case, we work on the honor system.

For the record, I do know that the unfortunate acronym for Special Homicide Investigation Team is S.H.I.T., an oversight some bumbling bureaucrat didn't understand until it was too late to do anything about it. In the world of state government—and probably in the federal government as well—once the stationery is printed, no departmental name is going to get changed because the resulting acronym turns out to be bad news. S.L.U.T. (the South Lake Union Transit) is another local case in point.

But for all of us who actually work for Special Homicide, the jokes about S.H.I.T. are almost as tired as any little kid knock-knock joke that comes to mind, and they're equally unwelcome. Yes, we laugh courteously when people think they're really clever by mentioning that we "work for S.H.I.T.," but I can assure you, what we do here at Special Homicide is not a joke. And neither is our boss, Harry Ignatius Ball—Harry I. Ball as those of us who know and love him like to call him.

Special Homicide is actually divided into three units. Squad A works out of the state capitol down in Olympia. They handle everything from Olympia south to the Oregon border. Squad B, our unit, is in Bellevue, but we work everything from Tacoma north to the Canadian border while Squad C, based in Spokane, covers most things on the far side of the mountains. These divisions aren't chiseled in granite. We work for Ross Connors. As the Washington State Attorney General, he is the state's chief law enforcement officer. We work at his pleasure and direction. We work where Ross Connors says and when Ross Connors says. He's a tough boss but a good one. When things go haywire as they sometimes do, he isn't the kind of guy who leaves his people blowing in the wind. That sort of loyalty inspires loyalty, and Ross gives as good as he gets.

That morning Mel and I both managed to survive the terminal boredom of the weekly staff meeting ritual. After that, we returned to our separate cubicle-sized offices where we were continuing work on cross referencing the state's many missing persons reports with unidentified homicides in all other jurisdictions. It was cold case work, long on frustration, short on triumphs and even more boring most of the time than the staff meetings.

When Squad B's secretary/office manager, Barbara Galvin, poked her head into our tiny offices and announced that Mel and I had been summoned to Harry's office, it was a real footrace to see who got there first.

Harry is a Luddite. He has a computer on his desk. He does not use it. Ross Connors has made sure that all his people have the latest and greatest in electronic communications gear, but he doesn't use that, either. It's only in the last few months that he's finally accepted the necessity of carrying a cell phone and actually turning it on. He and Ross Connors are really birds of a feather in that regard—they're both anti-geeks at heart. Occasionally we'll receive e-mail with Harry's name on it, but that's because he has dictated his message to Barbara who dutifully types it at the approximate speed of sound and then presses the send button. The same goes for electronic messages that come our way from Ross Connor's e-mail account. His secretary, Katie Dunn, sends out those missives.

In our unit, Barbara Galvin and Harry I. Ball are the ultimate odd couple in terms of working together. Harry is now, and always has been, an exceptional cop who was kicked out of the Bellingham police department due to a terminal lack of political correctness that survived several employer-mandated courses in sensitivity training. He would have been stranded without a job if Ross Connors, no P.C. guy himself, hadn't taken pity on him and hired him as Squad B's supervisor.

Barbara Galvin is easily young enough to be Harry's daughter. Her body shows evidence of plenty of piercings, but she comes to work with a single diamond stud in her left nostril. I suspect that her clothing conceals any number of tattoos, but none of those show at work. She's a blazingly fast typist who keeps only a single photo of her now ten-year-old son on an otherwise fastidiously clean desk. She manages the office with a cheerful efficiency that is nothing short of astonishing. She prods at Harry when he needs prodding and laughs both with him and at him. When I've had occasion to visit other S.H.I.T. offices, I've also seen how Squads A and C live. With Harry and Barbara in charge, those of us in Squad B have a way better deal.

When Mel and I walked into Harry's office he was studying an e-mail that Barbara had no doubt retrieved from his account, printed, and brought to him.

"Have a chair," he said, stripping off a pair of drugstore reading glasses.

Since there was only one visitor's chair in the room, I let Mel have that one. When Harry looked up and saw I was still standing, he bellowed, "Hey, Barbara. Can you round up another chair? Who the hell keeps stealing mine?"

Without a word, Barbara brought another

office chair to the doorway and then rolled it expertly across the room so it came to a stop directly in front of me.

"Sit," Harry ordered, glaring at me.

I sat.

Harry picked up the piece of paper again and returned the reading glasses to the bridge of his nose.

"I don't like this much, you know," he said.

Mel and I exchanged looks. Her single raised eyebrow spoke volumes, as in "What's he talking about?"

"I'm not sure why it is that you're always Ross's go-to-guy, but you are," Harry grumbled, sending another glower in my direction. "This time the Attorney General wants both of you in Olympia for the next while. It's all very hush-hush. He didn't say what he wants you to do while you're there, or how long he wants you to stay. He says you should 'pack to stay for several days,' and you should 'each bring a vehicle' which leads me to believe that you won't necessarily be working together. You're booked into the Red Lion there in Olympia."

"I'm assuming from that we probably won't be staying in the honeymoon suite?" I asked.

"I would assume not," Harry agreed glumly. "Now get the hell out of here. Time's a wastin'."